Bones littered the ground.

in blood, not so much as a scrap of flesh remained on the hundreds of skeletons strewn across the pasture.

"These bones weren't gnawed. They were pecked," said Helchen, "keep as far away from those trees as you can," she ordered.

"Too late," Gaiseric whispered, pulling Cryptblade from its scabbard.

Shareen followed the rogue's horrified gaze. The trees edging the pasture erupted into animation. A dark cloud rose from the branches, loose feathers drifting down as a black multitude swarmed into the air.

The bones, pecked clean of flesh, stripped of the last morsel. The birds were the culprits, a vast murder of crows. Shareen saw the gleam of bone showing through the rotten, feathery bodies. Not living animals at all, but a horde of winged zombies, ravenous for living flesh.

More Zombicide from Aconyte

Zombicide Black Plague

Age of the Undead by C L Werner

Isle of the Undead by C L Werner

Zombicide Invader

Planet Havoc by Tim Waggoner

Terror World by Cath Lauria

Death System by S A Sidor

Zombicide

Last Resort by Josh Reynolds

All or Nothing by Josh Reynolds

Do or Die by Josh Reynolds

CITY OF THE
UNDEAD

CL WERNER

First published by Aconyte Books in 2024

ISBN 978 1 83908 284 9

Ebook ISBN 978 1 83908 285 6

Cover art by Dany Orizio

Distributed in North America by Simon & Schuster Inc, New York, USA

Printed in the United States of America

9 8 7 6 5 4 3 2 1

ACONYTE BOOKS

An imprint of Asmodee Entertainment Ltd

Mercury House, Shipstones Business Centre

North Gate, Nottingham NG7 7FN, UK

aconytebooks.com // twitter.com/aconytebooks

The Old Kingdom

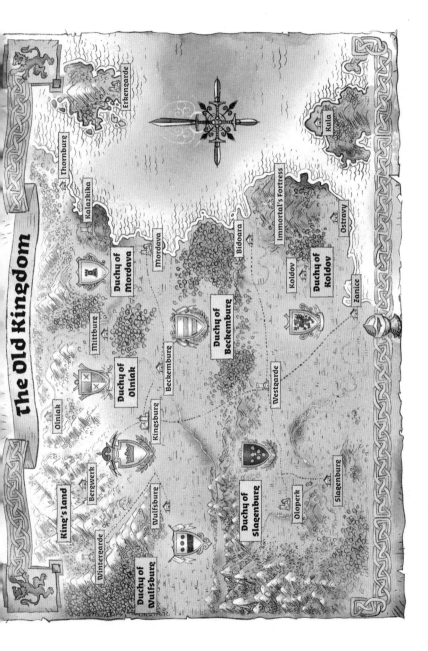

PROLOGUE

The surf crashed against the sandy beach, washing foam over rotting flesh and exposed bone. The stink of decay wafted across the island, seeping into every corner of the waterfront buildings and spilling out into the forested interior. The few seabirds that soared in the sky quickly fled when they dove landward and realized the nature of the carrion they thought to consume. The red-shelled crabs scuttling across the shore gave a wide berth to the enormous carcass.

Even the lowest forms of life were repulsed by the aura of black magic that saturated the carcass sprawled across the island's beach. Periapts crafted from human skin and inked in human blood were plastered to the rotting corpse, the charms serving to slow the decay. Other talismans such as spikes crafted from human bone and etched with infernal sigils had been hammered into the body at precise intervals. From these talismans, the malefic contagion of the Black Plague was drawn down into the carcass, spreading through its dead flesh, steadily swelling the infusion of necromantic corruption.

Lounging in the shadow of a boathouse, Gogol the necromancer sipped wine he'd found in the cellars of Yandryl's castle and waited for the energies he was gathering to completely saturate the carcass on the beach. The smell of decay was too strong to savor the wine's bouquet, and his long years practicing the black arts had left his body with a perpetual chill that negated the warmth of even the strongest liquor, but he could still savor the taste. That much enjoyment was left to him.

"For a half-mad elf-witch, you had an appreciation for wine," Gogol commented, turning in his chair and saluting the ruins of Yandryl's castle. "I'm sure you don't mind sharing, seeing as how you're dead now."

When exploring the castle, he'd found Yandryl's charred remains. The elven sorceress had been well and truly immolated, beyond even his powers to resurrect. A lethal case of dragonfire, for certain. He dipped his glass and turned his attention back to the beach. There wasn't any mystery about what had caused the sorceress to die as she did.

The carcass on the beach was the remains of Flamefang, the mighty wyrm that Yandryl had enslaved. It was an imposing monster, even in death. Leathery wings as wide as a galleon's sails, claws as long as pikes, teeth as big as swords … no, there was no mistaking the terrible power of a dragon. A crew of fifty zombies were pulling on ropes to drag the body up and away from the tide, but those nearest to the reptile's maw had to be frequently swapped out because the caustic drool that dripped from Flamefang's mouth gradually burned away their feet. Gogol had been stunned to discover that the brew was still potent after the dragon's immersion in the sea, so vitriolic that even his spectral walkers, immune to any mundane weaponry, were affected by the draconic spittle.

The wyrm had been a formidable beast. And now it belonged to Gogol. The thought brought a smile to his pale visage. He drained the last of his wine and reached for the bottle with his other hand.

"Caskets and coffins!" the necromancer cursed when the neck of the bottle shattered under his grip. He glared at the brawny green limb. Twice now he'd been forced to mend his body after an encounter with his hated enemy, Alaric von Mertz. This time, he'd replaced his missing arm with that of another necromancer, one that had happened to be an orc. An arm already exposed to occult conjurations was certainly beneficial, but he wasn't quite used to the increased strength it possessed. It would need some getting used to.

Gogol handed off his wine glass to one of the zombies standing beside his chair. He groaned when the hulking creature dropped the vessel, and it shattered on the wooden deck. "Orcs," he grumbled, glaring at the decayed brute. He was pleased to provide himself with a bodyguard of the brawny undead and had picked out seven of the biggest for that purpose, but he wished they were a bit more dexterous. Perhaps something to experiment with later.

For now, Gogol had grander and more important conjurations in mind. He was preparing to raise Flamefang from the dead, and he wanted something more than just a witless zombie incapable of acting with purpose unless under his direct control. What he needed was a deathless scourge that would be able to strike and kill his enemies from afar. A weapon to set loose upon von Mertz and his friends. The wider conquest envisioned by the great cabal of necromancers could wait. Gogol was focused upon revenge. He felt at liberty to indulge his desire after all he'd endured. When the last of the House of von Mertz was dead, then... then he could think about the downfall of the kingdom.

Gogol gazed out across the beach, biding his time while his zombies pulled the dragon away from the surf. The water might dissipate the magic necessary to animate Flamefang and he didn't want to take any chances. He wouldn't risk resurrecting the wyrm in a weakened condition. When the dragon took flight again, it would be as an undead engine of carnage.

The gleam of something shining further down the beach caught Gogol's notice and drew him out of his dark reverie. Ever cautious, he sent one of his bodyguards to investigate. With clumsy, ponderous steps, the zombie orc trudged across the sands. Gogol couldn't explain why, but he felt a sense of agitated excitement as the undead neared its goal. Closing his eyes, the necromancer transferred his sight into the brute, viewing the scene from the zombie's decayed orbs.

Shock nearly disrupted Gogol's spell. There was a body lying on the beach, buffeted back and forth by the waves. Someone who was not unknown to him. The armor, the torn tabard with its coat of arms depicting a dragon rampant, these could belong to only one man. Gogol didn't know the exact details of the battle, but having found Alaric's sword embedded in Flamefang's carcass, he knew the knight had been involved in the fight. Now he also knew that his enemy hadn't survived the encounter.

Dimly, Gogol knew he should feel exultant that Alaric was dead. Instead, he felt anger. The gods were laughing at him!

They'd cheated him of his revenge! His enemy was dead, and it was too late to exact satisfaction from him.

Gogol started to shake his fist at the heavens, but stopped even as he made the gesture. That was the hazard of anger; it clouded the mind and dulled reason. What was death to a necromancer? A nuisance, nothing more!

"The tomes," Gogol snarled at the zombies around him, snapping his fingers impatiently when the undead were slow to carry out his command. Yandryl had gathered an impressive collection of arcane lore and enchanted objects, although most of them had no bearing upon his own dark art. A few, however, involved necromantic formulae and rituals entirely new to Gogol. Among these was a spell that promised to fulfill his lust for revenge in a manner beyond his most sadistic dreams.

The zombies dragged the heavy chest containing the books to Gogol's chair. Excitedly he threw back the lid and began rummaging through them. He'd only briefly glanced at their pages before, intending to make a more thorough perusal later. Now he struggled to remember which of them had contained the spell that inflamed his imagination. He hesitated when he came to a slim volume bound in yellow leather, a nasty-looking symbol with three curled tendrils branded upon its cover. This was it unless his memory failed him.

Gogol salivated as his eyes roved across the pages, his enthusiasm finally escaping in a peal of demonic laughter. He hugged the book to his breast.

"Bring von Mertz here."

Gogol sent his command into the brain of the brute he'd left standing in the surf. He saw the zombie orc awkwardly lean over and heft the knight's corpse up onto its shoulders. Then it began the stumbling, clumsy walk back across the sands.

"Put him down there," the necromancer ordered, pointing at a spot only a few steps away from his chair. He stood up and moved to his dead enemy, studying the many wounds the knight had suffered. He must have followed the dragon down into the sea, Gogol decided, for the dragon's fire would have caused the water to boil. How else to explain the hideously scalded condition of Alaric's flesh? The distortions on the man's body indicated broken bones. His helm was gone, exposing a face that had been ravaged by aquatic scavengers. Something had bitten off the nose and it looked like claws had torn bits from the cheeks. The eyes, however, remained intact.

That was something. It wouldn't do for Alaric to be blind when Gogol forced his spirit back into his rotten flesh. He wanted the knight to appreciate the full horror of his condition. A broken, helpless shell…

Gogol stood up from his examination, a new devilish idea forming in his mind. He looked out to sea. He'd been able to watch the battle against Flamefang from a distance. He knew that the pirate vessel *The Demoness* had returned and taken on survivors from his own foundering ship. Certainly, Alaric had perished in the fighting, but some of his friends might have survived. That filthy thief Gaiseric and the witch hunter Helchen – they'd earned a full measure of his hate, too. It would be unthinkable for them to escape his wrath.

The necromancer looked down at Alaric's body, his fiendish idea now fermenting into a grisly plan. He could mend the damage that had been done to the knight, at least such injuries that would impair his ability to fight. What better way to triumph over his enemy than to make him serve as Gogol's own champion?

It wouldn't be enough, of course, to simply animate his body as a mindless zombie. No, he'd have to invest the man's spirit into that body. The yellow book held that secret. It described the technique to create what its author called a "zombivor," an undead that retained the mind and soul of its living self. Alaric would be incapable of doing anything contrary to Gogol's commands, but fully aware of what he was doing and his inability to resist.

Gogol would repair and reanimate the knight, then order him to kill all his old companions!

Almost tenderly, Gogol set his palm against Alaric's scalded brow. "You believed that when you died, you'd belong to the gods," he told the corpse. A cruel smile split the necromancer's face. His hand tightened in the knight's hair, and he pulled the dead face upward until it was only inches from his own.

"You don't belong to the gods, von Mertz," Gogol hissed at his enemy. "You belong to me!"

CHAPTER ONE

"Well, there's a welcome sight," Gaiseric said, as *The Demoness* rounded a bend in the river and he caught his first sight of Korbara, the fortified monastery where so many of the kingdom's survivors had fled to for safety. The wiry thief moved forward to the prow of the vessel, anxious to be back on land and able to avail himself of the security the refuge offered. Between ghost ships with zombie crews and fire-spewing dragons, he'd had enough seafaring to last him a long time.

The voyage had been undertaken with a goal both noble and desperate: find an orcish relic held by the elven sorceress Yandryl, which had the power to decimate the undead hordes roaming the kingdom and ensure the safety of those taking refuge in Korbara. On reaching the island, however, they found that it hadn't been spared by the Black Plague and Yandryl herself was dead. Striving against the zombie minions of an orc necromancer and eluding the feral dragon Flamefang, Gaiseric and his companions had managed to find the enchanted drum, Mournshroud. Getting the artifact away from the island had pitted them against the villainous Brunon Gogol and his spectral walkers, but the heroes had prevailed over their old nemesis.

"If only that had been the end of it," Gaiseric mused as he stared out over the river. Fleeing the island, they'd attracted the attention of Flamefang. The dragon pursued them out to sea, nearly destroying the ship and sending them to the bottom. It had taken everything they could throw at the reptile to fend it off, but making the wyrm retreat wasn't enough. Unless killed, the beast would return.

Alaric von Mertz knew only the dragon's death would ensure the survival of his friends and the success of their quest. Accepting his own doom, he'd leapt upon Flamefang as the monster tried to fly away, driving his sword deep into the scaly flesh. The dragon had strength enough to fly back toward the island with Alaric still doggedly hanging on and continuing his attack. Gaiseric blinked back tears when he pictured the moment Flamefang finally plummeted into the sea, taking the knight down to a watery grave.

"Of all the nobles I've had the misfortune to cross paths with," Gaiseric whispered, willing his words to carry into the ethereal realm beyond the mortal plane, "you were the only one who was truly noble." A sad smile pulled at his face as he considered Alaric's sacrifice. He refocused on Korbara. The best tribute any of them could render the knight was to see that his last ambition was successful and that the refuge was made safe from the Black Plague.

A deep cough turned his attention momentarily portside. Gaiseric wasn't the only one who'd reached their limit with regards to the sea. Ursola had her hands locked about the rail in a white-knuckled grip. The dwarf had bound her long hair back in a single braid that was tucked into her belt. Clearly, she didn't want it hanging down in her face when the need to stick her head over the side came upon her.

"We'll sink before we ever reach shore," Ursola growled. "By the beards of my grandfathers, I'll blast out the bottom of this scow if it doesn't stop rolling."

Gaiseric knew it to be an idle threat – the dwarf's grousing was simply her way of coping with being seasick. The pirates who crewed *The Demoness* weren't so certain, however.

He moved over to Ursola, resting his hand on her shoulder. "You might want to tone down the grumbling," he advised in a whisper. He looked around at the ugly faces of the pirates who were on deck. More than a few of them were glaring at the dwarf. "Some of these scalawags don't know you're joking. They're apt to heave you over the side."

Ursola grimaced. "Bad choice of words," she grunted before leaning over the rail and coughing part of her breakfast into the river. Gaiseric slapped her on the back to assist the process.

"I'll be glad to get my feet back on firm ground," Ursola said, turning back and wiping the corner of her mouth with the sleeve of her tunic. "There's only so much of this sloshing and swaying that a dwarf can stomach." The last word seemed to provoke her again and her head was thrust back over the rail.

Gaiseric patted Ursola's back again. "I agree. It'll be a relief to get back to Korbara."

"Take a closer look." The suggestion came from the captain of *The Demoness*, the ferocious Sylvia Samdei. The pirate's face, painted white to resemble a grinning skull, wore a grim expression. Gaiseric gave a start, for he hadn't heard her come up behind them. "Take a closer look," Sylvia repeated, pointing her spyglass at the high cliff above the monastery.

The thief took the instrument from Sylvia and pressed his eye to the lens. It took him a moment to spot what the pirate wanted him to see, but when he did a chill rushed through him, running from his toes to his scalp.

There were things moving on that cliff. A lot of things. It didn't take a royal scholar to deduce that the horde up there was formed of zombies. He watched in fascinated horror as bodies tumbled off the edge of the cliff, pushed into the empty air by the press of the mob. From this distance Gaiseric didn't know if he'd hear any screams, but from the stolid manner in which the undead plummeted through the void, he doubted there was anything to hear. The zombies didn't flail their limbs as they hurtled to the river. They might have been made of stone for all the reaction they exhibited. In just a matter of a few heartbeats, scores of the creatures fell into the river, their decayed bodies swept away by the powerful current.

"Let me take a gander," Ursola said, pressing Gaiseric for use of the spyglass. After looking through it for a moment, she chuckled. "They're saving the monks a lot of work."

"Look again," Sylvia said, her voice like ice.

Gaiseric did, after reclaiming the glass from Ursola. When he saw what Sylvia was talking about, his stomach lurched, and he thought he'd have to make his own dash to the rail. Most of the zombies falling off the cliff were sinking into the river, but not all of them. Some were striking the rooftops of the monastery and its fortifications. The violent impacts broke bones and tore flesh, but these weren't as disabling to the undead as they would be to living invaders. The battered zombies tumbled and rolled from the roofs to crash into the gardens and orchards below. Gaiseric's breath caught in his throat. There wasn't any way to guess how long ago the attack had started. It might have been hours, it might have been days. What he did know was that the mob of zombies stumbling and crawling out from the fertile acreage must number in the hundreds.

"Loaded dice and marked cards," Gaiseric hissed. "We're too late." As *The Demoness* sailed closer to Korbara, he could see templars and a rabble of armed refugees trying to keep the zombies from breaking out of the gardens.

"Why don't they just set fire to the orchards and gardens and take them all out?" Ursola grumbled.

"For the same reason they don't try to use magic against them." Gaiseric turned at the sound of Doran's voice. The battlemage had been below but must have gotten some inkling of what was happening and had come up on deck. There was an unnatural shine to his eyes, an indication that he'd used some sort of spell to enhance his own vision. Following close behind him was Helchen, her pale skin and the dark rings under her eyes giving mute evidence to how poorly she'd been resting.

Doran finished fastening the sword belt around his waist as he joined the others. He nodded his bearded chin at Korbara. "The provisional council can't risk anything happening to the monastery's crops. The food supply has already been stretched to its limit. Starvation would kill people just as surely as any zombie." He stared down at Ursola. "That's why they aren't setting fires and casting spells. They must use sword and spear to fend off the attack."

"Then Korbara's doomed," Sylvia stated. She pushed the side of the glass and directed Gaiseric's gaze to a section of the garden wall. Part of it had already given way and, as he watched, he saw more of it collapse under the weight of the zombies pushing against the structure. Debris spilled out into the lane that ran along beside the wall, flattening some refugee spearmen. Before the militia could regain their feet a tide of undead was sweeping across them. Gaiseric hurriedly surrendered the spyglass to Sylvia, not wanting to see the grisly details as the fighters were overwhelmed.

"Helmsman!" Sylvia cried out. "Bring the ship about!" Gaiseric had to grab the rail to steady himself as the vessel abruptly swung to starboard. The crew wasn't tardy about carrying out the command. They were close enough now that the pirates didn't need a spyglass to tell what was happening at Korbara. The sea dogs were quite happy to carry out orders that would have them steer clear of the beleaguered monastery.

"Sylvia! You can't do that!" Helchen gripped the captain's shoulders and turned her around. The witch hunter didn't need to look through the spyglass to know that Korbara was in trouble, either. "Those people are depending on us!"

"Some of them will get away." This came from Mendoza, Sylvia's first mate. He indicated the dock that served the monastery. Monks were hurriedly evacuating refugees to a small fleet of ships. Boats of every conceivable size and description were loading people on board, not pulling away until it looked like their gunwales were level with the water.

Gaiseric shook his head. "If the abbot is evacuating Korbara, he must feel the situation is hopeless. He's cutting his losses and saving what he can. The man must have been a gambler before he became a monk. Can't fault him for throwing in a losing hand." Only when he spoke the words did the thief truly feel their weight. They'd risked and lost so much to protect these people only to have it all be for nothing.

"It isn't hopeless," Helchen snarled at Gaiseric, the anger in her voice hitting him like a fist. Before he could say anything, the witch hunter turned back to Sylvia. "Please, take *The Demoness* in close. We can use Mournshroud to destroy the zombies." She looked over at Doran. "The drum's enchantment won't hurt the crops."

The battlemage thought for a moment, then nodded his hooded head. "You're right," Doran said, "sounding the drum didn't hurt any of the plants on the island. It shouldn't harm the ones here."

Excitement cut through the despair Gaiseric had felt a moment before. "Mournshroud!" He could kick himself for being so stupid. This was exactly the kind of situation the drum was made for. "Draw the right cards and a losing hand becomes a winning one. We aren't too late," he shouted. "We're just in time!"

Helchen gave him an approving smile. "Go below and tell Ratbag to bring the relic up." She looked back at Sylvia. "Try to bring your ship in as close to shore as you can."

The pirate captain grinned, warming to the plan. "Helmsman! Belay that last order! Hard to port and don't spare the canvas!"

Gaiseric snapped his fingers, hoping to catch a little of

the luck Helchen had invoked. He'd thought Sylvia wouldn't risk her ship or her crew any more than she already had. It warmed his heart to know he was wrong. Pirates, it seemed, weren't as callous and bloodthirsty as he'd always believed them to be. At least not when there wasn't a profit to be made.

The rogue scrambled below decks, doing his best to steady himself as the ship made another abrupt turn, this time toward the monastery. He passed a few buccaneers as they hurried up to the deck, then sprinted down the companionway to the cabin at the far end. In his haste, he didn't give the arranged knock before throwing open the door. It almost proved a fatal mistake.

"Ya tryin' fer der blip!" the guttural orcish jargon bellowed out from the cabin. Gaiseric ducked down as the gleam of metal swept past. He heard the scrape of steel against wood and saw the scimitar chew splinters from the doorframe. Only the combination of his quick reflexes and his attacker diverting his swing at the last moment kept the thief from losing his head.

The arm that gripped the saw-edged scimitar was massive, its leathery green skin rippling with muscle. The orc himself was huge, a head taller than the biggest pirate on the ship and wider across at the shoulders than the doorway he was guarding. Ratbag squinted at Gaiseric, his wide nostrils flaring as he smelled the thief's scent.

"Here I was thinking we were pals," the rogue scolded Ratbag. He tried to make his tone flippant, but he was shaking from his close call and could hear the frightened squeak in his voice. Trying to regain his poise, Gaiseric slipped into the cabin. "This isn't the frontier. Not everyone wants to lop your head off, you know."

Ratbag just glowered at him. "Ya wanna pull der brodie, lamp yaself anoth'r mug," the orc grunted. Gaiseric knew from experience that telling the rogue to find someone else to help him commit suicide was as near to an apology as he would get from the warrior.

"Helchen wants Mournshroud!" Gaiseric told the orc. "Korbara's being overrun by zombies!"

"Gonna croak cadavaz wid der tomtom?" Ratbag didn't bother to hide his glee at the prospect. Slipping the scimitar under his belt, he spun around and took up the enormous drum. The artifact needed someone of his strength to lift, much less carry, the gruesome relic. Gaiseric was just as happy to leave the job to the renegade. However beneficial the drum's powers, the orc shamans had covered the instrument in human skin, an aspect the rogue couldn't quite reconcile himself to. He supposed it had to do with its powers. To exert a destructive influence over the undead, maybe the relic had to itself be fashioned from the dead.

"Hurry," Gaiseric urged Ratbag as the warrior slipped an arm through one of the leather loops that hung from Mournshroud's side. The orc grunted back at him and thrust his chin at the doorway.

"Belly der chin-waggin' an' drift."

Gaiseric started to smile at Ratbag's appropriation of "belay" from the pirates but thought better of showing his amusement. Orcs weren't like humans or dwarfs; it was easy to do something they perceived as a slight and not always easy to tamp down the subsequent fury. He'd known Ratbag for several months and was better at interpreting the warrior's orcish patois than anybody else in their little group, but it was always good practice to avoid pushing his luck. He'd have saved himself many nights in cold dungeons if he'd always followed that practice.

The thief hurried ahead of Ratbag as they rushed down the companionway. There wasn't space in the narrow corridor for the orc to strap Mournshroud to his back, so he pulled it along after him by the leather loop. Gaiseric could imagine the scandal were Helchen or Doran around to see the precious relic treated in such a rough fashion. He felt some of that same indignation, after all they'd gone through to get it, but he knew better than to make an issue of it when the urge to battle was already rushing through Ratbag's veins. The orc needed even less provocation than usual when he was keyed up to fight.

When the pair emerged on deck, *The Demoness* had drawn much closer to Korbara. In fact, the helmsman was having a difficult time wending his way between the smaller ships and boats rushing away from the besieged monastery. This close to the shore Gaiseric could see the decayed horde of undead that was starting to pour out of the garden through the broken wall. Templars wearing the mantle of the Swords of Korbara were trying to block both ends of the alley-like pathway, locking shields and thrusting blades as they struggled to hold back the zombie mob.

"Ratbag! Over here!" Helchen's voice snapped across the deck. The orc lifted the heavy drum and marched over to join the witch hunter near the prow of the ship. Gaiseric trotted along after the warrior, as anxious as anyone to see if they could save Korbara.

Under Helchen's direction, Ratbag brought the drum to the very edge of the ship. She reached out with her hands, then hesitated. Gaiseric could guess the nature of her reluctance. Trained by the Order to despise anything that smacked of magic, and abhor all things necromantic, the necessity of sounding Mournshroud struggled against her deep-rooted loathing of the relic. Practicality would win out as it had back on the island – Helchen had even cast spells from Hulmul's grimoire to help them escape the castle – but right now there wasn't a second to spare. Gaiseric slipped around Helchen and slapped his palms against the ghoulish skin of the drum.

"I just have a normal, healthy revulsion of the thing," the thief told a surprised Helchen. "I don't have the handicap of whatever the inquisitors spent years filling your head with." The jab was perhaps harsher than intended, but Gaiseric retained a distrust of the Order and its witch hunters. He'd been happy to see Helchen divesting herself of some of the ideas she'd been conditioned to hold by her superiors, and it disturbed him to see her falter. It was only too easy to backslide into old habits and old prejudices.

The dolorous tremor that emanated from Mournshroud rolled out toward Korbara. The sound reached up to the spot where the templars were trying to hold back the undead pouring through the broken wall. At once the decayed creatures became still, easy targets for the knights fighting them. Not that such action was needed. As the booming note crashed against the zombies, their rotten flesh rapidly putrefied, dripping from them in greasy streams. Where a mob of vicious monsters had been only moments before, there was soon only a mire of filth and jumbled bones.

"I think that's the edge of the relic's reach," Doran said, waving his staff at the pathway. More zombies continued to stumble out from the garden, quickly freezing in place as Mournshroud's power smashed into them.

Helchen cursed under her breath. "There's no knowing how many more are up there." She turned to Sylvia and when she spoke, Gaiseric couldn't tell if she was pleading with the pirate or demanding her compliance. "Bring *The Demoness* in closer. The zombies are too far away."

Sylvia gave her a resigned nod and barked orders to her crew. "Make port! Smooth and easy!"

It was neither smooth nor easy, for several smaller boats were upset as the big pirate ship rushed ahead. There was a tense moment when the hull scraped against the side of a barge that was trying to reach the middle of the river, but both vessels survived the violent contact. Soon *The Demoness* was alongside the dock and armed pirates were forced to hold back the rush of panicked refugees who tried to clamber aboard.

"We'll have to carry Mournshroud ashore," Helchen declared. "Get it closer to where the zombies are."

"Swell!" Ratbag exclaimed. If the big orc hadn't been holding the drum, Gaiseric thought he'd have clapped his hands in glee. "Plenty cadavaz needin' der bump."

Gaiseric evaluated the situation at the wall before he stopped drumming. The stream of zombies staggering from the breach had slowed to a trickle. Few enough that he was sure the templars could hold their own without need of the relic's power for a time. "You're the only one strong enough to lug this thing around," the thief chided Ratbag. "No swordplay for you." A hurt look came across the orc's visage and Gaiseric felt like he'd snatched a toy away from a child.

"And no more music from you," Helchen said as Gaiseric stopped pounding the drum. "I'll take over." The look in her eyes seemed to say even more, telling him the witch hunter was ashamed of her earlier reluctance. She pointed at the sword hanging from Gaiseric's belt. "I need you to make sure nothing bothers us on the way. Some stragglers from Gogol's mob might be with this horde."

Gaiseric felt his blood go cold. He'd hoped they'd seen the last of the spectral walkers, a hideous new strain of undead developed by Gogol. These zombies couldn't be hurt by mundane weapons but while they were susceptible to magic, aside from the vulnerability of the crops, one look at the packed lanes and walkways was enough reason to avoid slinging spells around. The sword Gaiseric carried was a different matter. He'd found it on Yandryl's island, an enchanted weapon bearing the name Cryptblade, and it had already displayed its withering lethality. Although some of the biggest zombies, the horrors they'd taken to designating as abominations, were tough enough to keep going, their lesser kin were quickly reduced to lifeless husks after a single cut.

"Swell," Gaiseric said, with far less enthusiasm than Ratbag had.

Doran and Ursola joined Gaiseric in forming a vanguard for their tiny group, preceding Ratbag and Helchen down the gangplank the pirates lowered to the dock. Monks of Wotun held back the crowd with their staves, creating a pathway for the heroes. Once they were clear of the docks and they had firm ground beneath their feet again, Helchen started sounding the drum, sending its destructive enchantment rolling out across the monastery.

The crowds began to part of their own accord and Gaiseric noted the glimmer of hope that could now be found on the faces of the refugees. Some even applauded them as they made their way farther into Korbara and gave them shouts of gratitude or encouragement. The thief had to admit the attention made him almost as uneasy as the zombies did. A man in his profession fared better when he wasn't noticed.

"Somebody must have started wagging their tongue about what we brought back," Ursola huffed, fingers playing about the heft of the big hammer she carried.

"Maybe someone on the council has loose lips," Gaiseric responded, giving Doran a sidelong look. "A templar or mage who simply couldn't keep a secret."

"Be grateful they did," Doran retorted. "A rumor that spreads hope is a good antidote to panic."

"Let's just hope the drum's magic doesn't get exhausted," Helchen commented. Gaiseric glanced back at her and saw the sweat beading her brow. He knew sounding Mournshroud was a taxing experience and he wondered if she could maintain the pace. Had Alaric von Mertz been here, the knight would have already insisted on taking a turn at the drum. He, at least, wouldn't have been intimidated by Helchen's aura of authority.

Gaiseric shook his head, trying to refocus his thoughts. Now wasn't the time to remember his dead friend. There was enough trauma ahead of him. As their little group advanced through the monastery, they started to see signs of the zombie attack: refugees and monks who'd been injured by the undead, and who would have to be carefully monitored for any signs of infection. The odd puddle of filth and bones that marked the spot where a zombie had been struck down by Mournshroud's magic. Suddenly the crowd lessened and they started to see more knights in the livery of the Swords of Korbara, a pair of lightning bolts, emblem of the god of justice.

Just ahead were the gardens and orchards. As the sound of the drum came nearer, the press of zombies had been obliterated. The monastery's defenders were able to advance past the gates and the breached wall, pressing their advantage against the undead. For the most part, all Gaiseric could see was a morbid mire where the massed creatures had been destroyed. A troop of knights were fanned out through the garden, waiting as more zombies continued to plummet down from the cliff. Due to the proximity of Mournshroud, they were already starting to rot away before they even struck the ground.

"Krimp der ruckuz," Ratbag grumbled when he saw that there wasn't any fighting to be had. The orc resigned himself to acting as a platform for the drum and crouched a little lower now that they were in a fixed spot so that Helchen wouldn't have to stretch to pound the instrument.

For several minutes this tableau held. Gaiseric wondered how long they'd need to stay in the garden. Certainly, there didn't seem to be any end to the zombies on the cliff. Gazing up, it looked to him that the horde was as big as it had ever been despite all the undead that had already fallen off. He turned to glance at Helchen. She was too proud to say anything, but it was clear to him that she was tiring. He started over to take a turn at the drum, but as he did, he saw a group of templars rush into the garden. The foremost of them, a young man with dark hair and the gilded lightning bolts of a sergeant on his surcoat, hurried over to one of the knights keeping watch at the gate.

"If the enchantment is broken, can you cut any that drop down here before they can amass numbers?" he interrogated the other templar.

"Yes," the knight affirmed. "As long as they drop down the way they have been. If a group of them hit at once… or one of the big ones is with them…"

"You'll have to hold," the sergeant told him in no uncertain terms. Spinning around, he ran over to Helchen. "My name is Videric. The abbot sent me here to secure the relic."

Helchen gave Videric an incredulous look. Ratbag uttered a menacing growl. Gaiseric rounded on the templar. "Are you mad? The drum's the only thing stopping them!"

Videric didn't acknowledge the rogue's anger but maintained an icy composure. "You're destroying all of them that come within reach," he said, then nodded up at the cliff. "But you can't get the ones up there."

"So what's the abbot planning?" Helchen asked between beats of the drum.

"We're taking the relic into the hermitage," Videric replied. He pointed to a curious deformity in the cliffside. It took Gaiseric a moment to spot the small window that indicated some kind of chamber built high above the monastery proper. He knew that the cliff behind Korbara was honeycombed with tunnels. One of them must connect to the isolated hermitage.

"From there you should be able to get all of them," Doran mused as he pulled at his beard. He nodded to Helchen. "Down here we can only do so much, and we can't do anything if we wear out Mournshroud's enchantment. It's not a bad plan to get it even closer."

Helchen stepped back and the drum's rumble faded into echoes. "Take it and hurry," she said, motioning for Ratbag to remove the straps that held the drum to his back. Videric waved two of his templars to take up the burden, but in the end, it needed three of the knights to carry the relic comfortably. "Pray that Wotun smiles on us," Videric said as he turned to lead his men out of the garden.

"He already has, because I'm going with you," Helchen told the sergeant. She held up her hand to stay his objections. "You need someone who knows how to invoke the drum's power." Gaiseric had to smile at her audacity. It didn't take a genius to figure out how to beat a drum. He quickly hid his smile when the witch hunter turned to him. "Take charge here," she told the rogue.

"Of course," Gaiseric replied, "but just remember that while you're traipsing across Korbara, some of us will be over here fighting zombies."

Even as he spoke, a walker came hurtling down into the garden. It broke both legs when it landed, but the undead didn't hesitate to start crawling toward the nearest man. Ursola dashed forward and crushed its skull with a swing of her hammer.

Videric didn't answer, just waved his templars forward.

"Buttons be tak'n alla der watch." Ratbag grinned. He squinted up at the cliff as more zombies fell, scowling when they landed in the river. "Gimme der ruckuz!" He dragged out his scimitar and slapped its side, eager to start fighting the undead.

Gaiseric groaned in dismay. Once again, he couldn't share the orc's enthusiasm.

CHAPTER TWO

Helchen's chest tightened as she was led through the monastery's halls by Videric.

For several hours she'd been in the hermitage, a cave-like chamber isolated high inside the cliff. There'd been barely room enough for herself and the drum, and she'd felt the closeness of her surroundings press in upon her. She hadn't indulged her discomfort while she worked the drum, knowing that the least hesitation could cost people their lives. So, she labored on, feeling the stifling heat and stale air dragging at her stamina even more than the frantic pounding of the drum.

At length, a group of monks arrived to report that the danger was past, and she could stop. They took Mournshroud away, but Helchen was given no chance to rest. Videric told her that the council wanted to see her, and so they'd plunged back down through the tunnels to the more populated regions of Korbara.

The atmosphere within the monastery remained stifling. The stink of sweat and despair filled the passageways. In the weeks since she'd sailed away on *The Demoness*, it seemed that

Korbara's refugee population had doubled. There was barely a speck of floor that didn't have a bedroll or a blanket lying across it, or some ragged wretch sprawled there, weeping for those they'd lost or moaning over the unaccustomed privation they now suffered.

To their credit, the monks were doing everything in their power to help as many people as they could, but Helchen could see that their resources were stretched thin. The gruel the survivors were being served was more water than wheat and potato, the bits of fish parceled out were so small they couldn't feed a cat. It didn't matter if the sorry meals were doled out on gold plates from Wotun's chapel or wooden trenchers from the templars' mess, it was a question of portions. Helchen had spoken with enough veterans in her time to recognize the final stages of a collapse. When an army could no longer feed its soldiers, it was beaten before it ever reached the battlefield.

The refugees crammed into Korbara were an army. An army of the living struggling against the legions of the undead. For all she knew, these were the only living souls left in the whole of the kingdom. She hoped things weren't that bleak, but she'd always put her trust in facts more than hope. The people in the monastery and on the ships lying at anchor in the nearby river were the only ones she *knew* were still alive. The only ones who'd managed to escape the Black Plague.

The tightness in Helchen's chest grew more painful. The sensation had nothing to do with the closeness of the air, but with the sorrow in her heart. She thought the Order had whipped all the weaker sentiments out of her. Even when zombies slaughtered her brother's family – the only relatives she had in the world – her thoughts had been of retribution, not regret. But she was filled with regret now, her mind constantly returning to her last sight of Alaric von Mertz as he was carried away by the dragon, his sword thrust into Flamefang's scaly hide. Only when he was gone did she realize how important he'd been. She'd valued his judgment, even come to depend on his viewpoint in a world where the rigid strictures of the Order were no longer the iron law they'd been before. It was partly his encouragement that had enabled her to broaden her perspective, to see the good in those the Order had taught her to view only with suspicion and hate.

A part of her still wanted to deny that Alaric was dead, but reason dictated there was no way he could have survived battle with the dragon. Helchen knew Captain Sylvia had been right to sail away from Yandryl's island, to make all haste to get Mournshroud to the monastery. Had they tarried trying to find the knight's body they'd have been too late to save Korbara.

The survivors had annihilated the zombies on the cliff by setting Mournshroud in the hermitage. One of the wizards taking shelter in Korbara had sent his familiar to inspect the carnage afterward. It made Helchen think of Hulmul and his reptilian familiar Malicious, both dead in Singerva. The refugee wizard here was paired with an owl and the bird displayed a better capacity for numbers than Malicious had. The owl estimated something in the thousands of zombies decimated by the drum's enchantment, a horde well capable of massacring every person in the monastery. And Helchen reminded herself that, unless completely consumed, each person killed by one of the undead would rise again to join their ranks. Sparingly rare were those who could resist the diseased bite of a zombie.

"Your arrival was truly an answered prayer," Videric said as the two of them passed into the restricted section of the monastery, that part of Korbara where the monks and templars had relocated themselves and where the members of the provisional council had their quarters. Helchen expected that people of especial utility to the council were also accommodated here, such as the wizards and erudites who'd managed to reach the refuge. "A miracle sent by Wotun."

Helchen gave the slightest nod by way of reply. Not so long ago she'd have agreed vehemently on the subject of divine intervention. The Order had taught her that Wotun was an omnipotent deity and would unfailingly render aid to those the god deemed worthy. In the chaos of the Black Plague, she'd been forced to question many of her old beliefs and what she'd learned. The use of magic, for instance. How would her old commander Dietrich have reacted to her facility with the arcane or to the fact that she'd paired her magic with Doran's spells to fend off Flamefang? It wasn't too difficult to picture him ordering her arrested just for carrying Hulmul's grimoire.

No, with all that she'd seen, Helchen couldn't believe Wotun was as omnipotent as she'd been led to think. Either that, or he wasn't a just god. How could a just god have allowed Alaric to die the way he had after all he'd already suffered?

"The provisional council is anxious to see you," Videric continued as he led her up the steps to the council chamber. In better times it had served as a war room for the Swords of

Korbara to plan strategy. Cut into the white rock of the cliff, the long room was supported by twin rows of thick pillars. A pair of templars stood guard and saluted as the sergeant ushered Helchen past them.

The group gathered around the table were familiar to Helchen from her previous visit here. Or at least most of them were. There was a young blonde woman at the far end of the table who the witch hunter was certain she'd have remembered. There was a blue gemstone fused to her forehead, an obscure ritual that conjurers sometimes employed to open their arcane third eye and thereby increase their own magical ability. It was a rarely encountered practice not simply because it was an irrefutable mark that someone was a wizard but also because there was a genuine risk of occult power seeping out of the gemstone while the possessor slept. Sometimes the resultant manifestations were merely glowing wisps of light or the movement of inanimate objects. At other times the escaping magic would exhibit itself in more dangerous forms.

Another stranger to Helchen was a rough, grizzled-looking man with sunburnt skin and close-cropped iron-gray hair. He had an unsettling, sinister cast to his features and his eyes seemed to be narrowed into a perpetual squint. When he turned to watch her enter, she saw that the side of his face was deeply scarred, an old wound caused by some massive paw that had left his right eye a milky white and stretched that side of his mouth past its natural limits. He gave her a close scrutiny while she walked toward the table.

"Huntress Helchen, good of you to accept our invitation," the abbot of Korbara greeted her. He gestured to an open space on the bench, a position that would put her directly across from himself and the most prominent members of the council. Videric helped her to her place, then took a few steps back, standing at attention. Helchen wasn't quite sure if he was guarding her or guarding the council against her.

"Your return with the relic was most opportune," the abbot stated once she was seated. His speech was along similar lines to Videric's, giving thanks to Wotun for the monastery's deliverance.

"Yes, I'm sure the gods have lent a hand," the white-bearded wizard seated beside the abbot said once the holy man had finished praising Wotun. Helchen remembered him as the senior representative of the arcane among the refugees and that he enjoyed a superior position to Doran's. She glanced around, looking for the battlemage among the council. She hadn't seen him since the fight in the gardens.

An answer to this puzzle was soon provided by the elder wizard in the green, sylvan robes. "Whether divine providence or blind fortune, we owe our rescue to the powers of Mournshroud. My colleague Doran spent the most time with the relic, so he is leading our examination of the drum."

"Where is the relic?" the man from the Kingswatch wanted to know. Helchen hadn't thought much of the sweaty royal spy on their previous meeting. He didn't impress her now. "Is it ready for use?"

"It is safe, Philo," the dour templar captain seated at the abbot's other side assured. "But if you're worried, you could go stay on one of the ships in the river."

The remark evoked a bitter laugh from the noble Duchess of Mordava. She didn't deign to look at the spy while she disparaged him. "If you go now, you won't have to try to sneak aboard dressed as a woman to get to the front of the evacuation." Philo sputtered angrily at her remark, but from the way his face flushed, Helchen could tell the accusation wasn't baseless.

"Bickering gets us nowhere," the stern tones of Gunther, the master mason, cracked across the room. He gave duchess and spy alike a reproving stare, then looked over at the wizard. "Mournshroud will be ready if we need it?"

The wizard was quiet for a moment. His expression was grave. Helchen had a terrible feeling she knew what he was going to say before he even said it. "We've been forced to draw on the relic's powers for a prolonged period. Longer, I think, than the orc warlocks who crafted it ever meant for it to be used. There's a concern that its energy has been drained." He quickly raised a placating hand. "Not exhausted," he reassured the council, "but we are still trying to determine how much magic it has left."

"Can't you fix it?" the rotund guildmaster from the Brewers' League asked, his chins trembling with fright. "Can't you do something to refill it? Top off the barrel?"

"Something that's been enchanted can only be replenished through specific rites." Helchen spoke up, combining her knowledge from her training with what Doran had told her during the voyage. "Without at least a close approximation to those rites, there's little chance of restoring Mournshroud's energies."

"Wonderful," the blue-robed priestess of Darsina grumbled. Her fingers closed about the talisman of the sea god that she wore. "The drum was made by orcs. Who knows what bloodthirsty obscenities they performed to make the thing and keep it empowered?"

"There may be an answer to that question," the abbot said, glancing at the men seated to either side of him. He smiled when he looked across the table at Helchen. It was the sort of awkward smile she'd seen many times before, the uneasy look of somebody about to make a dangerous request.

The templar captain stood and addressed the council. "As Mother Magda has correctly reminded us all, we owe our victory over the undead last night to an orcish relic. The answer to Mournshroud's secrets *will* be held by those who made a careful study of orcs." He motioned to the scarred man with the predatory face. The man looked across the members of the council, his eye lingering on Helchen before he started to speak.

"My name is Rodolf Beelek," he introduced himself. "In my time I've been many things, some of which I fear would offend the delicate sensitivities of this august gathering." He managed a slight bow that had an air of crude mockery about it. "What is important just now is that I served as a trapper for the Royal Rangers. Helping secure material for their study." He shifted around and ran one finger down the center furrow of his facial scars. "Violent work, but the kingdom has only ever been kept safe through violence."

"You hunted orcs," Helchen said. She was getting irritated by Rodolf's manner. She knew his type, a small, petty man who suddenly finds his importance elevated and exults in his new status. "There are many who've done the same to protect the kingdom's border."

Rodolf scowled at her. "I didn't hunt orcs," he told her. "I captured them. Takes a lot more skill to take those brutes alive. I caught them and brought them back for the Rangers to examine." His eye glittered with challenge. "The Rangers were the ones trying to figure out better ways to kill them."

Helchen was surprised by the disgust she felt hearing the scout's speech. Most of her life, she'd believed orcs mindless, vicious brutes who had to be culled for the safety of the kingdom. Her time around Ratbag had softened those views, but until now she hadn't realized to what extent.

"All of which is beside the point," the old wizard said. "What matters are the things you heard while you were at the Ranger barracks."

"Of course," Rodolf apologized, and at least with regards to the wizard it seemed to Helchen that his tone was sincere. "The Rangers talked about a lot of the things they'd seen in the orclands as they scouted out the tribes' camps. They'd compare what they saw to what was already written down in their archives." He tapped the table with one finger as he drew attention to the detail that most concerned everyone in Korbara. "I heard them talking about a magic drum one of the scouts had seen the warlocks using, comparing what had been observed with what had been written down years before about a different drum. From what I heard, that older drum was certainly your relic."

"Then the Rangers may have a record detailing how the orcs used Mournshroud," Helchen pondered. She thought of how extensive and thorough the archives of the Order were and the exacting attention to detail the inquisitors demanded from their scribes. If the Rangers were even half as exacting, then there was a real possibility they'd learned the relic's secrets.

"That was our thinking," the abbot said, nodding to the templar and the wizard beside him. "The Royal Rangers may have written down the ceremony by which the warlocks maintained Mournshroud's power. Whether they did or not, it's a chance we can't pass up."

The look the abbot gave her was more than a hint about what he expected from Helchen. "You want me to go and find these documents for you," she said.

"You and your companions have already proven your capabilities," the wizard stated.

"Yes, and lost one of our group in the process," Helchen answered. There was such fire in her gaze that the wizard shrank back in his seat and averted his eyes. The witch hunter's gaze traveled across the other members of the council. "We've already endured many dangers to bring the relic here. You can't ask more of us."

The abbot nodded. "We know the risks we've already asked you to take have been extreme, and we can imagine the anguish you must feel over the death of Alaric von Mertz. But ask yourself, huntress, what he would do if this task were set before him. We would not make this request unless we felt that you were the only ones who could be trusted not to fail."

Helchen felt the abbot's words pierce her like a knife. He had to invoke Alaric's memory! Yes, she did know how the knight would have answered. It was, she reflected, the quality that had made her admire him, even when he was demanding she work with wizards or exert her familiarity with the arcane to cast spells. Alaric subordinated his own needs to those of the people he was charged to protect. In the end, it was what had gotten him killed.

Perhaps, Helchen thought, she'd get herself killed doing the same.

"All right," the witch hunter sighed. "I can only speak for myself. My friends will have to make their own choice, but whatever you want, I'll see it done."

The abbot gave her a grateful smile, then gestured for the templar captain to speak.

"The Royal Rangers maintained a barracks in Zanice, the largest of their hunting lodges outside of Wulfsburg." The templar pointed at Rodolf. "That's where Herr Beelek overheard his interesting conversation. What we need is someone to go to Zanice and bring back whatever the Rangers know about Mournshroud."

Helchen closed her eyes as she pictured the maps of the kingdom she'd seen. "It's a long way from here," she said. It was easy to imagine that the Royal Rangers had wanted a headquarters far away from the orclands in case of a major invasion by the tribes. At least by going to Zanice they'd be going south, away from the frontier and the potential of meeting hordes of zombified orcs and goblins.

"You could travel by ship down the coast," suggested Mother Magda, then surprised Helchen by adding, "Captain Sylvia and *The Demoness* have proven equal to the job."

"And you'll take along Rodolf to guide you once you reach the city," the abbot said.

"I know that part of the country nearly as well as I know the frontier," Rodolf bragged.

Helchen shook her head, remembering everything Alaric had told her about the great battle that had been fought in the south. "Zanice is even closer to the first outbreak of the Black

Plague. The king's army was wiped out by a colossal horde of zombies. By now the area around there must be completely infested."

"If Huntress Helchen is concerned about the safety of her mission, I'll go along to protect them." The offer sounded from behind the witch hunter. Videric stepped forward and bowed to the council. "I hope I've already exhibited my martial skill defending Korbara from the undead." He looked aside at Helchen. "You have my vow that so long as there's a breath in my body, I will not falter in my duty."

The templar captain hesitated for a moment, then slowly nodded at the sergeant. "The task is yours, Videric. Ensure the success of this mission."

"I'll need to keep Doran here," the old wizard spoke up. "He's crucial to our study of the relic. That would leave you bereft of magical protection... certain rumors notwithstanding." There was a gleam in his eye when he made the remark. Clearly it was known that Helchen had learned something of the arcane arts herself. She felt a chill run through her. Those were exactly the sort of rumors that a witch hunter would investigate back in more stable times.

"Shareen is a very capable acolyte," the wizard stated, pointing at the woman with the gemstone in her forehead. "She single-handedly evacuated her village and defended them on the journey to Korbara. You'll find her powers most useful."

Helchen felt her blood curdle at the idea. All her training as a witch hunter had taught her how dangerous wizards who'd opened their third eye were. Still, she had to concede that such raw power *was* useful, and with the kingdom thrown into complete chaos, there wasn't much left to worry about in terms of collateral damage. She pushed aside her reservations and nodded in agreement.

"I'll speak with the others," she told the council. "Once we've had a chance to rest, we'll embark."

The look the abbot gave her sent a chill rushing through Helchen. "You set out at once and get your rest on the ship," he said, a grave tone to his voice. "We don't know how much time we have before another horde of undead show up."

The old wizard made an even more worrying statement. "We don't know how long before Mournshroud's magic runs out."

Gogol stared at the corpse laid out at the middle of the cabalistic circle. The cardinal points were described by eldritch candles he'd looted from Yandryl's castle. Already endowed with arcane properties, they were almost made-to-order for his purposes. Knowing the macabre manner by which the candles must have been created, he wondered if the elf sorceress herself hadn't been a necromancer. Over their long lives, elves were capable of learning several occult disciplines. Maybe she'd included necromancy among her studies.

It was a moot point. Yandryl had been thoroughly destroyed, reduced to cinders by her own rebellious dragon. There was a lesson in that, Gogol thought. Never try to command what you can't control. She should have devoted herself to necromancy. The undead would obey their masters, even if it meant a second death.

He smiled as he traced out the last symbols on the edge

of the circle with powdered bone. Gogol had been forced to make that particular ingredient himself, rendering down some of the corpses scattered across the island that were too damaged to revive as zombies. Human and goblin bones were easy enough to grind down, but those of orcs took serious effort. Yet he'd needed all the bones he could get. It wasn't only the body in the circle he was going to bring back, but also the dragon's enormous carcass. His undead had finally managed to drag the wyrm far enough away from the surf that he was able to prepare it without fear that his work would be washed away by the tide.

The necromancer had never attempted to reanimate a dragon before. It was a feat that would be a true test of his powers. But so, too, was what he planned to do with the body of Alaric von Mertz.

Gogol checked the last of his preparations. There was a final ingredient he needed. Leaning down, he forced the knight's scalded mouth open. Taking out his athame, he raked the blade across his palm. He was forced to grip the dagger with his new arm, and the orc's greater strength caused the edge to cut deeper than he'd intended. It was necessary, however, to draw the blood from his own flesh, not that borrowed from a corpse.

Beads of dark crimson dripped down into Alaric's mouth, spattering across his teeth and over his tongue. Gogol held his gashed hand over the body for a full minute before drawing back and wrapping a bandage around his palm. Pacing three times around the dead knight, he began to chant, a slithering invocation of the Darkness itself. He could feel the malefic energy seeping into him. Through his mind ran the whispers of a primal force, beckoning to him, demanding his obeisance.

Gogol doubted any living creature could long resist the call of Darkness, but he only needed to endure for a few moments. Once he completed his third circuit of the body, he stopped at Alaric's feet and stretched forth both arms. From his fingertips, a shadowy miasma drifted down into the corpse, seeping through flesh and armor as he channeled the malignant energy into the knight.

"Arise, Alaric von Mertz!" Gogol hissed as the last dregs of shadow poured out of him and down into the knight. "Stand up from your grave and kneel before your master!"

For a moment, the necromancer thought his magic had failed, then a sneering smile replaced his worried look. The blank stare in Alaric's eyes vanished. There was an indefinable spark there; not the light of life, but neither was it the dull emptiness of the usual zombie. Yes, Gogol thought, there *was* awareness in that gaze now.

Alaric stirred, moving first one arm and then the other. Planting his hands against the ground, he pushed himself upward until he finally managed to stand. There was confusion in Alaric's eyes when he saw Gogol. He reached to his waist, no doubt seeking a sword that wasn't there. When he found himself without a weapon, his hands tightened into fists.

"That won't do," Gogol snapped. His confidence in his magic was emboldened by the obvious signs that he'd revived not merely Alaric's body, but his mind as well. The knight remembered who he was and who he wanted to kill.

The necromancer pointed at the ground. "Kneel before your master!" he commanded. Sardonic laughter rang out as the zombivor did as he was told. Gogol exulted in the subjugation of his enemy. He struck Alaric with his orcish arm, knocking the knight over. Clumsily, the zombivor picked himself up and resumed his former posture. Gogol laughed as he swatted his old enemy again and sent him sprawling.

"Only a taste of what I intend," Gogol told Alaric. There was a speck of defiance in the zombivor's eyes, but the undead was helpless to resist the necromancer's orders. He considered that a good sign. It meant the knight was cognizant of everything that was happening, but helpless to do anything about it.

Gogol kicked Alaric back into the dust. "This is nothing," he promised the zombivor. "My vengeance has barely even started." He pulled the knight back to his feet, staring into the semi-dead eyes. "Whatever I do to you will be nothing compared to what you're going to do to your friends."

The necromancer laughed anew when he saw a new flicker of emotion in Alaric's eyes.

This time what he saw there wasn't defiance. It was fear.

CHAPTER THREE

Ursola tugged at her braided hair, glad to feel the shiver of pain that went through her scalp. Maybe it would be a good reminder to her not to be such a stubborn idiot. She felt her stomach getting queasy again as she watched Korbara vanish around the bend of the river. Wasn't it only a day ago that she'd vowed to keep her feet on solid ground, the way any sane dwarf would? Yet here she was, back aboard *The Demoness* and heading down the river, and then out to sea. Sylvia's assurances that they'd stay near the coastline and avoid the deep water didn't mollify the demolitionist's black mood or the nausea the swaying deck was provoking.

"You could have said no," Gaiseric had to remind her. The thief was sat near the rail, scraping a whetstone along the edge of his sword.

Ursola's eyes narrowed into sullen slits. "And you might have sold that elf knife of yours," she retorted. "That burgomaster was ready to give you your weight in gold and throw in a Mordavan townhouse for it when things get better."

Gaiseric shook his head. "There's nowhere to spend the

gold and Mordava might have a zombie problem for a long time yet." He smiled at Ursola. "I might be greedy, but I'm not entirely stupid." He tapped his finger on the flat side of Cryptblade. "Just now, this sword's worth more than Ratbag's weight in gold."

"Are you calling me stupid, tall legs?" Ursola huffed. She stopped tugging at her braids and let her hand drop to the hammer hanging from her belt.

"Only if you didn't have a good reason for leaving Korbara," Gaiseric said. The seriousness of his tone caught the dwarf by surprise. For a moment she was at a loss for words. "Helchen feels obligated to carry on where Alaric left off," Gaiseric explained. "Ratbag, well, I wouldn't want to be the one to try to keep him out of a fight. Me? I don't have so many friends left that I'd sit back and let them head into danger. But what about you? What's your reason for going?"

Ursola's stare was steely when she answered. "Even if I forgot all my personal obligations to the man, I'd owe Alaric the deepest debt. All dwarfs do. He gave his life to kill Flamefang and many are the outrages that wyrm perpetrated against my people. For balancing that score, I'll do whatever it takes to honor Alaric. It's not so terribly difficult to guess what he would have done in this situation." She pointed over at Helchen. The witch hunter was in conference with Sylvia on the quarterdeck. "He'd have made the same choice she has. We help Kordava. Whatever it takes."

Gaiseric scratched his chin as he considered her response. "I'm not sure if that makes your reasons less or more selfish than my own."

Ursola smiled at the thief. "At least they're more noble

than his," she said, indicating Ratbag as the big orc lumbered up onto the deck. The levity left her face when she noted the intensity on the warrior's face. She followed Ratbag's gaze and saw that he was looking straight at Rodolf. The trapper was watching the shoreline, unaware of the orc. "Ratbag just wants a fight… and I don't think he's waiting for zombies to get one," she added as the renegade quickly marched over to Rodolf. Helchen hadn't told them much about their new traveling companions, but the witch hunter had asked the rest of them to do their best to keep Ratbag away from the scout.

"Just what we need," Gaiseric groaned, as Ratbag reached the trapper. Ratbag grabbed the man's shoulder and spun him around. The orc glared down at the startled scout while pirates scattered from the vicinity. The crew were ready enough to watch a fight, but they weren't eager to get caught up in one that wasn't of their choosing.

"Noodlin' der scars," Ratbag grunted, baring his fangs. "Noodlin' why der weedie croaker got der scars." The orc clamped one hand around Rodolf's arm when the scout tried to grab for his sword. The other reached to the man's face, splaying his fingers to match the old wound that scored Rodolf's flesh.

"Been 'nappin' der nippers an' molls," Ratbag growled. "Too yeller fer der propa ruckuz!"

"He says that Rodolf has been catching orc matrons and young in the tribal lands," Gaiseric translated for Ursola as the pair of them hurried toward the altercation.

The explanation didn't ease Ursola's mind. Dwarfs had a list of grievances against orcs every bit as long and detailed as those they had against dragons. She had a grudging respect for Ratbag as a fighter, but her regard for him didn't go beyond that. Yet if what he said was true, then Rodolf was a villainous swine.

"Maybe we'll get lucky, and they'll kill each other." Ursola stopped several feet away from the pair and grabbed Gaiseric so that his own advance halted. The thief responded with a shocked look. "A joke," she assured him.

"I don't take insults from marauder swine," Rodolf hissed. He couldn't free his arm from Ratbag's grip, but he drew the orc's hand away from his face. "The scars I have aren't half so bad as those your warlords have left across Wulfenburg! When did an orc ever spare our women and children?"

Ratbag gave the scout a toothy grin. He released Rodolf's arm and took a step back. "Scrap, if'n ya got der moxie." He drew the vicious scimitar and wagged it at the trapper, waiting for him to draw his own blade.

Ursola decided which fighter she sided with when, instead of pulling his sword, Rodolf produced a thin knife from under his sleeve and sent it speeding toward Ratbag. A sneaky, churlish act. The orc at least had given a chance for a proper duel.

Before the flying blade could strike, piercing cold snarled across the deck. The knife was buffeted by a blast of icy force, spinning away from its intended victim. Instead, it struck the mainmast and shattered, frozen so thoroughly that the metal was as brittle as a dead leaf.

"Enough of this!" Helchen shouted. Ursola was thankful that she wasn't the subject of the witch hunter's ire, for her face fairly glowed with anger.

The crew of *The Demoness*, rowdy and cheering on the fighters a moment before, fell silent now, as aware as Ursola of Helchen's anger. Shareen, the enchantress who'd joined them at Korbara, wore a look of amazement, perhaps even delight, and her fascinated gaze never left Helchen as she climbed down from the quarter deck.

"The orc started the trouble," Videric tried to explain as he moved to intercept Helchen. Ursola hadn't noticed the templar's presence on deck before, so she wondered if he'd truly seen the beginning of the incident.

"I don't care," Helchen said as she brushed past Videric. The templar bristled at her curt dismissal but didn't question her authority. She stalked toward Ratbag and Rodolf. Both antagonists stood glaring at each other but weren't so fixated that they didn't direct anxious glances at the witch hunter.

Ursola followed close behind Helchen. She didn't know Rodolf at all and couldn't predict how the trapper would react to what was coming. As for Ratbag, any orc could be vicious and unpredictable, more so when he'd almost been killed by an underhanded trick. If things went more awry than they already were, she wanted to be ready to help Helchen.

"Are you both stupid?" Helchen snapped at the pair. "There's not been enough death and slaughter already that you have to add to it?"

Rodolf scowled at her and wagged his finger at Ratbag. "I'm supposed to let this monster of yours cut me into bits? How anyone can take an orc into their company…"

Helchen talked over the scout's protests. "The Black Plague has made all of us keep strange company. It's enough that Ratbag's good in a fight and enjoys killing zombies." Her tone managed to become even more severe. "I've seen how he handles himself in battle, which is more than I can say for you."

Satisfied that she'd cowed Rodolf, Helchen spun around and glared up at Ratbag. The orc winced as her words lashed into him. "And you! I don't suppose you thought about what would happen after you killed our guide!" She pointed at Rodolf. "He knows how to get into the lodge the Rangers have in Zanice. Do you?"

"Rodolf used to catch orc matrons and children for the Rangers." Ursola was stunned to find that she was defending Ratbag's antagonism, but her own sense of honor couldn't be quiet.

"I know what he was," Helchen said. She gestured at everyone around them. "It doesn't matter. Pirates, thieves, witches or murderers, it doesn't matter who anyone was *before*. All that matters is what they can contribute *now*. Rodolf can get us into the lodge and find the archives we need. That is what matters. That is how we fight against the necromancers and the Black Plague. That's all any of us should care about." She turned and gave both Rodolf and Ratbag a sharp look. "Understand?"

"The abbot said that you're the boss," Rodolf replied, his expression making it clear he wasn't happy with the situation.

Ratbag slid the scimitar back under his belt. "Ya der abercrombie," he grunted. "Der mug wot sayin' wotz wot."

"Good, because if that's clear, I have some more news for all of you." Helchen motioned to the group – old and new – who'd agreed to undertake the expedition. "We won't be sailing into Zanice." She nodded at Rodolf. "So your job will be even more vital. I'll need you to lead us on the best overland path into the city."

"Why can't we just sail into port?" Ursola wanted to know. Much as she disliked being at sea, this sudden change of plans was even less to her liking.

"I'll explain that," Captain Sylvia offered, tugging at one of the gold rings that dangled from her ear. "Any ship going into Zanice must pass Snakehead Rock. I was just explaining to Helchen about the sea serpent that haunts those waters. Normally the Zanice Seaguard row out to the rock once a week to leave a goat for the serpent so it won't bother anybody. With the Black Plague, even if there are parts of the city that haven't fallen, I don't think anybody is too worried about seeing that their local monster is fed."

"This ship fought and killed a dragon," Videric reminded her with a nod at the massive ballista mounted on the quarterdeck. "Surely you can deal with an oversized eel."

Sylvia smiled at the templar. "My artillerists are the best in the Jolly Brotherhood," she boasted. "But you can't shoot at something that's under the water. A sea serpent likes to stove in a ship's hull from beneath. It's not going to dive down on us from above the way a dragon would." She shook her head. "We had small enough chance when we fought Flamefang and lost many good men doing so. Against Zanice's sea serpent, we'd have no chance at all."

"Maybe that ice spell," Shareen suggested. Her eyes were still filled with wonder when she looked at Helchen. "I've never seen magic like that before. You could freeze the water around the serpent…"

"I'm not so reckless as to depend on the fickleness of

magic," Helchen retorted, blunting Shareen's enthusiasm.

Ursola could tell that the decision had already been made during Helchen's talk with Sylvia. "So we go inland," she said. "How close do we get before you need to put us ashore?"

"Two, maybe three days of walking should get you to Zanice," Sylvia estimated.

The dwarf caught the uneasiness in the pirate's voice. "Depending, of course, on how many zombies we find in our path," Ursola said. "That's always something that makes the trip longer."

"Let's just hope it isn't too much longer," Gaiseric whispered under his breath, snapping his fingers as he tried to catch some luck. Ursola didn't take much with human superstitions, but her hope was that the thief would be successful.

The cold feeling in her bones made Ursola believe that they were going to need all the help they could get. It was as though her ancestors were trying to tell her things were going to get much worse before they got better.

From the shadows of an old storehouse, Gogol observed Flamefang's carcass on the beach. The more delicate preparations for the reanimation ritual were being carried out by his new slave. As a zombivor, Alaric possessed enough intelligence to perform complex tasks. Pouring the crushed bone onto the sand and using it to create the same intricate designs that had previously revived the knight was a labor Gogol wouldn't entrust to a lesser form of undead. Too much depended on it being done correctly.

Gogol's lust for revenge was too great to contemplate failure. Still, it was that same drive that made the necromancer relegate the duty to Alaric. The zombivor knew what he was doing and why. Gogol smiled when he thought of the agony that knowledge must be causing the knight. Every speck of bone that his dead hands stirred onto the sand and shaped into ankhs and octahedrons was one step closer to unleashing doom upon his friends.

Soon everything would be ready. The dragon's body was saturated with necromantic energies, spikes of bone drawing the dark power deep into its scaly flesh. The crushed bone Alaric was surrounding the carcass with would further inundate the monster with malefic magic. Having never attempted to reanimate something the size of Flamefang, Gogol wasn't sure how much energy it would take, so he ensured he did everything possible to invoke as much energy as he could. He'd even taken the extra step of rendering down many of his zombies so that it was their already polluted bones Alaric used to shape the cabalistic symbols. There would be no half-measures. This ritual would succeed.

Gogol drew back into the shadows, confident that the zombivor would fulfill his task. The necromancer had other preparations to make, ones that he might be too weak to undertake after reanimating Flamefang. He stepped over to a badly scored table that had once been used for cutting fish. Now, instead of cod the table supported a crystal sphere. Gogol had found the object while searching Yandryl's castle. No practitioner of the dark arts could fail to recognize what it was used for. It was the scrying stone the sorceress had employed to spy upon the mainland and seek places for her dragon to raid.

The necromancer laughed. He was going to use the crystal for much the same purpose.

Clearing his mind, Gogol set his hands to either side of the ball and fixed his gaze upon its depths. The sphere was completely transparent at first, but gradually a hazy mist began to swirl within it. He fixed his thoughts upon the haze, willing it to reveal what he wanted to see.

Gradually an image began to form inside the ball. At first it was a still picture, a moment frozen in time. Gogol recognized *The Demoness*, the pirate ship he'd pursued to Yandryl's island. Hate boiled up inside his heart when he thought about how many times the vessel had thwarted his efforts to destroy Alaric and his friends. Yes, here was a perfect opportunity to destroy his enemies while their ship was anchored off the coast. Though there were no markers he could identify, he had a sense of location, an impression of where this scene was located. Somewhere offshore between Ostravy and Zanice.

Zanice! There was a name that brought memories of its own. After being exiled, Gogol had spent several months in the port city, prowling its canals by moonlight in search of other practitioners of the dark arts. He'd found them, too. By dint of its location and the transient nature of its seafaring population, Zanice had proven an ideal spot for the cabals to rendezvous and evaluate potential recruits.

That usefulness was over, of course. The Black Plague would have decimated Zanice just as it had so much of the kingdom. Gogol had enough curiosity to want to see what was left but not enough sentiment to regret what had been lost to the zombie hordes.

Gogol focused his attention back on the ball when the scene in the crystal became animated. He watched as the pirates lowered a longboat into the water. A low gasp rushed past his lips as people climbed down into the boat. Some of them were strangers to him, but there was no mistaking the foes who'd opposed him ever since the destruction of Singerva. The slippery thief Gaiseric, the bomb-tossing dwarf Ursola, and the brutish orc Ratbag. But it was the woman in the leather armor wearing the broad-brimmed hat who aroused Gogol's deepest ire. Helchen, the witch hunter who hypocritically employed magic herself.

She was an enemy on many levels. The Order's entire existence was founded upon hunting down and executing necromancers, and in their zeal they weren't much concerned if the suspects they tortured confessions from were innocent or not. More specifically, though, Helchen was a confederate of Alaric's, a comrade-in-arms who'd been pivotal in helping the knight survive the many traps Gogol had set for him.

Well, Gogol smiled, he had an especially nasty surprise in store for Helchen. It wasn't going to be some rabble of unknown zombies that killed her. It was going to be the fingers and teeth of her old companion Alaric that stripped the flesh off her bones and reduced her to gory ribbons. Oh yes, he was going to see to it that she was a long time in dying. Long enough to know the full magnitude of horror and despair!

The image flickered for a moment and Gogol redoubled his concentration. It was too late, however, as the mists closed in once more. Before the picture was completely lost, he saw the longboat reach the shore and its occupants disembark. The meaning was clear. Helchen and her group were headed inland. From the size of their packs and the supplies they took with them, it was obvious this wouldn't be a short trip.

Gogol released the scrying stone and turned away. He'd have to delay taking revenge on *The Demoness*. Most of all he wanted Helchen and the others. It would be some time before he could consult the crystal again, which meant his enemies might find someplace they'd be safe from him. He was reassured that they no longer had the enchanted drum with them, but Mournshroud wasn't the only magic in the world that was antithetical to necromancy.

The necromancer emerged from the storehouse and hurried toward the dragon's carcass. He regretted spending so much effort on Flamefang now. He should have contented himself with a less ambitious ritual. If he had just half a day with the wyrm under his control the creature could have carried him back to the mainland and within reach of his enemies. The die, however, was cast. He'd started this complicated rite, now he had to see it through to the end.

"Faster, cur!" Gogol yelled at Alaric. He wanted to strike the undead knight but restrained himself. Any disruption of his work might spoil the arcane design and force them to start all over again. Instead, he folded his arms and watched with mounting impatience while Alaric methodically completed his labor.

When the design was finished, Gogol angrily waved Alaric away from the dragon. He'd spent too much effort creating the zombivor to have him destroyed now by standing too close during Flamefang's reanimation.

"Now we begin," Gogol hissed, his eyes burning with anticipation.

The necromancer drew a scroll from the corpse-skin bag slung over his shoulder. Like the satchel, the scroll was made from someone's flayed hide, only whoever had provided the material hadn't been human. The skin was scaly and retained a bluish hue. Gogol thought it might have been cut from the belly of a reptisaurian but having never seen one of the cold-blooded folk in the flesh, he couldn't tell for sure. Of one thing he was certain: to retain the power of necromancy, the scroll had to have been made from a sentient creature, something with a spirit aware enough to be entombed within the arcane letters.

A slow, hissing litany slithered off Gogol's tongue as he invoked the spell. He thought briefly of the prehuman ruins smothered in the southern swamps where the necromancer cabals had called forth the dread power that had started the Black Plague, the spark that had brought a cataclysm upon the kingdom. Perhaps he was wrong. Perhaps the scroll wasn't reptisaurian but from whatever ophidian breed first raised that eldritch and wicked city so long ago.

The necromancer felt biting cold rush through his body. It was as though a polar wind were passing through him, pulsing through his flesh as it wafted down from glacial wastes. He could see the dark miasma gathering around the draconic carcass, speeding into the bone spikes and pouring down into the scaly flesh. He felt something trickling down his face and when he licked his lips, he knew blood ran down from his eyes, crimson tears evoked by the blackest of magic.

Pain wracked the necromancer. Except for the undead arm attached to his shoulder, every part of Gogol's body begged him to relent, to abandon this enormous act of evil. Had he any respect for the gods left, he might have believed the pain was a warning from one of them, a last entreaty to him to forsake this outrage.

Gogol persisted. The hate inside him would not be denied. The twisted pride of a necromancer goaded him on. He had to see if his powers were equal to his ambition.

A sharp crack rang out over the beach. Gogol saw one of the bone spikes burst into splinters, unable to withstand the dark magic coursing through it. Another detonation and a second spike exploded. In quick succession, the other foci shattered in a chain of explosions. Unable to seep easily into Flamefang's body, energies stormed back into the necromancer. The feedback ended his conjurations in a tortured scream and Gogol fell to the ground.

It was several minutes before the necromancer stirred. Gogol was astounded to still be alive, so intense had been the rush of energy into his body. "Help me up," he snarled at Alaric. Dutifully, the zombivor reached down and picked up his master. The knight's reward was a slap to the face that broke what little remained of his nose.

"You reached too high, you fool," Gogol reproved himself. He brushed the sand from his black robes, then looked toward the beach. His eyes gaped at what he saw.

The dragon's body was much more decayed than it had been at the start of the ritual, with more exposed bone than before. The scales had turned a sickly green that darkened to almost black along the crest of its head and down its spine. Gogol could feel the dark magic clinging to the reptile, a greater quantity than he'd ever sensed emanating from one of the undead.

There was a quiver in Gogol's voice as he tested whether his hope had become a reality. "Flamefang, awake!" he commanded.

At his summons, the immense carcass began to twitch. The eyes, dead and unfocused before, now shone with a grisly awareness, a graveyard light both eerie and ethereal. The dragon flexed one of its claws, digging a deep furrow in the sand. Its uppermost wing unfurled, tatters of leathery flesh sloughing away from the bones. With a rumbling growl, Flamefang shifted itself upright, its wicked gaze locked upon the man who'd called it back from the dead.

"I am your master," Gogol declared, wondering who he was trying to convince more, himself or the dragon. "I called you back from the tomb so that together we can take our revenge."

A deep hiss sounded from the decayed wyrm, something Gogol took to be a sign of approval. A dragon was much more than a mindless reptile; it could understand the appeal of vengeance.

Gogol turned from Flamefang and exerted his will over the rest of his zombies. The dragon couldn't carry a large number of the necromancer's minions. At least, not externally. By probing Alaric's mind, Gogol received a detailed report of the battle with the wyrm and how it had disgorged partly digested zombies onto the ship.

The reptile's stomach was as dead as the rest of its body. There might be some acids left in its gut, but it wouldn't actively digest anything anymore. Flamefang's belly would make an ideal means to transport Gogol's zombies. Delighting in the perversity of the scene, the necromancer ordered his undead to march to the dragon. They stood unresistant as the reptile's jaws closed around them and they were sucked down into the monster's craw.

One after another, Gogol's zombies were consumed until two score of the creatures had been devoured. At last Alaric started toward the dragon. The necromancer laid a hand on the knight's shoulder and held him back. "No," he said. "We'll ride on his back."

Having taken such pains creating the zombivor, Gogol didn't want to risk the creature to the care of Flamefang's belly. Zombies were easily replaced. The remains of Alaric von Mertz were not.

There was a lot more Gogol wanted to do to Alaric von Mertz before he was through with the zombivor.

CHAPTER FOUR

A desolate silence held the countryside, making Helchen's skin crawl. It was, she knew, the effect of the Black Plague. Anything alive that had any instinct for survival fled from lands afflicted by the necromantic scourge. It was only supposedly intelligent creatures like humans who lingered in the domain of the undead.

She reflected on their parting with *The Demoness*. The ship would wait for them for three weeks since the pirates had provisions enough to last that long, and the strength to withstand any zombie attacks. Sylvia promised Helchen no more than that, though if she could secure more stores from Korbara, she'd try to come back and keep up the vigil for a further three weeks. After that, she'd have to give up the expedition as lost. Sylvia had been sincere in her emotional farewell to them, but Helchen sensed that this time the pirate was relieved not to be going the rest of the way. After their adventures on Yandryl's island, Helchen couldn't really blame her.

The region in which Sylvia disembarked them belonged

to the Duchy of Koldov. Historically this southern land was considered the safest and most stable in the kingdom, far removed from the threat of orc attacks and raids by giants. It was for this reason the Rangers had established their secondary headquarters in Zanice, a place to which they could regroup and reorganize should an especially great orc horde overwhelm Wulfsburg.

Yet it was here in the south that the zombie invasion had started. A vast legion of the undead had annihilated the king's army in the neighboring Duchy of Slagenburg. Koldov, so some of the survivors at Korbara claimed, had been overrun only days after.

Helchen could believe those claims just now. Passing through the fields and orchards, she detected no sign of life. No birds perched in the trees, no rabbits scurried through the brush. The only trace of human life they'd seen in the last hour was a donkey cart lying overturned in a ditch, a jumble of valuables strewn all around it. Bloodstains in the grass indicated what had likely befallen the owners.

"Looters, most likely," Gaiseric said after making a brief examination of the cart. He stuffed a jeweled necklace into a pouch hanging from his belt. "Probably should have been content with a little less than they tried to carry off, all things considered."

"You might show some respect for the dead," Videric reprimanded the rogue.

Gaiseric patted the pouch. "Sentiment is too expensive a luxury," he explained. He waved his arm at the field around them. "Since they're not lying around here, it's safe to say they're wandering around out there and what they're looking for now isn't gold and jewels." He snapped his teeth at the templar, mimicking the gnashing fangs of a zombie.

"Knave," Videric grumbled under his breath as he turned away from Gaiseric. Helchen was reminded of the way the thief had always managed to irritate Alaric. In the end though the knight couldn't have asked for a more devoted comrade-in-arms. If things came to a crisis, Videric would soon learn Gaiseric's value.

At the moment, Helchen was concerned about a more dubious member of their party. She spoke with Rodolf while the trapper was scrutinizing the horizon. "You do know how to get us into Zanice from here." Her words were posed more as a demand than a question.

Rodolf gave Helchen a surly look. "It'll be tricky, trying to stay away from the roads, but I can get you there," he assured her. A smug grin pulled at his mouth. "Naturally, it'll take more time going across country."

"It'll take even more time if we run into any zombies," Helchen reminded the man. "Any village or hamlet we pass through is apt to be infested with the undead." She thought back to the perilous exodus from Singerva when every sign of habitation had been fraught with danger.

"Just setting things straight." Rodolf shrugged. "It seemed to me that the abbot was anxious about us getting back to Korbara quickly."

"He'll be even more anxious if we don't get back at all," Ursola told the scout. "If we waltz into a nest of zombies, that could put a quick finish to this expedition."

Helchen thought the dwarf's mood dourer than usual. The empty satchel she carried was a good indicator why. Ursola had expended her last fire-bombs fighting Flamefang and there hadn't been the time or resources for her to make more. The demolitionist felt as vulnerable as an archer without arrows.

The scout didn't deign to reply to Ursola. Hitching up his belt, shifting his scabbard around so that it would be easier to reach, Rodolf prowled ahead of the small warband. Soon he'd put a good hundred yards between himself and the others.

"Nasty sort of cuss," Gaiseric opined, coming up beside Helchen. "Frankly, I found Sylvia's pirates more pleasant."

"Rodolf's a frontiersman," Videric reminded the thief. "He's more accustomed to working alone." The templar's tone was curt with Gaiseric, but the look in his eyes was actively hostile when he glanced over his shoulder at Ratbag. "Besides, he probably feels safer keeping his distance." The orc returned a toothy grin that was only slightly less menacing than drawing his scimitar. Videric's fingers tightened about the grip of his own sword.

"The Black Plague has forced many peculiar alliances," Helchen told the sergeant. Though she spoke to Videric, she wasn't looking at him, but rather at the person at the back of their little group. "Survival depends on overcoming those differences and being able to work together. We share a mutual enemy now."

The witch hunter scrutinized the tail-end of their party, the creeping gait that Shareen had adopted. It wasn't long after leaving the ship that the wizard had started to fall behind. Helchen had thought it was fear that made the enchantress linger at the back, but the more she watched, the less she believed timidity was to blame. A suspicion had been growing at the corners of her mind. Now she was convinced that her notion was right.

"Orcs and thieves, these aren't virtu…" Helchen didn't hear whatever else Videric was going to say. Instead, she walked back to Shareen. The wizard blinked at her in surprise, startled by the abrupt about-face.

"You can drop the glamour," Helchen ordered Shareen. The witch hunter planted her hands on her hips and glowered at the wizard. For a moment, Shareen wore an expression of confusion and innocence, but Helchen's demand wasn't to be swayed by the pitiable display. When working for the Order, she'd been unmoved by far more desperate entreaties.

"What's going on?" Gaiseric wanted to know. Ratbag lumbered along beside the rogue, fairly drooling over the prospect of trouble. Videric dashed ahead so that they wouldn't lose sight of Rodolf. Ursola, for her part, paused to puff at her pipe, taking advantage of the unexpected halt.

"Someone here isn't who she appears to be," Helchen told Gaiseric. Her eyes narrowed as she stared into Shareen's face. "Isn't that right?"

Shareen slowly bowed her head. She curled her fingers in a peculiar pattern, then made a circular motion of her hand. Helchen's view of the wizard became distorted for a moment, as though she were trying to look through a shimmering haze. When that peculiar veil dissipated, the woman Helchen saw was still recognizably Shareen. The clothes were the same, the build was the same, the gem set into the forehead was the same. The visage, however, was quite different. The features bore a stark resemblance to the wizard, but it was the face of someone many decades older.

"Loaded dice and marked cards!" Gaiseric gasped, taking a step back in alarm. Ratbag grunted in surprise. Helchen just shook her head.

"Vanity," she chided Shareen. "Did you really think you could pull off this illusion indefinitely?"

The wizard glared at Helchen. "I wasn't moved by vanity to work my spell," she growled. Her gaze shifted between the witch hunter, Gaiseric, and Ratbag. "I adopted this arcane mantle from necessity. I had to pose as my own daughter to convince my village that I was strong enough to lead everyone to safety. They wouldn't have followed someone who they thought was infirm."

"Why keep up the illusion in Korbara?" Gaiseric asked.

"Because I still wanted to help," Shareen said. "I wanted to do whatever I could, and I was worried the council wouldn't let me if they believed I was too old to do anything." Her eyes glistened with the dampness of tears. "My daughter was killed fighting the undead that crawled up from the village cemetery."

The look on Shareen's face was one that Helchen knew only too well. She'd seen it whenever she looked at Alaric. She saw it now whenever she stared in a mirror. It was the guilt of a survivor, the responsibility of the living to the dead, the compelling urge to atone for your own escape from death by becoming a surrogate for someone who hadn't been so lucky. It was that feeling that had caused her to study the grimoire Hulmul left behind, the same compulsion that drove her to act in Alaric's stead.

"You're trying to do what your daughter would have done if she were here," Helchen said, not without sympathy. Then she shook her head. "You can't hide who you are, Shareen. Maintaining the glamour will drain your magic..." She snapped her fingers when she realized why the wizard had dared such a taxing effort. Though her face was old, the gem set into her forehead was newly grafted. "The third eye! That's why you dared to open a perpetual window into the arcane."

Shareen nodded, a gesture not without a tinge of shame. "It was the only thing I could think of to ensure my disguise remained strong. There wasn't time to do anything else. The village wouldn't follow crazy Shareen the Elder, but they took inspiration from Shareen the Younger. I had to lead them away, take them somewhere safe."

"Ya work'd der tabletapp'r swell," Ratbag snorted. "Wotz makin' ya glom onta dis caper?"

"He wants to know why you decided to leave the refuge and go along with us," Gaiseric interpreted. "Honestly, that's my question, too."

"Doran had to stay behind to study Mournshroud," Shareen explained. "It was certain that the council would want a wizard to go along with you." She glanced aside at Helchen. "Someone who's made a proper study of how to channel magic," she added, almost apologetically. "I volunteered because I didn't want someone else to go. Someone more vital to Korbara's defense."

Helchen removed her hat and turned its brim between her hands. "You thought someone expendable should go. Someone old and with less to lose." She shook her head. "You might think this is a suicide mission, but the rest of us intend to make it back." The witch hunter frowned at the wizard. "You're here now and it would cost us too much time to take you back to the ship. So what you'll do is drop the glamour and just be Shareen the Elder from now on. I'm more apt to trust someone with the wisdom that comes from age rather than a person pretending to be someone she isn't. None of us are expendable, Shareen. Not me, and not you." She set the hat back on her head and pointed an accusing finger at her. "If you want to make good use of that magic seeping out of your third eye, weave a spell that'll make you vigorous. The reason I became suspicious of you in the first place is because you were tiring and lagging behind."

Shareen returned Helchen a defiant look. "I'll do better," she swore. "You won't have to wait for me."

The witch hunter turned away and walked off. She didn't trust her judgment at the moment. Her feelings were too muddled. Shareen had tried to deceive them, but from her claims she'd done so for all the right reasons. Helchen wasn't sure that mitigated the circumstances. It still showed a degree of selfishness rather than selflessness. Shareen's need to make good for her daughter's death clouded her perception. By taking the place of someone she herself admitted would be more qualified she'd already put the expedition in jeopardy.

Wizards! The Order was right to teach witch hunters to distrust them. Even at their most benign, they still resorted to deception and misdirection. Helchen only prayed that Shareen's lies wouldn't result in disaster.

After a few hours, Shareen no longer needed to concentrate on the energy pulsing through her third eye to vitalize her old bones. The process receded into the back of her consciousness, becoming instinctual. She was grateful once the magic became an instinctive element rather than something she focused on. It was a strain her mind could do without.

The countryside continued to consist of fields and meadows. The more distance they put between themselves and the coast, the warmer it grew. Now they encountered vineyards, the grapes ripening on short, intricate trellises of sticks. Shareen imagined the sound of workers harvesting the crop, their voices lifted in song to mitigate the drudgery of their labor. A footprint pressed into the rich dark soil was an echo of interrupted life, a shadow left behind by a world the Black Plague had consumed.

In the distance, the rooftops of isolated hamlets and farms were infrequently spotted, but whenever they appeared, Rodolf motioned them to change course and veer away. The scout seemed to know his business. Shareen knew her geography well enough to know that Zanice was in a southwesterly direction and from the position of the sun she could tell that after each diversion Rodolf would get them back on a track that would take them toward the city.

Shareen was confident in Rodolf's ability. It wasn't the trapper who puzzled her. The person who was an enigma to her was Helchen. A witch hunter who used magic. There was a contradiction that the Order had rarely permitted. Of course, in a crisis rules had to bend, so perhaps it wasn't so curious that Helchen would employ a power she already understood if only because that knowledge made it easier to oppose.

No, what confounded Shareen was the sort of magic she'd seen Helchen use. Fire and lightning were elements often wound into spells. Indeed, the king's battlemages were famed for their facility with these destructive forces. Spells that invoked frost, however, were far rarer, arcane secrets that were all but lost. From what Shareen had gleaned, Helchen had learned this magic from a wizard named Hulmul, a friend who'd died in Singerva. She wondered if the witch hunter appreciated the special power that had been entrusted to her. Before the collapse, there were mystics who'd have paid enormous sums to be taught such magic. Of course, that was why these kinds of spells remained rare; those who knew them seldom shared their knowledge because doing so made their own ability to cast them less special. It was a source of pride for a wizard to wield magic unknown to his contemporaries.

Ambition and pride. Shareen scolded herself for these vices in her heart. Of what importance was status now? Her daughter would have achieved far more than she ever dared to reach for, yet she'd sacrificed her life to save neighbors who distrusted and feared her. But they'd also respected the younger Shareen, far more than the villagers had ever respected her mother. Maybe that was because her child hadn't been so calculating and grasping. *She* helped people because she could, not because she angled for some kind of advantage. It was the magic the people had been afraid of, not the woman who used it.

Shareen blinked back tears when she considered that it had taken the death of her daughter to open her eyes to a concept so simple as responsibility. Being able to see beyond her own greed, to think about the suffering of her community. Well, she was going to make up for neglecting her duty. That was how she'd honor her daughter. Oh, if only she'd gone with her to battle the undead! Together they might have defended the cemetery.

Or at least Shareen the Younger might have survived and Shareen the Elder died in her place.

The wizard slowly tamped down the despair welling up inside her. It did no good to regret the past. That way lay only misery and madness. She couldn't change what had happened, all she could do was try to keep it from happening again.

"Hold here," Videric called out. The group stopped while the templar jogged ahead to join Rodolf. The scout looked out across a pasture. The tall grass in the meadow prevented Shareen from seeing whatever the trapper looked at. A moment later, Videric waved the rest of the party forward.

"There's a cheery sight," Gaiseric muttered when they reached the edge of the pasture.

Bones littered the ground. Though the earth was soaked in blood, not so much as a scrap of flesh remained on the hundreds of skeletons strewn across the pasture. An entire herd of cattle had been picked clean of the last morsel. An army of wolves couldn't have inflicted such carnage.

"Looks like going cross country doesn't mean there aren't zombies about," Ursola observed.

Helchen crouched down next to one of the bovine skeletons and ran her hand along the ragged bones. She brushed her fingers across the bloody earth. "This was recent," she stated, her voice grim.

"Half a day at most," Rodolf said. He looked up at the sky. "Probably shortly after sunrise."

Shareen stepped closer to get a better look. "Wouldn't zombies be more active at night?"

"More complex forms of undead prefer darkness," Helchen told her. "Some, like vampires, can't even endure sunlight.

Zombies, however, are among the simplest variety of undead. They don't need the darkness to sustain them. As a result, it makes little difference to them whether it is day or night. In fact, there are some kinds of zombies that are more dangerous in daylight." She looked over at Gaiseric. "These bones weren't gnawed. They were pecked."

All the color drained out of the thief's face. "Loaded dice and marked cards."

Shareen didn't understand Gaiseric's fear, but clearly, he had more than a suspicion about what had killed the cattle.

"What is it?" Videric demanded, uneasiness in his voice.

Helchen stood and studied the grove that edged the far end of the pasture. "Hopefully something we can avoid," she told the templar. She looked over at Rodolf. "Keep us as far away from those trees as you can," she ordered.

The scout shook his head, confused by the command. "The best way forward is straight ahead. If we go due south, we'll have to slog through a peat bog before…"

"Too late," Gaiseric whispered, pulling Cryptblade from its scabbard.

Shareen followed the rogue's horrified gaze. At once she shared his fear and understood Helchen's caution. The trees edging the pasture erupted into animation. A dark cloud rose from the branches, loose feathers drifting down as a black multitude swarmed into the air.

Only for an instant did Shareen delude herself that the birds were still natural creatures. No flock ever took wing with such uncanny silence, without a lone caw or squawk. The bones, pecked clean of flesh, stripped of the last morsel. The birds were the culprits, a vast murder of crows.

Like a dark storm, the crows flew toward them. Shareen saw the gleam of bone showing through the rotten, feathery bodies. Not living animals at all, but a horde of winged zombies, ravenous for living flesh.

"By Njall the Hunter!" Rodolf cried, stumbling over a skeleton as he sprang back. "Look at them!"

The undead crows came sweeping down, the rustle of their wings the only sound emanating from the hideous flock. Shareen quickly read through a scroll she drew from her satchel, focusing her thoughts upon a spell she'd had cause to use many times since the zombie invasion. She stretched out her hand and a snake of electricity danced from her fingers, searing into the birds. A clutch of the crows flopped to the ground, their ghastly bodies cooked and steaming. In the blink of an eye, she'd destroyed half a dozen of the monsters.

But there were more. Many more.

"Get behind me!" Helchen commanded, shoving Shareen back. Nearly mindless, the zombie crows were still capable of recognizing a threat. Until the witch hunter acted, Shareen hadn't noticed that the birds had shifted in their flight and now dove toward her. She started to defy Helchen's order, unwilling to let her perish because of the wizard's own mistake. Then she felt the hairs on her neck stand up, experienced the ethereal chill that accompanied any great exertion of magic. Her eyes widened with wonder as Helchen let the flanged mace fall from her fist to dangle by a leather strap from her wrist.

The witch hunter's hands were held wide apart, the fingers splayed. A low incantation rasped across Helchen's lips and then from each palm a burst of icy light blasted up into the black mass of undead birds. The frigid beam washed across the crows, freezing them in midair. The feathered bodies hurtled earthward, shattering as they slammed into the ground. Fixated upon attacking Shareen, the entire murder was caught by Helchen's spell. Scores of crows, frozen so brittle their decayed bodies were like glass, dropped from the sky to lie scattered among the bones of their late victims.

Suddenly the cold light winked out and Helchen sagged down to her knees, gasping from the tremendous effort of her conjuration. While she recovered, Gaiseric and Ratbag rushed into the field to stomp on any of the zombie birds that hadn't completely disintegrated on impact.

Shareen grabbed Helchen by the shoulders, her touch allowing her to redirect some of the vitalizing energies into the witch hunter. "That was magnificent," she declared. "No wonder you're so jealous of that spell."

Helchen turned her head and gave her a bewildered look. "Jealous?"

"It's very powerful," Shareen explained. "Though you should be more judicious about how much energy you put into it, or you'll be rendered too weak to do anything after you cast it."

"Jealous," Helchen continued to roll the word over on her tongue. Suddenly she laughed bitterly. "If I was ever jealous of anything, it isn't spells." A pained, haunted look crossed the woman's face.

It was Shareen's turn to feel bewildered. A mystic who wasn't jealous of her magic? But then she remembered that Helchen wasn't someone who'd studied wizardry as a discipline. She'd stumbled into the arcane. Something more than an amateur, to be sure, but neither was she an adept. Perhaps she wasn't as possessive of the frost spell as a real wizard would be.

The others joined Gaiseric and Ratbag in searching the field for any crows that looked like they might revive when the ice melted. For the moment Shareen was alone with Helchen. She decided to take a chance. "Will you teach me?"

Helchen was slow to answer, her eyes peering intently at Shareen. The wizard felt as though she were being studied, judged by the witch hunter. It dawned on her that it wouldn't be possessiveness on Helchen's part that would keep the workings of the spell a secret, but whether she felt Shareen was worthy of the knowledge. Whether Shareen could be trusted to use such power for good.

"After we make camp and have eaten, I'll explain the spell to you," Helchen said. A wistful look crossed her face. "I think that's what Hulmul would have liked me to do." Her hand caressed the grimoire chained to her belt. "Maybe we can teach each other," she mused. "I know how the spell works, but you might be able to tell me why it works."

Shareen nodded. "A deal."

She offered her hand to Helchen. Even amid the Black Plague, a tremor of fear rushed through the wizard when she shook hands with the witch hunter.

CHAPTER FIVE

No dwarf enjoyed camping under an open sky. It was uncomfortable enough to sleep in one of the ramshackle human buildings, all too aware that there were at best only a few feet of wood and stone over her head. Ursola was accustomed to tons of solid rock over her, of feeling the immensity of mountain and hill pressing down on her. She'd had a difficult enough time adjusting to the subterranean halls of Ironshield and Company, excavated only fifty feet beneath the streets of Singerva. Trying to get comfortable with naught but thin air above her was a fruitless effort and one she soon abandoned.

Rodolf had chosen the site for the camp, a small hillock set in the midst of several wheat fields. The peasants had maintained a shrine to some harvest goddess there, a rural deity unknown to Ursola, probably in the belief that doing so would encourage a divine interest in their crop. Whether it had or not, the goddess's favor hadn't protected the farmers from the undead onslaught. It was obvious no offerings had been brought to the shrine in weeks.

The scout was snoring away off to her right. Opposite her she could see Gaiseric curled up in his blanket. Nearby was Videric, the templar's armor neatly laid out on the ground next to him and his sword clasped in his sleeping hand. Ursola knew dwarf warriors who trained themselves to that trick, teaching their bodies not to twist or turn while they slept and developing their senses to such a degree that the least disturbance would snap them awake.

The bedrolls next to Videric were empty. Away at the edge of the camp, Ursola heard subdued voices. She recognized Helchen's and guessed that the whispered responses were those of Shareen. The wizard was trying to learn the frost spell Helchen had gleaned from Hulmul's spellbook. The dwarf chuckled under her breath. She wondered who was more eager between them, the student or the teacher. Helchen was uncomfortable practicing magic, a prejudice drummed into her by her years with the Order. Ursola imagined the witch hunter would be grateful to pass the knowledge along to someone else and let them take on the responsibility of flash-freezing flocks of undead crows.

Shifting around, Ursola tried to muffle the whispering of the women. As she did, she spotted Ratbag stalking around the hillock. Night was the natural element of orcs. They could see better and farther in starlight than they could by the harsh gleam of the sun. When choosing someone to keep watch, only Rodolf had offered any argument against Ratbag taking on the duty. The scout wasn't sure Helchen's orders would keep the orc from slitting his throat while he slept. Ursola wavered between wondering if that was Rodolf's guilty conscience talking or if it was simply the trapper's familiarity with orcs warning him. Whichever way, the scar-faced man had lost his fight to stay awake about an hour ago and Ratbag hadn't paid him the least notice.

Instead, Ursola thought, the orc renegade gave his full attention to the fields west of the hillock. Every time he made a circuit of the camp, he paused when facing west and hesitated, peering into the night before resuming his patrol. She got the impression that Ratbag sensed something out there in the darkness. Something he wasn't telling anybody about.

Ursola knew what a bold and relentless fighter Ratbag was, but it was impossible to forget that he was an orc. Where did his loyalties truly lie? What if the thing he sensed out there was a warband of orc raiders, not undead monsters like the ones they'd fought on Yandryl's island, but living marauders? Would Ratbag side with his companions against his own people?

The dwarf frowned as she pondered the subject. Softly, she drew back the blanket and reached for her hammer. Exhibiting all the silence she could muster, Ursola crept toward the orc as he stopped once more to stare off into the west. She peered past his elbow, straining her eyes to see whatever it was that so interested Ratbag.

"Der firebug ain't catchin' winkz," Ratbag grunted at her without turning around. It wasn't lost on Ursola that he had his scimitar clenched in one hand.

"Who can sleep?" Ursola replied, trying to keep her tone even. If Ratbag was plotting something, she didn't want to put him on alert and escalate the situation. "Humans and elves might be able to do this kind of thing, but this dwarf needs something solid over her head."

Ratbag uttered a brief growl of amusement. He partly turned his head to glance at Ursola. "Ya lampin' wotz Ratbag lampin'?" He rolled his shoulder off toward the west.

Ursola made another effort to stare into the dark, but the night refused to divulge its secrets. A dwarf could see across short distances in pitch blackness, but whatever Ratbag noticed was well past the limits of her own vision. "What's out there? What do you see?"

The orc sniffed the air, his wide nostrils flaring. "Cadavaz. Cadavaz wot was wulfen."

Ursola had a hard time understanding Ratbag's guttural speech, but she caught the meaning of that last word. *Wolf.* What he was watching out there in the night were wolves. Wolves that, like the crows they'd fought earlier in the day, had eaten the corrupt flesh of the undead and been transformed into zombies. The thought sent a chill through her veins.

"We should warn the others," she suggested.

"Nah," Ratbag huffed. "Der mugz'd set up der racket. Sure'n bring wulfen sniffin' 'roun' der bivwak." The orc gestured with his scimitar at the darkened fields. "Better'n ter dummyup an' let der cadavaz stroll off."

Ursola thought she understood the orc's meaning. If they kept quiet, the wolves wouldn't know they were around, and the zombies would pass them by. Waking everybody might cause enough noise to draw their attention.

"Helchen," Ursola gasped when she remembered that whispered conversation between witch hunter and wizard, and what the two were discussing. If Shareen decided to try the spell she was being taught...

The dwarf turned from Ratbag and hurried for the far side

of the camp. Ursola had only taken a few steps before there was a bright blue flash of light. A frosty slush drifted down to the ground as Shareen practiced the magic she'd learned.

"Stop!" Ursola hissed in as loud a voice as she dared. Helchen and Shareen turned around, both women staring at her in bewilderment. Their confusion didn't last long, nor did the dwarf's hope that the wolves wouldn't notice the icy light. Unlike the crows, the wolves retained some speck of their living instincts, for out of the night there suddenly arose a chorus of barks and howls.

The undead pack was on the hunt!

One benefit of his larcenous lifestyle was becoming a very light sleeper. Gaiseric snapped awake as soon as the first howl started. No fog of drowsiness clouded his mind. He was completely aware of his surroundings. He grabbed Cryptblade and drew it from its scabbard. Only with the sword in his hand did he try to assess what was happening around him.

Ursola had her hammer clenched in her fist and was rushing over to Helchen and Shareen. The witch hunter and the enchantress both wore confused expressions, but Helchen at least wasn't idle. She might not know what was happening, but she was fitting a bolt into her crossbow just the same.

Beside him, Gaiseric heard the rattle of armor as Videric hastily tried to don his mail. The thief shook his head. "I don't think you have time for that," he snidely advised the templar. With a sullen glower, Videric made a point of dropping his breastplate and grabbing his helm. His features soon vanished behind a mask of steel.

Rodolf, too, was scrambling into action. The scout fumbled about in his pack, pulling out what looked to Gaiseric like nothing so much as a big metal horseshoe with spikes along the inner curve. Rodolf took the peculiar object and set it at one end of the slim pole he'd been carrying since they disembarked. Until that moment the rogue had thought it was a walking stick, but now he saw it was part of some exotic weapon. With a twist, Rodolf locked the spiked horseshoe to the cap at the end of the pole. Then the man fell back toward the center of the camp, his darting eyes making it clear he was calculating his position so that from any direction there was someone standing between him and the dark of the night.

On the western side of the hillock, Ratbag wasn't in a timid mood. The big orc planted his feet, braced for the oncoming carnage. Moonlight glistened off his scimitar. "Cadavaz comin." He grinned at Gaiseric from over his shoulder before fixing his attention on the howling darkness.

"Wonderful." Gaiseric jumped to his feet. He gave one longing glance at his own armor, but the advice he'd given Videric was even more applicable to himself. If it took a knight five minutes to get into his mail, it would take a comparably untrained commoner like himself twenty. By then the enemy would be cracking his bones for the marrow.

The green shine of a dozen sets of eyes peered at Gaiseric from the night. Whatever possessed those eyes was lower to the ground than a human. That puzzled him before he connected the observation to the barks and howls he'd heard. Ratbag had warned of zombies, but the orc didn't mean human zombies. The camp was being attacked by undead wolves!

The first of the monsters sprang out of the darkness, its gray fur ratty and clotted with dried gore. Even before Ratbag cut it down with his scimitar, the wolf was a gruesome spectacle. The orc's swing cleaved through the snapping muzzle and split the canine forehead. Putrid blood and flecks of brain streamed from the gash and the wolf crumpled, its body sliding back down the rise.

A second lean gray shape lunged at Ratbag. Its head flew clear of its neck in mid-leap, hewn through by the scimitar's blade. The decapitated body crashed into the orc, staggering him. Gaiseric had no chance to see if the warrior recovered before the wolves closed in. More of the undead raced past Ratbag to attack the camp.

The sharp crack of Helchen's crossbow sounded from behind Gaiseric. One of the bounding wolves toppled, a hole in its head where the bolt had crunched through the decayed skull. Another wolf jerked about in midair, smoke billowing from its mangy fur as Shareen sent a string of lightning into its rotten flesh.

"Wotun's wrath is upon you!" Videric shouted, rushing past Gaiseric to meet the attacking pack. The templar looked somewhat ridiculous, a great helm over his head, steel greaves over one leg, but overall clad only in linen undergarments. The sword he swung, however, bit down into a wolf's head with such force that the skull split down the middle.

Another wolf skirted away from Videric and sprang at Gaiseric, mistakenly believing he would be easier prey. The zombie crumpled to the ground a heartbeat later, a slash from Cryptblade all that was needed to unravel the necromancy that endowed the brute with its unnatural mockery of life.

The wolf twitched and writhed as its body shriveled up like a dead leaf.

"Over here!" Rodolf called to Gaiseric, his voice panicked. The thief swung around to see Rodolf struggling with one of the undead. A huge wolf was caught in the mouth of the spiked horseshoe. A spring had caused the trap to close around its body when the monster lunged at the scout. Against a living animal, the wolfcatcher's spikes would have pierced it deep enough to start it bleeding, weakening it the more it struggled. The zombie didn't have such vulnerabilities. It remained as strong and vicious with the spikes embedded in it as it had when it first sprang at Rodolf.

"Help! I can't hold it for long!" Rodolf pleaded. The rogue nodded and ran over. The scout pivoted, swinging the wolf around so that he could chop into its spine with Cryptblade. The result was almost immediate. The zombie hung loose from the spikes as its body withered.

"Gaiseric! Watch out!"

Helchen's cry came too late. Gaiseric was flung to the ground by a terrific impact. He gagged on the foul stench of dead flesh and winced as he felt claws scratching at his back. He tried to bring Cryptblade around to stab at the monster pressing down on him but couldn't quite get the angle right. Moaning in dread, he clenched his teeth in anticipation of the zombie fangs that must soon be chomping down on his neck.

Instead, he heard a meaty impact and felt the weight pressing down on him drop away. He rolled onto his side to see Helchen standing over him with a huge wolf lying at her feet. Bits of fur and brain clotted the flanges of her mace. "Keep behind Rodolf," she told Gaiseric, repeating the command for the benefit of Ursola and Videric.

"Rodolf, catch them and swing them around for somebody else to finish," Helchen told the scout. "Gaiseric, watch his back in case any jump him."

Gaiseric scowled at the order. It was sound strategy; with Cryptblade he could bring down a zombie more quickly and more surely than anybody else. However, it wasn't lost on him that when he'd been helping Rodolf, the trapper hadn't warned him about the wolf at his own back.

Instead, Gaiseric voiced a different concern. "What about Ratbag?"

Well ahead of the others, the orc defended his part of the hillock all on his own. The wolves had enough awareness left that they'd eventually realize the fact and come at him from all sides.

"We'll move forward and make our stand with him," Helchen said.

Rodolf had another wolf snared and swung it around for Ursola to brain it with her hammer. "Holding this spot will be hard enough," he claimed, letting the slaughtered zombie fall and turning around so that he could catch another of the vicious creatures.

In the interval, Gaiseric clipped the leg out from under a wolf that had been ready to strike the trapper from behind. Rodolf turned in time to see the canine wither and fall. "You don't try to reach Ratbag, I'm going to stop watching your back," Gaiseric threatened. The way Rodolf's face paled told him the scout was in no doubt he meant what he said.

Yard by yard, the group moved across the hillock. Helchen

and Shareen watched their flanks, dealing with any wolves attacking from the sides. Rodolf held the point, snaring wolves and swinging the thrashing creatures around so that Ursola or Videric could overcome them. Gaiseric kept pace, hanging back until Rodolf trapped a zombie, then dashing forward to deal with any wolves that tried to come at him while his back was turned.

Slowly they drew nearer to the spot where Ratbag was holding his ground. The orc's leathery green flesh was torn in a dozen places, slashed by the claws of his foes, but around him were strewn the carcasses of a half dozen wolves.

"Ratbag! We're coming!" Gaiseric called out. The warrior still seemed terribly far away.

"Belly der dallyin' an' bump der cadavaz," Ratbag growled back. His voice was as fierce as ever, but Gaiseric discerned a note of weariness in his tone. The endurance of an orc far exceeded that of a human or dwarf, but it wasn't inexhaustible. He worried that Ratbag was reaching his limits.

For a moment, Gaiseric thought he saw a sly gleam in Rodolf's eye. The scout had another of the zombie wolves caught in his trap. He swung the undead back so that Videric could dispatch it. Taking a few steps forward, Rodolf snagged another enemy in his wolfcatcher. This time he stumbled as he tried to turn the animal so that Ursola could crush its skull. Instead of facing the dwarf, his spin brought him toward Ratbag.

Suddenly, the spikes withdrew from the wolf's body and the beast was flung out of the trap. It crashed into Ratbag from behind. The orc's knees buckled, and he spilled face-first into the dirt.

"No!" Gaiseric shouted. He ran down the side of the hillock, uncaring that he was deserting his role as Rodolf's protector. He'd seen that look and was convinced the wolf's release wasn't an accident. Rushing down the slope, Gaiseric reached the orc as a pair of wolves converged on him. Heedless of his own safety, he sprang into their midst, sweeping Cryptblade from side to side. The two zombies collapsed and withered, but he wasn't quick enough to avoid a third canine, the beast that had been freed from Rodolf's trap. The undead leapt at him, its fangs catching hold of his sleeve, barely missing the arm within.

The wolf thrashed its head, violently jerking Gaiseric off his feet. Cryptblade was knocked loose from his hand as he struck the ground. He cried out in horror as the zombie glared down at him, then shrieked in disgust as the creature's head burst in a spray of blood and brains. Ratbag grinned down at the thief and wagged his gory scimitar.

"Capital rumpuz, eh yegg?" the orc laughed.

Gaiseric trembled, comfortable only when he felt Cryptblade's grip back in his hand. He was relieved that Ratbag seemed unharmed. At least the orc wasn't surrounded by undead wolves now. The thief scowled up at the green-skinned warrior. "This might be your idea of a fun fight, but not mine."

Ratbag shrugged and squinted into the darkness. No more barks or howls rang out. It seemed like the last three wolves were just that – the last. Gaiseric only hoped that there weren't more packs of zombies near enough to have heard the fray. He could do without meeting any more of the vicious creatures. The undead wolves were even quicker and more savage than the most frenzied human zombies he'd encountered.

"That's all of them," Videric declared, assessing the carnage.

"Anyone hurt?" Helchen asked. Gaiseric knew the witch hunter wasn't asking about cuts and scratches. She wanted to know if anyone had been bitten. The bite of a zombie had proven to be not only deadly, but those who died from such wounds would themselves be infected by the Black Plague and join the ranks of the undead. He didn't know if the corruption could be passed on by an infected wolf, but it was prudent to err on the side of caution.

While the others called out whatever scrapes they'd suffered in the fight, Rodolf took a few steps down the slope. "That last wolf broke free of the trap," he informed Ratbag, a smug look on his face.

When he wanted to, Ratbag could move far quicker than his hulking frame would suggest. The orc closed on Rodolf before the scout could so much as blink. One beefy fist lashed out, mashing Rodolf's nose and knocking him over.

"Ratbag!" Helchen admonished the orc. "We need him to guide…"

"Ya der boss," Ratbag grumbled. "Jus' wise me if'n der stoolie ain't wanted nomore." He glowered at Rodolf before stalking away.

Gaiseric followed behind the orc, but tarried just long enough to whisper to Rodolf as the scout regained his feet. "Be grateful," he advised. "If you'd tried that stunt with me, I'd slit your throat, however angry that might make Helchen. Try that stunt again with Ratbag, and I'll still slit your throat."

Gaiseric didn't linger to judge what impact his warning

might have had. It wouldn't matter. He'd made up his mind to keep a close watch on Rodolf after this. It was only fair that if he was going to lose sleep worrying about the scout, then Rodolf should lose some sleep worrying about *him*.

Whichever way things turned out, Gaiseric was certain of one thing: they couldn't reach Zanice fast enough to suit him.

CHAPTER SIX

Helchen felt as though her head were on a swivel, so intensely did she watch the surrounding countryside. Every nerve was on edge and the bright daylight did nothing to ease her anxiety. True, it helped them spot any zombies that were prowling the area well before the undead could close upon them, but by the same token the creatures would be able to spot them.

Most of all, Helchen wrestled with doubt. She'd presented absolute confidence when she told the others that they'd stick to the roads after their deadly combat with the wolves. Between them and the crows earlier in the day, it seemed the countryside was as rife with zombies as any settlement could be. They might as well take advantage of the roads. If they weren't going to have safety, they should at least have speed and it would be much easier following a road than navigating fields and forests. She only prayed it was the right decision to make.

"We need to find a marker so I can get my bearings," Rodolf advised while he walked beside the witch hunter.

"I thought you said you knew this country," Gaiseric reminded the scout.

Rodolf shot the thief a dark look. "I'm not a walking map," he retorted, and then tapped his temple. "I keep everything up here. Big difference navigating the countryside and following the roads, or hugging the coastline. I need to see something that'll let me know how far from Zanice we are." He pointed up at the sky. "We're headed in the right direction, overall. Unless, of course, we've made better time than I calculated and we've gone too far."

Helchen scrutinized the trapper. She wondered if his claims that he didn't know precisely where they were was just an excuse to surrender the point to Ratbag. Rodolf was quite happy to let the warrior lead the way and it followed that the orc was pleased to be in the front where he'd be the first to get involved in any fighting.

"What do you need to see?" Helchen asked Rodolf as Ratbag took the lead.

The scout shrugged. "A milestone. A shrine. Failing that, any village could tell me what I need to know. There isn't one in the duchy that doesn't have some kind of fountain in its square, each of them with their own unique flourishes. Get me close enough to see a fountain and I'll tell you exactly where we are." He smiled in self-satisfaction. "Tell you exactly how far we are from Zanice."

The braggadocio, even when trying to cover for his own incompetence, stunned Helchen. It was truly a changed world when a man like Rodolf had the audacity to temporize with a witch hunter. In her days with the Order, she'd have threatened the scout with thumb screws to curb his duplicity.

Admitting a mistake or a failure was forgivable, trying to hide that he genuinely didn't know where they were with contrived assurances was something else.

Up ahead of them, Ratbag raised his fist, motioning that he'd found something around the next bend in the road. Helchen and the others jogged up to join the orc. The countryside here was bocage, pastures bordered by thick hedgerows. The farmers had cultivated their hedges so that the road was enclosed on both sides, lending it a tunnel-like quality.

Around the bend, the road opened somewhat. The broader vantage permitted a greater view of the country. Beyond the pastures, maybe a mile distant, Helchen could see a large structure surrounded by high stone walls.

"Ya noodlin' wotz wot?" Ratbag asked, nodding his chin at the building.

"Might be a manor house," Videric suggested. "The steading of some yeoman or petty noble."

"Looks more like a coaching inn," Rodolf said. "The byways near Zanice have a lot of them. Most are run by the Hospitality Guild."

"So that means we're close to the city?" Helchen asked the scout.

Rodolf frowned and shook his head. "The Guild always build according to set plans. One inn looks much like another. I'd need to see its sign to know which one this is and where it is."

"That would mean getting a lot closer than we are now," Gaiseric pointed out. He locked eyes with Helchen. "If there are zombies in there…"

The witch hunter weighed their options. The risk of encountering more of the undead against the hazards of wandering about the duchy with only a vague idea of where they were. "We can't afford the time to play safe," she decided. "Korbara is counting on us." She pointed at Rodolf. "Take over for Ratbag. The moment you're certain which inn this is, we'll draw back. There's no sense taking more chances than we have to."

Rodolf rolled his shoulders in a slow shrug. "As soon as I get the name, I'll know where we are," he assured her.

Only a few yards behind the scout as he prowled ahead on the road, Helchen felt a growing uneasiness. A suggestive silence hovered above the coaching inn. No sounds of activity rose from behind the walls. When they got closer, the gates leading into the courtyard were found wide open. Final proof, if any was needed, that no living occupants were around.

"If anybody was in there, they'd have tried to fortify the place," Videric said, echoing Helchen's assessment.

"Can you read the name?" Helchen asked Rodolf.

The scout gestured at a beam that projected from above the open gate. Two jagged strips of chain rattled forlornly in the wind. "Must have been blown down and fallen inside."

The report was hardly to Helchen's liking. Her eyes roved along the high stone walls. It looked like the gates were the only way in. That meant they were also the only way out.

"We've got to get our bearings," Ursola reminded the witch hunter, noting her hesitation.

"All right," Helchen said, "but be on the alert." She motioned everyone to follow while she led the way. She wasn't comfortable with the situation and wasn't going to have anyone take more risks than she took herself.

Behind the walls, they found a roughly paved courtyard. A well was at its center while off to one side was a corral and stables. Directly opposite the gate was the inn itself, a half-timber structure of three floors with a steeply angled roof and a couple of gables. Several wagons were drawn up against the left wall, tarps thrown across their beds to protect their cargo against the elements.

These details impressed themselves upon Helchen's mind, but her attention was immediately captured by the bodies strewn about the courtyard. A half dozen men were lying sprawled on the cobblestones. Each of them had a similar look, garbed in thick leather hauberks reinforced with iron. Horsehide caps trimmed in fur and adorned with a single steel spike covered their heads, made fast by straps that crossed under their chins. Near the outstretched hands of the corpses were strange weapons unlike anything Helchen had seen before. They resembled crossbows, but with a box-like carriage fitted above the string. Or rather, strings, for there were multiples of these.

The witch hunter scrutinized them, looking for the least hint of animation. The decay evident in their flesh made it obvious that they were dead, but death wasn't a conclusive condition since the onset of the Black Plague. Before she could warn him away, Ratbag lumbered over to one of the bodies. Keeping his scimitar ready, the orc gave the corpse a solid kick that sent it rolling a few feet along the cobbles. There was no reaction from the body. Had it been undead, Helchen was sure it would have been provoked by

Ratbag's aggression if not by the proximity of living flesh. Her tension eased a bit when she concluded the men were truly dead.

"Mercenaries from the borderland of the Eternal Empire," Rodolf said, noticing Helchen's interest in the bodies. "From the way they trim their beards, I'd say they were of the Kahgra nomads. Dead at least two weeks from the look of it."

"What would nomads from the Empire be doing here?" Gaiseric wondered. He shifted one of the crossbows with the tip of his boot, tripping its mechanism. The weapon shuddered and a bolt glanced off the cobblestones near where Videric was standing. The templar shot Gaiseric a dark look and the thief quickly backed away.

"The Rangers have a standing contract with a noble in the Empire," Rodolf answered. "Twice a year he sends them rarities from the far corners of the Empire. These nomads must have been guarding one of his caravans." The scout waved his hand at the row of wagons. "Some of those, no doubt, must have been on their way to the Rangers."

Ursola and Shareen walked toward the wagons, while Helchen gave a closer scrutiny to the corpse. It needed only a brief examination to divulge what had killed the nomad. There was a vicious wound in his neck, inflicted by teeth. "Zombies," she told Gaiseric when he leaned over her shoulder to see what she was looking at.

The thief took a step back, his eyes widening with alarm. "If they were bitten, they should have been infected. Why aren't they attacking us? Do we smell bad or something?"

Helchen frowned at Gaiseric and then she stared down at the guard. "They might have only been injured in battle with the undead. Knowing about the infection, maybe they took poison rather than risk turning into zombies themselves."

Gaiseric scowled at the grim suggestion. "That's a horrible choice to make. Not sure I'd have the stomach to do that." He shook his head. "No matter how nasty the situation, I always cling to the hope that luck can pull my bacon out of the fire."

"There have been people who've survived the bite of a zombie," Helchen said, but her expression was doubtful. "If there was any rhyme or reason to how they staved off infection, the Order never discovered it." Her eyes hardened when she recalled the methods the inquisitors had used to ferret the truth from such survivors. It might have been better had they not escaped from the undead. She shook the dark images aside and gave Gaiseric a half-hearted smile. "Maybe it was simply luck."

"Nah lampin' any cadavaz now," Ratbag grumbled. The big orc stalked toward the inn itself, squinting at its doors and windows.

"Maybe not now, but the undead were here." Helchen grimaced when she let the guard slip back down onto the ground. She looked around the courtyard. "If any zombies were still around, I think they'd have shown themselves by now. We've made enough noise."

The witch hunter was still ruminating upon the strange discovery when a cry of delight brought her attention over to the wagons. She looked over to see Ursola draw a big clay jar from the bed of one wagon. The dwarf's face was split by a wide grin.

"Dragon bile!" Ursola crowed. "All I need are some bottles and pots, and I can turn this stuff into dozens of fire-bombs."

She slapped her hand against the bed of the wagon. "There must be gallons of it here."

"A good day for a dwarf, then," Helchen said with a smile until Videric caught her attention.

"We could probably stand to get some rest," Videric reminded her. "This inn would be more defensible than an open camp."

Helchen slowly nodded. There would certainly be vessels inside for Ursola's dragon bile, probably some alcohol as well to dilute the combustible and render it more stable. And the argument against camping in the open carried a great deal of weight after their encounter with the undead wolves.

"All right," Helchen said. "We stay here tonight." She pointed at the inn. "But we keep to the ground floor and we keep together. If there's trouble, I want everybody ready to act." She looked over at Rodolf as the scout was searching the courtyard. A moment later and he found what he was looking for.

"The Red Unicorn," Rodolf laughed, holding up the fallen sign with its crude picture of a horned horse rearing on its back legs and kicking its forelegs. He turned and indicated the road outside the gate. "We keep following that road south, we'll be in Zanice tomorrow."

The news brought cheers from the others, but Helchen couldn't join in the celebration. Maybe it was the dour strictures of the Order preying upon her, but she was always uneasy when things started going too well.

It always meant that something bad was going to pop up and restore the balance.

•••

While the others started toward the inn, Gaiseric kept his eye on Rodolf. The scout started to drift back toward the wagons. Suspicious of the man, he quietly followed. Rodolf didn't notice the thief until he'd reached one of the tarp-covered carts. Guilt was written across his face when he looked at Gaiseric.

"Helchen said everyone should stay together," Gaiseric said.

The scout scowled for an instant, then a sly smile began to tug at the corners of his mouth. "If that's the way you want it, but I thought you were smarter than that." He thumped his hand against the side of the wagon. "The wares Tsao Yun sends to the Rangers would be worth a lot to the right people. The Black Plague won't last forever, and when it ends, smart people will have to make a living. People like you and me."

Gaiseric's distrust of Rodolf didn't inoculate him from the tempting picture the man presented. There was an argument to be made that one had to look to a world beyond the Black Plague. Simply because things were dire now didn't mean they would always be so. The old anxiety about existing in poverty, unable to maintain the slightest comforts, asserted itself again. Gaiseric had come from a poor family and had risked much to improve his circumstances. Rodolf was right. It wasn't enough to merely survive through the apocalypse, he had to aspire to the hope of a better world once the undead had been scourged from the kingdom.

"We'll split things even," Rodolf said as he started to draw back the tarpaulin. "Fifty-fifty."

"We split with everyone," Gaiseric corrected the trapper. He wasn't so greedy that he'd cheat friends. "Including

Ratbag," he added when he saw Rodolf wince at the notion of dividing any valuables. "They've risked just as much as we have."

Rodolf gave a sullen nod as he broke open a crate on the back of the wagon. "Not one of Tsao's wagons," he said, holding up a fistful of rabbit pelts. "Check the other ones."

Gaiseric turned to the next closest wagon and drew back the tarp. He expected to find a big pile of boxes beneath. Instead, to his surprise, he found a single massive cage with thick iron bars. As he pulled the covering away and sunlight shone upon the cage, he was shocked to see an enormous shaggy white bulk slumped in one of the corners.

"By Njall!" Rodolf gasped. The scout hurried over to the cage, pressing his face close to the bars. "You've really found something here. This was certainly from Tsao!"

"Whatever it was, it's dead," Gaiseric said. He wrinkled his nose at the stench wafting off the shaggy carcass. "As awful as it smells, it must have died long before it got this far. I don't think you'll get much for its fur, if you could stomach being that close to it long enough to skin it."

The more Gaiseric looked at the corpse, the more he thought it would need a far more callous conscience than his own to skin that hairy hulk. For all its prodigious size and thick white fur, there was a semblance of humanity to the thing that was unsettling.

He poked it to see if it would turn around and attack him, but most of the animals they encountered had to have eaten their share of zombie flesh to become undead. Locked up, it looked like this creature probably didn't have the chance and died of natural circumstances.

"Skin?" Rodolf scoffed. "Bah, the fur's the least valuable part of it. That's a yeti, one of the ice-men of the glaciers." He circled the wagon until he found the door to the cage. "They grind down the fangs and claws to make medicine, cures for everything from the pox to shingles. Any apothecary or alchemist would pay a fortune for yeti teeth!" Rodolf fumbled at the door for a moment, cursing under his breath when he found it locked. He inserted the point of his dagger between the door and its frame in an enthusiastic effort to pry it open.

"Let me," Gaiseric insisted, rounding the wagon and pushing the scout to one side. He removed a steel pick and a brass hook from a pouch on his belt and inserted them into the lock, grateful that it wasn't some complicated mechanism like the imperial puzzle box he'd once stolen from a guildmaster in Beckemburg.

Gaiseric felt the hairs on the back of his neck tingle while he worked. He kept a watch on Rodolf, but the scout didn't make any threatening move. Indeed, he appeared even more anxious than the thief to get the lock opened.

Risking a look across the courtyard, Gaiseric could see Helchen and the others entering the inn. It seemed the absence of the thief and the trapper hadn't been noticed. Or perhaps it had, for he suddenly saw Ratbag come lumbering back into the courtyard.

Gaiseric returned his full attention to the lock when he felt an inner spring give. "Ah, that's got it," he grinned, drawing back his tools and pulling open the door.

Rodolf tried to shove his way past the thief, but Gaiseric held firm on the door and glared at the man. "I opened it, I get first look."

"Listen, you cutpurse," Rodolf snarled. "It was my idea, I get..."

The trapper's voice trailed off. Gaiseric noticed that the man wasn't looking inside the cage now, he was staring through the bars at the courtyard beyond. Rodolf's face paled until it nearly matched the color of his scars. He stumbled away from the wagon, his good eye gleaming with fright.

Gaiseric followed the direction of his gaze and felt a chill run through him. The slaughtered mercenaries were starting to move!

"Loaded dice and marked cards," Gaiseric cursed. The nomads had certainly been dead when he looked at them earlier, but since the onset of the Black Plague, death wasn't as final as it usually was. Disturbing the wagon the guards had sworn to protect must have roused some fragment of their awareness, enough to respond to the necromantic infection.

"Help! Zombies!" Gaiseric screamed, hoping his cry was loud enough to warn the people inside the inn. He scrambled to drop away from the cage, but before he could move, he saw a wall of white fur rise up and launch itself at him.

Gaiseric slammed the door in the yeti's face and tried to dash for comparative safety. He didn't even manage to turn around before a clawed hand reached between the bars and clamped down on his shoulder. He shrieked in agony as the massive talons ripped into him.

Whether it had been dead before reaching the Red Unicorn or not was a moot point now. The yeti had revived as a zombie. Gaiseric could see the rotten flesh where some of the shaggy hide had rubbed away from the apelike body. The iceman's belly had burst open, loops of decayed guts hanging from the brute. It leered at him with a face that was almost reduced to a skull on one side. Beady eyes filled with deathly malice shone with a weird green glow. Tightening its grip on him, the yeti didn't try to leave the cage, but instead pulled the thief up against the bars.

"Help," Gaiseric groaned, terrified, looking for Rodolf. He spotted the trapper ducking under one of the other wagons. A crossbow bolt chased after the man, missing him by mere inches. Around the courtyard, the undead nomads were taking aim with their weapons. A sense of duty wasn't the only thing that lingered in these zombies. So, too, had the memory of how to arm and aim a crossbow.

The yeti's foul breath washed down across Gaiseric's face. He felt as though his chest would collapse under the excruciating pressure the abomination was subjecting him to. The zombie beast seemed intent on pulling him through the bars and Gaiseric knew his bones would snap before those iron rods would bend.

Sparks flashed before Gaiseric's eyes. The thief cursed himself for not drawing Cryptblade the very instant the yeti started to move. That initial moment of panic would doom him now. The opposing strength of his arms pressing against the wagon was barely keeping the monster from its purpose. If he relented for even a heartbeat, the yeti would crush him to pulp.

Gaiseric ground his teeth, trying to defy the anguish wracking his body. He had to stay conscious, he couldn't submit to the pain. If he did he knew the fate that was eager to claim him. One look at the yeti's yellowed fangs was enough to make him redouble his effort to fight back. Growling at the simian monster, he strained against the abominable grip that held him.

"Ya lampin' der boffo rumpuz!" Ratbag's bellow boomed in Gaiseric's ears. The thief's heart pulsed with hope. He knew Ratbag wouldn't relent until he was rescued. He saw the orc warrior leap at the cage and bring down his scimitar in an overhanded swing that chopped into the yeti's outstretched arm. It was a blow that should have chopped through an armored knight, but through Gaiseric's bleary vision it looked like it did little more than cleave a patch of fur and rancid flesh away.

Whatever the actual damage, it was enough to make the abomination release its hold on Gaiseric. The thief fell free, collapsing beside the wagon. He looked up to see the ape-beast gripping the bars of its cage and shaking them angrily. It seemed the zombie was too witless to recognize that the door was open and that only its hold on the bars was keeping the portal from swinging wide.

"Ya gotz der moxie mug," Ratbag grunted as he leaned down to help Gaiseric. The thief saw that the orc must have charged across the courtyard. There were two crossbow bolts sticking out of his body, the shots having punched through his armor as though it wasn't even there.

Gaiseric waved aside Ratbag's aid. "You don't… want… to bother… with me," he coughed. He reached for Cryptblade and pressed the sword into the orc's hand. "Take it… finish that… creature in the… cage."

At that moment, the sound of splintering wood and distorted metal exposed Gaiseric to a terrible truth. The yeti never did figure out that the door was open. Instead, the undead ape had ripped open the side of its cage.

The last sight he had before unconsciousness claimed Gaiseric was of a massive white beast dropping down from the wagon, beating its chest with its clawed hands and roaring its challenge to Ratbag. Even the orc renegade looked puny beside the shaggy abomination.

We're all going to die, Gaiseric thought as oblivion drew him down into its black abyss.

CHAPTER SEVEN

Videric was inspecting the common hall that fronted the coaching inn, coldly scrutinizing the evidence of past violence. That the place had been the scene of a terrible slaughter was evidenced by the copious bloodstains and the odd fragments of dismembered body parts. Any lingering idea of someone being alive in this charnel house quickly vanished.

Helchen and Shareen made a quick search of the back rooms, the witch hunter keeping a tight grip on her mace whenever she moved to open a door. Ursola, ignoring all other concerns, dashed behind the bar. Setting the keg of dragon bile on the counter, she snatched bottles from the shelves and poured their contents out on the floor. The demolitionist was impatient to replenish her exhausted supply of incendiaries. Despite his distaste for such weapons, Videric found himself sympathizing. He could easily picture his own distress if he lost his sword and had to make do without.

Ratbag posted himself near the door, his red eyes evaluating the room with a hungry, vicious gleam. The Swords of Korbara had fought orcs and goblins several times in the Duchy of Wulfenburg. Videric knew the orcish penchant for violence. He didn't understand Helchen's willingness to trust such a creature to control his savagery and obey her commands. True, Ratbag was a ferocious warrior and good to have on your side in a fight, but he thought Helchen hadn't given any consideration to what should happen if the orc reconsidered who his friends were. The very attributes that made him such an asset to their expedition would then be turned against them.

The templar was still watching Ratbag when the orc suddenly turned around and ran out the door. Videric could just make out sounds from the courtyard as he rushed over to see where the renegade had gone. "Trouble in the courtyard!" he yelled as he unslung his shield and left the inn.

Videric wasn't sure what he expected to see when he got outside, but it certainly wasn't the sight of the nomad guards lurching to their feet and working their crossbows with twisted, decayed hands. He couldn't imagine how or why the zombies had played dead, but he cursed himself for not taking precautions to ensure the corpses were harmless. Too eager to check the inn and secure it for the night. His father would have scolded him for such recklessness if he were here.

"Zombies!" the sergeant shouted, berating himself internally for not destroying the corpses while they were inanimate. A modicum of precaution he should have insisted upon no matter how distasteful.

Brushing aside self-recrimination, Videric focused on the immediate crisis. He spotted Rodolf and Gaiseric across the courtyard near the wagons, only now realizing that the two had lingered rather than following the rest of them into the inn. The scout was scurrying under the wagons, trying to take cover from the bolts the zombies were shooting at him. Gaiseric tried to scramble away from a large cage on one of the wagons. The templar winced when he saw the huge white ape inside the cage that had one of its claws clamped onto the thief's shoulder.

"Croak 'em!" Ratbag bellowed, his scimitar raised high. The warrior lunged across the courtyard, charging straight for the wagons. Videric was as impressed by the orc's fearlessness as he was revolted by his lack of strategy. Several of the zombies turned at the sound of Ratbag's war cry, shifting their aim from Rodolf to the orc. Bolts whistled at the renegade. Several shots went wide, but Videric saw one punch into Ratbag's shoulder. The undead weren't exactly precise marksmen but they were persistent and didn't hesitate to send another volley at the warrior. As he closed the distance between them, it could only be a matter of moments before Ratbag was ripped to shreds.

"Wotun watch over me," Videric hissed under his breath. He knew what he had to do, but he didn't like it. Boldly he marched out into the courtyard, banging the flat of his sword against his shield. "Here, you worm-feeding carrion!" the templar shouted, making as much noise as he could to draw the attention of the zombies away from Ratbag.

He sheltered behind his broad shield when the zombies reacted. All the guards turned Videric's way and sent bolts speeding at the templar. He felt the hard impacts against his shield, then grunted in pain. Looking down, he saw that the weapons the creatures were using had such an impact that some of the missiles were punching clean through the shield. One had transfixed his arm, another had continued on to embed itself in his abdomen. Whether that last one had dug deep enough into his armor to tear the flesh beneath, Videric couldn't tell.

"At least I kept them off you," Videric whispered, watching as Ratbag reached the wagons and went to help Gaiseric. He quickened his pace, running for the nearest of the zombies. He didn't think he could survive another volley from the creatures, but he was determined to take at least one of them with him before the end.

The templar was nearly knocked off his feet by a powerful gale that swept across the courtyard. He saw the zombies stagger, a few of them even dropping their weapons as they fought to stay standing. Any bolts that had been shot at him were swept away by the wind. Videric looked back over his shoulder and saw Shareen and Helchen emerge from the inn, the wizard's arms outstretched as she worked her spell.

"Get to cover!" Shareen cried out.

Videric knew enough about the ways of magic to know that the arcane windstorm was only a brief manifestation and that Shareen couldn't sustain its force indefinitely. Instead of rushing to cover, he resolved to take as much advantage of the gale as he could. Ignoring the pain from his pierced arm, he continued toward the closest of the zombies.

The gale dissipated just as he reached the creature. The undead awkwardly stooped to retrieve its weapon from the ground. Before it could rise, Videric brought the edge of his sword chopping down into the thing's head. This time when the guard collapsed, it wouldn't be getting up again.

Videric turned from his vanquished foe. Off to his right, he could see that Helchen had dispatched another of the zombie crossbowmen with her mace. Shareen shifted over to the frost spell she'd learned from the witch hunter, using the enchantment to immobilize two more of the undead nomads. That left four of the creatures… and the shaggy white ape-beast.

The hulking monster was confronted by Ratbag now. Videric had thought the orc was an imposing creature, but he was a runt next to the abomination. Big as an ogre and far more bestial, the white ape was a disturbing mix of man and animal, unlike anything Videric had seen before. It wasn't invincible, however, and a strike from the orc caused it to release Gaiseric. The injured thief slumped down beside the cage. The templar was impressed that the rogue retained enough coherence that even bleeding, he handed Cryptblade to his rescuer.

"The yeti! Kill the yeti!" Rodolf's cry rang across the courtyard. It looked to Videric that Ratbag was trying to do just that. The orc was using Cryptblade now, swinging the magic sword in awkward arcs that sizzled across the abomination's white pelt. Instant death to other zombies, the weapon's dweomer only seemed to enrage the yeti. The ape-beast brought both clawed hands smashing into the orc, flinging him into the nearby wagon with enough force that the bed splintered under the impact. Ratbag was soon buried in debris as the wagon folded and collapsed around him.

The loud crash had the zombie nomads swinging around and taking aim at the shattered wagon. Chances were that their shots wouldn't be able to find the orc at the middle of the wreckage, but Videric didn't intend to give the guards too much chance.

"No, you don't," he said.

While the creatures were turned, the templar rushed another of them, crushing its skull before it was even aware of him.

"The fires of Wotun take you!" Helchen shouted as she swept past Videric and charged the remaining nomads. A bolt from her own pistol crossbow punched through the forehead of one guard. A second zombie took a shot at her, the missile slashing her ear as it narrowly missed her. The undead never had the chance to make good its mistake, for the next instant saw the witch hunter's mace crunching down into its brain.

The last zombie took aim at Helchen, but the crash of Videric's sword and shield redirected the creature's sketchy awareness to the templar. He was too far away to reach the nomad and the only cover at hand was the dubious shelter of his own tattered shield. He bit back the tingle of fear that trembled through him. Death in service to a noble cause was an honorable end for a Sword of Korbara.

A blast of ice washed across the zombie crossbowman. Videric blinked in amazement, for he could actually see the bolt frozen in place as it was hurled away by the released string. He glanced over at Shareen, grateful for the wizard's timely aid.

The templar, however, wasn't the only one who noticed Shareen's spell. A savage ululation, part howl and part scream, boomed across the courtyard. The zombie yeti, its pelt savaged by Ratbag's attack, its decayed flesh withered by Cryptblade's magic, beat its huge fists against its chest and rushed toward the wizard.

"I still have more for you," Shareen promised, the gem in her forehead gleaming as she mustered energy for another spell.

Again, a blast of freezing vapor billowed from her hands. This time the spell didn't immobilize its target in a pillar of ice. Indeed, the yeti seemed invigorated by the cold, howling again as it rushed onward. Videric could see the panic in Shareen's face when she saw the apeman wasn't fazed by her magic. Instead of trying to conjure another spell, it was the wizard who stood frozen in place.

"Have at you, carrion swine!" Videric shouted, running to intercept the yeti before it could reach Shareen. The monster didn't even break stride, simply swatting him with a sideward swing of a long, apish arm. The templar rolled painfully across the courtyard. He slid near the gate, his shoulder cracking against the garden wall.

From his vantage, Videric could see the whole courtyard. Helchen was trying to deal with the first zombies Shareen had frozen as the undead quickly thawed. Gaiseric, now conscious, was crawling painfully away from the wagons. Shareen had rallied somewhat and was trying to burn down the undead yeti with a lightning spell, but electricity hardly hurt it. Another moment and the beast would be upon her. Videric tried to stand, but his battered muscles refused to obey him and he crashed painfully to the ground.

Springing away from cover, Rodolf now took a hand in the fray. The scout had assembled his wolfcatcher and charged at the yeti. The spiked trap closed about the monster from behind, digging deep into its decayed flesh. "I've got it! I've got it! Someone finish it while it's trapped!" Shareen quickly ceased her conjurations lest the trapper be shocked by spells intended to hurt the yeti.

Helchen moved to help Rodolf, but even as she did, the last of the nomads stirred from its frozen lethargy. It aimed its weapon at the witch hunter and loosed a bolt that caught her in the calf. The injured leg buckled under her, and she fell to the ground. The witch hunter's face contorted with fury. She opened the grimoire hanging from her belt, her eyes rapidly scanning a page. Helchen pointed her finger at the zombie and summoned a spell that engulfed its head in billowing flames and soon reduced it to a lifeless carcass.

"It'll get free!" Rodolf screamed, his voice now frantic. The hold he had upon the yeti was becoming more tenuous with each passing breath. The monster had its claws pressed upon the spiked jaws and was trying to force them apart. Its efforts were forcing the two combatants to dance around one another across the courtyard.

Videric knew the situation could only end in disaster. If Rodolf released the yeti, it would be on him an instant later. If things stayed the way they were, the beast was certain to break free with much the same result. The templar gnashed his teeth and prayed to Wotun for the strength to intervene, but his battered body still refused to obey him.

Then, from near the wagons, the unexpected occurred. A mass of wreckage and debris lurched upward and then fell aside. Bleeding from dozens of cuts and gashes, his face made even more monstrous for the gore spattered across it, Ratbag lumbered into view. The orc shook his head and smacked his palm against his scalp, trying to clear his dazzled senses. Videric observed the moment the warrior spotted the yeti, for his eyes narrowed with hate.

Videric felt hope well up inside him when he saw the orc charge toward the yeti. Then cold dread stifled that exuberance before it could take root. Both of Ratbag's hands were clenched into fists and neither of them held a weapon. In his daze, the warrior was attacking the ape-beast unarmed!

A crafty look came onto Rodolf's face. Videric hadn't believed the accusations about the scout during the fight with the wolves, but he couldn't deny the pleasure the trapper took when he pivoted the yeti toward Ratbag and the teeth of the wolfcatcher sprang open.

The released yeti stumbled toward Ratbag, its release taking it by surprise as much as it did the orc. As a result, its claws merely scraped across the warrior's armor and bowled him over. Fallen to his knees, Ratbag glared back at the beast.

Before either combatant could make another move, something went sailing through the air to crash against the yeti's side. Shards of glass and dark liquid spattered across the zombie's white fur. Videric looked over at the inn to see Ursola striding out into the courtyard. The dwarf took a long puff from the cigar in her mouth.

"I think that's just about enough from you," Ursola spat as she threw the lit cigar at the abomination.

The yeti's wailing howl rang out once more as the dragon bile covering it ignited and the ape-beast vanished in a pillar of consuming fire.

Ursola grinned when Gaiseric sputtered and coughed. "I

thought you boasted about how much you could drink." She tipped the bottle back toward the thief's lips.

Gaiseric tried to wave her away. "That isn't fit for human consumption."

He sprawled against one of the walls, his head propped up against his pack. A herbal poultice prepared by Shareen was tied to his shoulder where the yeti's claws had mangled him. Though the wizard hadn't been forthcoming, Ursola suspected there was magic as well as herbs involved in the mixture. Perhaps she was still exerting a degree of discretion, never forgetting that Helchen was a witch hunter.

"That kind of treacly grog is what dwarfs give to toddlers," Ursola chided him, pressing the bottle back to his lips. Gaiseric winced but submitted to the concoction. She frowned at the blood that stained the poultice. The undead might pass along zombification by biting, but that didn't mean there weren't more natural diseases that could be passed along by their decayed claws. She hoped Shareen's treatment would spare Gaiseric from such afflictions.

"How'd we do?" Gaiseric asked after managing to swallow the brew.

"Videric got knocked around almost as bad as you did," Ursola said. "Helchen took a few scrapes, but I don't think she'd tell anyone if she was hurt even if you caught her trying to sew her arm back on." The dwarf shook her head. "Pretty sure the same goes for Ratbag, but that ugly snow-ape mauled him so roughly that he couldn't do anything but lay there and scowl while Shareen used some kind of spell to close up his wounds." The dwarf tapped the side of the bottle with her thumb. "Lot more of this around to help everyone forget their hurts and doesn't seem like anyone was bitten. That's allowing Ratbag didn't get nipped when he was getting you away from the yeti. At least he hasn't said he did."

Gaiseric nodded, his expression turning grim. "Orcs don't tell anybody when they're hurt or sick. The other warriors are apt to abandon them and any hungry goblins that happen to be slinking around might decide they're weak enough to gamble against their empty stomachs."

Ursola turned her head and spat. Dwarfs had plenty of grudges against orcs, but at least they respected their courage. Goblins didn't even have that much valor. It wasn't surprising to hear that they had no compunctions about preying on their erstwhile orcish allies.

"Shareen needs to rest a bit before she feels she can work the same magic for you and Videric," Ursola explained. A note of admiration slipped into her tone. "Don't know how much of a view you had, but she really unleashed the whole book on those zombies."

"It didn't seem like Helchen was the same though," Gaiseric commented. He gave Ursola a hard look. "Seemed to me like she was reluctant to cast any spells herself. She had to get good and mad to use her magic."

"Maybe she was worried about disrupting Shareen's casting?" Ursola suggested. She didn't know enough about magic herself to have any idea if that was possible.

Gaiseric had a worried look in his eyes. "Or maybe Helchen's backsliding. Falling back on all the ideas the Order put into her head." He nodded as he considered the possibility. "Could be she's afraid of what she can do with her magic and is trying to draw away from it. Let Shareen take on all those responsibilities."

Ursola frowned. "I didn't see enough to tell you one way or the other." Her face colored with embarrassment. "I wasn't present for most of the fight."

Gaiseric raised a weak hand and gestured at the satchel hanging from Ursola's shoulder. "I saw enough to know you were staying busy. Must have been some kind of record whipping together a fire-bomb that fast."

"I was in such a rush, I wasn't sure I even had the ratio right," Ursola confessed. She patted the side of the satchel. "So I made a couple of backups just in case."

"Whatever you did, it burned up that yeti," the thief said. He clenched his fists in frustration. "I should never have listened to that sneak Rodolf. Trying to break into that thing's cage to take its claws and teeth is what started the whole mess." He locked eyes with Ursola, radiating worry. "Where is Rodolf?"

Ursola tilted her head, indicating the middle of the courtyard, just visible in the deepening twilight. "Over there, picking through the ape's ashes. Looking for claws and fangs, would be my guess." She bit her lip for a moment, wondering if she should clue Gaiseric in on her suspicions. "He had the yeti snagged in that trap of his during the fight. I think he deliberately let it loose to go after Ratbag."

Gaiseric's eyes narrowed to venomous slits. "Did he?" the rogue hissed. Ursola noticed his hand automatically reaching for the dagger he normally wore on his belt, but the blade had been lost during the recent fighting.

"I could be mistaken," Ursola tried to appease the thief. She'd only wanted to make Gaiseric wary, not incite him to retaliation. "Maybe he just wasn't able to hold his grip any longer." She prodded the poultice, drawing Gaiseric's attention with a pained gasp. "You know better than I do how strong that monster was."

Gaiseric clasped his hand to the injured shoulder, trying to rub away the hurt. "The first thing you learn when gambling is that coincidence is the tell for when the game is crooked."

"Maybe, but..."

Ursola swung around, all thought of Gaiseric and Rodolf, Ratbag and yeti driven from her mind. Her nostrils flared and she lifted her head, sniffing at the dark sky. A faint odor, but one that was unmistakable to her. She glanced at Gaiseric and saw only puzzlement on his face. Of course, a human's senses weren't that keen. But when she looked across the courtyard to where Ratbag had been searching the wagons, she saw that the orc was standing rock still and staring up at the sky. He'd caught the scent, too, and was trying to figure out what it was.

Ursola knew. It was mixed with other stenches, but underlying the rot and decay, the briny stink of the sea and the charred reek of boiled meat, there was the musky fug a dwarf would never forget once she encountered it.

The smell of dragon.

"Beards of my grandfathers," Ursola muttered. She turned back to Gaiseric and against his yelps of protest forced the man upright. "Take cover," she ordered him, all but shoving him behind the water trough next to the corral. "I've got to find Helchen."

"But what's wrong?" Gaiseric called after her as Ursola ran away.

The dwarf didn't pause to answer him. She kept running

toward the inn. "Take cover!" she shouted to the others in the courtyard.

The smell of dragon intensified. With it came the sound of gigantic wings fanning the air. Ursola had a firebomb in one hand, the bottle's neck rigged so that it would ignite on impact. There'd be no need for a lit cigar when she cast the incendiary at her enemy. She only hoped it would be hot enough to hurt a dragon.

Ursola's eyes scanned the darkened sky, trying to spot the winged reptile. Her heart froze when she did. This dragon was far beyond being hurt. The exposed bones, the sloughed scales, the decayed flesh. The monster swooping down on the Red Unicorn wasn't a living creature, but it wasn't just the existence of a necromantic wyrm that filled her with horror – it was the fact she recognized this beast.

"Flamefang!" the dwarf gasped in a horrified whisper. Her mind reeled with the recognition. The dragon had returned from its watery grave and its presence here could only mean that it had come back for revenge.

"Not that way!" Ursola yelled, grabbing Rodolf's arm as he ran toward the inn. He writhed free of her grasp and continued on his way, looking at her as though she was deranged. Perhaps she was, but after fighting this dragon before, seeing it savage the rooftops and towers of Yandryl's castle, Ursola knew if there was any speck of the wyrm's mind left in that undead bulk, the inside of the inn was the last place to seek shelter.

"Outside!" the dwarf shouted, hoping Helchen at least would hear. She added the words she knew would spur the witch hunter if she could hear them. "It's Flamefang!"

The rotting dragon made a single pass over the courtyard, circling like some gargantuan vulture. Ursola scrambled behind the stone-walled well, peering over its rim as the reptile dove down. As she'd expected, the wyrm attacked the building itself, much as it had Yandryl's castle. Here, however, there were no fortifications, no pillars to reinforce the construction, no arcane wards to repulse the beast. The roof exploded under Flamefang's bulk, collapsing into the upper floor.

People came rushing from the inn. Ursola saw Helchen leading the escape, followed close behind by Shareen and Videric. Rodolf stumbled out the door just as the lower story buckled under the dragon's weight. Debris pelted the courtyard, shards of glass and splinters of wood flying in every direction. Rodolf cried out as his arm was skewered by a sliver of timber.

The trapper's shout caught Flamefang's attention. The horned head whipped around and fixated on Rodolf. With a single flap of its mighty wings, the dragon landed in the courtyard. Rodolf's scream rose to an impossible pitch as the wyrm's immense claw slammed down upon him, grinding him into the paving stones.

"Wotun have mercy! It *is* Flamefang!" Helchen's tone held more panic than Ursola had ever heard the witch hunter express. She stood frozen in horror before Shareen took her by the arm and drew her away from the inn.

Ursola turned her head from the sickening sight of Rodolf under the dragon's foot. Doing so, she spotted Ratbag. The orc still bore Cryptblade and was rushing toward Flamefang in a charge that had more madness than strategy about it. The sword's enchantment might hurt the necromantic dragon, but Ursola doubted it could finish the beast before the beast slaughtered Ratbag.

"Don't be daft!" the dwarf snarled, bolting out and intercepting the big orc. Ratbag bared his fangs, but she didn't quail from him. "You want to kill it, or just annoy it?"

For the moment, Flamefang was occupied lashing its tail against the side of the inn. Perhaps believing there were more survivors inside, the dragon was trying to bring the rest of the structure down. Its distraction presented an opportunity, but Ursola would need Ratbag's brawn for the plan that suddenly came to her.

"Help me push that," Ursola told Ratbag, waving her fist at the wagon she'd taken the dragon bile from.

The orc squinted at it, then grinned. "Gonna torch der lizzerd. Swell gag," Ratbag growled. He rushed ahead of Ursola and was already putting his back to the job when she joined him.

Together the pair got the carriage moving, but Ursola worried they'd be unable to get it rolling fast enough. If Flamefang simply flew back into the air the ploy wasn't going to accomplish anything. Suddenly they were joined by two more sets of arms when Helchen and Videric charged in to help.

"Shareen's tending Gaiseric," Helchen informed Ursola. The witch hunter peeked around the side of the wagon to watch the monster destroying the inn. "That *is* Flamefang," she repeated in a composed but bewildered tone.

"No mistake," Ursola replied, teeth clenched in rage. She'd thought many debts had been repaid when the dragon was slain. Because of the Black Plague, those outrages were again unavenged. She could see the fury on Helchen's face. Alaric had died to kill this monster. Flamefang's return made a mockery of his sacrifice.

"We send this crashing into the wyrm?" Videric asked. "Then what?"

Ursola tipped her chin and indicated the satchel of fire-bombs she bore. "You run like hell. And don't go waiting around for anybody. Least of all Rodolf." She mentioned the last because she could see the trapper pinned under the dragon's foot, flattened like a bug.

Through their combined efforts, the wagon went rattling across the courtyard. The others broke away when Ursola felt the momentum would keep it rolling straight at their target. Death had dulled Flamefang's senses, it seemed, for the wyrm kept battering away at the inn long after it was just a pile of rubble. The dragon's obstinate fixation was going to be its downfall.

"This time, you stay dead," Ursola snarled as she ran behind the wagon. When it crashed against Flamefang's decayed bulk, she hurled the fire-bomb into the cart. Dragon bile, gushing from kegs broken in the collision, ignited at once. With a loud whoosh, the caustic material went up in a pillar of fire.

Ursola threw herself behind the well, covering her head as the billowing flames rushed past. She hoped the others had reached some sort of safety, but there wasn't anything that could be done about that now.

It was only a matter of seconds before the ignited vapor was exhausted. Dragon bile burned fiercely, but it soon consumed its fuel. Ursola was able to look over the seared edge of the well only a moment after taking cover. "Marked dice and loaded cards," she swore, mangling Gaiseric's favorite epithet.

The Red Unicorn was a smoldering heap of slag now, its timbers turned to ash, its stones fused into weird, blackened shapes. The wagon had been utterly annihilated and the paving of the courtyard was aglow from the intense heat it had been subjected to. Flamefang, however, was gone. With the crackle of leathery wings, the reptile took flight, rising into the sky.

Not destroyed, simply routed. The undead dragon retained some instinct of survival. Ursola could see the wyrm flying away to the north, patches of its rotten body still burning from the explosion. It was too much to believe the monster would succumb to its wounds. After returning from death, it would need a lot more to end Flamefang's malice.

Ursola looked aside when she heard footsteps. She saw Helchen and the others cautiously walking over to join her. All of them were staring up at the dragon as it flew away.

"He got away." Helchen scowled.

"At least the dragon's gone," Shareen observed, the hope of ignorance in her voice. Gaiseric turned his head and locked eyes with the wizard who was helping him stand.

"That was Flamefang," the thief explained. "It's bad enough that he's come back from the dead. What's worse is that he followed us here from Yandryl's island. Somehow that monster found us!"

Videric's face paled. The templar made the sign of Wotun. "If the dragon found you once, it can find you again," he said, clearly unhappy about the prospect.

"Then we need to finish our task before he can," Helchen

said through clenched teeth. It was obvious that her urge to see the monster destroyed was at odds with her duty to the people at Korbara. With her, duty would always win out over vengeance.

"How do we do that?" Videric asked, pointing at the destruction. "Rodolf was our guide. He was leading us where we need to go."

Ursola rounded and pointed at the road outside the courtyard. "We know that road takes us to Zanice," she reminded him. "That'll be enough to keep us going. Once we're in the city, we'll find the Rangers."

The templar shook his head. "With a dragon chasing us? What do we do about the dragon?"

The dwarf's gaze hardened until her eyes were like chips of steel. Ursola could feel the bitterness of her ancestors coursing through her. "We'll just have to figure out a better way to kill it," she swore. "If Flamefang is chasing us, at least it makes things a little easier."

"Wotz easier?" Ratbag said, puzzled.

Ursola's grin was as vicious as any the orc had ever displayed. "It means we won't have to go looking for the wyrm when we're ready for it."

CHAPTER EIGHT

The increased frequency of villages and hamlets was proof enough to Gaiseric that they were nearing Zanice. Every city in the kingdom acquired such neighbors given time. Indeed, as a city prospered and expanded beyond its old walls, such settlements would be absorbed into the urban sprawl, vanishing into the warren of streets and alleyways. Often, after a few decades, all that would be left of the old village would be a chapel or cemetery hidden among rows of warehouses and workshops. Such was the nature of progress.

Helchen directed them to keep clear of the villages. The prospect of finding provisions in the houses and farms had to be balanced against the likelihood of also finding zombies lurking in the desolation. More than that, Gaiseric feared they might run into Flamefang again. Ursola had managed to drive the dragon away, but it was too much to hope the beast was injured too badly to take up their trail again. Whatever vengeful urge had the undead wyrm hunting them all the way from the island, it wasn't going to stop because the dwarf had given it a hot foot. No, Flamefang would come looking for them and might even be keeping tabs on the villages to do so.

Though that brooked the question of how the dragon had found them in the first place. Gaiseric winced as he walked along, although the expression had little to do with pain. After Shareen tended to him with a few spells, the injuries he'd suffered at the yeti's claws had healed up entirely. They didn't give him any worries now. What troubled him was that Flamefang, having risen as some kind of necromantic abomination, had access to magic of its own. It was hard enough to hide from a dragon – how did you hide from a dragon with magic on its side?

"Figure that out in time," Gaiseric said. He looked out across the overgrown wheat fields ahead of them. In the distance, the stone walls of Zanice reared up, stretching across much of the horizon. He could pick out a few red-tiled towers and rooftops. This far out, however, he couldn't spot any signs of life.

Videric studied the view. "Well, Rodolf was right, all we had to do was follow the road." The templar scowled at the clusters of buildings that lay scattered between the farmland. "Of course, with Zanice so near, we don't need anything to guide us now. We can *really* stay away from the settlements now."

Helchen removed her hat and ran her fingers through her hair. "It's a hazard we can avoid. There'll be risk enough when we get into Zanice."

Gaiseric didn't like the fatalistic acceptance in her voice. He could see that Helchen was rattled by Flamefang's return. He wasn't an especially zealous man, so he wondered how injustice and misfortune affected someone who was. The Order had taught Helchen that Wotun's justice was the supreme law of the land, but if that were true then how could the dragon be back? How could Alaric's sacrifice have been for nothing? The witch hunter's faith was shaken, and with that upheaval went that cool surety she exuded, that unspoken confidence that good would ultimately prevail over evil.

"Maybe the citizens of Zanice fared better than those of Singerva," Gaiseric suggested. "Maybe they kept their city from being overrun."

Helchen shook her head and gave Gaiseric a weary look. "You heard Sylvia. They haven't been feeding the sea serpent. Surely if the people had successfully defended the city, they'd ensure their route to the open sea remained safe." She donned her hat and drew its rim low over her face. "Maybe a few pockets of survivors here and there struggling to keep back the plague but the city as a whole must be lost to the undead."

Gaiseric felt goaded into defying her gloomy speech more from emotion than logic. "Until we see for ourselves, you don't know anything for sure."

Helchen sighed. "You've seen enough to know that preparing for the worst is the only prudent thing."

Shareen sided with the thief. "The monks at Korbara provided a refuge, the citizens of Zanice could have done the same."

"Korbara had the benefit of isolation," Videric said. "That gave us time to be aware of the Black Plague before we came under direct threat." The templar shrugged and looked aside at Helchen. "Still, the burghers of Zanice would have access to far greater resources than we did at Korbara. They *might* have been able to fight the zombies back."

"Bucko gabbin'," Ratbag grumbled. The orc shook his fist at the distant walls. "Ya mugs gonna be lampin' wotz wot?"

Ursola rolled her eyes. "It takes a bunch of humans arguing to make the orc the voice of reason. We're not going to settle anything talking about it and whichever way things stand, we still need to get into the city." She shifted the satchel with the few remaining fire-bombs so it rested easily in the slope of her arm. "So let's get to it already."

Helchen nodded her head. "Let's get to it," she repeated. "Victory or death," she added in a grim whisper before starting off across the fields.

Gaiseric hurried after the witch hunter. The somber vow was far from inspirational. The necromancer cabals had made death a more doubtful resolution than victory. There was a certain macabre comfort in finding a heroic doom. There was none in the prospect of ending up a decayed zombie staggering across the kingdom.

The rogue was still trying to rekindle some degree of optimism several hours later when the little band reached the end of the fields and found the thick walls of Zanice rising before them. This far south in the kingdom, such fortifications weren't built to defend against orcish invasions, but rather against the militaristic ambitions of other humans. Gaiseric's grandfather had told him about the last Ducal Wars, when half the kingdom was fighting, noblemen struggling to expand their own wealth and power by laying claim to the lands of their neighbors. Zanice, an important and wealthy trading hub even in those days, had been vital to controlling the south. After ousting the Duke of Slagenburg's vassals, the Duchess of Koldov had immediately set about securing her claim on Zanice by turning it into a mighty stronghold. A bastion that the armies of Slagenburg would hesitate to besiege.

Looking upon the immense walls, Gaiseric could appreciate why the Duchy of Slagenburg had forfeited all claim on Zanice. The enormous gray stone blocks they were constructed from, stacked five high, were each ten feet tall and twice as wide – and there was no telling from this vantage how deep they might be. Timber hoardings ran the length of the battlements and every few feet there was a crenelation to provide cover for the city's soldiers as they shot arrows or hurled stones down on attackers. Fortified towers sprouted from the walls every hundred feet or so, their narrow windows too small for even a goblin to slip through, but wide enough for an archer to loose missiles at an enemy.

Gazing down the length of the wall, Gaiseric could see one of the giant gate houses that afforded entry into the city. Even from a distance, he could see that the double portcullis was lowered, the iron gates barring all passage.

"Maybe there's someone holed up in the gatehouse," Gaiseric suggested. He gave Helchen a pointed look. "When we entered Singerva, we could tell that some of the guards had tried to barricade themselves in their post. Maybe the soldiers here had enough supplies to hold out longer."

The witch hunter stared up at the gatehouse with its dark, narrow windows. "If anyone is in there, they've probably seen things that have pushed them to the limit." Her expression grew solemn. "They might not be able to tell the difference between the living and the undead. They might not even have enough sanity left to care."

"We should still try," Shareen said. The wizard started to walk along the road, picking her way between the abandoned carts and junk spilled all along the path.

Gaiseric dashed forward and drew Shareen back. "My idea, my risk," he told her. "Helchen just might be right and, well, I still owe you for fixing up my shoulder." He patted the piece of anatomy in question and gave her a lopsided grin. The wizard looked unconvinced, but stepped away so that he could proceed. He gave her a knowing wink. "I've risked shaking hands with the hangman for a few pieces of silver before, so I'm used to making bad choices."

Despite his show of bravado, Gaiseric felt his hackles rise as he contemplated the silent gatehouse. He swaggered as he approached the city, making an ostentatious roll of his shoulders and whistling a jaunty tune. In short, he tried to do everything possible to assure anyone watching him from inside the fortification that he wasn't a zombie.

He was still thirty yards from the wall when Gaiseric heard the twang of an arrow being shot from a bow. Leaping to one side, he saw a shaft slam into the road, its point snapping as it hit the paving. The thief was back on his feet in a second, shouting at the unseen archer. "Idiot! I'm not a zombie!"

Another arrow came whistling down, this time passing so close to him that Gaiseric could feel its momentum against his cheek. He could see movement behind that narrow window. Such sunlight as was able to get inside revealed the gleam of naked bone.

A fleshless figure that held a bow in its hands.

The occupants of the gatehouse *were* aware that he wasn't a zombie… and that was the problem.

Gaiseric remembered the skeletal walkers they'd fought in the Order's dungeons, undead that had retained some fragment of their old awareness the same as the nomad guards at the Red Unicorn. The ability to aim and shoot a bow was a skill they'd kept even as zombies.

"Get back!" Gaiseric shouted as he turned and ran away from the wall. "Deadeye walkers!" he added, an explanation he knew would make sense to Helchen, Ursola, and Ratbag. For a dozen yards, arrows continued to chase after the rogue, but none managed to strike home.

"Zombies on the walls," Ursola swore. She drew one of her fire-bombs and contemplated it. "If I could get close enough, I could burn them out."

"You'd have to lob it through that little window," Gaiseric told the dwarf between gasps for breath.

"A bit of magic then," Shareen suggested.

Helchen motioned for the wizard to look at the other towers. "You'd never get them all," she said. Stirred by the agitation of the zombies in the gatehouse, more of the skeletal archers were shuffling around inside the other strongpoints, showing themselves at the apertures and loosing the occasional arrow in a mindless display of hostility.

"Then we can't get inside," Videric cursed. "We don't dare build a raft and go in by water because of the serpent and we can't get past the walls because of the zombie bowmen."

"The Rangers themselves might be zombies," Shareen speculated, adding to the sense of despair.

Helchen growled at the wizard, "Even if they are, we must go on. Getting those records from their archives is crucial to Korbara's survival."

Gaiseric spun around and pointed at Videric. "Something you said." The thief beamed. He turned to Helchen. "There's another way for us to get inside. It'll mean getting wet, but it will get us past the walls."

"Wotz der yegg speelin'?" Ratbag grunted in confusion.

"Another way into Zanice," Gaiseric insisted. "Though I don't think it'll be the most dignified route."

Ursola snapped her fingers, realizing what Gaiseric was suggesting. "The sewers."

Gaiseric nodded. "Zanice might dump a fair bit of their refuse into the canals, but I'm willing to bet at least part of the city is sending the stuff inland."

"All right, gambler," Helchen said. "I'll take that bet. Let's see if we can find a culvert leading into these sewers of yours."

Once, many decades ago when Shareen had been naught but an apprentice learning magic from the conjurer Marcellus, she'd been present at the summoning of a devil, Boroborith, one of the lesser counts of the netherworld. The scorpion-like entity, its body coated in dripping slime and its face combining the worst qualities of bat and spider, had been a horrible enough sight but what had stayed vivid in her mind down through the years was the rancid stench the devil exuded. The reek had billowed out from the summoning circle that confined Boroborith, saturating every corner of the conjurer's tower until it brought tears from Shareen's eyes. She'd had to shave her head afterward, unable to get the stink out of her hair.

Incredibly, the sewers of Zanice smelled even worse than Boroborith had. Shareen wished now that Gaiseric had never spotted the culvert or that Ratbag hadn't been strong enough to wrench the iron grating free from the opening at the base of the city wall. Challenging the skeletal bowmen on the battlements or daring the attentions of the sea serpent would have been preferable to enduring the dark, dank, dripping foulness of the sewer. Thigh-deep in the semi-liquid sludge that gurgled through the underground channel, Shareen cringed every time a lump of semi-solid filth bumped against her legs. She'd disabused herself of the notion of looking down at the odious flow, keeping her eyes locked on the vaulted ceiling that arched only a foot or so above her head.

"Please do find a way out of here soon," Shareen enjoined her companions. "We're certainly past the walls by now."

Gaiseric was at the head of their little procession, lighting the way with a lantern. "Believe me, I'm looking," he assured her. The thief looked as though he regretted entering the sewer every bit as much as Shareen. Still, he wasn't the one leading this expedition. That role belonged to Helchen and the witch hunter's dour determination was as resolute as ever.

"There'll be access points," Ursola declared. The filth came up to her waist and she'd taken the precaution of holding her satchel of fire-bombs well above the sludge. "Dwarfs probably designed these sewers, but they didn't build them." She spat against the wall in a display of contempt. "Human work, and done on the cheap. Needs a lot of maintenance to keep this kind of construction from wearing out and buckling." She chuckled to herself. "Wonder how often some happy little merchant prince woke up one morning to find his villa had sunk down into this muck and his art gallery was gone to the rats."

"Thanks for that," Videric scolded. The templar had removed his tabard and had it wound around his shoulders to keep it away from the waste. "Just what I need to make things worse, the image of this tunnel collapsing on my head."

"Just hope you're crushed before you get a chance to drown," Gaiseric suggested, looking back at the templar.

"Pedeque lampin' der escarp'r, mug," Ratbag growled at the rogue, angrily motioning for the man to focus on finding an exit. The orc was having an even worse time than Shareen, she had to admit. Too big to comfortably fit into the tunnel, he was bent nearly double and moving sidewise like a crab. Ratbag had several layers of cloth wrapped around the bottom of his face in an attempt to shield his keen nose from the sewer smell. Even to the orc, this stench was extreme.

Shareen saw Gaiseric shrug and continue trudging his way through the sewer, but her attention was soon arrested by something beyond the thief. A hint of movement just outside the reach of his light. Before she could be certain it wasn't simply a trick of the bobbing lamp, she heard what sounded like a furtive rustle of claws against stone.

"Gaiseric…" Shareen hissed at the thief, trying to get his attention. It was too late for any kind of warning, however. She heard the sharp crack of a crossbow followed closely by the shattering of glass. The tunnel was plunged into darkness an instant later as the broken lamp fell from Gaiseric's startled hand.

The darkness now erupted into bedlam. Shareen could hear the filthy water sloshing wildly as unseen bodies moved rapidly through it. There were voices, too, shrill and grating, though she could make no sense of the sharp words being uttered. To this was also added the shouts and cries of her companions, alarm and confusion in their tones.

"Ya got der rumpuz!" Ratbag bellowed, vicious glee in his roar. "Give dese bimbos der bump!"

Shareen was heaved to one side and knew the big orc was shoving his way past her. Ratbag's vision was better in the dark than any of them. He could see whatever it was that had ambushed them, but he was the only one. Well, a wizard had ways of changing that.

Invoking a simple cantrip, Shareen caused a sphere of pulsing white light to erupt only a few feet away. The arcane glow wouldn't blind anyone as it violated the darkness but would soothe the eyes even as it illuminated the tunnel. In a crisis such as they now faced, Shareen knew even a second of weakness could be fatal.

The wizard wasn't prepared for what her spell revealed. Shareen had expected that they'd been attacked by some manner of undead, perhaps similar to the zombie crossbowmen at the Red Unicorn. Instead what she saw in that first glimpse were revolting, monstrous shapes, things that had never been human but which were very much alive. They were as tall as a grown man and their lanky bodies were arrayed in a confusion of ragged clothing and armor. Any part of them that was exposed didn't display skin but fur. The hands that gripped crooked swords and jagged spears ended in thin fingers tipped with sharp claws. The heads that leered from between hunched shoulders were long and narrow; their faces weren't those of anything remotely human. They were the verminous countenances of enormous rats!

Shareen had never seen such creatures in the flesh before, but she'd read of them in her mentor's books. Ratlings, foul scavengers who infested tunnels and mines, stealing from their less feral neighbors. The realms that suffered from ratling depredations were far south of the kingdom's border. She'd never heard of them ranging this far north before. Perhaps they'd arrived in Zanice hidden in the holds of ships and then infested the sewers as a natural lair.

All of these thoughts rushed through Shareen's mind in an instant, then the crash of sword against sword snapped her back to the chaos unfolding around her. The light spell had startled the ratlings more than her companions, but the creatures were still intent on attack. She saw one lunge for Gaiseric, the thief's sword only narrowly blocking the strike. Man and vermin strained against each other, the agility of the former vying against the frantic speed of the latter. Soon both combatants took a step back, scowling at the minor nicks and cuts they'd received in the fray.

Ratbag was a different matter. Howling an orcish war cry, he waded into the fight. A crossbow bolt from one of the man-rats crunched into his forearm, but he ignored the wound, just as he barely acknowledged the spear that stabbed into his midsection. His size forced him to use the tip of his blade rather than its cleaving edge as there simply wasn't space to allow for a killing sweep of the scimitar. The warrior's weapon thrust forward at the vermin who stabbed him, piercing its chest. The orc bellowed again and a quick flick of his blade sent a spatter of blood into the eyes of the sword-rat charging at him. The blinded ratling was run through by the renegade's scimitar, the furred body seeming to fold around the steel as it ripped flesh and broke bone.

The crack of another crossbow, but this time it was Helchen who sent a bolt speeding through the tunnel. One of the ratling crossbowmen – specifically an arbalest – collapsed against the wall, his weapon vanishing into the muck as he clapped his clawed hands to the missile embedded in his throat. The vermin thrashed about in agony before sinking into the filthy water.

Videric struggled to join the fighting, sword and shield at the ready. "Vile monsters! Brave my sword, curs!" Though unable to slip past Ratbag and Gaiseric to reach the ratlings in the narrow tunnel, the templar's shouts added to the turmoil. The man-rats had expected to overwhelm their enemies in a swift ambush under cover of darkness. Now that things weren't going their way, their commitment was faltering.

The vermin still outnumbered Shareen and her friends. From what she could see, there were still at least a dozen of the monsters. They seemed to rediscover their resolve when a man-rat to the rear of the murderous pack started screeching at them. He was arrayed in a long black cloak and had a cowl-like mask covering much of his face and head. From the way he brandished the curved daggers clenched in his paws, he looked ready to carve up the other ratlings if they broke away from the fight.

Shareen focused her attention on the gray-furred creature, meeting his beady red eyes. She had the satisfaction of seeing the man-rat flinch when she pointed a finger at him and started to invoke a spell.

"No flames!" Ursola yelled, tugging at Shareen's sleeve. The dwarf made a show of sniffing. "This air's so rank it's like firedamp! Set anything alight and you're liable to turn the whole tunnel into a furnace!"

Shareen grimaced at the warning. Perhaps it wasn't just to plunge the sewer into darkness that the ratlings had eliminated Gaiseric's lamp. Maybe they'd also been removing the threat posed by the flame inside.

The wizard hesitated, feeling helpless as she watched the battle. Did she risk using lightning against the ratlings? If the shock should ignite one of the rags they were wearing or some of the filth caked into their fur…

The ratling Shareen had decided was the leader bared his fangs in a wicked grin, apparently guessing the reason for her hesitation. He started to squeak new orders and she saw one of the arbalists aim a crossbow at her.

Abruptly the man-rat chief swung his head around, ears pressed back against the sides of his head and his eyes wide with fright. The squeaks that now spilled from his fanged mouth had a frantic quality to them. As suddenly as the ambush had started, the ratlings now turned tail and fled, practically trampling over one another as they hurried down the tunnel. Before they were beyond the reach of Shareen's spell, she saw the creatures turn a sharp corner to the left. Then their attackers vanished in the darkness.

"C'mon back, yellerbellys!" Ratbag raged, shoving the carcass of a dead ratling toward his fleeing foes.

"Why'd they break off?" Helchen wondered.

Gaiseric made a fumbling attempt to retrieve the lantern from the sewage, but gave up the effort after a moment. He rose and stared at the tunnel ahead of them, his expression one of intense concentration. "Maybe they had a good reason to run," he whispered, drawing back toward the others.

Softly, faintly, new sounds drifted back to Shareen, noises that the man-rats must have heard and which had sent them into flight. They were sinister plop-scratch sounds. Ratbag fell back to join the rest of them. There was uneasiness on the orc's face.

All too soon the reason their ambushers had retreated squirmed into view. The tunnel ahead of them was crawling with animation, a tide of hideous bodies swimming through the sludge and scrambling over the more solid detritus bobbing in the water. Rats! Rats by the score! Rats by the hundreds, their eyes shining green in Shareen's light. Not normal, natural rats, but animals that had glutted themselves upon diseased carrion, creatures that had become tainted by the Black Plague.

From wall to wall and swimming straight toward them, the sewers were swarming with zombie rats ravenous for living flesh.

"Back!" Helchen ordered the others, fear shining in her eyes. Shareen watched the witch hunter take a step forward, her hand outstretched. She knew what Helchen intended, yet it was clear an instinctive loathing of magic made her hesitate to invoke the spell. Helchen was reluctant to conjure spells unless forced.

Shareen suffered from no such prejudice where spellcraft

was concerned. Biting down on her fear of the rat swarm, she put herself between Helchen and the undead. Gesturing at the zombies, she conjured the spell that would end their menace.

The cloying humidity of the sewer suddenly turned frigid. Shareen could see her breath as she spoke the last element of the incantation. From her hands, a chill blast swept down the tunnel, freezing the foul sludge in the direction of her spell. The swarm of rotting rats swimming through the filth were frozen in place, trapped within the icy sewage.

Shareen gasped when she finished her spell, grateful when Helchen came over to support her. This magic was still new to her and she wasn't accustomed to the toll it took upon her stamina.

Videric moved past the two women and studied the ice. "We'll have to chip away at it to move forward," he said, demonstrating his words with the pommel of his sword. "And we should brain as many of these as we can while we're doing it," he added, smashing the skull of a zombie rat.

"It'll be slow," Gaiseric said consideringly, "but better than waiting for the rats to thaw out."

"Then you'll just need to find the way out," Ursola goaded the thief.

Shareen fixed a sympathetic gaze on Helchen, trying to let her know that she understood why the witch hunter had hesitated. The overture made Helchen uncomfortable, and she quickly turned toward Gaiseric. "When you get through the ice, give the left wall a close look," she told him, reminding Shareen of how the ratlings had escaped. "There should be something to find there, whether it's obvious or hidden."

"If it means getting out of here before anything else happens," Gaiseric said, "just let it try to hide from me."

CHAPTER NINE

Gogol finished his inspection of the enormous reptile, wiping the residue of charred scales from his hand in the dead grass. The undead dragon's presence in the fallow field had poisoned the ground, though the necromancer was uncertain if that was caused by the dark magic concentrated into Flamefang's body or the draconic fluids seeping from the wyrm's wounds.

Gogol was more confident on one point. He was glad he'd sent Flamefang off by itself to track down Helchen and the others. He could tell from the creature's injuries that it had been attacked with dragon bile. It was a testament to how powerful the undead monster was that it had survived the experience and simply been driven off. Had Gogol accompanied the beast, he knew his own fate would have been sealed.

"Probably the dwarf," Gogol hissed as he looked over the dragon one more time. "What do you think, von Mertz?" He glanced over at the knightly zombivor and sneered at his undead slave. The same prudence that made the necromancer keep out of harm's way had also applied to the tortured husk of his most hated enemy. "We'll have to make sure we kill her first. Be a shame not to take more time with her, but I can't risk it." He smiled when he saw the unspoken anguish in Alaric's eyes. The knight wanted to defy him, but that wasn't going to happen. Gogol's spell was too strong to be broken.

The necromancer laughed and directed Flamefang to test its tattered wings. If the dragon couldn't fly, then its utility was greatly diminished. Fortunately, the beast was able to lift itself into the air. A gesture from its master, and the reptile descended once more.

"Let's figure out where your friends have gone," Gogol told Alaric.

He pointed at Flamefang. Without uttering a sound, the zombivor marched over to the wyrm. The dragon shifted to one side, holding still while the decayed knight climbed onto its back. Gogol waited a moment longer, then joined his creations. Firming his hold on Flamefang's body by digging his hands under the rotten scales and gripping the sinews beneath, he ordered the beast into the air.

Like an enormous vulture, Flamefang described everwidening circles as it climbed into the sky. Gogol kept a careful watch on the land below. Many details he recognized only because he already knew what they were. Away on the coast was a little black blot that represented *The Demoness* at anchor. There was a problem that could be settled later. He didn't want to risk Flamefang against the ship's artillery, at least not at this point. The pirate scum would wait. The enemies who'd disembarked from her wouldn't.

Much closer was the pillar of smoke rising from the ruins of the Red Unicorn, site of the recent fray between Flamefang and Helchen's band. The fire caused by the dragon bile was still smoldering, feeding off the rubble. Gogol knew better than to waste time looking for his enemies there. After driving off a dragon, only the biggest fool in the world would wait around for the wyrm to come back. No, Helchen's group was gone. Where they'd gone to was the riddle he needed to solve.

Higher and higher the soaring circles took Flamefang, expanding the view afforded to its riders. Gogol gasped in delight when he spotted the dark swathe away to the south. The Red Unicorn had been to the south and west of where the pirate ship was anchored. The urban sprawl he saw in the distance lay in the same direction.

"Zanice," Gogol chortled, recognizing the city he was looking at. He looked over his shoulder at Alaric. "Your old friends are heading to Zanice. Let's see about providing them a warm welcome when they get there." The necromancer's eyes glittered with a vengeful light. "After all, we wouldn't want them to feel lonely in the big city."

Urging Flamefang onward, Gogol sent his dragon into the south. This time, when Helchen faced the beast, it wouldn't be the mindless attack of an undead monster. Gogol would be there to guide the wyrm. Gogol would be there to savor every scream, every rip and tear as Flamefang obliterated his foes. Perhaps, if the dragon left enough to salvage, he'd even add a few more zombivors to his retinue. There was something deeply satisfying about forcing your worst enemies to obey your least command.

"Don't lose heart," Gogol advised Alaric. "When I'm done, you might have some company."

•••

At least there's light, Helchen thought when she stood on the surface again. Their exit from the sewers had been by means of an access-way that opened into the cellar of a wine shop. The business had been thoroughly ransacked and there wasn't a soul to be seen in the shop itself – a fact that was of some relief to everyone since the ratlings had preceded them along this route.

Stepping out of the wine shop's battered doors, Helchen had her first view of Zanice. The city was unlike any she'd visited before. The buildings were tall and packed close together, throwing deep shadows across the facades of their neighbors. The walkways that squirmed along the edges of the structures were cramped, narrow affairs, often fashioned from wooden planks and supported by timber piles. At a glance she could see that these paths were but an afterthought, a concession to utility by the city planners. The proper streets that served the city were the wide canals that flowed through Zanice. She could see many quays and docks where barges remained tethered. Many buildings had doors built out over the canals themselves so that the inhabitants might receive goods and visitors directly from passing boats.

Helchen couldn't speak to the normal condition of the canals. The existence of the sewers would argue that the burghers made an effort to keep the water relatively clean. In the chaos of the Black Plague, however, the channels were foul with morbid debris. Wrecked boats bobbed about in the slow tide, bumping against the fundaments that supported the city. Bloated bodies in all stages of mutilation floated in the murky water, undead crows still picking at them in a mindless hunt for living flesh. Zombie rats swam through the flow, their naked tails drifting behind them. The stench in the sewers had been that of waste; the miasma that wafted up from the canals was the reek of death.

"I guess the citizens decided drowning was preferable to being mauled by zombies," Ursola commented when she stared down into the canal. "Can't say I really blame them."

Helchen turned from the dwarf and tried to get some sense of Zanice's dimensions. The winding canals, however, offered no perspective, cutting off any view of more than a quarter mile. From the street level there was simply no vantage to be gained.

"Now we see why we needed Rodolf," Videric stated, as though reading Helchen's thoughts. The templar pointed at the sign hanging over the entrance to a beer hall on the other side of the canal. "He'd have known how far the Pike and Pint was from the Rangers' lodge and what direction we'd need to go."

"Well, the swine isn't here," Gaiseric hotly put in. With effort, the thief reined in his temper and instead nodded at the buildings around them. "Only way I can see to get some idea of where we are is to try and get up above all this. Get a view from higher up."

Helchen nodded. She'd reached the same conclusion. "That villa, across the way, looks promising," she said. From where they were, they could see a mass of green vines hanging over the edge of the flat roof. It was a good indicator that the home boasted a rooftop garden, a sign that the place got more sunlight than shade and therefore stood above its neighbors.

"There's a footbridge a bit further on," Shareen observed. "We can use that to get across."

"A better idea than taking a swim," Ursola agreed, scowling down at the ghoulish canal.

Ratbag swung his scimitar up and rested the curved blade against his shoulder. "Less gabbin' more doin'," he grumbled and started lumbering away toward the bridge.

"I guess that settles it," Helchen said, shaking her head as she watched the orc march away. Patience was a virtue Ratbag had in very short supply. She'd have thought the skirmish with the ratlings would have sated his appetite for violence, at least temporarily, but instead it seemed to only pique his bloodlust. The worrying thought came to her that maybe all the fight had done was remind the orc how much more satisfying he found it to maul living foes rather than the undead.

The narrow bridge was still a few hundred yards away when Helchen spotted movement on the other side of the canal. Surging out from a desolate storefront came a mob of ragged, rotten figures. Not all of Zanice's inhabitants had drowned themselves in the canals, it seemed. There were still zombies prowling the ruins and these had obviously noticed the living intruders.

"Walkers." Helchen hissed the alert to her companions, drawing their attention to the undead. Some of the creatures mindlessly stepped off the footpath and plunged into the canal, but most of them had enough awareness stirring in their decayed brains to shamble off toward the bridge. The macabre procession marched past other buildings, rousing the undead lingering inside. All too soon, instead of a handful of zombies, there was a mob a dozen strong. Worse, some of them weren't the shambling, lethargic walkers. A few were frenzied runners and these charged past the rest of the cadaverous throng to strike out across the footbridge.

"We need to stop them before they cross," Shareen said. She gave Helchen an imploring look before taking a position at the edge of the pathway. The wizard gestured at the zombies on the other side. From her fingertips, a curl of lightning shot forth and crackled through a half dozen of the undead. Smoke billowing off their shocked bodies, the zombies crashed to the ground, an impediment to the walkers shambling behind them.

Helchen scowled, knowing what she had to do but resenting the fact. She'd have preferred to delegate the spellcraft to Shareen and keep her own hands clean. It was a selfish indulgence but recognizing it as such didn't make the urge any easier to resist. She found that she had to consult Hulmul's grimoire to ensure that she cast the spell correctly.

In that time, Shareen did her best to stem the zombie mob. A wall of frost followed the lightning bolt, freezing in place another clutch of the monsters. Her magic wasn't enough to keep several runners from reaching the bridge and starting their rush across the span.

An obstacle of a much different sort awaited the frenzied undead. Ratbag charged ahead of the others and out onto the bridge, ready to meet the zombies with his massive scimitar. The first of the creatures was ripped in half by the orc's blow, legs tumbling off one side of the span while the torso went splashing down into the water on the other side. A second zombie was impaled on the crescent blade. Lifting the runner off its feet, Ratbag used his enemy as a makeshift shield to block the clawed fingers and gnashing teeth of the mob.

Gaiseric and Ursola rushed in to protect the orc's flanks. Cryptblade withered any zombie that tried to slip past Ratbag's advance while heavy blows from the dwarf's hammer knocked the decayed creatures into the canal.

"They're holding the bridge," Videric reported. The templar looked anxious to join the fray but was holding himself back so that the two spellcasters wouldn't be left without protection while they worked their magic.

Videric's commitment to duty compelled Helchen to act. Reading from the grimoire, she gestured at the far side of the canal. The spell she invoked summoned a powerful windstorm. Water was whipped up in a fury, rolling high against the opposite bank in an ever increasing arc. When it was sweeping over the very ground the zombies were walking across, she quickly changed her conjuration. Now it was the chill power of the frost blast she summoned, directing it against the waters she'd churned into such chaos. The rolling waves were frozen in an instant, creating an icy slope that stretched across the channel.

Helchen's head reeled with the unaccustomed strain of rapidly switching spells. She staggered and would have fallen had Videric not been there to support her. The templar's eyes were wide with shock when he looked at her. "What have you done?" he accused.

The walkers on the opposite side were turning now, taking advantage of the ice that created a path between themselves and their intended prey. Dozens of zombies stumbled out onto the frozen slope, intent upon the living flesh they sensed so near. A few of the creatures lost their footing and went sliding along the ice, but their misfortune only sped their passage over the canal.

"Made things easier," Helchen answered the templar. She drew the flanged mace from her belt and slid its leather loop around her wrist. She smiled at Videric and added, "Easier for us." Bracing her legs, the witch hunter brought her mace cracking against the ice just below the pathway. At first there wasn't any reaction. For a horrible instant she wondered if she'd misjudged the strengths and weaknesses of the spells she'd employed.

Then there was a dull snap and Helchen saw a slender fracture start snaking its way through the ice. Other cracks splintered away from the initial one, groaning and burbling as they spread through the frozen patch of canal. Helchen knew how transitory the frost was in the best of conditions, but here, with the warm waters of Zanice's canals flowing against and beneath the patch she'd frozen, she knew the effect would be even less durable.

The zombies, though, with their decayed brains, were oblivious to such things. In their dull understanding, the ice simply represented a new bridge for them to use to reach their prey. The undead didn't hesitate to try to cross. They didn't even think to retreat, to save themselves by turning back to the other side. They simply continued their shambling, stumbling advance even as the surface under their feet shattered.

The closest of the walkers was still a dozen feet away from Helchen when the ice split and whole sections sloughed away. Zombies plunged into the water below, sinking beneath the surface, swept away by the current. With each fracture, the integrity of the remainder was further compromised and the destruction escalated rapidly. In a matter of moments, the whole span shattered, spilling scores of the undead into the canal. One section, bobbing like an iceberg in polar seas, carried away a half dozen walkers as it floated off into the far reaches of Zanice.

Helchen looked on with satisfaction as the combination of spells wrought doom upon so many of their foes. It was the indulgence of only a moment, for then she snapped her focus back to the far more stable stone bridge where her companions remained locked in battle. While the witch hunter had been laying her trap for the walkers, Shareen had continued to use her magic to whittle away the zombies converging upon the crossing. The far end was littered with decayed corpses, shocked, burned, and frozen by the wizard's craft.

Ratbag continued to press the fight for the bridge. The orc, with his enormous size and brawn, was in his element. The melee saw gashed and dismembered zombies spilling off the sides to join those already lost to the charnel waters below. The frenzied assault by the runners was thwarted by the confines of the span. Direct attack was blocked by the ragged, torn creature impaled on Ratbag's blade. Efforts to slip around the warrior's guard were undone by the punishing efforts of Gaiseric and Ursola. With the greater part of the zombie mob drawn off by Helchen's trick with the ice bridge, the living survivors were soon able to triumph over those that remained and win their way to the opposite side of the canal.

"There's your villa," Gaiseric said when Helchen joined them on the other side. He started forward, but only managed a few yards before an arrow whistled down at him and drove him back. "Whiskers of a nameless cat," he cursed at the nearness of the shot.

Helchen held a hand over her eyes to shield her vision

from the sunlight bearing down on them. "More deadeyes," she said, staring up at the villa with its tall tower and narrow windows.

"Zanice has been raided by pirates in the past," Shareen said. "Some of the older structures were constructed more like forts than homes." She looked over at Gaiseric. "Be grateful the zombies aren't more restrained and decided to shoot at you the instant you came within range." The wizard indicated the other arrows coming from the tower as they clattered uselessly against the ground well away from their own position.

Videric removed his helm and scratched his chin while he appraised their situation. "We've still got to run the gauntlet if we're going to get inside that villa."

Helchen frowned as she made her own calculations. "Not if we do something they aren't ready for." She pointed to Ratbag and indicated the doorway of the shop beside them. "Find something big enough to provide cover, heavy enough to block arrows, and portable enough to carry."

The orc scowled back at Helchen, frustration in his gaze as he tried to juggle the assortment of directives. Ursola shook her head. "Come on," she told Ratbag. "I'll pick it out for you, you just lug it along."

The pair soon returned with a large oak bench, a leather-worker's table from the look of it. The furnishing was big enough that Videric had to help Ratbag manage it. Between them, the two warriors carried the table like an oversized pavis. Once they had a firm hold on it, Helchen motioned Shareen to join her behind the bulky shield.

"This will keep the arrows off until we get close enough to the villa," Helchen told the wizard. "Once we're near enough, we'll have to direct our energies to blocking up those windows."

Shareen shook her head. "Even if we combine our magic, the frost won't hold for long."

Helchen stared up at the tower and the skeletal figures that were moving about within. Already there were more arrows shooting down from the villa. "It doesn't have to," she assured Shareen. "We only need to stop their attack long enough to get inside." She nodded at the doorway leading into the residence. A mob of zombies had already taken care of that problem for them. The heavy panels lay on the ground, battered off their hinges.

"Once we get in close, I'll deal with them," Videric swore.

Helchen grinned at the templar. "That depends on whether Ratbag doesn't deal with them first," she said. She doubted the fight to cross the bridge had sapped much of the big orc's stamina. She was certain it had done little to satiate his aggression.

There were moments when Helchen could almost pity the undead.

CHAPTER TEN

Videric kicked open the door and sprang into the tower room. His sword crunched into the fleshless skull, dropping the zombie archer.

There were four other skeletal bowmen in the room. Until the moment Videric burst through the door, the undead had maintained silent vigil at the windows where traces of ice continued to linger. The zombies lacked the cognition to appreciate that while those apertures had been frosted over, their enemies had entered the villa.

"Der bump fer ya, cadavaz!" Ratbag bellowed as he charged past the templar and slammed into the nearest of the undead bowmen. The walker was sent reeling by the brutal impact, thrown into its comrades even as they started to take aim with their bows. Before the creatures could try to recover, Videric and the orc were upon them, hewing and hacking until the zombies were delivered a permanent death.

"That makes seven," Gaiseric commented from the doorway. On their way up from the front hall, they'd encountered a walker in the livery of a valet and a runner that had somehow locked itself in a closet and needed the sound of living people to motivate it into freeing itself.

"Shouldn't that be a lucky number?" Ursola asked the thief, leaning against the wall and taking a deep breath. "Might mean these are the last undead hanging around the place. Though I'd dearly like to introduce my hammer to the head of whatever cur designed that stairway."

The dwarf was of the opinion that, for purely capricious reasons, the architect had put the steps just far enough apart that she wasn't able to ascend them at a natural pace but had to exert herself in short hops. It hadn't improved her attitude when Ratbag decided the jumping dwarf was something to laugh at.

"Always reckless to assume there are no more enemies," Videric cautioned the others. He wiped the residue of brains and blood from his sword on the tattered uniform of the last zombie he'd destroyed. "It's unwise to relax in enemy territory."

"You almost sound like an inquisitor of the Order," Helchen told Videric as the witch hunter entered the room, Shareen following in her wake. "Of course, they also taught us that *everywhere* was enemy territory," she added as she looked over the remains of the fray.

Gaiseric clucked his tongue and frowned. "Vigilance through paranoia. No wonder you're such an intense personality, Helchen."

Videric spun around and pointed his finger at Gaiseric. "The abbot made Helchen responsible for this quest. She's your leader and you *will* respect her authority."

Even as the outburst cracked off his tongue, he regretted his loss of control. His only excuse was that the thief's sneering flippancy was grating. It was undisciplined and dishonorable. He knew Gaiseric was brave enough in a fight, but he couldn't reconcile that knowledge with his belief that a warrior should always exhibit a certain reserve, a dour demeanor that reflected the obligations of duty. Helchen had such qualities. In his savage fashion, so did Ratbag.

But Gaiseric? He seemed incapable of evolving beyond a trite, juvenile perspective that held *any* authority in contempt. Such a mindset, Videric felt, was what undermined the strength of the kingdom and created the very chinks in the armor that had enabled the necromancer cabals to inflict the Black Plague upon the realm.

Gaiseric returned the templar's ire. "The monks put Helchen in charge," he said. "You they sent along just to be rid of."

It was the worst thing the thief could have said. Videric stormed toward Gaiseric and would have struck the rogue had Helchen not stepped between them.

"Enough of this stupidity," she scolded the men. "We've enough problems. As you pointed out, sergeant, it's unsafe to presume there aren't any more zombies in here. I suggest we make sure and get up to the roof while there's still enough light to see by."

Videric lowered his head. "As you command," he said, not entirely able to keep a sullen hint from his tone. Aspersions against his capabilities as a templar hit too close for comfort. All his life he'd wrestled with self-doubt, questioning his own merit. How many of his accomplishments were earned and how many had simply been given to him? Videric was the son of Captain-curate Seitz, acting commander of the Swords of Korbara in the absence of their grandmaster. When he'd risen to the rank of sergeant, he'd wondered if it was because of his abilities or his pedigree. Being sent on this quest, was that a testament to his fitness as a knight of Wotun or was it just a means by which Seitz could elevate Videric's prestige and heap accolades upon his son?

The templar threw himself into the task of clearing the rest of the villa. Videric was nearly as eager as Ratbag to find something to kill, to silence the doubts that rankled him in the din of battle. Unfortunately for him, the deadeye walkers in the tower proved to be the last undead in the residence. Soon he was mounting the broad steps leading to the top of the villa.

The roof was unlike the sharply angled shingles that characterized the buildings of Korbara. Here, in Zanice, the style was to have a flattened expanse. With space at ground level cramped and compacted, the burghers didn't squander real estate on gardens and parks. Such greenery as the city possessed was therefore hidden above the canals and pathways, surviving in pots and planters on the roofs of villas and palazzi.

Videric half-expected to find a mob of zombies waiting for them when he cautiously advanced onto the roof. Instead, all he found were potted palms and soil-filled troughs blooming with flowers of every shape and hue imaginable. Even to an untrained eye it was clear that the owners of the villa had expended a good deal of money and effort to curate their garden, which made the equally obvious neglect all the more poignant. Brown weeds had sprouted in many of the flower beds, gradually supplanting the intended occupants. Other plants, more delicate and requiring daily attention, were developing splotchy blemishes, shedding petals and leaves as they slowly died. The marble walkways through the garden were littered with dead leaves and spilled dirt. Mold coated the sides of basins and fountains, clouding their waters.

"Nobody up here," Videric called down the stairs while Ratbag continued to poke around the garden in a vain attempt to expose any zombies with sense enough to lurk in ambush.

The templar's encouragement brought Helchen and the others up the steps. The witch hunter gave only the briefest consideration to the garden itself. Her mind was fixed on their purpose in coming here. She worked her way past the flower beds and stunted palm trees to the vine-covered ledge that ran around the periphery of the roof.

Videric joined her. The vantage afforded by the villa wasn't everything that they could have wanted, but it was better than wandering aimlessly at canal-level. They could see over the tops of the adjacent buildings and onward for several blocks before taller structures blocked off the view entirely.

"I don't see anything that looks like it's a headquarters for the Rangers." Helchen sighed in frustration.

Videric expected the lodge to be marked with the iconography of Njall the Hunter, a deity the Rangers considered to be their patron god. Failing that, they'd certainly have marked the lodge with the crossed arrows that were the badge of the Royal Rangers. In his time with the Swords of Korbara, he had had some dealings with the Rangers. He suspected that Helchen had done the same when she was with the Order of Witch Hunters. In the wilderness, the Rangers were so discreet that they could utterly disappear, but in an urban setting they squandered no opportunity to boast of their organization and its royal charter. There would be no doubt that they were looking at the lodge when they finally found it.

Unearned or not, Videric held the rank of sergeant and knew what it was to lead others into perilous situations. He could sympathize with Helchen's position. Right now, she was thinking the risks involved in invading the villa had been unwonted. But that was because she was thinking about immediate rather than incremental success.

"We're not up high enough," Videric said. He directed Helchen's attention to a building in the distance, a structure so tall that it towered over the intervening blocks. It was the cathedral of Wotun. Zanice, like any prosperous city in the kingdom, had built an extravagant temple to the God of Justice as a means of expressing their piety and of flaunting the wealth of their community. The templar considered such exhibitions vulgar, almost blasphemous. Under the circumstances, however, the zeal of Zanice was also useful.

"The spire above the cathedral is the highest point around," he told Helchen. "From there, you can probably not only spot the Ranger lodge here in Zanice but also see clear back to Korbara."

"We'll strike out for the cathedral," Helchen decided after a moment of consideration. There was a grateful smile on her face when she turned toward Videric. "You continue to prove your value to this expedition," she told him.

The templar shook his head. He should have known he wasn't duplicitous enough to hide anything from a witch hunter. Helchen had probably guessed his problem the moment he reacted to Gaiseric's quip. He wavered between offering an explanation or an apology.

Before he could offer either, the moment was lost. Videric and Helchen both spun around when they heard Ursola's cry echo across the roof, a name infused with terror even in the dwarf's harsh tones.

"Flamefang!"

Sight of the dragon, slowly winging its way above the rooftops, paralyzed Helchen with horror. Despite knowing that the wyrm was unlikely to have died from the damage it had sustained at the Red Unicorn, to have the beast's survival confirmed in such an abrupt and terrifying manner wasn't something she could adjust to. She was only able to watch in ghastly fascination while the reptile soared over Zanice like a colossal hawk.

Helchen dimly recognized the voices of Ursola and Videric asking her for orders, but she didn't respond. All she could do was stare at Flamefang's monstrous form, at the tattered wings and charred scales, the necrotic decay that had changed the dragon's colors from red and yellow to rotting green and diseased blue. She gazed at the long saurian face, the flesh peeling away from the fanged jaws, the eyes consumed by a necromantic glow. It was clear to her, from the way the beast glared back, that it had spotted them, that the wyrm was coming to kill them all.

Her horrified fascination was broken only when Flamefang abruptly dodged in midair and diverted from its approach.

"What's that grave-cheating lizard doing now?" Gaiseric asked, his voice cracking with fear.

"You can be sure it bodes ill for us," Helchen said.

She watched the dragon alight upon the top of a nearby tenement. She saw two figures drop away from the reptile, sliding off its back to reach the rooftop. Hate and revulsion swept through her when she recognized one of the dragon-riders as the necromancer Brunon Gogol. Even with the brawny arm of an orc fitted to his shoulder, she couldn't mistake the villain she'd thought slain back on Yandryl's island. In Gogol, she was certain, was the explanation for Flamefang's hideous resurrection.

The necromancer's companion was hideous in his own right. No living man could be the owner of that scalded, almost skeletal countenance. Yet the man moved in a manner that was more alert and deliberate than the dull shamble of the usual undead. Helchen didn't know what that peculiar animation portended, but she did know what the familiar armor and tattered surcoat meant. There was only one knight she knew of who bore that coat of arms displaying the sword and dragon. As desperately as she wanted to deny the proof, she knew who this creature had been in life.

"Alaric."

Despair clawed at her heart just by whispering the name. Just as the return of Flamefang was Gogol's doing, she knew this atrocity was also the necromancer's handiwork.

"Alaric?" Gaiseric came up beside Helchen and stared at the other rooftop. His jaw tightened with a rage Helchen had never seen him show before. "That corpse-snatcher! Murderous maggot! He's found Alaric's body and turned it into one of his stinking zombies!"

"Gogol will pay for this," Helchen vowed, unsure if the words were for Gaiseric's benefit or her own. Simply speaking them was enough to numb some of the horror she felt.

"Helchen! Gaiseric! Snap out of it!" Ursola shouted, shaking the witch hunter's shoulders. "Alaric is gone. That is just another zombie under Gogol's control!"

With a start, Helchen shifted her focus away from the frightful sight of Alaric's undead body. The dragon lifted away from the tenement after depositing Gogol and the knight on the rooftop. The wyrm was now soaring toward the villa.

"We should retreat inside," Shareen implored Helchen, the wizard twitching with fear.

Helchen shook her head. "We make our stand here. The dragon could collapse this building the same way it did the inn." She shook her fist at the black-clad form of Gogol. "And with that scum on hand to give it orders, Flamefang would make a much more thorough job of it." She reached for the grimoire, her jaw set with fierce resolution. Loathed by the Order or not, magic was the only chance of opposing the undead wyrm. "There's no running from the fiend. We fight the beast here."

Gaiseric turned and dashed back to the stairs after Helchen voiced her decision. Videric scowled at the running thief. "For all his faults, I at least thought him brave."

"He is," Helchen assured the templar. She didn't know why Gaiseric was rushing back inside, but she was certain it wasn't to save his own skin. His ethics might be questionable, but not his devotion to his friends.

The witch hunter had no more time to consider Gaiseric's actions. Flamefang dove down on the villa, claws spread like a phalanx of pikemen. She wasn't sure if the dragon could spew fire in its undead condition, but she knew there wasn't anywhere on the roof to shield them from the reptile's flames if it did. The only course was to spoil the monster's attack before it could begin.

The words and gestures of the wind spell came easily to Helchen this time. She barely glanced at Hulmul's book before she sent a tempest slamming into the flying wyrm. The howling gale blasted Flamefang, arresting its forward momentum. It took all the dragon's strength simply to maintain position.

The dragon hung in midair. Then the reptile opened its fanged maw. Helchen conveyed a prayer to Wotun, begging the god that the wind would blow Flamefang's fire back into its face.

Instead of fire, however, the reptile disgorged a mass of slimy flesh that splashed down on the rooftop. Helchen remembered the dragon's distress when it attacked *The Demoness* and spewed a bunch of partially digested zombies onto the ship's deck. That instance had been affliction rather than a deliberate effort. This, however, appeared to be Flamefang's intention. The wyrm drifted back after spitting up the zombies, letting the gale carry it away toward Gogol.

"Five hexes of a mad witch," Shareen gasped, recoiling from the undead. Ratbag plunged in to put himself between the shocked wizard and the zombies. His scimitar lopped the head off a burly brute as it tried to stand. His second swing glanced to one side when he tried to cleave an emaciated, almost skeletal creature. Helchen grimaced when she saw the eerie glow suffuse the withered zombie.

"Spectral walkers," Ursola growled, backing away before swinging her hammer at the zombie.

Helchen grimaced. "Don't waste the effort," she warned

Videric. "The glowing ones are protected by a phantom shell. Only magic can hurt them."

"And Gaiseric ran off with Cryptblade," the templar snarled. He circled around the undead mob and intercepted a feral runner that seemed to have the same idea. A low sweep of his blade took the legs out from under the creature. A stab to its skull ended the zombie's menace.

Shareen recovered from her surprise to send a ripple of lightning into one of the spectral walkers. The creature's eerie dweomer vanished as its decayed flesh smoldered under her spell. Soon there was only a smoking corpse sprawled over the flower beds.

But there were more. Flamefang had vomited ten zombies onto the roof, half of which were spectral walkers. Helchen directed her attention to the other glowing creatures, unleashing a wave of frost that locked the undead in place. Ursola employed her hammer to brain a zombified orc brute that staggered away from the spell with one arm frozen solid. Lacking the ectoplasmic shell that guarded the spectral walkers, the hulking orc fell with a head reduced to pulp.

"The dragon!" Videric shouted.

Helchen turned to see Flamefang speeding to the villa. She knew Gogol gave the reptile directions now, keeping the beast back until she was busy staving off the spectral walkers. Before the witch hunter could unleash another gale upon the dragon, its body described an arc and it rose above the roof.

"Scatter!" Helchen shouted to her companions. She scrambled to follow her own command, leaping behind a marble basin, throwing her arms up to cover the back of her head. The next instant the entire building shook as Flamefang came plummeting down. When Helchen looked up, she saw the beast crouched in a crater of its own making. Potted palms were strewn everywhere. The frozen zombies were reduced to so much gory debris by the dragon's impact.

Flamefang fanned its tattered wings, buffeting a dazed Ratbag and flattening the orc to the ground. A claw licked out and flung Videric halfway across the roof. Shareen lay sprawled on the ground, her head bleeding from a gash caused by flying debris.

Only Ursola was on her feet. The dwarf glared death at Flamefang, the ancient hates of her people rising to the fore. She unslung her satchel and snatched a fire-bomb. "This time I make sure you burn," she swore before hurling the incendiary at the dragon's face.

Flamefang made no effort to dodge. It opened its mouth and spewed another clutch of zombies onto the roof. Ursola's bomb crashed against the slimy undead, igniting as it did. The decayed creatures were incinerated by the bomb, but their destruction left the dragon unharmed.

Again, Helchen saw Gogol's hand in the necromantic dragon's enhanced cunning. After blocking the fire-bomb, Flamefang dug a claw under a fountain and tore it free of its foundation. The broken fixture went spinning straight at Ursola, viciously battering the dwarf and almost knocking her over the edge. The stunned demolitionist scrambled for a handhold, any notion of renewing her attack lost in the crisis.

The sound of running feet caused Helchen to glance back to the stairs. She felt a thrill of wonder when she saw Gaiseric charging up to the roof. Despite her confidence in his courage, she was shocked to see him now, throwing himself into a battle that was all but lost.

"Keep the beast busy!" Gaiseric yelled.

Helchen noted the objects clenched in the thief's hands. He'd ducked back inside to retrieve a bow and arrows from the vanquished deadeye walkers. Helchen gave him a grim smile and an approving nod as he charged past her. Fighting Flamefang was only part of their problem. The rogue was going to try to eliminate the other part.

Focusing her mind, Helchen sent an icy blast into Flamefang. The dragon's inner heat had given it considerable resistance to the spell before, but it occurred to her that the zombies it was hacking up were far more intact than the partly digested undead it had spat onto *The Demoness*. The lack of any draconic fire added to her belief that death had chilled the wyrm's body and that now it might be vulnerable to her magic.

She realized her mistake as soon as she cast the spell. A conjuration that could freeze a pack of human or orcish zombies simply lacked the power to do the same to a beast the size of a dragon. All it managed was to put a coating of frost across one of Flamefang's legs. And to draw the monster's attention to her.

The dragon turned away from Ursola; the villa quaked as the reptile stepped toward Helchen. She knew only too well the difficulty any normal weapon would have against Flamefang. A glance to one side showed her that Gaiseric was taking aim with the looted bow. To distract him now, to try to bring Cryptblade against the reptile might be to spare Gogol a speedy death. Not even if she was in the dragon's jaws would she risk the necromancer getting away again.

There was, however, another weapon she could draw upon. Something Helchen dreaded resorting to more than even the darkest spell.

Hidden in her boot was the Dragon's Kiss, the profane relic she'd taken from the Order's vaults in Singerva. Its obscene power had destroyed the treacherous Archmage Vasilescu; now she prayed it would do the same to Flamefang.

The dragon's foul exhalations washed across Helchen as Flamefang lurched toward her. As the reptile came within reach, her hand wrested the evil relic from her boot. "Wotun's mercy," she begged her god as she drove the fanglike dagger into the wyrm's outstretched claw.

Helchen could feel the wicked energy of the artifact pulse through her, the black shadows that swam through her mind while she held it in her hand. She knew its murderous history, how all those who'd carried the blade were driven mad by it, viciously preying upon the innocent.

At the same time, the witch hunter beheld the awful power of the Dragon's Kiss. Stabbing into Flamefang's claw, its destructive energies seeped into the wyrm. Helchen watched as the scales blackened and sloughed away, as the flesh beneath dripped from the beast's bones like melting wax. The monster's entire foot was soon denuded, reduced to bare bones. Even the skeletal structure began to dissolve, eaten away as though infused with some terrible acid.

Shivering from the awful power she held, Helchen withdrew the dagger and backed away. Though undead and inhuman, there was a look of agonized horror on Flamefang's face. The dragon raised its foreleg and twisted its neck so it could bring its jaws snapping into the flesh above the corroded foot. With a powerful wrenching motion, Flamefang bit off the member and let it tumble over the edge of the roof. Still bearing an expression of fear, the dragon fanned its wings and retreated back into the sky.

Helchen watched the wyrm flee, then stared in awe at the profane dagger. Was it really possible that its diabolic corrosion would have spread to consume Flamefang entirely had the reptile not bitten off its own leg? Shuddering at the implications of just how powerful the Dragon's Kiss was, the witch hunter slid it back into the sheath hidden in her boot.

Whipping around, Helchen turned her attention to the roof where Gogol and Alaric were. She saw neither the necromancer nor the knight. What she did see was Gaiseric crouched down by a flower pot, pale and shaking. He looked up when he heard her walk toward him.

"I shot him," Gaiseric cried. Angrily the thief tossed the bow and remaining arrows down into the canal. He stared at Helchen, his eyes filled with self-reproach. "I tried to stick an arrow in Gogol's gizzard, but my first shot fell short." He paused, struggling to face what had happened. "My second shot would have had him, but it never hit Gogol." There were tears in the rogue's eyes. "Helchen, before the arrow could hit him, Alaric deliberately stepped in the way. I shot Alaric, put an arrow through his chest." He slammed his fist against the rooftop. "There's no question. No doubt now. Alaric's one of that cur's zombies."

Helchen laid a sympathetic hand on Gaiseric's shoulder. "You did him a mercy," she consoled him.

Gaiseric frowned. "No, I didn't because he didn't die… get destroyed… whatever happens to a zombie. He just plucked out the arrow and followed Gogol when the scum ran into the building." He ground his teeth in fury.

"We'll free him," Helchen said. "We'll free Alaric." She meant her words, though she didn't know how they were going to accomplish the feat. Did a necromancer's domination end at death, or would Gogol's magic persist in the afterlife? She wished she knew.

Helchen turned Gaiseric and motioned for him to help Ursola. "Right now, we need to help the others and get moving. I want to reach the cathedral before Gogol or Flamefang decide to take another crack at us."

It was another untruth. Looking back at the tenement, what Helchen really wanted to do was go over there and find Gogol. Her devotion to duty demanded otherwise. Korbara was depending on them and she wouldn't risk the mission to give battle to the necromancer.

Not even for Alaric's sake.

Ratlings weren't a breed renowned for their courage. Khurr Darkwalker usually found that to be a limiting quality, a flaw that hindered his kind from true power. Of course, there were exceptions, like himself, man-rats whose hunger for power was stronger than any craven inclination. Only the boldest would seek to serve the Darkness, to share in the infernal might of ancient evil.

Khurr's gray paw caressed the talisman he wore beneath his cloak, an obsidian disc honed to such a polish that it was like a lightless mirror. He never failed to feel a thrill run from neck to tail when he touched the amulet. It was a token of the Darkness, proof that he was beyond the petty squabbles and bickering of other ratlings. He could aspire to things beyond a full belly and a lavish nest.

Takwit Slashstab and her warriors were slinking around somewhere nearby. They'd been willing enough to follow Khurr after leaving the sewers, trusting that the sly Darkwalker would devise an even better ambush to deal with the humans and their allies. No ratling was above indulging a vengeful inclination provided the odds were in their favor and there was some prospect of plunder to be had. They'd stayed with him as he led them through a wineshop and into the apartments above, slinking through the building adjacent to the villa where the humans had gone.

There was a great deal of plunder to be had. Takwit was hoping to claim some of the weapons and armor for herself. The blade the vicious orc carried was a perfect size for the hulking Grobox Spinesnap. Even old Kraknik Chantchew had an avaricious gleam in his bleary eyes, drooling over the prospect of stealing the magic they'd seen the human females use to cross the canal. Khurr didn't know how Kraknik would manage that theft. There might be ways a real sorcerer could do that, but in all the months he'd been in Zanice, he'd yet to see Kraknik perform anything that wasn't pure charlatanry. If Kraknik had any real magic, he was good at keeping it hidden.

Kraknik was also good at turning tail and sneaking away with the others the moment the dragon showed up. The ratlings weren't going to take even the slightest risk of getting the reptile interested in them, and so they'd retreated back down into the cellars.

Normally Khurr would have cursed such cowardice, but right now he was thankful for it. It meant he was the only ratling who'd seen the fight… and how it had ended. The woman in the hat had used a very special weapon to fend off the dragon. That weapon was of keen interest to Khurr.

The dagger exuded an energy that was quite familiar to Khurr. It was Darkness, the power that he served. His heart had almost stopped when he saw the relic disintegrate the dragon's foot. Never before had he witnessed such a concentration of destruction. With that artifact in his paws, in the paws of someone who understood its nature and potential, there was no limit to what he could achieve. He'd rise to become the greatest disciple of the Darkness, holding power never claimed by any ratling.

Khurr bared his fangs while he watched hat-woman muster her companions. He'd hoped at least a few of them had died in the fighting, but it seemed they were all still alive.

This complicated matters, but nothing he couldn't overcome. Takwit and her warriors were down in the cellars. So long as he could convince them the dragon was gone, they'd be pliable enough. There was plenty of loot to spread around among them… or at least for those who were strong enough to keep their plunder away from their fellow ratlings.

Of course, the hat-woman's dagger was going to be Khurr's part of the spoils. If any of the others contested that claim… well, theirs wouldn't be the first throats to be slit by one of Darkwalker's knives.

CHAPTER ELEVEN

Well before the sun fully set, the canals of Zanice were plunged into darkness. Only those waterways maintaining a straight course for an appreciable distance managed to receive any light. For the rest of the city, the tall buildings acted like the walls of artificial canyons and blocked the descending sun. In better times, Shareen realized, lamplighters would have drifted down the canals, igniting the oil lamps hanging from iron posts every few hundred yards along the track. She could picture the effect in her mind, thousands of flickering lights to drive back the shadows and transform Zanice into glittering magnificence.

That beautiful image, like so much else, was lost to the Black Plague. Zanice was no longer a vibrant, wondrous place, but a scene of brooding desolation. The shadows clung to the buildings like mammoth bats, slowly stretching their wings to draw more of Shareen's surroundings into darkness. The shadows were everywhere, advancing and expanding to plunge the city into an early night. The shadows, where even the least of them might conceal an undead figure ready to resume its cannibalistic rampages.

The gurgle of the canal was the only constant as the expedition drifted through blighted Zanice. The barge on which they traveled wasn't the most elegant of boats, compared to the shapely gondolas and sleek skiffs that they might have appropriated – ones still floating, that is. None of them, however, could have easily accommodated so many people and certainly not a huge orc.

Helchen and Videric had decided that the strength of the vessel was more important than its speed. Neither of them were absolutely certain that the sea serpent couldn't swim into the canals or that it might not have progeny small enough to do so. Shareen agreed that having a boat that could survive an attack at least for a few minutes was essential.

Looking into the polluted waters made Shareen think she'd prefer being killed outright to sinking into that morbid morass. The barge continually bumped into floating corpses, either brushing them aside or pushing them under. Abandoned boats, smashed crates and casks, wrecked furniture, all the debris made for a slow passage. Ursola and Videric kept busy pushing away such obstacles while Ratbag exerted his inhuman stamina to pole the barge through the murky water. Gaiseric kept at the ready, Cryptblade clenched in his hand, leaping into the fight when a zombie crow would fly up from the dead bodies to try its luck against living prey.

Twice, larger human zombies grabbed Ratbag's pole and tried to climb up from the canal. Though the undead were dispatched almost as quickly as the lone crows, they were a stark reminder of the threat lurking underwater. With no need to breathe, the zombies that ended up in the canal wouldn't drown. They simply lingered on the bottom, reacting to whatever disturbed their mindless lethargy. The vision of swimming through the polluted muck only to have decayed hands grab her from below was a constant fear pulsing through the wizard's veins.

Of course, the shore offered no safety, either. When it became too dark to easily navigate, Shareen conjured an arcane light to guide their way. This display of magic was novel enough to attract the zombies prowling in the ruins. The edges of the canal soon boasted scattered mobs of walkers that reached out to the passing barge with rotten fingers. A few, more mindlessly vicious than the others, even stepped off the banks and plunged into the canal when the tantalizing prospect of gnawing living flesh was too great to resist.

The water wasn't entirely devoid of life of its own. Shareen once saw a blue-scaled pike as long as an ox go swimming past the barge. Eels, dark green mottled with yellow specks, often decided to show themselves. The snake-like fish appeared to have developed an appetite for the crows picking at the floating corpses. Whether alive or undead mattered little to the eels and Shareen would see them slither up from the depths to snag an oblivious bird and pull it under. The sight made her think about Helchen's observation that the Black Plague itself was restricted to sentient creatures like humans and orcs, but that by consuming diseased flesh animals could be infected. Even now, there might be a chain reaction going on in the canals as the eels became infected and passed their corruption on to the larger fish that ate them.

Perhaps the spread would go so far as to even affect the sea serpent that guarded Zanice's harbor.

"Shareen. Tower." Ursola indicated the darkened facade of

a fortification that clung to the roof of a palazzo they would soon pass. It was clearly of more recent construction than the rest of the colonnaded building, raised with an eye to robust durability rather than the refined styling of the structure beneath it.

The fear of pirates must have been hammered into the citizens of Zanice, Shareen thought. They'd passed by several towers now and found that even death hadn't been enough to make the guards abandon their posts. They lingered on as skeletal zombies, the horrific deadeye walkers. Let a living soul stray too near their watchtowers and a volley of arrows would soon be flying down at them.

The frequency of such attacks caused Helchen to develop a strategy for dealing with the undead archers. Shareen could see that the witch hunter was already poised to do her part. Helchen would conjure a windstorm to knock away incoming missiles. Shareen's role was to use a frost blast to seal up the tower windows and prevent further attack.

"Black cats and broken mirrors!" Gaiseric swore as an arrow thunked into the hull only a few inches from where he was standing. He spun around and glared at Helchen. "You can stop thinking like a witch hunter and start using your magic to blow away their arrows!"

Helchen scowled at the thief, but Shareen thought she saw more than a hint of guilt in her eyes. "Magic should not be deployed frivolously," she scolded Gaiseric.

Shareen could appreciate Helchen's view and even to a degree sympathize. The rogue, however, was having none of it. The anger with which he spoke made it clear he'd been suppressing his concerns for a long time.

"I see. So it's perfectly fine to exhaust Shareen's magic, but not your own?" Gaiseric pointed at Shareen as she was opening her grimoire to look up a wind spell. "Somehow it's different if she does the conjuring but not you."

"Shareen has the greater experience," Helchen returned. "She knows what she's doing."

"So do you," Gaiseric hissed.

"Gaiseric, it's all right," Shareen told the thief, touched by his concern. She stretched out her hand and sent an enchanted gust toward the tower. The force of the spell wasn't enough to stop the arrows, but it did slow them enough that they glanced off the hull and plunked into the canal.

"No, it isn't," Gaiseric told the wizard. He turned back to Helchen. "I've been watching you. The farther we go, the more you're content to let Shareen do all the spell-casting." He gestured at the witch hunter's own grimoire hanging from her belt. "Hulmul entrusted that book to you so it could be used. Not so long ago you understood that. Understood that the world is more complex than the Order wanted you to believe. I thought you were at risk of becoming a better woman than the inquisitors were turning you into. Someone who'd do the right thing." He made a helpless gesture with his hands. "I guess I was wrong. Helchen Anders wants to revert to type. It's easier to let the Order do her thinking for her."

Helchen gave the rogue a withering look. "You don't know what you're talking about." Perhaps Shareen imagined it, but she thought there was a trace of doubt beneath the witch hunter's anger.

"Prove it," Gaiseric challenged her.

Shareen could feel the chill as Helchen drew upon arcane

forces. She felt an unnatural breeze waft through her hair as the witch hunter extended her arm and directed an aerial discharge in the direction of the tower. The spell was far more powerful than Shareen's own efforts. It was too dark to see any of the arrows that were buffeted away, but it was obvious that something would need the power of a ballista to force its way through the gale.

It needed a few more minutes of poling before the barge was close enough to the tower for Shareen to cast a frost spell. She could see the strain on Helchen's face as the woman struggled to maintain the windstorm. A further reminder to Shareen that Helchen wasn't a true wizard, despite what Gaiseric might believe.

In stabler times, she'd be considered the very thing the Order would hunt down with unwavering resolve: a self-taught sorceress, an amateur whose ability with magic came not from careful apprenticeship and training but from untutored research and blind experimentation. She hadn't been taught the discipline and restraint that enabled a wizard to safely harness arcane power and guide it to beneficial purposes. Maybe, Shareen wondered, Helchen's hesitancy to use magic wasn't simply the repugnance she'd been taught by the Order, but an awareness of her own lack of skill. Something, she was sure, a witch hunter would never admit, perhaps even to herself. It could be that the backsliding Gaiseric implied was more complicated than the thief thought.

The tower drew close enough for Shareen to cast her spell. She saw the thick layer of ice form across the windows. At one of them, a walker had been leaning out to take a shot. The skeleton was flash-frozen, caught in mid-attack, arrow drawn back against its fleshless cheek. It would remain that way for a good many minutes before the magical ice began to thaw. By then the barge would be long gone.

But to where? As the darkness continued to grow all around them, Shareen worried about their plan to reach Wotun's cathedral. Could they reach the temple before night completely covered Zanice? And what would they find when they reached the site? Helchen's objective was to climb up to the spire and look across the whole city, to pick out the Rangers' lodge from among all the other buildings.

Would that even be possible? They might not be able to get up to the spire if the area was infested with zombies, and if they could, would they be able to hold their position until daylight when Helchen could make her survey of Zanice?

There were so many unknowns and all of them depended upon the thinnest of margins to bring the expedition success. Shareen wasn't an overly religious woman, but she offered a prayer to Wotun that the god would grant them good fortune.

"We certainly need something to work in our favor," Shareen concluded, gazing up into the darkening sky.

The great cathedral of Wotun was far easier to pick out from the urban sprawl than Gaiseric had expected. Night was full and the true master of Zanice now, for the sun had retreated in earnest several hours ago. This time, however, the darkness was in their favor. A bit of luck the thief thought was long overdue. The cathedral stood out among its desolate neighbors for one simple reason: the cathedral had light.

"Someone has sought refuge in Wotun's temple," Videric commented, offering the obvious explanation. Gaiseric scrutinized the templar for a moment. There was a catch to his voice that he'd encountered before, the tone of a man who expresses a belief of which he's no longer certain. The Swords of Korbara were templars devoted to Wotun, militant monks who went to battle in their god's name. Certainly they'd been taught to trust in the power of Wotun, yet the magnitude of destruction and despair unleashed by the Black Plague was such that even the most zealous might question the presence of their god.

A bitter pang ran through Gaiseric when he thought about another knight who'd expressed doubt. Alaric von Mertz had truly lived by a code of chivalry that wasn't simply an excuse to belong to a privileged elite but rather carried with it an obligation to defend the people entrusted to him. The peasants died while he was serving in the king's army, his entire family and all their retainers had been massacred by Gogol's undead, many of the survivors of Singerva he'd taken responsibility for had fallen victim to the zombie hordes roving the countryside. He knew how keenly Alaric had felt every death and how his own helplessness to save everyone had caused him to question everything he'd been brought up to believe.

In the end, Alaric had given his life to save everyone aboard *The Demoness*, bravely sacrificing himself to kill Flamefang. In better times, the thief and the knight would have never seen eye to eye, but the Black Plague had thrust them into situations where he couldn't fail to appreciate Alaric's valor. Some of the man's selflessness had rubbed off on the rogue. Certainly, he'd taken risks he never would have before and for the sake of people he barely knew. It pained him to question Alaric's intentions in those last moments, but Gaiseric wondered if his friend had been willing to go to such lengths because he thought his own quest for revenge had been satisfied.

It was a sadistic twist of fate that the necromancer Brunon Gogol had survived. Not only that, but he had revived Flamefang as a draconic abomination, making a further mockery of the hero's sacrifice by turning Alaric into one of his zombies.

If there was any justice that Wotun had domain over, then Gogol most certainly avoided it. Gaiseric would give just about anything to see the necromancer pay for his many outrages.

"The cathedral's a good choice," Ursola responded to Videric, drawing Gaiseric away from his own brooding. "Thick walls. Stout doors. A handful of survivors could put up a good resistance in there."

"Der ginkz got plenty cadavaz," Ratbag said, removing one of his leathery hands from the pole to point at the plaza around the cathedral.

Gaiseric felt a chill rush down his spine. "Looks like Singerva," he commented when he saw the horde of zombies that filled the plaza. The scene was much like the one that had greeted them when they'd led some of the town's survivors to the supposed refuge of Vasilescu's tower. The open square around the archmage's fortress had likewise teemed with undead trying to feast on the living flesh sheltering inside.

"Only there's no trench around the place to fill with dragon bile and burn those walking atrocities," Helchen said. The witch hunter glared at the besieged temple and shook her head. "There's certainly no way we're getting through that mob and even if we did, we'd have the same problem the zombies are having. We'd need to force a way inside."

Shareen looked at her aghast. "Surely anyone inside would let us in," she gasped.

Gaiseric smiled at the wizard's innocence. "Don't bet on it," he advised. He thought again of Singerva and the moneylender who'd fortified his house and forced Alaric to break in to take shelter. "Sometimes, people are so determined to survive that they'll happily let somebody else do the dying for them." He frowned at his own remark and sighed. "You don't even need an undead invasion to make them that way."

"Steer us around the cathedral," Helchen directed Ratbag. "We can see only two sides from here. Maybe the zombies won't be as numerous…"

She let the thought drift, unconvinced by her own idea. Gaiseric understood her frustration. She'd been entrusted with this mission. Ultimately the success or failure rested on her decisions. For the witch hunter to be clutching at the flimsiest possibility spoke to how dire the situation had become.

"Ya der boss, abercrombie," Ratbag said. The big orc poled the barge into a side channel, following it along to the right of the cathedral. Slowly the barge began to turn a corner. After several minutes, the back of the temple came into view.

Gaiseric had to do a double take. It made no sense at all, but there weren't any zombies flocking to this side of the cathedral. It took a minute before the light from Shareen's spell was close enough to show them why. While the other sides of the building were fronted by an open square, this part of the cathedral had been built right up against the edge of the canal. The undead weren't swarming around this side of the temple because there wasn't any ground for them to gather on, just a sheer drop into the water below.

"It seems like Wotun smiles on you," Gaiseric told Helchen. "There's our cathedral and the only zombies in sight look intent on taking a swim." He nodded at several decayed creatures that were groping about the edge of the building, trying to find a way around. Invariably, they'd lose their balance and fall into the canal.

Helchen studied the layout for a moment. "If you can get the barge up between those two buttresses, we'll be far enough away from the corners to avoid any zombies falling into the boat." The orc nodded in understanding and began to angle the barge for the approach they needed.

Ursola poked her elbow into Gaiseric's ribs, a mischievous grin on her face. "You know what comes next, right?" She pointed at the stained glass windows that decorated the cathedral. The lowest of them was more than a hundred feet from the base of the structure. "Somebody will have to climb up there, and guess who somebody is."

There wasn't any need to guess. Gaiseric's agility made him the only choice. He'd become used to taking on the perilous task of making long climbs, braving heights that no amount of loot could have tempted him to risk when he was simply a thief. Now he was a protector of innocent lives and there was much more than pilf at stake. Still, he wasn't so resigned to these ordeals that he couldn't indulge his own bitter humor in the face of Ursola's amusement.

"Yeah," Gaiseric told the dwarf, "I'll be the one making the climb, but I won't be the only one. Even if whoever's inside is overjoyed to see me, they're not about to open the front doors while those zombies are out there. That means that anyone else who wants to get in there is going to have to make the same climb." He almost felt bad at the way Ursola's eyes bulged. He could practically see her making mental calculations about the height she'd have to ascend.

"Once I'm at the top," Gaiseric said to Helchen, "you come up next."

"Why is that?" Videric demanded, his sense of chivalry offended by the notion that he should wait while Helchen exposed herself to danger. "I should go in case there's trouble."

"The trouble will be when Gaiseric drops you on your head," Helchen informed the templar. "He's not strong enough to pull you up on his own."

Gaiseric frowned at the statement. "There's probably a less harsh way to say it, but, yes, I'll need help to get you and Ratbag up." He glanced back at Ursola. "You, too. That thick dwarf skull of yours isn't going to be easy to lift."

She made a rude gesture at the thief. If looks could kill...

"All right," Helchen said. "Me, then Shareen, then Videric."

"Ursola should be last," the thief advised Helchen.

The dwarf set her hands on her hips and glowered at Gaiseric. "And why would that be? Aside from your wanting a black eye, that is."

"You're more afraid of heights than I am," Gaiseric replied frankly. "If you freeze up and don't want to go all the way, I don't want anyone stuck on the barge. Besides, if the alternative is to be left alone, that might be enough extra incentive to get you moving."

Ursola sputtered angrily, but there was too much truth in Gaiseric's reasoning for her to raise a serious objection.

"That's settled then," Helchen declared. "Ratbag after Videric and Ursola last. You'll signal from the window when you're ready for the next person to start climbing. Whoever's on the barge, remember the order and wait until Gaiseric tells you to start up."

The closer Ratbag brought the barge the more agitated the zombies at the edges grew. Dozens of walkers slipped and fell, quickly sinking in the canal. A few runners attempted to leap onto the boat, even managing some frantic strokes in the water before slipping under. Gaiseric was thankful that the distance wasn't any narrower or the orc any slower about bringing the barge up to the base of the cathedral.

Helchen turned to the thief. "I know this will be difficult..."

Gaiseric ran his hand down his forehead. "Difficult? No. Terrifying? Yes."

He scowled up at the buttresses with their heavy ornamentation and compared them to the regular blocks of the cathedral proper. "I'll have a better time going up the support and then using a grapple to reach the window. If all goes well, I'll drop a line from there and pull everyone up one by one. If we're really lucky, there will be a platform on the other side of that window that we can stay on while we decide where to go from there." He removed the rope and grapple from his pack, then motioned for Ursola and Ratbag to give him the ropes that they carried. Estimating the lengths he'd need, he lashed his rope and the dwarf's together and then wound the remainder around his shoulder. Fixing the grapple to the end of the longer rope, he motioned everyone away from the center of the barge. He'd need some open space to make his cast.

"Wotun watch over you," Videric said.

Gaiseric frowned at the templar's words. "Considering that, even if this works, I'm breaking one of his windows, I'd be happier if Wotun's busy doing other things right now."

Swinging the rope and slowly feeding out more line, Gaiseric built up momentum until he thought he'd have enough force to reach the height he was aiming for. When he made his cast, he was thrilled to see the grapple snag on an ornamental spur on his first try. Bracing his legs, he gave the line a sharp tug. The result made him smile. The rope held fast.

Gaiseric didn't allow himself time to think before he swung up against the buttresses and planted his feet against the masonry. Hand over hand he began a rapid ascent. To pause would mean giving himself the opportunity to look down, and he didn't want that.

Reaching the spur, Gaiseric freed the grapple. He repeated the process by which he'd made the initial climb. From the greater height, he was able to feed even more rope before making his cast. A granite gargoyle thirty feet above him was where the line finally caught. Another rapid climb, another long cast, another ornamental spur.

It was on his fifth round of cast-and-climb that Gaiseric was at the height he wanted. He unfastened the grapple and secured the original line to the weathered statue of a bearded saint. If something went wrong now, he wanted a direct route back to the barge.

The sound of glass shattering made Gaiseric wince when

he threw the grapple with Ratbag's rope attached to it. The hook failed to catch when he tugged on it and he was forced to withdraw the line and try again. More of the delicate window broke each time he cast the line. Sweat dripped from his brow as the thief wondered who else had heard the noise. The zombies trying to claw their way into the cathedral *might* be making enough racket that whoever was sheltering inside couldn't hear him, but what about the undead? Those in the plaza he wasn't worried about; there wasn't any way they could reach him up here. But a flock of zombie crows? Or worse, what if Flamefang took notice?

"Crack that strongbox when you have to." Gaiseric snapped his fingers to catch some luck and made another cast. The grapple noisily smashed through one of the windows. This time, however, the hook found something to hold on to. Laughing with relief, the thief secured the other end of Ratbag's rope, then unfastened the longer line and tied it around his waist. Firmly keeping his face staring upward, Gaiseric scrambled across the rope to the shattered window.

The jagged glass leered at him with its crystal teeth. Gaiseric had to kick more of it free before he could climb inside the window. He saw why the grapple had encountered so much trouble. Three quarters of the window was backed by nothing, only empty space lay between it and the cathedral floor a hundred feet below. The last quarter, however, had a wooden platform behind it, part of a series of walkways that wound around the upper reaches of the temple. He could see the great bells hanging below the vaulted ceiling and the narrow stairway that switch-backed its way up into the spire itself.

"Enough of that," Gaiseric chided himself. "Get everybody else inside first, then start making plans."

Feeding the longer rope out from within the window, Gaiseric soon had a line that reached to the barge. He hoped the light from Shareen's spell was good enough that Helchen could see him when he pointed at her.

When Gaiseric glanced down, he saw that Helchen was making the ascent. The witch hunter made the climb with such speed that he promised himself he'd remember it the next time he was asked to do something like this.

When it was Ursola's turn the dwarf validated Gaiseric's worry. She managed the first dozen feet well enough, but after that she froze with fright. It took the brawn of Ratbag to raise her dead weight up to the window. She staggered through the aperture and onto the platform within. She moved over to the walkway connected to the platform where the others waited. Sight of the sheer drop to the cathedral's floor didn't restore her equilibrium and she grabbed Gaiseric's arm to steady herself, dragging him with her as she stepped back from the edge. So deep was Ursola's fear that Gaiseric couldn't make any quips, but simply left the dwarf alone until she regained her composure.

"We'd best leave the rope secured here," Videric said. He pointed down to the floor of the cathedral where several fires had been lit. They could see pews and furniture piled up against the doors and some people milling around behind the barricade. "We don't know what kind of reception they're going to give us." The templar laid his hand on the rope. "It'd be best to have a way to make a quick exit if they don't like us here."

Gaiseric laughed at Videric. "Now you sound like a thief." He didn't needle the man further, but looked to Helchen. "We could stay up here until daylight, then take a gander from the spire. They'd never even need to know we were here."

The witch hunter considered the argument, but finally shook her head. "Anyone in here is more familiar with Zanice than we are. They could tell us things we need to know."

Gaiseric shook his head. "All right, but let's do like Videric says and leave the rope here just in case."

CHAPTER TWELVE

Helchen started down the walkways, finding stairs at the back of the cathedral that gradually cycled down to the ground floor. Videric accompanied her in the descent while the others hung back in case of conflict. He reasoned that a templar of Wotun might put the refugees in the cathedral more at ease. Helchen couldn't argue with that. Besides, it was probably going to be easier to warn the survivors about Ratbag before they saw the big orc.

The interior of the cathedral was opulently adorned with soaring pillars and rich fixtures of gold and silver. Though their candles had long since been exhausted, Helchen was impressed by the extravagant chandeliers that were suspended between the support columns by interconnecting chains. It wasn't hard to imagine the temple illuminated by this network of lights. Statues of saints and heroes graced niches cut into the walls and pillars, alternately extolling the virtues of simple piety and battlefield courage. Though she'd been schooled by the Order of Witch Hunters, the people represented by some of the sculptures were enigmas to Helchen. Local legends whose acclaim had never spread into the north, or perhaps southern variations of figures she did know.

As they neared the marble floor of the cathedral, Helchen appreciated the full extent of the damage the survivors had inflicted. There wasn't a pew, table, or chair in sight, all of them removed to either barricade the doors or to be broken up as fuel for several bonfires. Reliquaries seemed to have been spared, though tapestries had been torn down to provide bedding for the refugees. She could see dozens of makeshift bedrolls that had been assembled from religious hangings. Only at the end of the nave was there no evidence of scrounging. The altar of Wotun looked to be intact, its gold goblets and bowls glistening with reflected light from the bonfires. Of course, instead of the litany of a priest or the harmony of a chorus, the sound of zombies clawing at the outside doors echoed through the building, a morbid dirge that promised death for those within.

It was only when Helchen and Videric actually stepped down onto the marble floor that the survivors noticed them. A bedraggled woman wearing the tattered finery of a courtesan was carrying a bucket of water toward the group standing watch behind the main doors. She happened to glance toward the steps as the newcomers descended. Her eyes went wide with shock and she dropped the bucket when she spotted the strangers.

"Someone's inside!" the courtesan screamed, turning and running toward the doors. The alarm brought immediate response. People emerged from every corner of the sanctuary, scurrying out from beneath piles of improvised bedding or forcing their way through slapdash fortifications.

"Easy, we don't mean them harm," Helchen reminded Videric. Though their intentions weren't hostile, both of them made sure to have their weapons drawn. They might not mean trouble, but she knew it was important to drive home to the survivors that their visitors weren't defenseless either. Any mistreatment by the refugees was going to cost them.

In a matter of heartbeats, a few dozen men and women converged on Helchen and Videric. They appeared to come from all strata of society. She recognized the rolling gait and loose clothes of sailors, but alongside them were those whose lingering finery and delicate complexions denoted lives that had previously been sheltered from physical labor and privation. There was a slim woman still wearing the bell-capped hat of a jongleur, a stocky man whose long leather apron marked him as either a smith or a butcher, a couple of soldiers arrayed in the serpent and ship livery of Zanice's Sea Guard, and a grizzled limping man who wore a monk's habit and had a billhook clenched in his gnarled fingers.

Most distinctive of all, however, was a sinister figure cloaked in leather. A hood covered his head, and a beaked, birdlike mask hid his face. Helchen felt the intensity of his gaze as the plague doctor studied her from behind the glass lenses of his mask.

"Who are you and how did you get in here?" The question was asked by a tall, stern man with a curled mustache and plaited blond locks spilling across his shoulders. There was a trace of accent in his speech, but Helchen couldn't place it. From the look of him, she'd have taken him for one of the hillmen from beyond Wintergarde, but his clothes were those of a sea captain. He had an imposing physique but there was a sharpness in his eyes that told the witch hunter that here was a man of brains as well as brawn.

"I'm Helchen Anders of the Order of Witch Hunters…" she started to explain. The sea captain quickly waved away the introduction.

"How did you get in here?" the hillman repeated. He glanced at the anxious faces of his fellow survivors. "Did you leave a way that *they* could get in?"

Helchen didn't like the accusatory tone or the assumed authority in the sea captain's attitude. "Unless the zombies can both swim and climb, you've nothing to fear," she retorted. Her eyes roved across the survivors, the withering stare that was a witch hunter's best asset. The sea captain and the plague doctor didn't balk, but she soon had the rest of the crowd cowed.

"Helchen Anders," she said, tipping her hat to the sea captain. It was clear to her that he was the leader of this motley gathering of survivors. "This is Sergeant Videric of the Swords of Korbara."

The hillman nodded to Videric. "Ulfgar the Vanirian. In my time I've fought both beside and against templars of Wotun. You make fine warriors." He shifted his gaze to Helchen. "I've less use for witch hunters." There was no overt insult in his voice, only a statement of fact. "I can put the templar at full rations, but you'll have to be content with half of that." He pointed at each of them in turn. "Your weapons you keep, but any food you're carrying goes into the community store. That's not open for debate."

"We don't intend to stay," Helchen told the hillman. That

statement brought murmurs of disbelief from some of the crowd. "Tomorrow we'll leave."

"Only the two of you?" the plague doctor's voice was muffled by his mask. With his face obscured, Helchen tried to glean some hint of his attitude from his voice, but it was too distorted to reveal anything.

"We have some friends with us," Videric said. "They'll be upset if you try to detain us… or rob us."

Ulfgar's eyes turned upward, guessing where more intruders would be lurking. He didn't spot anyone but just the same a knowing smile pulled at his face. "So that's how you came in. Up the wall and through a window. I should have thought of that." He laughed and let out a sigh of relief. "I was afraid you'd found a way up from below. We lost a number of good people securing the crypt. The last thing I needed was for it to be opened up again." He pointed at a pile of timber and loose stone lying off to one side.

Helchen could easily imagine that there were steps underneath that led into the sacred crypt below the sanctuary. She wondered if the undead Ulfgar had fought were simply those who'd been buried there or if other zombies had dug their way in. Without a necromancer to guide them, she didn't think the creatures were smart enough, but she remembered that the treacherous Vasilescu had bragged that there were entire cabals of his ilk harnessing the Black Plague.

"We came by way of the canal," Helchen told the hillman. She held his gaze for a moment before adding, "It might offer you and your people a way out of here."

"So, you came here to rescue us?" Ulfgar had a doubtful look.

"I didn't say that," Helchen said. She went on to explain about Korbara and the mission that brought them to Zanice, how their motive for coming to the cathedral was to gain the vantage offered by the spire. "Finding anyone alive was more than we'd expected," she admitted.

"You're really going to try and reach the Rangers' lodge?" the plague doctor asked.

"Some people aren't content to sit back and hide," Helchen snapped, the fury in her tone causing him to take a step back. "Perhaps you think that mask and those gloves will protect you from the Black Plague. They won't."

The plague doctor took two steps toward Helchen, as though to show that he'd been surprised rather than intimidated. "Brave words," he said. "I wonder if you have the spine to back them up." He waved his hand to draw attention to the sound of the zombies outside. "Courage isn't enough. You need brains, too. Otherwise, you'll soon become one of them."

"You'll excuse Doctor Stormcrow's eccentricity," Ulfgar advised. "His lack of social grace would be crude even in a Vanirian outpost. He prefers to keep to himself... unless something attracts his interest. Just now, that means you." The hillman pondered that point for a moment, then expressed the idea that had occurred to him.

"I think I can offer you better than just a look from the spire. Doctor Stormcrow here used to work with the Rangers. Had a chymistry right there in the lodge."

Helchen suddenly developed a keen interest in the plague doctor. "Is this true? Could you guide us there?"

Doctor Stormcrow nodded his hooded head, looking more

birdlike than ever. "If you're truly intent on going there, I'd go with you. You see, I left certain... materials... behind when I evacuated to the cathedral. The zombie outbreak hit Zanice with such abruptness that we didn't have much warning." He clasped his gloved hands together and nervously cracked his knuckles one after the other. "I mean, I'd like to go with you if..."

"What the chymist is trying to say is he'd be willing to go with you if he felt safe to do so," Ulfgar explained. "Seems he's worried that some of the Rangers might still be hanging around there. As zombies, of course."

"We managed to come through fine so far. Courage and brains," Helchen added for Stormcrow's benefit. She felt a bit guilty about leaving out some details of her story, such as the vindictive presence of Gogol and Flamefang or the hideous fate that had befallen Alaric. If a vengeful necromancer and an undead knight weren't enough to make Stormcrow stay put, she knew that the threat of a dragon would.

"Perhaps it would make you more comfortable to meet our friends," Videric said. He looked over at Helchen. "They should be here if we're going to make any plans."

Ulfgar gestured at the rest of his survivors. "We'll offer you such help as we can, but you'll have to promise to take everyone to Korbara. The monastery sounds like a more stable refuge than this place."

"Agreed," Helchen said, taking the hillman's hand. Her smile dipped into a frown as she considered another problem. "Captain Ulfgar, before I ask my friends to come down here, I think I should warn you about Ratbag..."

•••

Khurr Darkwalker waited in the cellar of a grog shop, watching through the barred window while the other ratlings scurried ahead onto the street. He was mostly confident that the noisy contraption of pots and pans they'd assembled and set down in a chandler's around the block would draw off any zombies in the vicinity, but it was always prudent to let somebody else take the risks when possible. Only when he was sure none of Takwit's underlings were in jeopardy of having an undead creature jump out at them from the shadows did Khurr emerge from hiding and join the other man-rats.

"Went up wall, enemies did," Takwit informed Khurr when she noticed the cloaked ratling. She gestured with her crooked sword at the cathedral across the canal. Khurr was too late to see their foes actually making the climb, but he began to salivate at an incredible stroke of luck. The stupid humans had the temerity to leave the rope they'd used to climb the wall still dangling down from the window.

"Takwit is going looking," Khurr ordered the chieftain. He closed his paw around the bottom of her muzzle and turned her head to ensure she was gazing where he wanted her to. "Provides does Darkness," he chittered in amusement, flicking his scaly tail from side to side.

Takwit twisted free of Khurr's grip and bared her fangs. "Audacity, Khurr has," she hissed. She pressed the point of her sword against Darkwalker's belly.

Khurr saw the intense gleam in the eyes of Takwit's followers. Even old Kraknik had an excited look. "Forgetting, Takwit is," Khurr whispered. He was sure of his own position, confident that the chieftain's display was nothing but a bluff.

The other ratlings obeyed her because they were afraid of her, but they were more afraid of what would happen to them without Khurr. They credited their survival to the strange powers of Darkwalker, his ability to succor the Darkness and hide them from the zombies. Takwit could kill Khurr, but her own life would be a matter of heartbeats after that. The rest of the pack would tear her to pieces.

Darkwalker was pleased when Takwit Slashstab backed down. It showed good sense on her part. A stupid ratling was of no value to a leader.

"Forgetting water, Khurr is," Takwit snarled at him. She swung her sword around and gestured at the canal. "Forgetting swimteeth."

Khurr preened his whiskers for a moment. Long before the zombie outbreak, the ratlings of Zanice had learned to shun the canals. The sewers were safe enough for them, but in the canals there were big fish that took an unsavory delight in feeding on rodent flesh.

"Plan Khurr has," Darkwalker informed the armored chieftain. "Picking most worthless warrior, Takwit is. Stabbing worthless warrior, Takwit is. Dumping in canal, Grobox is." Khurr looked over at the oversized ratling bully. "Eating bait, swimteeth are. Then crossing canal, Takwit's useful warriors are."

The chieftain nibbled her lip while she considered the plan. The rest of the pack eyed each other suspiciously, each trying to decide the relative value of their fellow ratlings. Grobox looked unconcerned – having heard that he was to carry off the victim, he knew he wouldn't be the one sacrificed. Kraknik, on the other paw, was fumbling about with his talismans and making a point of curling his fingers into occult gestures as though to remind the other man-rats of his supposed powers.

Takwit turned and motioned with her finger at one of the warriors. "Helping Takwit pick, Draknik is." The warrior bobbed his head excitedly and gave his fellows a smug look. He scurried over to join the chieftain and confer with her in rapid whispers.

Even Khurr was stunned by what happened next. Draknik was Takwit's best fighter, yet she suddenly drove her sword through his belly in mid-whisper. The warrior had a shocked look on his face as he fell, paws clutching at his wound. Khurr understood then. Worried that she'd have to fight, Takwit had chosen the one member of the pack who'd be least suspicious of betrayal and therefore the easiest to betray. He had to remember that. Slashstab wasn't just cunning, but she was unhesitatingly ruthless, too.

"Carrying fishbait," Khurr ordered Grobox. The bully loped over and picked up the wounded Draknik, holding him under his arm. Darkwalker directed the huge man-rat to a spot several hundred yards upstream, a place from which Draknik's blood would carry for a long way. Without ceremony, the writhing ratling was pitched into the canal. He floundered at the surface, trying to keep himself afloat. Then the sleek shapes of eels and pike began to converge on him.

"Quick swimming, ratlings are," Khurr snapped. The distraction presented by Draknik wouldn't last too long. By the time the ravenous fish were through with him, the rest of the pack needed to reach the barge the humans had been using.

"Waiting, ratlings are," Takwit imperiously declared. Khurr watched with angry impatience as the chieftain stripped off her armor and divided it among her followers to carry. Steel plate and iron chain stolen from ships and shops across Zanice were rapidly parceled out among the man-rats. An angry snarl from Slashstab prevented her underlings from foisting off their burdens on weaker members of the pack. She didn't want to swim with the bulky armor, but she also didn't want to lose any of it because a minion was overburdened.

When Takwit's armor was finally dispersed, the first of the warriors scrambled over the edge of the canal and started to swim across. Khurr waited until a good number of them were in the channel before taking the plunge himself. The most dangerous places to be in such an endeavor were first and last. A secure place in the middle was best. Takwit dropped in beside him and kept close to the agent of Darkness. It made Khurr uneasy having her so close. It would be a simple thing for her to stab him while they were swimming and then claim he'd simply drowned.

"Finding blood, swimteeth are," Khurr commented as they swam. "Chasing swimteeth, zombies will," he added to allay any fears about the undead at the bottom of the canal. It was both a reminder that they had to hurry while Draknik could still distract the fish and a warning that the zombies would be drawn to them if Takwit tried anything. From the disappointed way her ears curled against the sides of her head, Khurr felt he'd nipped a bit of treachery in the bud.

The first of the ratlings to reach the barge was the brutish Grobox. Khurr didn't know what threats or promises Kraknik had made, but the big man-rat had carried the pseudo-sorcerer across on his shoulders. Irritation gnawed at Khurr when he saw the old charlatan standing on the boat and inspecting his talismans to ensure none had been lost in the canal. Darkwalker was furious that Chantchew came up with the idea first. Intelligence was an asset in an underling. Initiative wasn't. The correct thing to do would have been to suggest the idea to Khurr first.

The rope was still there, hanging down the side of the cathedral when Khurr climbed onto the barge. He could see the window far above to which the line had been secured. He wasn't particularly worried about the ascent, only the potential that the humans had placed a guard there. One quick cut, and anybody climbing the rope would suffer a lethal fall. Best to let Takwit send somebody first.

"Choosing most worthless warrior, Takwit is," Khurr whispered to the chieftain when she was aboard the barge.

Takwit looked up from strapping a vambrace to her arm. She nodded in agreement, appreciating the reason Khurr wanted an expendable underling. This time she picked out a truly useless ratling, Slabbrix, a scrawny arbalest who would be hard-pressed to hit the belly of a giant at forty paces. Slabbrix knew better than to argue, and after grinding his teeth in dread he started up the rope.

Slabbrix scurried up the line at a rapid pace, covering the hundred feet before the last members of the pack were across the canal. Khurr watched as the man-rat gingerly poked his head over the edge of the shattered window. He saw the scaly tail that drooped from under the arbalest's robe wriggle in excitement. Wrapping one claw around the line, Slabbrix made a chopping motion with the other. The meaning was clear. The humans hadn't left any guards. The delighted ratling crept over the shattered panes and disappeared inside.

Khurr waited a moment for any tell-tale scream. It was just as possible that Slabbrix would run into the undead rather than living humans. It would take some concentration to pick out a shriek from the noise the zombies around the cathedral were making. He debated sending another ratling up, but against his caution he had to weigh his need to possess the dagger. That urge won out over his fear. "Climbing next, Khurr is," Darkwalker told Takwit when she started toward the rope. He wanted to get inside first and assess the situation. "Waiting for armor, Takwit is," he added, reminding the chieftain of her vulnerable state. She glared at him but sat back down and impatiently motioned for her warriors to bring the rest of her gear.

The climb didn't bother Khurr. Ratlings were deft climbers and even better jumpers. If, for some terrible reason, he lost his grip on the rope he was confident he could leap to the buttress that supported the cathedral. No, the thing that worried Darkwalker was what he'd find inside. He knew the woman who carried the profane dagger was here – they'd followed the barge all through Zanice. What he didn't know was what else he'd find. The humans came here for a reason, and he had an idea what that reason was.

After driving off the dragon, they obviously wanted to brag about it to the rest of their pack. The presence of so many zombies outside the temple indicated that there were living humans inside. That was something the ratlings had quickly realized and used for planning their own raids through the ruins. Wherever living humans were, it followed that they'd also find stores of food to steal. And, after all, humans were slower than ratlings, so if any zombies did break in, they'd go after the humans first. A very equitable state, Khurr thought.

Khurr's concern was how many humans would be inside this building. The place was big enough and the horde of zombies outside was large enough that there could be hundreds of humans hiding here. That was going to be a problem if he wanted to kill the woman and get the dagger away from her. He might have to think about a different strategy.

Scrambling through the broken window, Khurr joined Slabbrix on a wooden platform that overlooked the vast hall below. He picked out his target easily even if she was too far away to pick out her scent. The big black hat gave her away. He clenched his claws in annoyance that she was quite some distance away. She was talking to a bunch of other humans, and he'd have liked to know what she was saying. Likely she was boasting about driving off the dragon, but it was possible she was up to something else. Maybe she'd somehow figured out that the ratlings were following her and she was gathering reinforcements.

"Too many for ratlings attacking," Slabbrix chittered, his crossbow clenched in trembling paws.

Khurr hated to agree with the underling, but in this instance he was right. There were only a dozen ratlings left in Takwit's pack and at least three times that many humans down below. The nasty orc was there, too, a monster large enough to make Grobox look like a whelp. He also wasn't forgetting the dwarf and the wizard; both had shown terrible powers when fighting the dragon. No, the more he evaluated their chances, the less Khurr cared for the prospect of giving battle to these particular enemies. He'd need to think of something else.

While he was thinking, Takwit and the rest of the man-rats finished climbing through the window. There wasn't room enough for all of them on the platform, so Khurr irritably ordered the warriors to spread out into the adjacent walkways and stairs. He was especially anxious to get Grobox somewhere else after the way the boards groaned under the bully's weight.

"Too many for ratlings attacking," Takwit said, making the same evaluation as Slabbrix.

Khurr rolled his eyes. "Knowing, Khurr is. Plotting, Khurr is." He pulled at his whiskers, trying to devise a ploy that would exterminate the humans without risking the dagger. It would also need to be a plan that offered minimal risk to the ratlings.

The anxious murmurs of the other man-rats vexed Khurr. Not only did it make it harder to think but there was a chance their enemies might hear. "Quiet ratlings being," he snarled, spinning around to chastise the warriors. As he did, he noticed for the first time the enormous bronze bells that were hanging from the roof of the cathedral.

Inspiration struck Khurr, a devious plan that formed rapidly in his twisted brain. He looked below at the barricades the humans had raised. The sound of the zombies outside the cathedral was loud enough to reach them even up here a hundred feet above. Darkwalker bared his fangs in a malicious smile.

"Why ratlings attacking?" Khurr asked Takwit. "Letting zombies attacking, Khurr says."

Kraknik sputtered in protest. "Forgetting loot, Khurr is! Wanting magic paper, Kraknik is!"

Khurr soothed the old charlatan's worry. "Not looting, zombies are. Yes, eating humans. Not looting. After zombies leaving, looting bodies ratlings can." His eyes gleamed at the simplicity of the notion. The zombies would kill their enemies but had no interest in any of the plunder. Once the undead wandered off, Khurr could go down and claim the dagger at his leisure.

"Outside, zombies are," Takwit said. "Getting zombies inside, how Khurr is?"

With a triumphant flourish, Khurr pointed up at the bells. "Needing Grobox," he said. Still pointing at the bell, he made a quick gesture at the wall far below. "Needing Grobox and warriors," Khurr amended, considering the difficulties of getting the huge bronze mass to fall at the angle he needed it to. "Keeping zombies out, humans are." He snarled with vicious laughter. "Letting zombies in, ratlings will."

CHAPTER THIRTEEN

The square outside Zanice's Cathedral of Wotun teemed with decayed corpses, all of them animated by the baleful might of the Black Plague. Gogol knew that to bring about such a concentration of the undead there would have to be a concentration of the living. Someone had taken shelter inside the cathedral. Many someones, in fact. Probably the biggest group of survivors in the entire city, at least from what he'd seen.

The necromancer wasn't having the best of days. His attack on Helchen and her friends had been a fiasco. Not only had he failed to kill his enemies, but the witch hunter had routed Flamefang. Gogol hadn't been able to find the undead dragon and reestablish control over it. He'd made a mistake letting the wyrm get so far away from him. It seemed his influence over the monster was dependent on proximity, something he'd need to bear in mind. He wondered how close the necromancer had been when Flamefang first attacked. But now wasn't the time – there hadn't been the luxury of considering that possibility.

Then, that thieving wretch Gaiseric had shot arrows at him. At *him*! Fortunately, Alaric was firmly under his domination and had blocked the missiles with his own body. That, at least, brought a smile to the necromancer. He could see on what was left of the zombivor's face how much the knight was angered by the actions Gogol compelled him to perform, preserving the life of his enslaver.

"Worry not," Gogol told his undead bodyguard. "When I find your friends again, I'll make you do things that you'll have even more reason to be angry about." He laughed when he saw the tremor that passed through the zombivor. Alaric was trying to resist, but it was a futile effort. Gogol had brought him back from the grave. The knight was his to control, a puppet to dance to his every whim.

Gogol savored Alaric's agonized efforts to defy him, then returned his attention to the cathedral and the zombie horde laying siege to it. The creatures weren't getting anywhere in their attack. It would take more resources than their nearly mindless hostility could muster to break into the sanctuary and slaughter the people inside. At present, the best the undead were doing was trapping the living within. No doubt, in days or weeks they'd starve the survivors into doing something desperate.

Gogol didn't have the patience to wait for that. His pride stung from the double failures of losing Flamefang and letting his enemies escape. He needed an outlet for his frustrations. The massacre of the people inside the cathedral would satiate his urge to inflict misery.

"Let's see if there's a way we can speed this up," Gogol said to Alaric.

He motioned the zombivor to accompany him as he walked into the square. The aura of death magic that surrounded a necromancer made the undead regard him as one of their own. A closer inspection of the cathedral might reveal some weakness that the creatures could exploit given the proper direction. The necromancer could establish complete control over a few score of the zombies and command them to such an undertaking. Once a way inside was created he'd have no further need to influence the horde at all. Their own instincts to rend and slay would take over. Then the killing would begin.

Still relishing the visions of slaughter that raced through his mind, Gogol was slow to notice the loud crash that rose from inside the cathedral. The crash was followed by a booming clamor, the chaotic clang of a great bell. He felt a tremor pulse through the stones under his feet. He watched in amazement as a part of the exterior wall buckled and spilled into the square. Dozens of zombies were crushed by the debris. Many more were smashed into pulp by the enormous bronze bell that rolled into the plaza. The rest of the horde didn't react to the destruction of so many of their own. They didn't even notice something far more important. The walls of the cathedral had been breached.

Gogol started forward, intending to give the horde direction. Then he remembered the stump of an arrow lodged in Alaric's chest. The survivors in the cathedral would be in a panic, but without anywhere to run, it was certain that they'd fight. There wasn't any sense putting himself in harm's way. One of those doomed wretches might get lucky and take a shot at the necromancer.

"Show these dolts the way," Gogol ordered Alaric, pointing at the shattered wall. The zombivor hesitated, but then dutifully pushed his way through the horde, forcing a path to the breached wall. As the knight advanced, other zombies followed him. Such lowly undead were imitative, following any of their kind that displayed even the least hint of purpose.

"We'll kill these fools," Gogol said, his words echoing in Alaric's mind by dint of their occult bond. He wouldn't let the zombivor stray far enough to lose control the way he had Flamefang. "Then we'll get back to the job of tracking down your insufferable friends."

Somewhere in Zanice, the necromancer was certain, Helchen and her companions were still creeping around. When Gogol found them, he promised his enemies would wish they'd been here instead. Torn apart by a horde of zombies was a merciful fate compared to what he had in store for them.

A choking cloud of dust billowed across the cathedral. Helchen's head pounded with the deafening clamor raised by the great bell as it came crashing down. Dazed and coughing, it took her several precious moments to realize the enormity of the catastrophe.

There was a huge hole in the north wall.

"Syrtin and Yamar!" Ulfgar howled, his curse loud enough to penetrate the ringing in Helchen's ears. "The zombies have a way in now!" The sea captain turned to his horrified refugees and by gesture and shout tried to redeploy them to defend the massive breach. Chunks of masonry continued to fall from the weakened wall, forcing the survivors to retreat.

Someone grabbed Helchen's elbow. She turned to see the beaked mask of Doctor Stormcrow only a few inches away. "They'll never hold the gap," he yelled. "The undead won't care about getting killed by falling debris. These people will and they'll stay back. They can't save this place."

"Stormcrow's right," Videric agreed bitterly. "We've got to get out of here while we can." He waved his armored hand toward the stairs. "We can't forget the quest!"

The cloud of dust filling the gap gradually settled, becoming a gritty fog. Through that gray veil, Helchen saw the shambling figures of walkers. The zombies would be inside in a matter of moments.

Guilt twisted her guts, but Helchen knew what she had to do. Videric was right. Too much depended on them getting that research from the Rangers and bringing it back to Korbara. If there was one thing the Order of Witch Hunters drummed into every initiate it was maintaining perspective. Simple, brutal numbers. She couldn't risk the thousands of refugees at the monastery to try to save a few score here in Zanice.

"Get moving," Helchen told her companions, pointing to the stairs.

Shareen stared at the witch hunter in horror. "No! We must help these people!"

The wizard's expression evoked desperation and disgust within Helchen, who knew how ruthless her choice was. She also knew it was the only choice to make.

"Drop it," Ursola grumbled, grabbing Shareen's arm and turning her toward the stairs. "How many people do you think that barge can carry? They'd be fighting each other –

and us – for space. Better they should make their ancestors proud standing against a real enemy."

Shareen was obstinate. "I won't abandon these people."

Before the wizard could do anything else, a brawny green arm curled around her and lifted her off the floor. Carrying Shareen as though she were a kitten, Ratbag loped toward the stairs. "Nah time fer der high hat," he grunted.

Helchen was stunned. Of anyone, she'd have expected the orc to want to stay and fight, but instead even he saw the necessity of escape.

"Come with us," Helchen told Ulfgar. "We can't take everyone, but we can get you and Stormcrow out of here."

The sea captain smiled and shook his head. "You've got bigger things to do. My place is here. I swore to lead these people." He nodded at the survivors. A few of them stood at the breach, waiting for the first zombies to enter. "Besides, if I'm not here, they'll panic worse than they already are. I don't want to kill people I tried to save." He clasped the witch hunter's hand. "Avenge us," Ulfgar said. The hillman swung around and hurried over to the breach.

Helchen watched, admiring Ulfgar's resolution. He knew it was a hopeless fight, but he went anyway. Such courage was all too rare in the kingdom. A courage she was determined to remember and to honor.

The others were already making their ascent, racing up the switchback stairs. Gaiseric kept the lead, with Videric close behind him. Ursola had taken the role of guiding Stormcrow, the only one among them who was unfamiliar with the turns they'd have to make once they entered the network of walkways and platforms suspended beneath the cathedral's ceiling. Helchen prayed the bell's fall hadn't broken any of the sections they'd need to cross or weakened the stability of the scaffolding. It was a long way to the floor and no mystery what would happen to someone who made that precipitous descent.

Helchen stopped at the first bend in the stairway to look back at the survivors holding the breach. She spotted Ulfgar bolstering the flagging courage of his followers. She saw the walkers shambling over the rubble. Then her eyes locked upon the decayed figure leading the zombies.

Alaric's armor and surcoat were too familiar to Helchen for her to mistake them. The man himself, however, had been utterly destroyed. What was framed by the steel of his mail coif was more skull than face, soft tissues scalded away in his battle with Flamefang. The gaping eyes shifted their attention away from Ulfgar and his fighters and she could feel them staring at her with a dreadful intensity. The undead knight took a few steps into the cathedral. Unlike the other zombies, Helchen knew there was intention beyond the mere urge to rend living flesh. Alaric was coming for her.

The knight was forced to take notice of Ulfgar when the sea captain rushed at him with a raised axe. Alaric's reaction wasn't that of a mindless zombie. He twisted to one side when Ulfgar swung at him. Expecting his foe to make no move to dodge the blow, the hillman overbalanced and lost his footing. Alaric swatted him with the flat of his sword, knocking him prone.

The knight made no attempt to finish his enemy, instead looking back at Helchen and resuming his advance. The other survivors hesitated to close with Alaric, preferring to fight the ungainly walkers who were now marching into the breach. Ulfgar, however, wasn't willing to let matters rest as they were. Shaking his head, he rose from where he'd fallen and rushed the knight from behind.

The duel between the two combatants was a blur, so quickly did the enemies engage. Helchen saw that Ulfgar's initial charge didn't surprise Alaric. The knight spun around and parried the axe with his blade. What followed was a blinding flash of steel against steel. Only when the foes separated could Helchen tell the trend the fray had taken. Alaric's shoulder was deeply gashed, the mail of his armor hanging in a tattered strip. Ulfgar's chest was a gory ruin, slashed from ribs to belly. He made a fumbling effort to renew the fight, but his axe slipped from his weakened grip. A final shout of defiance, and the brave sea captain collapsed.

The death of their leader snapped the tenuous courage of the defenders. The fighters holding the breach broke away in ones and twos, and as more of their comrades deserted, the retreat became a complete rout. Zombies trudged their way into the cathedral, the original mobs of walkers now joined by massive brutes and frenzied runners.

Alaric paid the influx of zombies no attention at all, nor did the undead bother with the decayed knight as they pursued the survivors through the sanctuary. He was, after all, one of them. With staring eyes fixed upon Helchen, he marched for the stairs.

Helchen felt her heart hammering as fear coursed through her. The nameless hordes of the Black Plague didn't phase her so much as the sight of someone who'd been her friend intent upon her slaughter. The thought of fighting Alaric disgusted her at the core of her being. She'd managed to destroy the zombies that were once her brother and his family, but somehow she couldn't find that strength now.

Rather than hold her ground to engage a foe she wasn't sure she could even fight, Helchen turned and climbed after her companions. Lingering to watch the battle between Alaric and Ulfgar had allowed the others to put a good deal of distance between themselves and the witch hunter. She could just see Ratbag and Shareen twenty feet above her, the orc warrior still carrying the old wizard.

Suddenly, Ratbag reeled and dropped Shareen on the stairs. The renegade caught himself on the rail before he could fall. Helchen was wondering what had happened to him when she heard something strike the steps just inches from his foot. In the darkness she couldn't see the object that went clattering away, but she was familiar enough with her own crossbow to recognize the sound of a bolt ricocheting.

Shareen raised her hand and quickly conjured a spell. An orb of light sprang into being, throwing a bluish glow across everything, including their attackers. On walkways and platforms above and adjacent to the stairway was a motley pack of verminous creatures. Ratling arbalests were perched in the rafters, their crossbows clenched in furred paws. Helchen spotted a wizened man-rat waving a splintered staff and snarling orders to the creatures around him. From higher above, the witch hunter now detected shouts of alarm from Gaiseric and Videric, quickly followed by the clash of steel.

Helchen didn't wonder where the ratlings had come from or why they were here. Such questions could wait. All that mattered now was that the man-rats had ambushed them and unless she did something fast their quest would end right here and Korbara would be lost. Holding her crossbow at the ready, she sprinted up the steps, hurrying to help Ratbag and Shareen.

Only when Helchen turned the next corner did she realize the insidious cunning of their ambushers. The ratlings were poised to close their trap from both sides. There were four of the monsters clinging to the underside of the stairway. They'd let the others pass by them so that they could drop down and surround their prey once everyone went past.

At least such was Helchen's theory. She quickly discovered that the tactic was even more deliberate. One of the ratlings pointed a clawed finger at her as she rounded the corner. "Mine, black hat is!" As the creature squeaked this reminder to his minions, Helchen recognized the hood and cloak. This was the same pack of ratlings they'd fought in the sewers. It wasn't an accident they were here: they'd followed Helchen's group to the cathedral!

Helchen's chest felt cold when she considered that the ratlings were probably responsible for the bell falling. Fury and guilt made her take aim and shoot a bolt at the cloaked man-rat. The creature chirped in fright but exhibited terrifying agility by squirming up and over the side of the stairway to avoid the shot. "Killing black hat, ratlings are!" he screeched orders to the others while scrambling for safety.

The other ratlings dropped down from the underside of the flight of stairs above Helchen. They wore ramshackle armor of boiled leather, uncured hides, and whatever metal they could tie or stitch to the motley arrangement. Each of these creatures had a curved sword thrust under their belts, cutlasses stolen from sailors, Helchen assumed. As they landed on the steps, the man-rats reached for their blades. The witch hunter's flanged mace crushed the arm of one enemy before the cutlass could be drawn. The ratling yelped in pain and sprang away. He misjudged his leap, however, and crashed through the railing.

Helchen's other foes weren't so slow to draw swords. They rushed in even as their comrade fell to his doom. The witch hunter blocked one of the blades with her mace, but the other ratling darted in low and slashed her leg. Dropping to one knee, she was barely able to avoid a strike that would have opened her belly with an upward sweep of her bludgeon that gashed the man-rat's hand and forced her enemy to dart back.

Before she could try to recover, Helchen felt something slam into the side of her head. She slumped against the stairs, struggling to stay conscious. She saw the cloaked leader drop down from the staircase above. She knew it was her blood dripping off the knife the ratling leader held. He'd hit her in the head with the blad of the blade.

"To Khurr giving dark dagger, black hat is," the cloaked man-rat snarled at Helchen. He started to come at her with his knife, but even as he began to move, his ears flattened against the sides of his head, and he gnashed his fangs. Something had frightened him, and he lost no time shoving the other ratlings into danger.

That danger brought a heavy sword crunching into the skull of the foremost ratling. The blade caught in the rodent's body and dragged the weapon with it as the man-rat slumped on the stairs. The other verminous warrior sprang for the now unarmed interloper, driving her sword into the center of his chest.

By rights it should have been a killing blow, but Helchen knew the man the ratling had stabbed was already dead. With the sword lodged in the center of his chest, Alaric seized his enemy by her furred throat. The terrified creature struggled in the knight's grip, the claws of her hands and feet scratching futilely at his armor and undead flesh.

Khurr darted in while Alaric was struggling with the warrior. The ratling's knife slashed down at Helchen's leg, trying to cut her boot. The blade failed to slice into the thick leather and before he could stage a more determined effort, the witch hunter swung her mace in a vicious arc. The flanged edges chopped into Khurr's foot, breaking bones and severing toes. The man-rat sprang back, grabbing onto the underside of the next flight of stairs. He glared at Helchen for an instant, then awkwardly scurried away, blood streaming from his mangled foot.

Helchen had only a moment after Khurr's retreat before she heard the sharp crack of a snapped neck. She twisted around to see Alaric drop the lifeless body of the ratling warrior. Up close he made for an even more hideous sight. His staring eyes had no lids to cover them; his face had neither nose or lips and such flesh as remained was pocked with scars. His complexion was the dull gray of decay and no blood oozed from his wounds, only a scabby crust that clung to the ends of severed veins.

The witch hunter dragged herself away from the undead knight. She left off the mace and reached for Hulmul's grimoire. Dark magic had brought Alaric back; in her desperation she thought only magic could end her friend's ghastly existence.

Alaric reached down and recovered his sword from the first ratling he'd killed. Now, Helchen knew, it would be her turn. The undead had saved her from the man-rats only so he could please Gogol by killing her himself. The knight started to raise the sword, his eyes still fixed on her.

Then a strange look twisted those decayed features. The gaping eyes dilated wildly, the rotten body trembled and shivered. Helchen forgot the spell she'd intended to cast as she watched Alaric struggle. She recognized that here was a chance to overcome an enemy while he was helpless, but there was more than that. Alaric was more than just a zombie. Something yet remained of his spirit in that undead body. Something that was trying to break free of Gogol's control.

A battle was being waged between the knight's honor and the necromancer's magic. Helchen could feel the turmoil raging inside Alaric's body as he fought to break free. By commanding his undead slave to kill her, Gogol had overestimated his domination. He'd stirred up the essence of the man and forced it to resist.

Whether Alaric could free himself, Helchen didn't know, but the shapes that came rushing up from below made the question moot. Two frenzied runners were charging up the stairway. It wouldn't need the knight's sword to kill her, the teeth and claws of the runners would be just as effective.

With no time to prepare a spell, Helchen lashed out with her mace and smashed the face of the first zombie as it slipped past Alaric and sprang at her. The creature fell onto her, its unnatural life stilled by her attack. In dying, however, it pinned her bludgeon between its body and hers. She was helpless against the second runner, unable even to raise a hand to conjure a spell.

The runner dashed past Alaric, ignoring the knight entirely. It was the last mistake the zombie would ever make. Breaking free of his own struggle, Alaric brought the edge of his blade crunching through the neck of the creature. Head and body pitched over the rail, careening down into the sanctuary far below.

There was a flicker of the mortal man in the lidless eyes when Alaric stood over Helchen and lifted the destroyed zombie off her. He reached down and pulled her to her feet. "Zombies…" His voice was a dry, cracked rasp. The sound of it seemed to sicken him and after the first word he simply gestured with his head at the horde streaming in below.

Helchen thought she understood Alaric's meaning. "There's another way out," she muttered. Even if he'd just saved her, it wasn't easy to adjust to the horrible sight of her friend in his condition.

Alaric could certainly see the revulsion in her face. Helchen could see the pain that flashed through his eyes. He turned away and started down the stairs. Fighting back her disgust, she reached out to him, her hand clasping the cold, dead flesh of his arm. "No, don't go."

The knight shook his head. "Gogol," he hissed, making a thrusting motion with the sword.

Helchen couldn't imagine how greatly Alaric wanted the necromancer dead, but she feared that if he tried to confront the villain that Gogol would regain control over him. "Help us," she said, desperate. "Mournshroud may lose power. The secret to maintaining its strength is here in Zanice. Help us find it."

If there was truly more than a trace of Alaric's spirit in the undead, Helchen knew the appeal to his sense of duty would be stronger than the urge for revenge. The knight had forsaken his vendetta against Gogol before in order to help others. She hoped that appeal to honor would carry through again.

Alaric hesitated for a moment, then gave a slow nod of agreement. "Later... Gogol," he rasped. He motioned Helchen to go ahead of him. She soon realized why. There were more runners coming up the stairway. The zombies didn't react to Alaric, trying instead to dash past him to reach her. Only when the knight struck at them did the other undead recognize him as an enemy. By then their efforts to pull him down were too little and too late. He had no need to fear infection from the gnashing teeth, and the clutching claws only raked dead flesh even when they found a spot that wasn't covered in armor. It was a simple matter for Alaric to eliminate the zombies and, at least for a time, remove the threat of pursuit.

Ascending the stairway, Helchen saw the signs of combat. Crossbow bolts were embedded in steps and rails, dead ratlings were scattered about the platforms. She could see the lingering traces of frost where Shareen had cast her spells. Whether the wizard had killed all the man-rats or simply routed them was impossible to tell.

The witch hunter's goal was the broken window and when she came in sight of the platform, she found Gaiseric on guard there. The thief lifted Cryptblade the moment he spotted

Alaric, horror crawling across his features, but Helchen made placating motions with her hands.

"I know what he looks like," she said, "but Alaric's still here. Gogol made a mistake and revived his spirit as well as his body." Helchen looked over at the undead. "He's broken free and wants to help us."

"No." The thief shuddered. "Alaric's dead. This… this is just a zombie."

"Not zombie… zombivor," the knight hissed, the unfamiliar word dropping from his tongue like poison.

"Alaric's mind is still here," Helchen tried to convince Gaiseric, to pierce the terror the rogue felt. "He's not like the other undead."

There was just a flicker of uncertainty, then Gaiseric firmed his hold on Cryptblade. "Another of Gogol's tricks."

Alaric bowed his head, his mouth curling with regret. "When I… no longer…" He pointed at Cryptblade. "Use for me… when I don't… help." He grasped his throat as though to force his voice to obey him.

"He saved me from the ratlings and the zombies," Helchen explained. She fixed a penetrating look on Gaiseric. "Where are the others?"

"Already climbed down to the barge," the rogue replied, his eyes still locked on the zombivor. "We had to fight our way through the ratlings, but everyone made it through. Ratbag got the worst of it, but Shareen and Stormcrow are tending to him. He wasn't so bad off that he couldn't climb down the rope." Gaiseric's expression became somber. He looked over at Helchen and posed a question of his own. "Ulfgar and the rest?"

Helchen shook her head and glanced at Alaric. There wasn't any need to talk about the zombivor's part in the tragedy. "They didn't make it."

Gaiseric nodded. "Then there's no more use waiting around." He darted a suspicious look at Alaric. "Might be better for *it* to climb down last. Let the others know first." He turned to Helchen. "Or maybe you should explain things. I'm not as sold on this thing still being Alaric as you are."

"Some things you feel more than you know," Helchen said, amused at her own statement. "Sometimes you have to trust."

"Trust is an indulgence I've never permitted myself," Gaiseric said as he climbed out the window and started down the rope. "But right now, it doesn't look like I have much choice."

CHAPTER FOURTEEN

The canals of Zanice were a bewildering maze to Videric. By using waterways as their streets, the city builders had constructed a complex network of arteries and channels that flowed into one another, spreading away from the main streams like the threads of a great spider's web. Within half an hour of leaving the cathedral, the templar couldn't even tell in what direction the building was.

Of course, it wasn't vital that Videric knew where they were, only that Doctor Stormcrow knew. The plague doctor was up at the front of the barge, his masked face peering into the pre-dawn gloom. At each branch of the canal, he would gesture with a gloved hand and let them know which course their boat needed to take. So far, at least, he appeared to be a confident guide, though the efficacy of his directions wouldn't be known until they actually spotted the Rangers' lodge.

The task of poling the barge had been surrendered to the undead creature Helchen brought with her from the doomed cathedral. Videric wasn't convinced of the trustworthiness of Alaric von Mertz. Whoever he'd been in life, now he was a decayed monster, barely even a step removed from the zombies that threatened to destroy the kingdom. That a witch hunter could suffer such an abomination to exist made him again wonder about the stability of Helchen's reason.

Videric was far from the only one who doubted how far the zombivor could be trusted. Ratbag's first impulse was to attack the knight and he might have done so had Shareen not dulled his senses with a spell so that she might tend to the orc's wounds. The renegade had taken no less than six bolts from ratling crossbows during the ambush and the wizard couldn't heal him while the missiles were still embedded in his flesh. Gaiseric was only a little less hostile than the orc. The thief sat a few feet away from the undead Alaric, Cryptblade resting across his lap and one hand laying on the sword's grip. His eyes never left the knight's decayed figure and Videric suspected that the least suspicious move would have Gaiseric lashing out at the zombivor with his enchanted weapon.

Ursola and Stormcrow had accepted Alaric's presence with more aplomb. The plague doctor seemed more intrigued than frightened by the undead knight. Videric supposed that if the process of instilling awareness into zombies could be harnessed then it could turn the tide against the necromancer cabals, pitting their deathless legions against creatures with the intelligence to remember who they had been and why they should defend the realm being destroyed by the hordes.

Ursola's own view was framed by an obscure dwarfish custom. "In the strongholds we have the Tomb Watchers," she stated. "There aren't many who choose to join their ranks, but doing so is the greatest act of devotion any dwarf can extend to the ancestors. Sometimes a dwarf who has been crippled by accident or battle, or who has brought on some terrible dishonor, or who simply has too much grief over a lost relative, will decide to become a Tomb Watcher. A deadly elixir is provided to the dwarf, which is then taken daily in small doses. Over the course of several years the poison is imbibed, and so gradually does death creep over the dwarf that the line between the living and the dead is blurred. Not always, but sometimes, that line is so blurred that when death does finally come the dwarf doesn't truly die but becomes a Tomb Watcher, an eternal guardian to patrol the crypts of the ancestors."

The practice of allowing some dwarfs to willingly become undead gave Ursola a peculiar acceptance of Alaric's condition, but Videric couldn't share it. There were no such traditions among the people of the kingdom. The dead were the dead and the living were the living. Anything that trespassed over those boundaries was unnatural and evil.

The barge moved more slowly than it had when Ratbag was poling it, but the journey was smoother. Tireless and unrelenting, the zombivor propelled the boat with the steady rhythm of a machine. Videric had to concede that much to the undead knight.

Dawn shimmered ahead of them, at once putting Videric on the alert. After the enveloping shadows of the canals where the tall, clustered buildings created urban canyons, the abrupt illumination was unsettling. But it wasn't just the light that alarmed Videric. It was the reason for the light. What lay before them wasn't a narrow channel, but a wide expanse of water.

"He's guided us to the harbor!" Videric exclaimed, turning toward Stormcrow.

"The sea serpent," Shareen gasped, her face pale with fright. The forbidding monster that lurked in Zanice's waters was a menace they'd risked much to avoid. Now it seemed the plague doctor was leading them straight into the beast's jaws.

Stormcrow bobbed his hooded head, looking more than ever like some grisly carrion bird. "The lodge is near to the port," he said. "Easier for the Rangers to receive materials from distant lands." He glanced aside at Helchen and then at Videric. "We needn't go into the bay and rouse the serpent." He pointed at a side channel that was a few hundred yards to their right. "We take this course."

"You'd better know what you're doing," Ursola warned Stormcrow.

The plague doctor made an ostentatious bow to her. "By all means, mistress dwarf, if you know a better route to the lodge then feel free to take over."

Ursola glared at the man, but his rebuke silenced her threats. Videric didn't like it either, but they'd gambled everything on Stormcrow's claims that he could get them where they needed to go.

After the shimmering view of the harbor, the channel the barge moved into seemed darker and more foreboding than any they'd navigated. Shadows from dilapidated tenements and tall warehouses stretched over the whole canal, only the narrow ribbon of sky directly overhead betraying any evidence of the growing dawn. Undead crows fluttered about floating corpses, mobs of zombies crept along shoreside pathways, gazing hungrily at the passing boat. Videric could feel the malevolence of their surroundings pressing in around him.

Zanice wasn't a city of the living. It was a city of the undead.

The templar strove to retain his composure. The unrelenting threat he'd been surrounded by for the past day was wearing on him. It was worse than withstanding a siege, for at least in a siege there was no mystery about where the enemy was. Here, in this blighted place, the foe was everywhere, needing but the least provocation to reveal itself in sudden violence. The situation was far different from what he'd expected. Videric's valor was being tested, and it was a trial he feared he would fail.

"There," Stormcrow announced, extending his hand toward a timber-framed building that rose on their left. There was a wooden jetty that projected slightly into the canal, a set of oaken doors just behind the quay. Above the doors was a massive coat of arms, crossed arrows flanked by the figures of a stag and bear, their rampant forelegs reaching for the missile. The insignia of the Rangers.

"At last," Helchen said. She removed her hat and wiped perspiration from her brow. Until that moment, Videric hadn't considered that she might be under every bit as much strain as he was: the burden of leadership, the responsibility for bringing their quest to a successful conclusion.

"The archives you want are on the lower floor," Stormcrow told the witch hunter. "Not so very far away from where my... materials are kept." He helped tie the barge to the jetty when Alaric poled it close to the lodge.

"Exactly what are these materials you want so badly?" Videric asked the plague doctor. The eyes behind Stormcrow's mask transfixed him with a sullen stare.

"Rare components that the Rangers provided me for my experiments," Stormcrow finally said. "They'll be quite useful, I assure you."

"What kind of experiments?" Gaiseric asked, but before he could get an answer, Helchen cut him off.

"There's only one thing I want to be assured of," she told the plague doctor, "and that's whether the records Korbara needs are in these archives. Anything else is secondary." Helchen climbed off the barge onto the jetty. Now it was Stormcrow who was fixed by a piercing gaze. "Secondary, you understand?"

"If he doesn't, I'll make sure that he does," Videric said, stepping forward and standing right beside Stormcrow. The menace of his posture wasn't lost on the plague doctor.

"Everything we want will be inside," Stormcrow assured them. Then he paused and lowered his beaked head. "Unless…"

Videric pounced on Stormcrow's expression of doubt. "Unless what?"

The plague doctor shook his head. "Unless zombies have already destroyed what we're after."

"Zombies won't be looking for loot, just people to kill," Ursola stated. "Everything else should be intact as long as said things didn't get in their way."

"Only one way to find out," Videric said, bristling that the plague doctor had waited until now to suggest the grim possibility that the lodge had been vandalized. "We go in and look for ourselves." He shoved Stormcrow onto the jetty and toward the doors.

"Since you know this place, you go first," the templar told Stormcrow.

It was painful for Alaric to look at his companions. The vitality coursing through them had a hurtful brightness that stung his eyes. Everything else was hazy and indistinct, as though he were looking at the world through a carnival charlatan's trick mirror. He could see well enough to navigate, but the only real distinction was the blazing glow of the living. Small wonder that zombies sought out mortals to kill. The lifeforce was the only light in the hazy shadow world of the undead, a light that brought only pain and perhaps the agonizing memory of their own condition. It wasn't to feed on flesh that the zombie hordes attacked the living, but to extinguish the tormenting light the mortals exuded.

Alaric was the last to disembark. He was hurt to see Gaiseric lingering behind the others as they climbed onto the jetty. The thief was clearly waiting for Alaric to pass him, to ensure that the zombivor wasn't at his back. After the onset of the Black Plague, Gaiseric had become a close friend of the knight, a last link back to the von Mertz domain and the home they'd both lost. To now have the rogue openly and overtly hostile toward him deepened the sense of loss that tormented him. There could be no acceptance of the undead among the living, only a guarded tolerance.

"Let me ... lead," Alaric suggested to Helchen. "Zombies ... not ... attack," he explained.

Helchen motioned for Stormcrow to move away from the

doors. "Tell Alaric where to go," she said to the chymist. He looked doubtfully at the knight, but finally nodded his head in agreement.

The doors into the Rangers' lodge proved to be unfastened and easily opened when Alaric shoved his hands against them. The Rangers and their servitors must have been in a hurry to evacuate if they left the doors unsecured. The hallway inside showed that they likely had good reason for such hasty flight. Debris was strewn everywhere, proof of the violence that had unfolded here. Among the litter were a few bodies, their leather hauberks adorned with the insignia of Rangers. The skulls of each man had been shattered, crushed to pulp by a tremendous weight. No threat of these corpses reanimating as zombies. With the brains destroyed there wasn't a nexus for the necromantic energies to focus upon.

Stormcrow drew back when he saw the bodies. Alaric thought the plague doctor was more agitated than he'd been before. That suspicion intensified when Gaiseric stepped forward and examined the corpses. "Looks like someone dropped a heavy barrel on them." The thief demonstrated his meaning by holding his hand over the wounds and describing an arc with his fingers. The depiction made Stormcrow recoil.

"If you know what did this, you should tell us," Helchen advised the chymist.

"No... I... it's just... I knew these Rangers," Stormcrow stammered.

"Sawbonez givin' der spiel," Ratbag grunted. The big orc's body was swaddled in bandages, but his head was clear enough that even he saw Stormcrow was trying to hide something.

Alaric didn't think the plague doctor would be forthcoming. The chymist had his own reasons for coming here. From what he'd gleaned listening to Helchen on the barge, Stormcrow only wanted them along to provide him with protection. He had no interest in the records they were looking for. Whatever secrets the man was protecting, it would take more than their disapproval to get him to expose them.

"Which… way?" Alaric asked Stormcrow, waving his arm at the hallway ahead of them. The light from Shareen's spell revealed numerous doors opening into the wide central hallway as well as a few connecting side passages.

Stormcrow didn't hesitate when he pointed at one of the passageways. "There. The steps lead down to the cellar where my laboratory is… and your archives."

"And maybe something else?" Gaiseric pressed. He pointed at the dead Rangers. "Like maybe whatever did that?"

"We need to be on our guard," Helchen agreed with the thief. "You and Alaric stay in front, Ratbag and Videric move to the rear, just in case whatever's lurking in this place comes up behind us."

"Ya der boss," Ratbag said. Clearly, the warrior didn't know whether to be pleased or upset over the duty, given the uncertainty as to which direction the trouble he wanted would come. Or perhaps he was simply annoyed that he wouldn't be close enough to strike at Alaric if the zombivor betrayed them.

Alaric chose not to ruminate upon the distrust of his old companions, and focused on the task ahead of him. Marching into the side passage, he soon found a set of stairs that plunged downward. He was reminded of the temple-fort of the witch hunters in Singerva, with their dungeons and catacombs beneath the building. The stairs here were broad, wide enough to accommodate large cargo brought into the lodge. He wondered why the Rangers would need the space but then speculated that perhaps the structure was one they'd acquired rather than designed and the large stairway was a legacy from when the place had housed some manner of mercantile enterprise.

The zombivor was partway down the steps before the sound of Gaiseric choking caused him to spin around. The thief was leaning against the wall, waving a hand before his face and making gagging sounds. He directed stern looks at Alaric and Stormcrow.

"Can't you smell that?" Gaiseric snarled at them.

Stormcrow brushed a finger along the beak of his mask. "This is filled with a pomander of invigorating aromas to stave off the ill-vapors of the Black Plague," he said. "It would be a failing of my design if any smell could seep in."

Alaric shook his head. "Nothing," he rasped, but the answer made him anxious. He knew his sight was reduced and strange after becoming a zombivor. How much were his other senses likewise impacted? He thought of the zombie mobs he'd walked among but couldn't recall if he'd smelled the stench of their decayed flesh.

"I'm not surprised," Gaiseric said as he started to wrap a cloth around his face. "You're ripe enough that you wouldn't notice." He gestured with Cryptblade at the passageway at the bottom of the steps. "There's something dead down there. Either it's big or there's a lot of them."

Doctor Stormcrow flinched when he heard Gaiseric's

description. Whatever the chymist was hiding, Alaric thought the thief had struck pretty close to the truth.

"We... find out..." the undead knight declared, resuming his descent. Shareen was at the top of the steps now and sent her light down to guide his way. It was considerate but unnecessary. Alaric's unnatural sight was no worse in complete darkness, a slight compensation for its hazy indistinction.

Reaching the passageway below, Alaric was again struck by the resemblance to the temple-fort in Singerva. The hallway was lined with barred cages, long cells that stretched a good forty feet along the wall on both sides. By the light he could see a huddle of shapes lying in those cages, but he didn't have time to scrutinize them closely, or to wonder about the doors further down the hall. One of those doors was swaying open on its broken hinges and a shape emerged from the room beyond, a figure so massive that it had to crouch and move sideways to fit through the opening.

The creature somewhat resembled a minotaur, being of a roughly human shape but twice the size of any man. The legs were smaller in proportion to the long, powerfully muscled arms. Much of the beast was covered in black fur, but there were stretches of bare skin around the belly and under the arms that was dun-colored. The head that rose between its broad shoulders looked like that of a monstrous goat with curled horns and a mouth that was bulging with long fangs. Alaric glanced down at the fiend's feet and saw that they were hooved. The answer to what had crushed the skulls of the Rangers was exposed.

The goat-ogre was no undead thing. Its nostrils flared when it caught the scent of the intruders and its red eyes shone with vicious hunger. A low, ragged bray came from deep in its throat and it stamped one hoof angrily against the floor.

"Monster," Alaric tried to cry in warning, but his withered voice wouldn't carry up the stairs. Locking his hands around the hilt of his sword, he braced himself for the goat-ogre's charge. To threaten the others, it would first have to come through him.

That was a prospect that didn't faze the monster at all. Braying again, it lowered its head and barreled across the passageway. Alaric struck the thing with his sword, gashing it along one of its massive arms, but the beast's charge didn't falter in the least. Its horned skull slammed into him and a twist of its neck flipped him through the air. He crashed against the bars of the cells with bone-jarring velocity.

"Help! Help! The specimen is loose!" Stormcrow's shout was muffled by his mask, but it carried farther than Alaric's raspy warning. The zombivor looked over to the stairs in time to see the chymist fleeing up them. In his wake he left Gaiseric to stand alone against the furious goat-ogre.

The thief slashed at the hulking monster with Cryptblade, but the sword's enchantment held no power over a living foe. His weapon was only a normal blade as far as the goat-ogre was concerned, and Gaiseric lacked the strength to inflict more than a glancing cut across the beast's furry hide. The monster swung at him in retaliation, the enormous fist cracking the stone step as the rogue squirmed out of the way. From above came the sounds of the others rushing down to support Gaiseric.

Alaric picked himself up and charged the goat-ogre from behind. His sword bit into the back of the creature's knee, tearing through tendons and causing the beast to stumble as it took another swipe at Gaiseric. The monster turned its head, bleating in rage at the knight. It struck at him with a clawed fist, but the zombivor dodged the attack and delivered one of his own. His blade pierced the goat-ogre's side, slipping between its ribs to puncture the lung behind them.

The sudden pain made the goat-ogre rear up onto its feet again. It roared, but this time blood as well as sound erupted from its jaws. By now the others were in the passageway. Videric and Ratbag rushed at the monster, slashing it with their blades. Ursola was behind them, but before she could swing her hammer, the beast staggered back. Blood from its punctured lung was dribbling down its face. It made a final, futile effort to reach Alaric, then collapsed to the floor.

"Any more surprises like that?" Helchen demanded of Stormcrow, holding her crossbow at his head.

"I didn't expect it to still be here," the chymist protested. "It broke free when we were trying to evacuate! That was weeks ago!"

The plague doctor's deception was set aside when Shareen noticed movement in the cells. Her light shone into the cages, and what it revealed was an even greater horror than the goat-ogre. The cages were filled with orcs. Scabby, scrawny, their green skin faded to a necrotic yellow, their flesh mottled with decay, it was clear to anyone that these weren't living creatures but more victims of the Black Plague. Alaric shook his head in wonder. The orcish zombies hadn't so much as stirred when he was right against their cages, but now, with living flesh nearby, they were roused into animation. No wonder the goat-ogre had been careful to keep itself in the middle of the hallway.

The undead orcs were unable to break free of their cells, but there was one orc in the building who wasn't caged. Ratbag gave vent to a howl of bestial fury at the sight of the zombies. He rounded on Stormcrow, seizing the chymist and lifting him off the floor.

"Stinkin' gut-rippin' croak'r!" Ratbag raged. "Ya skinn'd out! Left der mugz ter starve!" He shook the plague doctor from side to side. Alaric could see the man's eyes wide with fright behind his mask.

"Ratbag! Calm down!" Gaiseric urged the orc. The renegade slapped the thief aside when he came too close.

"Belly der gab!" Ratbag snarled at Gaiseric. "Alla ya bimbos alike! Na gonna get der prop'r scrap, ya jus' let der mugz starve!" He shook Stormcrow again, ready to smash his head against the ceiling.

"Ratbag, whatever he's done, we still need him." Helchen tried to reason with the orc. Unlike Gaiseric, she kept her distance. Ursola and Videric circled around the warrior, ready but not eager to rush in and attack.

"Ya ginkz been playin' der high hat!" Ratbag shouted. "Ya gonna…" The orc's speech faltered, and his grip suddenly slackened. Stormcrow found himself abruptly dumped to the floor. He scrambled away before Ratbag's eyes rolled back and the renegade pitched forward onto his face.

Alaric turned toward Shareen. The wizard stood near the dead goat-ogre, her hands curled into an arcane gesture. She shrugged her shoulders. "A sleeping spell. It was the only thing I could think of to make him stop."

"Done… good," Alaric rasped, but it was an approval without emotion. He recognized that he should feel something, but instead there was only a dull recognition that the spell had been helpful. He stalked over to the shaken Stormcrow and stood him upright. The zombivor's skeletal features leaned against the chymist's mask, his gaping eyes glaring into those behind the lenses. "Why?" he demanded, pointing at the cells. The anger he experienced was far less than the rage he knew he should have felt toward the ruthless experimenter.

"The Duke… the Duke of Wulfenburg," Stormcrow explained. "He engaged the Rangers to find a way to control the orcs. Keep them from swarming across the frontier. I… I was using specimens to… test… to find…"

"A poison that would exterminate orcs but leave everything else alone," Ursola guessed where the chymist's speech was going. She nodded at the somnolent Ratbag. "You think he's mad now, wait until he hears that. Better to leave him here to sleep it off."

Stormcrow shuddered in Alaric's grip. "You… you won't…"

Helchen came forward and glared at the plague doctor. "That depends how quick you show us to the archives and what we find there."

Alaric released his hold on Stormcrow. He turned and nodded his head at the sleeping orc. "Ratbag?" he asked.

Gaiseric shook his head, aghast. "We can't leave him here, even if he's going to be trouble when he wakes up."

"We'll deal with that problem when we have to," Helchen stated. Her eyes narrowed as she looked back at Stormcrow. "We might have someone to throw to him so he can work out his anger."

CHAPTER FIFTEEN

"I was performing a service for the kingdom. I've nothing to feel guilty about," Stormcrow insisted as the group hurried down the hallway toward the doors at the end of the vault-like passage.

Ursola thought that, for a man with a clean conscience, he certainly talked about it a lot.

"My people have been fighting orcs since before your kind piled logs together and called it a house," the dwarf said. She helped Gaiseric drag the unconscious Ratbag along the floor. Ursola nodded her chin at the cages of now zombified orcs that reached out hungrily for the passing mortals. "But this is a disgrace."

Stormcrow stared down at her. "Had I discovered the right mixture, I would have secured the frontier of the kingdom! Wulfenburg's people would never again have needed to fear orc raids against their villages and towns."

"And, of course, you'd have opened all the territory held by the orcs to settlement," Gaiseric put in, his face looking like there was a foul taste on his tongue.

"Would that be so bad?" Stormcrow countered. "It would be a boon to everyone to expand the borders of the kingdom. Much good would have come of my discovery."

Ursola scowled at the chymist. "A so-called good result doesn't make a despicable means any less despicable."

The plague doctor waved his arms in exasperation. "You dwarves are always looking behind you instead of ahead. That's why you limit yourselves to your mountains. Your civilization is older than ours, yet you've been overtaken by humans in virtually every area of development. The future is ours because dwarves won't stop living in the past."

Helchen, leading the advance through the Rangers' extensive vaults, lost her patience. "You can justify yourself all you want after you've shown us the archives," she told Stormcrow.

"Of course," Stormcrow said, the arrogance temporarily subdued. Ursola thought there was even an element of fear in his tone. Among humans, alchemy was near enough to magic that those who conducted such experiments often attracted the attentions of the Order of Witch Hunters. After his last remarks, she found a delicious irony that the chymist would have had a much more secure position if he were in one of the dwarf strongholds. They would no doubt value his abilities.

The plague doctor showed intense interest in the door from which the goat-ogre had emerged, but his eagerness to see the state of the room was tempered by his fear of the witch hunter. Stormcrow pushed on down the passageway, past several other doors. Some of these were open and Ursola could see that they were used to store the lodge's supplies. The condition of some of the contents was proof that Stormcrow's escaped specimen had been sustaining itself on the grains stockpiled by the Rangers. Sacks and barrels had been savagely torn open, their contents strewn across the floor with the marks of the beast's hooves visible in the spilled millet and barley.

"There," the chymist finally declared, pointing out a nondescript door further along the hall. "This is where the Rangers stored their records and studies."

Alaric moved to the door and tried to open it. "Locked," his brittle, ragged voice hissed.

Stormcrow shrugged. "The chief archivist has the key. Wherever he is now. You'll need to find your own way in."

"I can attend to that," Gaiseric said. He reached for the bundle of steel picks and wire hooks that had been so useful in his life as a thief.

"So can I," Ursola stated. She shifted the burden of Ratbag's weight onto the rogue and walked to the door. Taking up her hammer, she brought the weapon crashing against the lock. The door shuddered in its frame. The second blow shattered the latch and the portal swung open. "Much faster this way," she said, smiling at the thief.

"Noisier, too," Videric said. The templar cast a worried look back toward the cells. All of them could hear the zombie orcs shaking the bars, trying to free themselves. The loud noise had agitated the undead.

"If those cages could hold them when they were alive, they'll hold them now that they're dead," Helchen said. She turned to the yawning portal. "Let's find what we've come all this way to get." The sphere of light shot past the witch hunter, illuminating the darkened room and leaving the hallway in a nebulous half-shadow.

When Ursola stepped into the room she found that it wasn't overly large, but was crammed with cabinets and shelves. Helchen and Videric were already at work leafing through the nearest documents, hurriedly searching for the Rangers' records that would unlock the secrets of Mournshroud. Slowly, almost timidly, Shareen joined the hunt.

"Gaiseric, give a hand here," Videric called to the thief. As gently as he could, Gaiseric leaned Ratbag against the wall and left the orc snoozing beside the open door.

The impact of a mailed fist against the side of a cabinet interrupted the search. Everyone looked over to see Alaric staring at a handful of parchment that he slowly returned to its shelf. He turned toward Helchen. "Eyes... no good," he said, waving a hand before his skull-like face. Ursola couldn't begin to imagine what the world looked like to one of the undead, but it seemed being able to perceive letters on a page wasn't among the capabilities of a zombivor.

"You can send him with me," Stormcrow was quick to say. "He can't see well enough to help you here, but he could keep a look out while I examine the condition of my laboratory." He cocked his head to one side and stared at Helchen. "You promised I would have a chance to recover my supplies if I led you to the lodge."

The witch hunter didn't bother to disguise her distrust of the plague doctor. "All right. I wouldn't want to leave you alone. Alaric, go with Doctor Stormcrow." A sly smile pulled at the corners of her mouth. "Ursola, go with Alaric. Just in case he needs any help."

Stormcrow made no protest over his double escort, but it was obvious to Ursola that the man was far from pleased.

Turning on his heel, he left the room, carefully avoiding the
spot where Ratbag was sleeping. The plague doctor waited
outside for Ursola and Alaric to join him, then ignited a
chemical lamp he fitted onto his belt. She wondered if he
realized it was a device invented by dwarves. "Let's go," he
said, starting back down the hall. As she'd expected, he led
them to the chamber where the goat-ogre had been hiding.

"Infernus take that damn beast!" Stormcrow exclaimed
when he stepped through the doorway, invoking the elemental
spirit alchemists believed to be their guiding patron.

The room was a shambles and a pungent reek clung to it
worse than musk to a dragon. Tables and shelves had been
smashed to splinters, books ripped apart and strewn across
the floor. The remnants of jars and bottles of every size and
description littered the ground, liquids and powders of every
hue puddled amid the broken glass. Zombies might have left
the material alone, but the monstrous specimen hadn't.

In her capacity as a demolitionist, Ursola had more than a
passing familiarity with alchemists and their laboratories and
recognized that the wreckage she was looking at would once
have represented a considerable asset to any chymist. Even
while wrinkling her nose at the lingering fumes, she couldn't
curb her curiosity.

"You should probably stay in the hall," Stormcrow advised
her when she followed him into the room. "You don't have
protection," he said, running his finger down the beak of his
mask. "Like I do." He pointed at Alaric. "And our friend here
is beyond being harmed by anything in here."

As Stormcrow spoke, Ursola noticed his head turn ever
so slightly to a bronze keg lying among the debris. "Sure of

that, are you?" the dwarf laughed. She recognized the nature of that metal vessel. Walking over the spilled mixtures and broken glass, she pulled the keg upright. Its side was slightly dented, showing it hadn't escaped the goat-ogre's rampage, simply survived it. By its weight, she could tell it must be full. The runes etched into its lid removed the last doubt over what was inside.

"Blasting powder," Ursola mused. She placed her thumb under the runes. "Mixed by the Stonecracker clan, fellows who know their business. You could send this whole street sliding into the canal with that. Just a pinch would be enough to destroy Alaric."

The plague doctor quickly turned to the zombivor. "That wasn't my intention at all," he protested. "You're much too unique and valuable as a specimen to destroy. A zombie that remembers who and what he was …"

Alaric moved toward the chymist, forcing Stormcrow to retreat from him. "Threaten… to control," the knight hissed. Ursola could sense the anger rising within the zombivor. He'd managed to break free of Gogol's domination. He wasn't about to be enslaved again.

"No, nothing of the sort. This is the only thing I wanted!" the plague doctor insisted. Stormcrow swung around and darted to a heavy iron chest lying on the floor. Like the bronze keg, it had proven too strong for the escaped monster to destroy, though its battered condition made it clear the beast had tried.

Digging into his robes, he produced an iron key and soon had the box open. Within was a big clay pot with an iron seal. "My work, the poison I was developing for the Rangers and the Duke of Wulfenburg." He carefully lifted the pot out of the chest, both arms wrapped around it to steady the vessel. "I wanted to salvage my work. That stupid akerbeltz ruined my ingredients, but with the mixture itself to draw from, it won't be a total loss."

"It isn't orcs the kingdom needs saving from right now," Ursola reminded the chymist. She gestured with her hammer at the pot of poison, fighting the impulse to smash it and have done with the vile concoction. Another thought suddenly occurred to her. "How is that stuff against zombies?"

Stormcrow's eyes had a befuddled look when he stared at the dwarf. "I… I don't know."

"Maybe we should find out," Ursola snarled. "Alaric, help the doctor with his work. It looks too heavy for him to carry." Stormcrow let out the briefest squeal of objection before surrendering the clay vessel to the zombivor. "We'll take this to Helchen and see what she thinks." Ursola glanced back at the keg of blasting powder and took it under her arm. There wasn't any sense in leaving it behind. She glanced around at the ransacked room. "Anything else that beast left that might be useful?"

Stormcrow shrugged his shoulders, a gesture that made him look like a human vulture. "Possibly, if it hasn't been ruined by all the potions splashed all over the place." He looked at the wreckage, then sighed. "No, I don't think so."

Ursola started to tell the chymist to make a more detailed inspection, but at that moment she heard a shout from the hallway. Firming her grip on the bronze keg, she rushed out into the passageway. Alaric and Stormcrow were close behind her.

The dwarf's eyes were sharp enough to see a figure running through the dark toward the plague doctor's laboratory, but it was only when Stormcrow emerged into the passage with his lamp that she had enough light to see who it was. Ursola lowered her hammer when she saw Gaiseric coming toward them.

"Shareen found it!" the thief yelled, his jubilation evident on his face. The loudness of his voice caused the caged zombies to rattle their bars even more violently. Gaiseric glanced in their direction and softened his speech. "Shareen was looking through one of the cabinets and found a sheaf of papers that describe what has to be Mournshroud. The Ranger who made that report must have watched the orcs for a long time, because he describes the rituals the warlocks used to consecrate the drum."

Ursola smiled and nodded her head. "Excellent! Now we can leave this cursed half-drowned, zombie-infested slum and get back to Korbara."

Gaiseric returned her smile with a frown and his demeanor became sheepish. "Not yet," he said. "Helchen wants to make sure there aren't more manuscripts pertaining to Mournshroud. She sent me back to get you and Stormcrow to help in the search."

Until that moment, Ursola wasn't conscious of just how much she wanted to get out of Zanice. She'd just about overcome her fear of drowning during her voyages on *The Demoness*, but this strange city was something else entirely. There was a wrongness about it that offended the dwarf at a primal level. A city was meant to have its foundations firmly set in rock and stone, not squatting over murky water like some colossal toad. Just as she'd resigned herself to accepting the idea of drowning, now she had an entire city around her that she felt would sink at any minute.

The demolitionist scowled as she tempered what she recognized as irrational fears. "Let's get to it then. The sooner Helchen's satisfied, the sooner we can all get out of here."

As they started back toward the archives, Ursola noticed Alaric lingering behind. He was staring into the darkness toward the stairs. The dwarf had to nudge him to get him moving. "Come along," she said. "Maybe you can't help look, but you can take a turn dragging Ratbag when it comes time to leave."

Almost reluctantly, Alaric turned and walked down the passage, still carrying Stormcrow's pot of poison. Now it was Ursola who lingered, gazing toward the stairs and wondering what had drawn the zombivor's attention.

Gogol kept to the shadows, waiting for his enemies to leave. When he sensed the withdrawal of Alaric he felt confident enough to start back down the steps into the vaults below the Rangers' lodge. A few dozen zombies, recruited from the horde around the cathedral of Wotun, accompanied him. The orcish zombies locked in the cages were making so much noise that he didn't think anyone would be able to hear the shuffling steps of his rotting entourage.

What the necromancer hadn't counted on was the sensitivity Alaric exhibited. Gogol was able to key into the zombivor's presence – indeed, the arcane link had allowed him to track the rebellious knight across Zanice – but he hadn't thought the bond would go the other way. Though it seemed Alaric hadn't realized what he'd sensed, the zombivor had detected that Gogol was near. A vexing problem for the necromancer, but not an insurmountable one.

More bothersome was that Alaric had broken free of his control. Gogol had been careful to keep the zombivor closer than he had Flamefang, but he hadn't reckoned upon the knight's willpower. He hadn't compelled the dragon to do anything that went against its nature, but when he'd commanded Alaric to kill Helchen, the conflict inside his soul had been enough to strengthen his resistance and slip free. Even now, trying to regain control, the necromancer found Alaric's defiance too great to overwhelm. He'd need to find some other way to bring the zombivor to heel.

Gogol moved down into the passage. He paused when he reached the base of the steps and saw the goat-ogre's corpse. Already he could feel the malefic energy of the Black Plague seeping into the carcass. In a day or so it would be great enough to animate the beast as a zombie. He, however, would speed the process and improve upon it. Lingering over the dead monster, Gogol drew a cabalistic pattern around it in crushed bone and dried blood. Pricking his palm with the tip of a ritual dagger completed the preparations. Nine drops of fresh blood fell upon the horned head.

Giving one last look at the lighted room far down the hallway, Gogol made sure none of his enemies were coming back. He didn't want to be disrupted while casting his spell. At a gesture, his entourage of zombies spread out along the hall, putting themselves between the archives and the necromancer.

"Restore this heart to tenderness, make supple these

sinews…" The incantation slipped from Gogol's tongue in a reptilian hiss. As the necromancer wove his spell, the hulking body of the goat-ogre began to twitch. Suddenly one of its clawed hands turned and pressed against the floor. The other followed suit a moment later and then the beast was pushing itself upright. The legs kicked at the ground, finding purchase for the thick hooves. Its eyes gleaming with a feral awareness unlike the vacant stare of a normal zombie, the abomination stood upright.

"Yes," Gogol approved. "You should give them some trouble. You've enough necromantic power pulsing through you that it'll need several solid blows from that relic Gaiseric's carrying to put you down again. A nice surprise for the thieving fool."

At the necromancer's gesture, the bestial abomination followed him over to the cells. Gogol pointed at the locked doors. It needed only a swat of the monster's clawed hand to break the locks and free the orc walkers inside. The undead started to shamble into the hall. There were too many for Gogol to command entirely, but he was able to place a single directive upon them, coercing them into keeping near the stairs. He didn't want any of the zombies straying too close to the archives and alerting his enemies to their danger before the necromancer was ready to attack.

Gogol deployed the abomination to the other cells so that it could free the rest of the undead orcs. The ruffians who'd captured orcs for the Rangers had certainly been busy. By the time the cages were opened, the necromancer had nearly a hundred zombies in his horde.

"I hope you found what you're looking for, Helchen

Anders," Gogol whispered to himself. "It will add an extra savor to your despair when I take my revenge." He clenched the hand of his orcish arm into a fist. "It'll make it so much more satisfying when I take it all away from you."

The necromancer's eyes studied the lighted room. "Before I'm finished with you, you'll learn there are far worse things than death that await my enemies."

CHAPTER SIXTEEN

Gaiseric had misgivings about Helchen's decision to search the archives for more information about Mournshroud. It was possible, perhaps even likely, that the Rangers had made further forays into the orclands to investigate this powerful artifact. At the same time, they'd found what they needed to find. They should get the reports Shareen had discovered back to Korbara as fast as they could. Not only would it get them out of Zanice before anything else happened, but there wasn't any telling when the monastery might come under attack again.

Videric echoed the thief's thoughts when he set down the sheaf of parchment he was looking through and addressed Helchen. "This is reckless," he told her bluntly. "We've found what the abbot and the captain sent us here to find. Rodolf never mentioned any other documents."

"I hardly think a scout and trapper like Rodolf, a scoundrel who was only a hireling of the Rangers, would be privy to their secrets," Helchen said, not bothering to look up from the papers she was studying. "If there's more here, we should look for it now rather than letting someone else undertake the dangerous task of coming back to Zanice. Or were you hoping to make a second journey so you could attach even more renown to your name? Maybe catch the notice of your captain and gain a promotion."

The templar's face flushed with emotion at such an accusation. "That would be a disgrace to the Swords of Korbara to engage in such deception. My fa ..." He stumbled over the slip of the tongue, especially when Helchen snapped her head around and fixed him with a curious look. "The captain would never reward that sort of dishonorable conduct."

Gaiseric scratched his chin while he considered Videric's fumble. He'd certainly been about to say "father." So, the captain of the templars was Videric's father. That complicated things in all sorts of ways.

Helchen slowly set down the documents she'd been examining. "I did you a disservice, sergeant," she said contritely. "It was wrong of me to cast aspersions on your sense of duty. I remain, however, in command of this expedition. My decision is that we stay and make a thorough search while we are already here."

Everyone was paying sharp attention to the dialog between the witch hunter and the templar. Except, that was, for Alaric. Gaiseric noticed that the zombivor was watching the doorway. It struck the thief that his fixation wasn't simply that of a sentinel keeping a lookout. There was something eerie, almost obsessive, in the way Alaric stared into the hall. Gaiseric was minded of a hen that knows a hawk is nearby.

Replacing the papers he'd been looking through, turning them around so he'd know where he'd left off, Gaiseric walked over to Alaric. He had conflicted emotions about the zombivor. After saving him from the goat-ogre – Stormcrow called it an akerbeltz – Alaric was less suspicious to the thief. That didn't make the undead knight any less disturbing though. Just being around the creature made Gaiseric's skin crawl. Alaric had been his friend; despite the difference in their social status the two of them had developed a mutual respect for the skills and experiences of the other. When he'd sacrificed himself to kill Flamefang, Gaiseric had mourned for the knight. To have Alaric come back in such a monstrous state wasn't an easy thing for him to reconcile himself to. He couldn't equate the zombivor to the living man he'd followed ever since leaving their devastated village.

"You're keeping an intense vigil," Gaiseric stated when he stepped up beside Alaric. There was a pungent stink of decay exuding from the knight. He was surprised the reek hadn't roused Ratbag from his sleep.

"Something… out there." Alaric rasped his reply, gesturing with a mailed hand.

"You see something in that darkness?" the thief pressed him.

The zombivor's face twitched, trying to smile with lips that were no longer there. "Dark… not for… me," he said, pointing at his lidless eyes. Gaiseric shuddered when he noticed the tiny scars left by the fish and sea life that had nibbled at the knight before he was resurrected by Gogol. He quickly looked away.

"Does it… do you hurt?" he asked.

"Hurt… here," Alaric replied, touching his heart. "Knowing what… I am." The crackling voice managed to convey the grim melancholy the undead felt, the constant awareness of a lost life and the abominable condition that had supplanted it.

Even as they talked, Alaric kept facing the hallway. Whatever peculiar sense had him on alert wasn't relenting. Suddenly the knight reached for his sword. "See movement... tell others." He didn't wait for Gaiseric to act, but immediately stepped out into the darkened hallway.

Gaiseric's first instinct was to shout an alarm, but he resisted the urge. If there was something in the hallway – and he had every reason to believe so – then a lot of noise would warn them that they'd been spotted. By himself, with no need for light, Alaric might take whatever was out there by surprise. Either way, it would be better to make some plans before forcing an enemy into action.

"Alaric's spotted somebody out in the hall," Gaiseric informed Helchen, drawing close to her so that his words wouldn't carry.

The witch hunter gave him her full attention. "Zombies? Ratlings?"

Gaiseric shook his head. "I don't know. I can only say that Alaric thought they were a threat and has gone out for a closer look." He frowned as he considered something. "Before he actually saw anything, he was acting disturbed. Like he already knew somebody was out there."

The discussion had drawn the others nearer. When she heard Gaiseric describe the zombivor's agitation, Ursola spoke up. "Alaric seemed unsettled when we were leaving Stormcrow's laboratory," she said, nodding to the plague doctor. "Not that I know how a thinking undead is expected to act, but it struck me as peculiar."

"The bonds of life have been severed," Shareen said. "The undead no longer see the world as they did when alive. Much that we're aware of is hidden to them, but there is much that is hidden to us that they can sense."

"He certainly saw something out there in the dark," Gaiseric agreed. He gave Helchen a concerned look. "What do we do?"

"It would be really reckless to assume anything in Zanice is friendly until we know otherwise," Helchen said. "So the prudent thing is to brace ourselves for a fight." She wagged a finger at Shareen. "Hold on to the documents and keep behind the rest of us. No matter what, those papers have to get back to Korbara."

"Wait," Stormcrow said, holding his arm across the doorway. "Listen. The subjects aren't rattling their cages."

A cold shiver went through Gaiseric. Until the chymist pointed it out to him, he hadn't noticed the absence of sound in the hallway. He glanced at the others and saw that the same dread was racing through their veins. Something had silenced the creatures.

The rotting figure of Alaric stepped out from the darkness, sword in one hand and a severed head in the other. "Zombies," he reported, tossing the head into the light. It was the decayed head of an orc.

"Wotun," Helchen gasped. "The orcs are loose."

Gaiseric's eyes went wide with horror. "Zombies wouldn't know to do that. Not unless someone told them to. Otherwise they would have freed themselves long ago."

Ursola stamped her foot and spat on the floor. "Gogol," she growled.

Alaric swung around, staring back into the darkness. "That... what... I feel," he hissed. Gaiseric at once understood the zombivor's meaning. The sense of wrongness that had been dogging the knight wasn't baseless. Some occult tether bound him to the necromancer and he was picking up on Gogol's presence.

"Hundred... maybe more..." Alaric expanded. "Fifty feet... from..." He ended the statement by pointing at the ground at his feet.

"Is there another way out of here?" Helchen asked as she turned to Stormcrow.

The plague doctor shook his head. "None. To get out we need to go back the way we came."

"Through Gogol and his undead," Gaiseric shuddered. "That's the only reason they haven't swarmed us already. The scum's playing with us." One thing that rattled the thief like nothing else was the feeling of being trapped. Just now he felt like a shepherd who'd been treed by a pack of wolves.

Alaric turned to Shareen. "Light... change light?" he asked, waving his sword at the arcane sphere she'd called into being. He gestured at his decayed face. "Make hurt... dead eyes."

Shareen caught the knight's meaning. "I'll try," she said, rustling through the pages of her grimoire. "I'm sorry," she apologized. Following designs inked on the pages, her fingers curled into strange patterns. She made passes with her hands, causing the light to alter in color and intensity.

Gaiseric was impressed by Alaric's resolve. The zombivor kept his face turned to the light, defying the pain the experiment would cause him if it succeeded. It was sound strategy, something that the Alaric of old would have devised.

Whatever hurt the undead knight would be sure to hurt Gogol's horde.

"We don't need to maim them, just stun them," Gaiseric told Shareen, suddenly worried that the wizard would go too far.

"Whatever you're doing, do it quick," Videric called to them. The templar had taken on the role of lookout at the doorway. "There's movement out there and it's close enough now that *I* can see it."

"When we start, don't stop," Helchen warned. "Don't try to help anyone if they get caught. The only way through is to keep moving. Remember the quest."

Gaiseric spun around. "What about Ratbag? We can't just leave him like this!"

"I… carry," Alaric said, still looking up at the light. "Blind… if works."

The rogue hadn't considered that facet of the plan. Alive or undead, the knight was a formidable fighter. If he was blinded, even temporarily, it would stack the odds even more against them. Realizing he wasn't helping their chances, Gaiseric spoke to the zombivor. "You carry him and I'll guide you through."

"I'll keep the grave-cheaters off you," Ursola promised. The dwarf was finishing a harness to strap the keg of blasting powder to her back. She smiled at the concern everyone showed. "With this, Gogol's not going to have long to gloat if he wins. I've always lived by the mantra that if you're going to lose, then make sure everybody loses."

"What about my poison?" Stormcrow asked, pointing at the big clay jar. "That represents two years of work! Worth a small fortune to the Duke of Wulfsburg! We can't just leave it."

"Unless you can carry it by yourself, that's just what we're going to do," Helchen snapped at the chymist, impressing on him that the decision was final.

Doctor Stormcrow glared at her from behind his mask, but he could tell that further argument would be futile. His gloved hands toyed with the vials he wore on his belt, slim tubes of steel and copper. He turned to the pot of poison. Gaiseric could guess the idea he had, to draw off some of the concoction into one of the vials. Whatever he'd created, however, was so potent that the plague doctor hesitated to break the seal on the jar.

"Cheer up," Gaiseric advised the chymist. "You don't even know if the duke is still in any condition to buy your creation. Kinda hard to get gold out of a zombie." He could imagine the face behind the beaked mask scowling when Stormcrow looked his way.

A low, rattling moan rang out suddenly and Alaric covered his eyes with his arm. The zombivor cringed away from the arcane sphere. The orb had taken on a dull, pulsing scarlet hue. Shareen wavered between the satisfaction of success and sympathy for the ally she'd harmed in the process. Helchen had no time for either emotion.

"Dull the light and keep at the center," Helchen ordered the wizard. "When I tell you to do so, call the light back with as much power as you can endow it with." The witch hunter glanced over the members of the expedition. "We go. Now."

Gaiseric felt his stomach turn at the declaration. He snapped his fingers, trying to catch a wisp of his fleeting luck.

"Loaded dice and marked cards," he grumbled as he pulled Ratbag away from the wall and into Alaric's grip.

There was always a feeble line between a fool and a gambler. Gaiseric wondered which side of that line he was on as he stepped out into the darkened hallway.

The near-complete darkness of the hallway beneath the Rangers' lodge produced its own disorienting effect on Helchen. It would be only too easy to get turned around in the gloom and lose all sense of direction. Keeping to a set course was easy enough… until the fighting started. She knew how wild the scrum of battle could be.

The witch hunter felt equal measures of frustration and guilt that she'd allowed everything to depend upon Shareen's magic. Magic was a fickle servant under the most ideal conditions. The light spell she'd tested had been under the crudest circumstances. They were risking it all on the premise that what impaired the senses of a zombivor would also afflict a more unsophisticated form of undead. From her training, Helchen knew that the opposite was often the rule. Things to which a vampire or banshee were vulnerable held no special power against a simple zombie. It was, perhaps, a way by which the gods punished such transgressions by mortals. The lesser undead were beneath divine notice, but more powerful varieties incurred their wrath. At least such was the principle expounded by the Order.

Even with the arcane light reduced to the merest flicker, there was no mistaking the presence of the undead all around. The sounds of shuffling feet. The reek of decaying flesh. The impression of movement in the pitch darkness. The zombies were there, Helchen knew, and their very restraint proved that a greater intelligence was controlling them. That could mean another necromancer, for the twisted wizards were operating in cabals to further the destruction wrought by the Black Plague, but she felt in her heart that Alaric was right. The enemy before them was Brunon Gogol.

"Wait," Helchen whispered, her hand tight about the grip of her mace. She could dimly see her companions around her and the fear in their faces. All of them knew they were walking into the lion's den, danger closing in around them with every step they advanced. Yet they *were* advancing. The stairs were some four hundred feet farther on, if her estimates were right. Gogol was waiting to spring his trap, but by waiting he was letting them get closer to the stairs and freedom.

And they had a surprise of their own for the necromancer. She hoped.

The moment came when Videric, off to her left, cried out in alarm. Helchen saw him spin around, saw the ragged sailor-zombie clawing at his armor, heard the impact of the templar's sword as he brought it chopping down into the walker's head.

"Shareen! Now!" Helchen yelled, twisting to fend off the zombie that chose that instant to lunge at her with bony fingers and yellowed teeth.

The wizard's voice rose for an instant, invoking her magic. The faint sphere blazed into scarlet brilliance, bathing the hallway in a pulsing, hellish illumination. Zombies howled in pain, pawing at their eyes as the intense light flooded their vision.

Helchen crushed the skull of her foe as the zombie was blinded. The creature flopped to the floor at her feet. She looked up from its destruction to see the situation into which they'd been thrust. There were at least thirty zombies around them, all but surrounding the group – human undead that Gogol must have brought with him, but they weren't the only resources at the necromancer's beck and call. Between them and the stairs there stood a huge mob of green-skinned orcs, all of them in horrible states of mutilation and decay. The zombified prisoners the Rangers had left to starve in their cells when they evacuated the lodge, the subjects Stormcrow had callously used in his experiments. Gogol had released the monsters from their cages and deployed them as an army.

The necromancer himself was behind the ranks of the orc walkers, poised upon the stairs. Helchen cursed when she saw the huge beast that crouched beside the man. Gogol always availed himself of a bodyguard – this time it took the shape of the goat-headed akerbeltz. He'd revived the dead monster as one of his undead abominations. For all its size and strength, however, the monster was every bit as disrupted by Shareen's light as the human and orc zombies. It cringed away from the scarlet glow, a clawed hand clamped across its eyes.

Gogol, a living man for all his necrotic activities and the rotten arm stitched to his shoulder, wasn't fazed by the arcane light. He glared from across the hall, his face pulling back in a contemptuous sneer. "You're going to suffer for that little trick," he threatened, weaving a bit of dark magic so that his voice echoed down the hall.

"Destroy them while they're blind!" Helchen spurred her companions on. She swung her mace at the stunned zombies around her, smashing faces and cracking heads. Videric and Ursola staged their own attacks and even Stormcrow got into the action, plying a slender stick with a rounded spike at its tip to pierce the hearts of the undead and leave them lifeless on the ground. Gaiseric, leading Alaric while the zombivor carried Ratbag, could only look on. Shareen, focusing on her light spell and remembering the order to keep out of harm, stayed close to the thief and the knight.

Abruptly the color of the light changed. Helchen looked up to see Gogol making gestures with his hands that resembled the arcane passes Shareen had used. She remembered something Alaric had told her about the villain, that he'd been convicted of sorcery and was exiled by Baron von Mertz. He'd returned later as a necromancer, but he'd known different spells before plunging fully into darkness. Gogol was drawing on that old magic to counter Shareen.

The changing color brought relief to the zombies. "Hurry, they're snapping out of it!" Helchen shouted, braining a decayed stevedore with a missing lower jaw. The next undead she closed with proved to be one of the orcs and it had recovered enough to swat at her with a beefy fist. She dodged the clumsy attack, but the blow she'd intended for the zombie's skull failed to connect. She staggered back while the orc walkers surged forward.

"Ya doub'-deelin' bimbos!" Ratbag's familiar roar bellowed from behind. Helchen spun around in time to see the big orc, awake and enraged, lift Alaric and hurl the knight into the nearest zombies. The armored zombivor struck with the impact of a ballista, bowling over a half dozen of the creatures. "Ya ginks gotta rumpuz!"

The orc started to lunge toward Stormcrow. The plague doctor was torn between defending himself against Ratbag or the undead now closing in on him. Videric darted in to keep the zombies off his back while Gaiseric interposed himself between the warrior and the chymist.

"Use your head!" Gaiseric shouted at the orc. "Killing Stormcrow won't help anything! All you'll be doing is helping that swine Gogol!"

Of them all, Helchen knew Gaiseric had the best rapport with the ferocious orc renegade. Ratbag glowered at the smaller man, but he retained enough restraint that he didn't swing the scimitar in his fist. The tableau held for only an instant, then Stormcrow made a dash back for the archives. Snarling, Ratbag charged after him.

"Stop!" Gaiseric called after Ratbag, but before he could pursue the warrior, he had entirely different orc problems. Several walkers converged on him, trying to encircle the thief. Slashing at them with Cryptblade, he was able to extricate himself, but only just.

"Helchen, we've got to fall back!" Ursola cried out. The dwarf resorted to one of her fire-bombs to fend off the undead that were closing in on her.

"I can't… get control… again," Shareen gasped through clenched teeth. Her body shook from the effort of fending off Gogol's counter spell. Videric turned away from the zombies he fought to help the wizard back toward the doorway.

Ahead of them, Helchen saw the mob of orc walkers marching toward them, gradually mixing with the human zombies. Looming over the rest of the undead was the horned head of the goat-ogre. Gogol, sure of his victory, had sent his abomination to finish the job.

"Fall back," Helchen ordered, the pang of defeat twisting

her gut. She saw Alaric fighting his way back through the zombies. It looked as though the undead would ignore him only until he began to fight against them. That was when the creatures took full, vicious notice of the zombivor.

Seven of them against Gogol's horde. Bad odds, especially since Ratbag was battling against all sides, it seemed. Helchen whispered a prayer to Wotun as she joined the others in a gradual withdrawal.

The zombies closed in, pushing them back. The decayed remains of humans and orcs lurched toward them in an unrelenting mob. The akerbeltz, its eyes gleaming with the hateful purpose of an undead abomination, lumbered ever closer.

"No! You can't do that!" The scream rang out from inside the archives, distorted but hardly muffled by Stormcrow's mask. Helchen turned her head to see a peculiar reversal of the situation from a moment before. The plague doctor chased Ratbag out of the room, shaking his gloved fists at the orc. The warrior had the big pot of poison in his hands and an expression of unyielding rage on his face.

"Ya mugs bett'r dangle!" Ratbag howled at Helchen and the rest. There wasn't any mistaking his intention or the reason for Stormcrow's desperation. The huge orc lifted the jar of poison and flung it into the oncoming zombies.

Helchen quickly ducked back into the room. Over her shoulder she saw the pot shatter when it slammed into the undead, releasing a billowing cloud of green gas. The nearest zombies collapsed, their bodies tearing themselves apart as spurs of bone ruptured their flesh.

"Not sittin' fer der bone-calla makin' mugs inta cadavaz,"

Ratbag growled as he dashed back into the room. All eyes turned to the hallway, anxious about the poison the orc had unleashed. The slight draft in the vault caused the gas to drift back toward the stairs and across the undead mob.

"It would seem your mixture does have an effect on the undead," Helchen told Stormcrow. "Maybe it will be useful after all."

The plague doctor clenched his hands in outrage. "That lummox just lobbed my entire supply into those zombies. I don't have any more!"

"Be thankful Ratbag did," Gaiseric said. "Otherwise, we'd be dead."

Helchen studied the drifting green cloud. Something moved beyond the gas. She wondered if the poison had settled Gogol's fate or if the necromancer had managed to fend off its effects. "We still might be," she cursed.

She could see why Stormcrow had considered his brew incomplete. It was strong enough to make a human body rip itself apart, but not powerful enough to destroy that of an orc. Creatures lumbered through the toxic fog – orcish walkers, but now zombies that had undergone a horrible change. Parts of the orcs were grossly bloated, as though they might rupture at any moment. Horrible spikes of bone pierced them from within, spurs that the poison had caused to rapidly erupt from the orcs' skeletons. In eerie silence the twisted zombies marched toward the archives, sensing the living flesh within.

"Maybe wait before trying to sell that mixture," Gaiseric advised Stormcrow.

"Keep away from them," the chymist warned. "They're full of poison! It's seeped into them and inundated their veins!"

Helchen put Stormcrow's warning to the test. Aiming her crossbow, she sent a bolt into the head of the nearest zombie. The tainted walker stumbled back, blood jetting from its wound. Wherever the blood sprayed, it steamed and sizzled.

"It's like they're filled with acid," Ursola cursed.

"We'll use magic," Shareen suggested. "Hold them back with spells." She started forward, but Helchen held her back. The green fog dissipated and now she could see something else in the hallway.

The akerbeltz hadn't been destroyed. Like the orcs, the goat-ogre had been too strong to be consumed by Stormcrow's brew. Its body had the same distorted state, flesh bulging with internal poisons, spikes of bone stabbing out from its shaggy hide. The same infernal intelligence shone in its eyes, however.

Stamping its hooves, the tainted abomination charged the doorway.

CHAPTER SEVENTEEN

Videric didn't hesitate to place himself between the others and the charging abomination. The icy grip of fear flowed through him, but the templar pushed it down, fought it back. Courage wasn't the absence of fear, his father had always taught him, but rather the ability to deny the emotion, to never let fear supplant duty in his heart.

His duty, his task, was to the expedition, to give his life so that they could have a chance to get the records back to Korbara. That was the eventuality that Videric had accepted when he was chosen by the captain to join the quest. The Swords of Korbara weren't motivated by the vain pursuit of personal glory but the search for humility, to lose the sense of self in service to Wotun. It was why the idea that his father had sent him over a more qualified knight was particularly anathema to Videric, and he was ready to do anything to prove it wrong.

"Wotun's justice be upon you," Videric snarled in defiance as the tainted abomination rushed toward the archives. The goat-headed beast pushed through the last of the undead walkers, its hate-mad eyes fixated upon the defiant templar. Videric decided he wouldn't simply wait for the monster but would rush out to meet it. He had no illusions that he would be able to destroy the akerbeltz, but maybe he could buy enough time to give his companions a chance.

Only Videric never got his chance. Before he could run at the goat-ogre, the templar was shoved roughly aside. "Sure, ya can shit der castle, too," Ratbag grunted as he stormed past, insulting Videric's bravado. The orc renegade glared at the tainted abomination with a gaze that matched the ferocity of the undead monster. "Der shiv's gonna open ya brain buck't, gink," Ratbag snarled, charging straight into the goat-ogre.

Despite the orc's boast, his swing wasn't directed at the horned head, but rather his scimitar swept low and slashed across the beast's leg. Videric wondered if that had been intentional, an effort to deceive the abomination. Intentional or not, the strike ripped through the monster's polluted flesh to scrape the bone beneath. The akerbeltz stumbled and nearly fell, its own rush broken by the vicious assault.

Ratbag screamed when the abomination's caustic blood splashed across him, searing his green skin. Videric felt his gorge rise when he saw smoke sizzling off the orc's body. One of Ratbag's ears dripped to the floor as the acid ate at his flesh.

"You can't help him." Ursola's reprimand sounded in Videric's ear. He felt the dwarf's strong fingers pulling at his arm. Only then was he aware that he'd tried to charge in to rescue Ratbag.

"Idiot!" Stormcrow exclaimed, shaking his hooded head. "I warned you all what would happen if you got close to the poisoned zombies."

"Yes, you did," Helchen snapped at the chymist. "Now you can shut up." She loosed a bolt into the abomination, but the missile glanced harmlessly off its horned skull.

"You can't help him that way," Shareen told Helchen. The wizard pointed at the oncoming tainted walkers. Ratbag was in a doubtful enough position against just the akerbeltz. He'd be overwhelmed in a heartbeat if the other zombies got to him.

Videric saw the grim nod Helchen made. "Take the right. I'll take the left," the witch hunter said.

The intensity of the light faded when Shareen redirected her focus upon another spell. Pointing her fingers at the orc zombies, she sent a spear of lightning crackling through them. There wasn't a release of caustic blood when the electricity incinerated the walkers. Helchen's effort was less permanent but affected a wider swathe of undead. From her outstretched palm a mighty gale surged through the left side of the hall, pushing the walkers back as though they were being dragged by horses.

Without the threat of being surrounded, Ratbag renewed his attack. Videric was amazed by the orc's hardiness. The side of his face that had been splashed was hideous, a dripping mess of exposed muscles and jawbone. A sweep of the scimitar removed three of the abomination's fingers when it struck at him. The renegade managed to avoid the remaining claws, but not the bone spikes that protruded from the monster's arm. One of these raked across Ratbag's chest, tearing his armor and gouging his flesh.

Ratbag ran a finger along the bleeding furrow. "Baked wind, chippie," he growled at the abomination, scorning the severity of the attack. Videric thought it was the tone rather than the orc's mangled speech that incited the goat-ogre to lunge at the warrior.

The akerbeltz's momentum drove it upon Ratbag's scimitar. The orc howled in pain as the abomination's arms closed around him, driving the bony spurs into his body. Smoke billowed from the warrior as tainted blood gushed from the beast's wound. Such was the orc's fury, that even in his agony he maintained his grip on the blade. Gnashing his fangs against the wracking torment, Ratbag worried the scimitar back and forth, expanding the hole in the bestial zombie's chest.

Videric understood now why Helchen and the others kept company with the vicious orc. It wasn't the raw strength Ratbag possessed or even his feral boldness. There was, in the renegade, an unwavering determination that neither pain nor fear could break. His body was pierced by the spikes, his ribs were cracking under the crushing arms that held him, his flesh was dissolving in the acidic blood, and still Ratbag fought.

"You can't help him," Ursola repeated, drawing Videric back. The templar felt ashamed to just stand and watch, even if he knew the demolitionist was right. There was nothing he could do however desperately he wanted to. All he'd accomplish would be to share in the orc's fate.

"Ratbag!" Gaiseric cried out. The thief was being restrained by Alaric to prevent him from making a futile gesture to help the orc. Videric saw the gleam of tears in Gaiseric's eyes.

"Raddabrag!" the orc shouted back. He ducked his head to the side when the akerbeltz tried to bite him, then drove his forehead into the beast's chin, cracking the exposed bone there. Ratbag's tenacity prevailed at last; the wound he was expanding in the beast's chest finally reaching the monster's heart. The tainted abomination staggered, its arms loosening their hold on its foe as it pawed at the air. The horned head tilted back and a ragged, braying cry sounded from deep within its shaggy frame.

Released, Ratbag slopped to the floor in a pool of gore. His legs, what was left of them, buckled under him when he tried to stand. The orc managed to sit up and stare at his reeling enemy. With the renegade's scimitar still lodged in its chest, the tainted abomination took a few steps backward before it fell, its weight slamming down on the weapon and driving the blade completely through its body to erupt from its back. The beast shuddered once and then was still.

"Peddle ya papers, yegg," Ratbag snarled in victory as the abomination died. The orc gave a bark of laughter, then his ravaged body slumped back in the mire of caustic gore. Smoke sizzled off the dead warrior as the tainted blood continued to dissolve his flesh.

"Ratbag!" Gaiseric shouted, anguish in his cry. The thief slipped free of Alaric's grip but had enough sense not to rush over to the orc's body.

Stunned silence held the observers. Videric felt a sense of awe at Ratbag's sacrifice. Never would he have believed an orc capable of such valor. "After everything. What he saw Stormcrow and the Rangers doing to his people…"

"You can never tell about an orc," Ursola said, a grudging respect in her tone. "Maybe he did consider us friends. Maybe he just wanted to die in a way he could brag about when he goes into the afterworld. You never can tell about an orc."

The spells from Helchen and Shareen faltered for a moment and the tainted walkers began to advance once more. Without the distraction of the fray, the zombies again fixated on the archives. The two spellcasters started to resume their conjurations, but Alaric's raspy voice called out to them.

"Gogol… gone," the zombivor said, making a vague gesture with his hand. "Feel it," he added. From what Videric had heard about the villain and from what he'd observed for himself, it would be like the necromancer to flee when his abomination was destroyed. Gogol liked to be around to watch his victims suffer, but he wasn't shy about quitting the field when things turned against him.

"Light," Helchen told Shareen. With the necromancer gone, there wouldn't be any counter magic to disrupt the scarlet pulse the undead found so debilitating.

The wizard lost no time in adjusting her spell. The arcane sphere expanded and changed hue. Moans rose from the tainted walkers as the light seared into their eyes.

"Make for the stairs," Helchen commanded.

"Don't strike any of the walkers," Videric added, sheathing his own sword so that he didn't forget his own warning. The zombies wouldn't need to see them to bring one of them down; the tainted blood from their wounds would be enough to do the job.

The group hurried through the carnage, avoiding the steaming pools of blood that were everywhere. The blinded zombies staggered and stumbled around the hallway, making no deliberate effort to hinder them. Videric took the lead, using a shield scavenged from one of the destroyed human zombies to push aside any of the tainted walkers that got in his way. He glanced back to make sure the others were following. He spotted Gaiseric when the thief paused over Ratbag's corpse and saw him press something into the dead orc's hand.

"What was that?" Videric asked Gaiseric when they reached the stairs.

Gaiseric gave the templar a sad smile. "A gold coin. I don't know if orcs have to pay Charon to cross into the land of the dead, but I didn't want to take the chance." He turned his head and stared back into the passageway. "I owed that much to Raddabrag," he said, deliberately lingering over the orc's real name.

"We all do," Videric agreed. He clapped the rogue on the shoulder. "Now let's get those papers back to Korbara and make sure his sacrifice wasn't for nothing."

Ursola felt relieved when they found the barge where they'd left it. She'd been afraid that Gogol might have stolen the boat. Probably more work than the necromancer was willing to put in, poling the vessel along the canals. That was the kind of labor he'd leave to his zombies and it would take the cur some time to gather together another mob of undead. By that time, she hoped, they'd be long gone from Zanice.

"We'll make our way back toward the wall," Helchen said as they boarded the barge. "Go back the way we came in."

"Give the ratlings another crack at us when we go into the sewers," Gaiseric pointed out.

"If they're still creeping around, they can get at us wherever we are," Ursola reminded the thief. The humans had an understandable loathing of the vermin, but it seemed to her that they had a blind spot when it came to their capabilities. Dropping the bell and collapsing the cathedral wall was no mean feat. That had taken some incisive calculation and planning. It was audacious continuing to underestimate the man-rats after that catastrophe.

"The sewers then," Helchen decided. "That, at least, is ground we're familiar with."

Alaric took on the task of poling the craft. The zombivor wasn't as strong as Ratbag had been, but he was tireless. Passing away from the squalid waterfront, the barge traveled back up the main channel. Stormcrow gave the knight directions. They'd have to head toward the cathedral and use that landmark to retrace their path back to the sewer entrance.

The warehouses and tenements of the port soon gave way to palatial villas and palazzi. Ursola had a grudging appreciation for the magnificence of this part of the city, even if its builders wanted to see it all sink into the sea. Zanice flaunted its prosperity with marble statues and elaborate finials along the facades of the homes. In some places, slender bridges that were so delicate they might have been lattices in a garden stretched across the canal, joining structures on opposite sides of the waterway. She wondered if the narrow spans were functional or merely ornamental. A dwarf wouldn't build in such a fragile manner, but humans were sometimes as bad as elves when it came to putting aesthetics ahead of durability.

The barge was passing through an avenue of ostentatious guildhalls, the extravagant adornments of their walls uniformly depicting the nature of the guild. Scrollwork on the corners and around the windows of the Shipwrights' Guild displayed the hulls of barques and galleons in various stages of completion. In place of gargoyles there were miniature ships sculpted along the roof, their figureheads ready to spill rain down into the canal. So it was with the guilds of the chandlers and the ropemakers, the harpooners and the navigators. Each profession, it seemed, had its palatial guildhall, loudly proclaiming its trade in the most visual manner. Ursola knew how proud the clans in the strongholds could be about their chosen line of work, but there was something tawdry and cheap about the way the people of Zanice went about it. Maybe it was because it smacked more of the braggart and less of the craftsman to her.

The halls of the fishing guilds dominated the next block of buildings. Here, as expected, the decoration was devoted to the animals each trade specialized in. Though some of the adornment was sculpted, there was an equal amount that had been cunningly crafted from the bones and shells of the aquatic creatures themselves. The Lobstermen's Guild had framed its doors and windows with an edging of polished and lacquered carapaces. The Sharker Guild had portals enclosed by the jaws of sharks; the immense example that surrounded the entrance was of such scale that Ursola hoped it was a fabrication. She didn't want to think there might really be a fish that big swimming around somewhere.

The Guild of the Serpentiers lay just beyond that of the whalers. Ursola shivered a little when she saw the design of water snakes that characterized the building. The guild had done the sharkers one better by stretching the dried skin of

an enormous sea serpent across the side of the building. Red
and black, the scaly hide wrapped itself along the front of
the structure and around the corner. From what she could
see, the reptile it had been harvested from had been ten
feet wide and at least a hundred feet long. She glanced over
her shoulder in the direction of the harbor, appreciating
for the first time how formidable Zanice's serpentine guard
would be.

"That place makes my skin crawl," Shareen said, echoing
Ursola's thoughts. The wizard pointed at the roof. "They put
the biggest snake up there." A quiver came into her voice
when she spoke, a note of frightened uncertainty.

Ursola lifted her eyes and looked to the rooftop. Terror
closed around her heart when she saw the figure that had
provoked Shareen's ophidiophobia. It wasn't a snake, and it
wasn't a sculpture.

"We need to turn around," Ursola whispered, her eyes
locked onto an immense, but horribly familiar, reptilian head.

"This is the quickest route back to the cathedral of Wotun,"
Stormcrow objected.

"It's the quickest route to death," Ursola hissed back. All
eyes were on her now. "Nobody make a sound," she warned
before pointing out the thing sprawled across the roof. She
watched as eyes widened in horror and faces paled in fear.
Shareen hadn't recognized it for what it was, but the others
did. Lying on the roof was a colossal dragon.

"Flamefang," Gaiseric breathed, then bit his lip as though
speaking the wyrm's name might draw its attention.

Helchen studied the dragon for a moment. Only its head
and claw were visible from below. "Maybe he's dead. I did

stab him with the Dragon's Kiss and you saw what that did to Vasilescu."

"Flamefang looked well enough when he flew off," Ursola returned. "No, I think the brute's sunning himself. Dragons are, after all, big lizards."

"Would an undead dragon need to sun itself?" Videric asked.

Helchen shook her head. "The undead, especially the higher forms–" here she couldn't help but look toward Alaric "– will ape the habits they possessed in life, however pointless they might be. A vampire might continue to have its servants prepare meals for it even though it can no longer digest solid food. No, it wouldn't be surprising that a necromantic dragon would maintain the habit of sunning itself."

Alaric stopped poling and fixed his gaze on the rooftop. He shifted his position and tried to hand the pole off to Videric. "Go. I stay... finish Flamefang. Collect... debt."

"Getting yourself killed won't settle anything," Ursola scolded the zombivor, wondering if "killed" was the right way to phrase it. "If the Dragon's Kiss couldn't destroy that lizard, you won't even be able to scratch it." She turned to Helchen. "We should go back and find a different route to the cathedral. Fast, too, before anything disturbs..."

But the barge had already been too long in one spot. Sensing living flesh nearby, zombies began to stagger out from the guildhall. The serpentiers presented a barbarous aspect, their clothing adorned with fragments of sea serpents. Snakeskin boots, belts, vests, and gloves were common among them. Some of the men had sewn on fangs and bones to lend flair to their appearance. Somehow, the serpentine accouterments made their cadaverous and decayed state more hideous. The zombies offered no immediate threat, limited to the pathway outside the guildhall. It was when some of the creatures mindlessly stepped off the path and plunged into the canal that disaster struck.

Flamefang lifted its head, roused by the sudden noise. The reptile flexed its claws, tearing into the side of the roof and sending tiles splashing into the waterway. The dragon stared down, its eyes narrowing when it sighted the barge.

"If anybody has an idea, now would be a good time to share it," Gaiseric quipped.

Shareen looked to Ursola. "Can he still breathe fire, do you think?"

Ursola shook her head with uncertainty. "Haven't seen him do it since he… came back," she said. "Doesn't mean he can't, just that we haven't seen it."

The wizard bowed her head. "I have an idea, but the dragon has to come close to get it to work." Shareen pointed at the shadowy canal. "It's not dark enough here, so he has to come close."

"If he breathes fire, we're all dead," Stormcrow reminded them, an edge of panic in his muffled voice.

"Any idea you'd like to share, I'd welcome," Helchen told the chymist.

"Not as though we have any choice about what Flamefang's going to do," Ursola pointed out. It was too late to try and sail away and the dragon would make short work of any building they tried to shelter in. Their only chance, slight as it might be, was whatever scheme Shareen had in mind.

"Now we're in for it," Videric said, pointing up at the roof.

Flamefang had withdrawn from the edge. They could hear massive wings fanning the air and a moment later they saw the wyrm climbing into the sky. The necromantic dragon circled high above them twice, then dove down into the canal, its wingtips stretching nearly across the entire span.

Ursola drew one of the fire-bombs from her satchel. She knew it wouldn't cause the dragon much hurt, but it was the only way she knew to fight back. It wasn't in the dwarf to give up without trying to make a stand.

Flamefang's rotten reptilian musk washed over them as the dragon swooped down on the barge. The wyrm was only a few dozen feet away when Shareen unleashed her spell. A sphere of scarlet light billowed directly in the creature's path. Blinded, Flamefang wheeled away in a hiss of pain. With little room to spare in the canal, the dragon crashed into the building on the other side of the waterway. The impact drove the beast through the facade. A loud crash boomed across Zanice as the ceiling gave way and the whole structure collapsed upon Flamefang.

"That should…" But Videric bit off his triumphant words when he noted the dragon's tail projecting out from the rubble. The member lashed angrily from side to side, hurling bits of debris in every direction.

"It'll take more than that," Helchen told the templar. "When he was alive, Flamefang took a lot of killing. Being undead, he's only gotten worse." She smiled at Shareen. "But you've bought us some time to get away."

Gaiseric pointed at the trapped dragon. "Get away? He's going to dig himself out and *really* start looking for us."

Doctor Stormcrow coughed loudly, trying to catch

everyone's attention. "I suggest we repair to a place too strong for the dragon to batter down." He made a dramatic flourish at the channel ahead of them. "Make for our original destination, the Cathedral of Wotun. Only we won't just pass it by. We will take shelter inside." He looked at Shareen. "We can bide our time there until it is dark enough that you can try that trick again when the dragon doesn't have to be right on top of us."

"What about the zombies? Are they just going to sit back and let us take up residence?" Gaiseric pressed the plague doctor.

"We keep to the walkways," Helchen said. "They can only come at us a few at a time there and at worse we can block off some of the stairs to keep them away. But we need to find a place where we assess the threat. And not leave a zombified dragon to pillage the countryside."

Ursola scratched her chin and looked at the destroyed guildhall. The rubble was gradually shifting as Flamefang dug itself free. "I like the plan, Stormcrow, but with a little help, I can improve on it."

The dwarf didn't explain herself further. That would wait until she had the opportunity to really study the cathedral and figure out how she was going to get rid of Flamefang for good.

CHAPTER EIGHTEEN

"The cathedral will be full of zombies," Helchen cautioned. "The horde that overwhelmed Ulfgar's people would have had no reason to leave after they massacred the survivors." She felt sick considering the awful fate that had befallen the refugees. She tried not to think about how it was Alaric who'd brought death to the heroic sea captain, knowing that the zombivor had still been Gogol's slave at the time.

The barge was within sight of the mighty temple. The first thing Helchen noticed was the emptiness of the square outside. Before, the plaza had been teeming with the undead. Now it was utterly desolate. There was no question where the monsters had gone. Gogol had brought a handful of them away with him to ambush them at the Rangers' lodge, but it was certain most of them were still inside the cathedral.

"I… draw them… away," Alaric said. He rubbed at his throat, trying to force his voice into its old vivacity. Some of the dead skin came away under his fingers. "Not care… undead."

Helchen nodded. It was a bold ploy Alaric proposed, and

one that had a major flaw. They would land the zombivor a good distance from the cathedral and let him approach on his own without the betraying presence of living companions. He'd get inside the sanctuary and then start making noise, getting the zombies to follow him away from the building. Being undead himself, the creatures would have no reason to attack him unless he attacked them first; they'd just mindlessly follow the noise he was making.

Helchen's worry was that somewhere in the horde there might be an enemy not so easily taken in. A necromancer or abomination would recognize Alaric as an adversary and they'd react accordingly. If that happened, Alaric wouldn't have anyone to help him. He'd be completely on his own. She shivered when considering the possibility that Gogol might regain control over him.

"Did you consider the other problem?" Gaiseric asked the witch hunter. He nodded at the upper levels of the cathedral. "What if the ratlings are still scurrying around in there? We'll be coming in the same way we did before…" The thief scowled as he mulled over the part of the plan he disagreed with the most. He'd lost the argument about finding another route into the building. It would take time and with the threat that Flamefang might have already freed itself from the collapsed guildhall, time was something they couldn't waste.

"If it worries you so much, I can go first," Videric offered.

Gaiseric shot the templar an insulted look. "That's not what I'm saying," he protested. "Of course I'll climb up first. I'm getting used to that." He turned back to Helchen. "Just don't blame me if the rope gets cut by a ratling when I'm halfway up."

"They wouldn't do that," Stormcrow told the rogue. "They'll wait until you get inside, then slit your throat. That way they can steal your stuff and carve steaks off your corpse."

Ursola shook her head at the plague doctor. "Don't think that was exactly reassuring."

"Grim or not, it's what he should expect if the man-rats are still hanging around," Stormcrow said with a shrug. "I think they'll be long gone though. The ratlings have just as much reason to fear the zombies as we do and no reason at all to be heroic. They'd have no reason to stay in the cathedral. After we escaped, they probably made themselves scarce while the undead were finishing off everyone in the sanctuary." He noticed the shocked looks the others gave him and cocked his head to one side. "Small sense in mourning the dead when we might be joining them soon."

"Maybe it would help evaluate the risks better if we knew why we were doing this," Shareen said. Everyone turned to look at Ursola.

The dwarf just shook her head. "Not until I know," she said, stubborn as ever. "I don't want to raise any false hopes."

Helchen pondered those last enigmatic words. She had a feeling she knew what Ursola intended, but, like the demolitionist, she didn't want to buoy anyone up by letting them indulge an impossible hope. She'd abide by the dwarf's policy and not say anything until they knew for sure.

The barge pulled close to a quay several hundred feet from the side of the cathedral on the same block of land where the building had its foundations. Alaric turned the pole over to Videric and stepped onto the little jetty. Once he'd disembarked, Helchen handed a strange object to the knight: Videric's upended helmet with a blanket stuffed into its neck. The cloth was there to trap the motley collection of objects donated by the members of the expedition. Cutlery, coins, rings, and other small pieces of metal. Taken together, the curious array would turn the helmet into a noisemaker once the blanket was taken out and they had room to move. Muffled as it was, she could hear a slight rattle when she gave it to the knight.

"Not… fail," Alaric vowed, saluting her before he turned and marched off into the gathering gloom. Night was again stretching forth its shadowy hand to take possession of Zanice.

"Think it'll really work?" Videric asked Helchen in a whisper when he started to move the barge away.

"Pray to Wotun that it does," Helchen answered him. "Pray that it does."

"Still no trace of the dragon," Shareen offered. A spell lent her vision a reach far beyond normal, so she'd been appointed as lookout. She did a small circle, turning her eyes in every direction as she stared at the sky. "It's getting too dark now," she warned. "Already I can't make out much to the east."

"If it's dark, you can blind the beast again," Stormcrow suggested.

"That's if Flamefang will fall for the same trick again," Helchen told the plague doctor. "More likely, if he spots us out in the open, he'll rip the top off a house and drop it on us. Sink us before we can do anything."

Gaiseric flinched at the imagery and peered over the side at the murky, corpse-strewn water. "Ratlings be damned, let's get to the cathedral already."

From where they'd let Alaric disembark, it was a short trip to the canal-side face of Wotun's cathedral. Helchen was relieved that the rope was still hanging from the broken window. When the barge drew close, she took the cord in hand and tested to see if it was secure.

"All right," Gaiseric said, tying down Cryptblade so that the sword wouldn't come loose from its scabbard. "Let me start up."

Helchen pressed her hand against his chest and pushed the thief back. "Not this time," she told him. "This time I go first." Before Gaiseric could recover from his surprise, she started climbing the line. She knew if she'd spoken of her intention beforehand, he'd have contrived some way to be first. For all his grousing and complaining, Gaiseric had a noble heart and would put himself at risk to spare his friends from danger.

Only Helchen felt the danger was less for her than it was for anyone else. She'd downplayed the possibility that the ratlings were still around, but she knew they were a very real threat. One that was especially focused on herself. Their verminous leader had made it clear he wanted the Dragon's Kiss during their previous encounter. That meant he wouldn't risk losing the dagger by cutting the line and dropping her in the canal. The man-rats would wait until she was at the window before trying anything. That gave her an edge nobody else would have in dealing with them.

The witch hunter had another edge as well. Strapped to her left arm and hidden under the folds of her cloak was her pistol crossbow, loaded and ready to shoot. If she did find enemies waiting for her, the first vermin to show his face was in for a nasty surprise. From the fragile courage they'd displayed last time, the sudden death of one of the pack might be enough to scatter the rest. At least long enough for Helchen to be in a position to better defend herself.

The rising moon glistened from the remaining panes in the broken window. Helchen watched the opening for any hint of movement, but either there wasn't any or it was too dark to see. She regretted that she hadn't borrowed Stormcrow's lantern or asked Shareen to cast one of her light spells, but she just didn't dare take the chance. Light would surely alert the ratlings if they were around and, worse, it might distract the zombies Alaric was trying to lure outside. She strained her ears, listening for the sound of the knight's noisemaker but there was only the flow of the canal and the wind whistling through the buttresses. Either the zombivor wasn't in position yet or she was too high up to hear him.

When she reached a spot just below the broken window, Helchen paused. Straining every sense, she tried to pick up the least hint that the ratlings were waiting for her. The faintest sound, the slightest whiff of their mangy pelts... but there was nothing. Taking a deep breath, the witch hunter finished her ascent and swung her leg over the sill.

The darkness wasn't quite complete inside the cathedral. A dim light filtered down through the westward facing windows. Helchen could make out the platforms and the stairways, the destruction where the bell had plunged down into the sanctuary below. She didn't see any trace of the ratlings, but that could mean that the vermin were keeping to the deep shadows.

Faintly, from far below, Helchen started to hear the rattle of metal against metal. It was too dark to see, but from the way the sound moved through the sanctuary, she was certain it was Alaric shaking the noisemaker and catching the attention of the lurking undead. She prayed again that the trick would work and that there weren't any intelligent creatures in the horde to alert the rest to the deception.

The witch hunter waited for a full minute, searching for any sign that the ratlings were around, before she gave three sharp tugs on the rope. It was the signal Gaiseric would anxiously be waiting for down below, letting him know it was safe to come up.

But was it safe? Helchen spun around when a scratching sound reached her ears. The scrape of claws against wood? Had the ratlings been watching, waiting for her to give the signal before they sprang into action? She drew back her cloak and raised her arm, ready to loose a bolt at the first enemy to show himself. She fixed her eyes on the darkness, trying by force of will to make them pierce the shadows and expose whatever was hiding there.

The sound came again. Helchen shifted her gaze downward and had an impression of motion on the steps below. She was ready to shoot but could make out just enough of the outline to doubt whether what she was looking at was a ratling. It looked human. A human who made slow, agonized steps, ascending the stairs in painful increments. A lone survivor? Someone who'd managed to escape the zombie horde?

That thought made Helchen hesitate. The dim light exposed a distinctly human silhouette. A few steps more and she realized what was coming toward her wasn't human. Not anymore.

The moon had risen enough that now its rays shone full

upon the platform. By its light, Helchen saw the undead creature that was creeping toward her. Horror churned her stomach. The body was grotesquely mutilated, chunks of flesh torn away to expose naked bone and raw sinew. But that wasn't the reason for her horror. There was enough left of the face to recognize who the zombie had been. The thing was Ulfgar.

The hillman still held on to his axe, dragging it behind him as it shambled toward Helchen. The zombie was ten feet away when she snapped out of her shock and sent a bolt speeding into the creature. The missile struck true, punching into the mutilated head. She was sure she'd pierced its brain... but Ulfgar kept coming. Worse, the zombie dropped the axe it was dragging and abandoned the ambling, slow gait it had maintained during its climb. Ulfgar rushed her in a berserk charge that had in it all the rabid ferocity of a runner.

Helchen was taken by surprise by the sudden, vicious attack. The hillman slammed into her, knocking her off her feet. She crashed down on her back, the platform creaking ominously under the impact. Quickly she brought up the unloaded crossbow, wedging its steel frame between herself and Ulfgar's gnashing teeth. She had to stay quiet as she struggled with the creature lest she draw attention away from Alaric and attract more undead onto the walkways.

The zombie straddled the witch hunter, pinning her down and ripping at her with its claws. A crazed, feral attack that took all Helchen's strength to fend off. By degrees, the creature was prevailing. The clawed fingers tore her brigandine and raked the flesh beneath. She felt blood oozing from her cuts and knew it was only a matter of time before Ulfgar dug his claws still deeper and began to inflict real damage. She tried to work her legs up under the undead berserker, but found her enemy was too close to manage the maneuver.

"Helchen, are you there?" Gaiseric's voice called from outside. The thief was probably only a dozen feet below the window. Caution made him pause before climbing any higher, lest there was an enemy waiting for him. By the time he grew impatient and climbed in anyway, there would be.

The sound of Gaiseric's voice drew Ulfgar's attention away from Helchen. The zombie turned its head and for just an instant, the pressure pinning her down relaxed. The witch hunter seized the opportunity. In one motion, she hooked her leg under the berserker and threw it over. Helchen grabbed her mace and brought it slamming down into Ulfgar. The zombie twisted beneath her just enough that instead of bashing in its skull, the weapon slammed down into its throat, the sharp flanges digging into the flesh.

Ulfgar thrashed underneath Helchen, trying to throw her off, but there was no coordination behind the zombie's effort. She was able to keep him pinned. Not daring to relax the pressure on the creature's neck by withdrawing her mace, she instead raked the cutting flanges deeper, gradually sawing through the throat. After a minute, the head was severed and rolled away from the body. Ulfgar fell still and Helchen stepped away from the motionless corpse.

"Black cats and broken mirrors!" Gaiseric gasped as he came through the window, Cryptblade clenched in his fist. He stared for a second at the headless zombie, then turned concerned eyes toward Helchen. "Are you all right?"

The witch hunter took a deep breath and recovered her hat

from where it had fallen during the fight. "It's always rougher destroying them when it was someone you knew," she told the thief. She made a quick examination of her wounds. They felt worse than they actually were. "Yes, I think I'll be all right. In a way we should be grateful Ulfgar attacked me."

"How is that?" Gaiseric wondered.

"It means the ratlings aren't scurrying around up here somewhere," Helchen stated. "If they were, the zombie would have been hunting them instead of focusing its attention on me."

The thief chuckled at the remark. "A silver lining if I ever heard one." He paused for a moment and smiled when he heard the rattle of metal below. "Of course, Alaric's noisemaker sounds even better."

Helchen returned Gaiseric's smile. "We'll check up on his part of the plan later. Right now let's see about bringing the others inside. I'll feel better when they're somewhere Flamefang won't spot them."

Ursola did her best to appraise the structure of the cathedral from her perch on the stairway, impatient for Alaric to finish gathering up all the zombies. Shareen had come up with a way to conjure light that wouldn't upset the zombivor's role as a distraction, anchoring the arcane sphere right above the knight's head while he was circling through the cathedral below. It was the normal, soft blue color, not the scarlet pulse the undead found so debilitating. The idea was to lead the creatures away, not have a horde of them stumbling around blindly in the devastated cathedral.

Devastated was the right word, too. Ursola thought the

zombies must have pulled apart every pew and table in the place. She was amazed there'd been enough left of Ulfgar to reanimate given the gory scraps the rest of the survivors had been reduced to. The entire floor looked to be littered with bloodied limbs and butchered trunks. It was a somber reminder of the havoc the undead could inflict when gathered in large numbers.

"So, Mistress Stonebreaker, what's your plan?" Videric asked Ursola. The templar had posted himself a few steps lower so that he could intercept any zombies that lost interest in Alaric and decided to head their way. Several of the undead had looked up at them, but always they'd turned back to the zombivor when he rattled the helmet.

Ursola squinted as she stared at the support columns, evaluating their thickness and how much of the structure they were bolstering. Much of the building's weight was conveyed into the exterior buttresses, but it would be too much of a job to bring those down. She had to try to make it work with just an interior demolition.

"Once Alaric leads the zombies away from here, I need to take a closer look at those pillars," she said. She looked up at the rest of the expedition and saw that she had their full attention. "The blasting powder I took from Stormcrow's laboratory should be barely enough to do the job."

"What job?" the plague doctor wanted to know.

Ursola grinned at Stormcrow. "Haven't you guessed? We're going to lure Flamefang in here and then collapse the cathedral on top of him. If that doesn't settle the wyrm, nothing will."

Everyone looked to the ceiling, envisioning the roof crashing down. Shareen ended that speculation with an alarmed cry that she quickly smothered with her hand. She pointed at the shattered window they'd climbed through.

The moonlight revealed the immense shape of the undead dragon as it soared through the sky. The tattered wings fanned the air as Flamefang's neck twisted from side to side. The reptile was searching for them. It was only a matter of time before it spotted the barge and narrowed down the scope of its hunt.

"Well," Gaiseric said, "the lizard's heard the dinner bell. Now we just need to get the trap ready."

Ursola pointed at Alaric down on the floor below. The zombivor was starting out through the broken wall, hundreds of undead shambling after him.

"It's like some profane religious procession," Helchen observed.

"I was thinking of the elf mage Theriel and how he wove a spell to lure all the goblins away from the Goldgap Mines," Ursola said.

"Sounds like one elf you dwarves should be thankful for," Gaiseric commented.

Ursola scowled at him. "We would be if the faithless maggot hadn't then decided he wanted twice the fee we'd agreed to pay him. The cur came back in the night and used the same spell to abduct every child in Granitefist Stronghold." She shook her head as she considered the outrage done to her people. "We settled with Theriel. A bounty hunter caught up with him in Blackwater Canyon. Brought his head back to the thane wrapped in the mage's own robes."

Videric tapped Ursola's boot with his hand from where he was posted several steps below. "Looks like Alaric's cleared out the last zombies." He looked past the dwarf to where Helchen was standing. "How far is he taking them?"

"As far as they'll follow," the witch hunter said. "He'll know when to stop and make his way back. I don't think there'll be any mistaking when Ursola springs her trap." She motioned to the dwarf. "Let's see about placing those charges."

Ursola smiled and patted the bronze keg. "This'll settle a lot of scores my people owe that murdering wyrm."

Shareen watched with growing anxiety as the charges were being set. She understood magic, but the delicate process of measuring out powder and laying down fuses was too complex for her to follow. She'd given up when Ursola insisted on chipping out furrows in the columns that were at specific heights and angles. None of it made sense to her.

The wizard restricted herself to maintaining the light by which the dwarf and her helpers were working. Videric kept guard at the broken wall, but the rest were doing their utmost to help Ursola get the explosives placed. They'd briefly considered keeping a lookout up near the window, but decided against it in the end. Doing so might cause Flamefang to notice them before they were ready and, in any event, if the dragon did decide to attack, there wasn't much good a warning would do them.

She looked toward the double doors that served as the main entrance to the cathedral. The improvised barricades had been hurriedly pulled down and the doors themselves rigged with charges, ones that could be detonated separately from those Ursola was placing in the pillars. The reasoning was clear enough. The hole caused by the falling bell wasn't big enough for the dragon to get through, so when they were ready, they'd blast open the doors. The explosion would serve two purposes. It would create an entrance for Flamefang and the noise would draw the wyrm in.

Sound reasoning, but Shareen was getting nervous. Things were going a little too well. Maybe she'd caught some of Gaiseric's pessimism, but she couldn't shake a sense of mounting dread.

The wizard expended some of her power to maintain the light in her absence and paced across the length of the chapel. A hint of motion drew her attention to the pile of debris that blocked off the crypt beneath the cathedral. She thought she'd seen some of the rubble shift. Shareen was about to chalk it up to imagination when it moved again, sending a few bricks clattering away from the pile. She opened her mouth to shout a warning to the others when the entire heap suddenly collapsed into the crypt below. A massive cloud of dust billowed upward, sweeping over Shareen and pouring into her throat. Coughing and hacking, she staggered away from the open hole, leaning on the altar to support herself.

A shape moved behind the cloud of dust, climbing up from the hole. Even as a vague shadow, she recognized the outline of Gogol with the brawny orcish arm attached to his shoulder. She tried to conjure a spell, but couldn't get an incantation past her coughing fit.

The necromancer emerged from behind the veil and smiled at her. "At a loss for words?" he taunted. Gogol glanced back at the opened crypt. "I'm afraid my minions were crushed in the collapse, but don't worry. I never travel alone."

Still coughing, Shareen reached for the golden vessels on

the altar behind her, hurling them at Gogol. A plate gashed the necromancer's cheek as it glanced off his face.

Gogol dabbed his finger into his own blood and pointed the dripping digit at Shareen. "Die," he hissed.

The next instant there was a terrible roar and the cacophony of shattered glass. Shareen felt her body slashed by a hundred shining slivers as the stained glass windows behind her were obliterated. Her last sight as she fell to the floor was of an enormous scaly body diving down into the chapel.

Gogol wasn't alone. He'd renewed his hold over Flamefang and brought the dragon with him.

Before Ursola's trap was ready.

That bitter thought tormented Shareen as her world sank into darkness.

CHAPTER NINETEEN

The sudden opening of the crypt brought Videric spinning around. "Keep working!" he shouted to the others while he dashed toward the chapel to investigate the disturbance. Through the cloud of dust, he spotted Gogol climbing out of the hole. The templar tightened his grip on his sword and ran forward to confront the villain.

Before he could get in close, Videric was nearly knocked off his feet when a terrific tremor swept through the cathedral. The impact was every bit as intense and violent as what they'd experienced when the bell came crashing down. Only this time, the violence brought with it a thick, stifling stench. The rotten musk of an undead dragon.

"Flamefang!" Videric yelled. The next instant Shareen's arcane light winked out, plunging the sanctuary into shadow. Only the moonlight streaming down through the shattered windows illuminated the cathedral.

The templar felt guilt stab at him. He'd noticed Shareen walk into the chapel, the very place where Gogol and the dragon chose to make their entrance. He could see her body sprawled on the floor. But there was more than just the loss of Shareen to feed Videric's shame; it was knowing that the documents were still with her. The death of the wizard could also mean the doom of Korbara.

The floor trembled under Videric's feet. He heard stone crack as the dragon landed. By the moonlight he watched the great reptile come stalking forward, crawling through the sanctuary like a mammoth lizard. Terror gripped him as Flamefang lumbered ever closer. The beast appeared oblivious to his presence. The thought entered his mind that he could lie low and slip out the breached wall before the wyrm found him.

Disgust curled Videric's lip, revulsion at the cowardice that tempted him. He was a Sword of Korbara. He would not disgrace the traditions of his order nor the faith his father had shown in him. Beside dishonor, death was a thing to be desired. There was just a chance he might still be able to recover the papers from Shareen's body. Running now would be abandoning everyone in Korbara who was depending on the quest.

Firming his hold on his sword, Videric continued to wait, but now it was for the dragon to come even closer. To reach Shareen meant getting past the reptile. Flamefang's snout cleared the cloud of dust, its horned head oscillating from side to side as it hunted for prey.

"Here I am, wyrm!" Videric snarled, swinging away from the column he'd been using for cover. He slashed his sword at the reptile's face, trying to strike at the gruesome eye. The blade bit into the scaly ridge above the eye socket and glanced off, unable to cut into the dragon's armored hide.

Flamefang spun toward Videric, jaws snapping at him in

retaliation. The templar ducked back, the fangs closing only inches away from his body. The reptile pressed its attack, lunging forward to make another bite. Videric dodged behind the column again, wincing when he felt the pillar shudder as the dragon drove its horned head against it.

"You only prolong the inevitable," Gogol jeered from the shadows. "Let the dragon have you and end this farce."

Videric leapt away from the pillar. Flamefang snapped at him as he rushed past the wyrm, but the undead monster was partially blocked by the obstruction. The templar did his best to ignore the reptile's attack. He'd already seen that there was little he could do to hurt the dragon, but there was another enemy nearby who he didn't think would shrug off the sting of his sword so easily.

The templar charged toward Gogol's voice. Dimly he could make out the necromancer's figure in the darkness. Before he could close on the man, Videric was struck a tremendous blow and hurled across the chapel. He saw the dragon's ridged tail swing around for another strike. His head swimming from his rough collision with the stone floor, it was nothing shy of a miracle when he managed to roll away from the descending tail. Chips of stone went flying from the impact. Flamefang glared at him from where its head poked around the edge of the pillar.

Before the dragon could whip its tail again, Flamefang was beset by new foes. Focused upon killing Videric, it wasn't aware of its other enemies until they were already on it. Gaiseric slashed the beast's foot with Cryptblade, the anti-undead enchantment searing into the reptile's flesh and causing scales to rot right off its body. At the same time,

Helchen wove a frost spell that froze the ground on which the wyrm was standing. When it twisted its body around to confront Gaiseric, it found no purchase on the slick floor. The entire cathedral shook when Flamefang's legs slipped out from under it and the dragon fell.

Sprawled on the floor, another enemy ran in to attack the undead behemoth. Stormcrow had a vial in one hand and his slender staff-sword in the other. The plague doctor dashed the contents of the vial into one of Flamefang's eyes. The orb turned a leprous color and the gelid mass stiffened. Then the chymist's sword stabbed into the afflicted eye, bursting it like a boil.

The dragon reared back, snapping its jaws in a crazed display. Its attackers scrambled to get out of the way. Half-blind, Flamefang could still crush them by mere chance.

Or was it blind? Videric noted a change sweep over the necromantic dragon. Its mad thrashings turned into deliberate attacks against Gaiseric and Helchen. The two narrowly avoided being stomped by the reptile's clawed feet. The templar whipped around. He spotted Gogol, no longer lurking in the shadows but standing in the open and making gestures with his human hand. Videric could guess what the necromancer was doing. He was giving directions to Flamefang, helping it to find its enemies.

"Not today, you blackguard," Videric hissed through clenched teeth. The pain was excruciating when he forced himself up off the floor. He was certain some of his ribs had been broken by Flamefang's tail. It was an effort to draw breath and there was blood in his exhalations. He suspected that a sliver of rib had punctured a lung.

Struggling past his pain, Videric rushed the necromancer. Gogol heard him coming and spun around to meet his charge. He felt the dark energy of the villain's magic sear into him. His nose and throat started to clog up, the blood from his lung clotting under Gogol's spell.

Videric thought of his father and their god, and all the innocents they'd sworn to protect in the name of Wotun. There were things more important than life, things stronger than pain, things mightier than fear. He drew upon those things now, duty and honor and love. They gave him the determination to fight through the smothering agony.

Gogol had an incredulous look when Videric refused to fall. Too late to run, he raised the brawny orcish arm to block the strike that was aimed at his head. The templar's blade pierced the green limb, stabbing through the necrotic flesh and digging into the bone within.

The necromancer cried out in horror and twisted away like a wounded snake. Gogol's panicked exertions wrenched the sword from Videric's grip. The templar stood there for a moment with empty hands, trying to understand why his enemy had his sword through his arm. The sounds of battle, the fight against Flamefang, were receding into the distance, but whether that was because the fray was moving deeper into the sanctuary or because his hearing was starting to fade, he couldn't tell. All he knew was that Gogol had his sword embedded in his arm and the templar wanted it back.

"Get away!" Gogol snarled at Videric, retreating before him.

Videric felt his strength waning. He forced himself to pursue Gogol as the necromancer made for the yawning opening to the cathedral's crypt. But that forced him to come across Shareen, so still upon the altar. And he remembered he had a greater duty.

Videric abandoned the idea of catching Gogol and instead used his last strength to stagger over to the dead wizard. Guilt gnawed at him when he saw the horrible way she'd died. He almost lacked the conviction to do what he knew he had to do. As gently as he could, he rolled Shareen onto her back and searched her cloak for the precious papers she carried. He almost laughed in relief when he found them. His fingers clenched tight around the documents that would save Korbara and its refugees.

The templar tried to stand, but he found that the effort was too much now. Instead, he slumped against the altar, his breath coming in ragged gasps. He looked back to the sanctuary, watching as Flamefang pursued Stormcrow and Gaiseric. The chymist and the thief took it in turns to attack the beast. The potions of the plague doctor had burned away patches of the scaly hide while Cryptblade had left denuded, leprous swathes of bare flesh along the wyrm's belly and legs. Without Gogol's magic to guide it, Flamefang was constantly turning, trying to bring its good eye to bear upon its foes. Whenever it did, the man who wasn't the target would dart in and attack.

Two fighters. Videric stared at the scene, concerned that Helchen had fallen prey to the beast. He couldn't see her body, but that might be because Flamefang had swallowed her whole. "Wotun, don't let this be," he prayed as he continued to look for the witch hunter.

Suddenly Helchen ran up to the altar and leaned over him.

Like the templar, she'd broken away from battling the dragon as soon as possible to look for Shareen and the invaluable papers she'd been carrying.

"She doesn't have them," Videric said when Helchen looked away from his injuries and glanced over at Shareen. He held up his hand and the papers clenched in his fist. With his other hand, he grabbed the witch hunter's arm and pressed the documents into her grasp.

Helchen's face was grave when she took the papers from him. "Videric… your wounds…"

A choking laugh bubbled up from the templar, blood dribbling down his chin. "Doesn't matter. Get the papers to the abbot. Tell my father that I was true to my duty and I have honored my vows."

Helchen tried to draw him up from where he sat, but Videric shook her off. "I can't leave you like this," she admonished him.

"Yes, you can," Videric told her. He put a finger in his mouth and showed her the dark blood that coated it. "Flamefang's already killed me. At least from here, I'll be able to see the dragon die when Ursola sets off her trap." His gaze hardened when he looked up at the witch hunter. "Get the papers back to Korbara. I've done my duty, now you must do yours."

"I will. I promise." Helchen lingered only a moment longer. "We will succeed," she said before she turned away. He watched her for a time as she crept through the devastated cathedral, slipping behind pillars and piles of debris. The documents she was carrying were too important to risk having the dragon notice her and make her a target. Videric supposed the others would be leaving soon.

Then it would just be him and Flamefang… and the trap Ursola had prepared. Videric fought to control his breath, to try to defy the death he felt stealing over him. He only wanted a little more life, just a little longer.

Ursola drove the sounds of battle from her mind. Flamefang had decided to put in an appearance before she was ready for it. Well, there was nothing she could do about that except to hurry and cut a few corners.

The strategy she'd designed in her mind called for the mining of six pillars, but now the dwarf would make do with four. That would be enough to bring down the roof. That would crush the dragon, but to ensure the beast couldn't escape, she moved the charges away from the doors. Flamefang was already inside, so there wasn't a need to make an opening for it. There was a need for the material the refugees used to build their barriers though. Ursola set the charges in the middle of the smashed pews and broken tables. Then she doused them with the whale oil from the supplies Ulfgar's people had collected. An explosion was nice, but fire would help even more.

The noise of Flamefang's rampage increased in volume. Ursola thought Helchen and the others must be giving the wyrm the very devil of a time. Maybe they had the dragon so enraged that it wouldn't stop to think about the trap she'd set for it.

"Well, I've done all I can do," Ursola told herself when she finished pouring the oil over the piled wooden scrap. She plucked a fire-bomb from her satchel and turned toward the fighting. "Now let's get this ball rolling."

The dwarf jogged toward the fray. She waved her arms at Gaiseric and Stormcrow, the only people she could see. They couldn't mistake her gesturing. She wanted them to back away from the dragon. Flamefang was reluctant to let Gaiseric sneak away and started to pursue the thief when he darted behind an alabaster statue of Wotun. Ursola decided it was time to give the wyrm something else to think about.

"We've a score to settle, carrion-licker!" Ursola cried out. Flamefang ignored her shout, but it couldn't ignore the fire-bomb that struck its jaw and sent flaming liquid splashing over its snout. Alive, the reptile had been immune to such an insignificant fire; in its undead state it was slightly less invincible. The incendiary charred its flesh wherever the thick scales failed to protect it, cooking the meat. She saw strings of grease drip away from the dragon's face before it brushed its snout along the floor and put out the fire.

"More where that came from, egg-sucker!" the dwarf mocked before throwing a second bomb. The dragon was able to extinguish it rapidly, but now its focus was firmly locked upon Ursola.

"Get out of here!" Ursola screamed at her unseen companions before she turned and started running back through the sanctuary. The whole building shuddered as the enormous dragon lumbered after her, its claws tearing chunks from the floor.

The dwarf barely avoided Flamefang's snapping jaws before reaching the entryway. She swung around and lobbed a last fire-bomb into the heap of scrap timber, then dove for the protection of a stone fountain.

The oil-soaked timber ignited with a loud whoosh. Ursola

could see Flamefang turn toward the sudden conflagration. The next moment, the flames reached the blasting powder nestled deep within the pile.

A deafening roar boomed through the cathedral. Ursola hunkered low, covering her head with her arms as fiery debris went flying through the temple. When the echoes of the explosion dissipated, she stood up, her clothes and hair soaked by the fountain. Flamefang had been knocked back by the detonation, thrown down on the floor almost precisely at the midpoint between the hollowed columns. Slivers of burning wood were all around the dragon, but only a few had pierced the gaps in its scaly armor.

Ursola hadn't thought the first explosion would do much to the wyrm. It was the second detonation that was going to visit doom upon the beast. While Flamefang was still confused by the blast, she rushed across the sanctuary to reach the fuses. Her soaked clothes insulated her from the burning debris that was all around. Fire was spreading from the wooden scrap, igniting carpets and tapestries. She even saw a finger of flame starting up the stairway and into the rafters.

She wasn't sure if she should call it good luck or bad that none of the debris had touched off the fuses, but they remained intact when she reached them. Striking steel to tinder, she lit them, waiting a moment to be sure the individual lines were burning. The fuses had been laid out like a spiderweb, coiling across the sanctuary to each of the four pillars. The charges she'd set had not one but four lines leading into them, any one of which would be enough to detonate the explosive. Ursola tried to leave as little as possible to the caprices of random chance.

"Time to go," the dwarf muttered. Ursola started to run for the hole in the wall left by the falling bell, but even as she started to move, a caprice of random chance fell upon her.

Flamefang's foot came stamping down, catching the dwarf and pinning her under its claws. The dragon leaned over her, its fanged jaws only inches from her face. There was hate and rage in the dragon's remaining eye. At least until Ursola started to laugh at the reptile.

"We meet our ancestors together!" she mocked the undead monster.

The dragon still possessed enough awareness to understand Ursola's tone if not her words. Sensing danger, Flamefang reared back and unfurled its wings, ready to fly up through the roof to escape. The wyrm might have managed the feat, except for the injuries its body had suffered in the first blast. Splinters of wood had ripped through its pinion. Unprotected by thick scales, the leathery membranes had been shredded, reduced to tatters that hung uselessly from the wingbones.

"Not this time," Ursola snarled at Flamefang. "This time you don't get away. This time my people will be avenged."

The dwarf heard her own bones break as Flamefang pressed its weight down on her. She was still alive, however, when the charges went off and the pillars fell. The last thing she saw was the ceiling spilling down, tons of stone supports and lead roofing that would crush the dragon the same way it was crushing her.

It was a good death for a dwarf.

Gogol wasn't certain what the deafening noise that roared above him was, but he knew it wasn't anything he wanted any part in. Perhaps without his guidance Flamefang was running amok. It would serve Helchen and her cohorts right if such was the case. The dragon was fully capable of obliterating them without the necromancer's help.

The crypt below the cathedral went well beyond the boundaries of the temple itself. One of the first things Gogol had learned about the priests of the kingdom was that none of them were above stealing a little land in the name of their god. The priests of Wotun in Zanice had carved out subterranean vaults that extended the length of the block. They'd probably have delved even further if not for the surrounding canals.

He'd thought it an amusing idea to have his minions dig their way up so he could take his enemies by surprise. Bad luck that Gogol's surprise wasn't as complete as he'd intended. Now his zombies were buried in the rubble and he was retracing his passage through the catacombs alone. He didn't like that, not one bit. If any of the corpses lying in the niches and shelves he passed had been complete enough, he'd have expended some of his magic to raise them up. Of course, any viable corpses had already been turned into undead by the Black Plague itself weeks ago.

Gogol winced in pain and scowled at the sword that was still embedded in his arm. He regretted now the effort he'd put into making the orcish limb feel like part of his own body. He'd gained greater functionality from it, but in return it had become more sensitive. It wasn't quite an undead thing now, but shared a quasi-life with the necromancer. That meant it could feel pain and convey that pain to Gogol.

"Of course that idiot had to stab the strong one," Gogol cursed, ignoring the fact that it was he who'd used the brawny arm to block the templar's attack. With the orcish arm he was certain he could have pulled the sword free from the bone it was caught in. Attempts to remove it with his natural arm had proven hopeless.

A few zombies could have done the job, and that would be the first task he'd set them to once Gogol found some and brought them under his control. If he could ignore the pain long enough to manage such a simple act of necromancy. He found he was unable to maintain his focus with a few feet of steel lodged in his body.

A powerful quake rocked the catacombs. Gogol had to brace himself against the wall while the entire passageway shook. He could hear the crash of stone as sections of the crypt behind him collapsed. It sounded like Flamefang was tearing down the whole cathedral. Hopefully the dragon would bury Helchen and the rest of them in the rubble.

"I hope you rot," Gogol said, staring up at the ceiling.

"I... already... am," a cold voice rasped from the darkness ahead.

Gogol drew back as a shape marched toward him from the shadows. He was stunned when he recognized the shape as belonging to Alaric von Mertz.

A dry rattle rose from the zombivor, the closest he could manage to laughter. Alaric appreciated the shocked expression the necromancer wore. "Wound... disrupts... You not... sense me," the knight said, pointing at the sword lodged in Gogol's arm. Alaric drew his own sword, his lidless eyes glaring at his enemy. "I... sense... you. Follow and... find."

The necromancer tried to turn and run. Before he could take even a few steps, he felt something sharp strike his neck.

Then he was falling, rolling along the dusty, bone-strewn floor. He collided with the wall and came to rest. He watched something take a few staggering steps before it collapsed. It took him a moment to appreciate that it was his own decapitated body.

The unnatural vitality of a necromancer sustained Gogol's head for hours. He watched Alaric march off, moving toward the same exit he'd been trying to reach. In their game of vengeance, it was the knight who'd prevailed at the end.

Once the zombivor's footfalls vanished in the distance, Gogol was left to wonder whether the dark silence that surrounded him was life or death. For a necromancer who'd blended the two so often and trespassed across inviolate boundaries, there was something bitterly ironic about his final moments.

If he'd still been capable of speech, Gogol would have cursed the gods with his last breath.

CHAPTER TWENTY

The explosion rocked Zanice. Across the square from the cathedral of Wotun, Helchen was knocked to the ground by the tide of force rolling from the devastated structure. From where she was thrown, she watched in awed fascination as Ursola's charges brought down the immense building.

The spires on the roof shivered for an instant, then the roof folded and sank inward, collapsing into the sanctuary below. Buttresses and exterior walls followed suit, their upper sections crumbling into the temple. The lower parts of the walls fell afterward, struck by an avalanche of unstable rubble from the interior. The debris spilled out onto the square, broken statues and individual blocks of stone rolling across the plaza. Stained glass windows shattered as their frames twisted and contorted before sinking away into the general demolition.

"Ursola," Helchen whispered sadly. She could see that Gaiseric and Stormcrow had escaped the cathedral, both men close behind her in running away from the temple. Videric was already dying before the explosion, his fate sealed one way or the other. But the dwarf? She hoped against hope that Ursola would emerge with one final trick up her sleeve to survive.

A wave of dust swept away from the heap of broken stone where the cathedral had stood. When it cleared away, only the northernmost walls and a handful of buttresses still stood. They looked like the broken teeth of a titan jutting up from a shattered jaw. The scope of destruction went far beyond what Helchen had believed possible. Gazing upon the carnage, she felt sick to her stomach. There wasn't a chance anything had survived.

That meant the dwarf every bit as much as the dragon.

"Vengeance for your people," Helchen said, solemnly hoping that Ursola's spirit would hear her and know the trap had worked. Flamefang was destroyed.

Gaiseric and Stormcrow spotted Helchen and hurried across the plaza to join her. "She's not dead. She can't be. She's too tough," Gaiseric insisted. While he kept a stubborn watch on the rubble, the plague doctor came close and advised Helchen against lingering.

"Mistress Stonebreaker is past any help we could render," Stormcrow said, leaning his beaked face close to the witch hunter's ear. "The longer we stay here, the more danger we put ourselves in. However far Alaric led the zombies, he won't keep their attention after that noise." He waved a gloved hand at the collapsed cathedral. "Every zombie in Zanice has heard that racket and will be drawn here. Our only hope of getting away is to make sure we're gone before they show up."

Helchen knew Stormcrow was right. As much as she shared Gaiseric's reluctance to accept Ursola's death, she knew they had to be practical. Too much rested on getting the papers back to Korbara. The papers documenting how to recharge Mournshroud. Her hand patted the pocket where the documents were secured. "Gaiseric, Ursola's gone," she said.

The thief turned toward her. He clenched his fists, anger written upon his face. Then his shoulders slumped, and he sighed in defeat. Gaiseric knew she was right.

"Let's get out of here before zombies start wandering this way," Helchen said.

"What about Alaric?" Gaiseric wanted to know.

Helchen wasn't sure about that question. "We can't wait. He'll have to catch up."

Inwardly, she wondered if the zombivor would even be allowed into Korbara. Whatever he'd done and whoever he was, Alaric was also now one of the undead.

The trio started along one of the pathways edging the block where the cathedral was situated. What had been fashionable villas rose on the other side of the square and workshops where everything from vestments for Wotun's priesthood to souvenirs to sell to pilgrims were manufactured. All the buildings were empty shells now, ransacked for supplies by survivors and ravaged by zombies looking for living prey. Helchen directed her companions toward the clustered structures. They'd provide some cover from undead eyes and delay their discovery by the zombies she was certain were on the way.

"We can slip through the alleys, then cut across back to the canal," Stormcrow suggested. "If it looks feasible, we can have a try at recovering the barge."

Helchen studied the narrow, gloomy walkway ahead of them, searching for the least trace of lurking zombies. Satisfied there weren't any around, she looked back at the plague doctor. "Forget about the barge," she advised. "Even if it wasn't crushed by a falling buttress, the only way to reach it would be going toward the ruins. The very place we can expect the undead to head for."

"We'll have to find another boat." Gaiseric reached the obvious conclusion. His tone wasn't optimistic. In their journey along Zanice's canals, they'd seen only a handful of still-floating skiffs. Many were obvious wrecks, others were swamped and recoverable if the companions had the leisure to bail them out.

"Difficult, but not impossible," Helchen said. "We can look for one while we try to go overland to where we entered the sewers."

She frowned at that last possibility. Zanice could be teeming with zombies, and those creatures would all be drawn to the ruined cathedral. The undead would sink in the canals, but they'd be dangerous on dry ground. The city's reliance on waterways meant only a few land routes existed through its quarters. The zombies would be funneled into those avenues – the very same ones that Helchen and her companions would need to use.

"Sufficient to the hour are the evils thereof," Helchen whispered, trying to calm her own thoughts. It would be enough to find a way back to the sewer; she could worry about zombies when she had to face that obstacle.

The narrow alleyway slithered between the villas, a dark and dank course too cramped for the moon to shine into.

What little light the stars provided was just enough to pick out the deeper shadows of the surrounding walls. Furtive scurrying noises set the witch hunter's nerves on edge – feral cats, starving dogs, or scavenging rats the likely culprits. Since the sounds grew more distant rather than closer, she didn't believe whatever made them were zombies. The last thing they needed was to run into another swarm of undead rats.

"We need to risk a light," Helchen told Stormcrow. She thought the alleyway was sheltered enough that a zombie would have to be standing directly adjacent to one end or the other to spot the glow.

Stormcrow tinkered with the lantern on his belt and soon had a soft yellow light spilling across the soot-blackened walls and decaying litter that surrounded them. The people of Zanice took great pains about the exteriors of their homes, but that only applied to those parts that could be seen by their neighbors. A place like the alleyway was neglected, left to become as dingy as the elements cared to make it.

The light startled a big brown rat. Its eyes gleamed red as it scurried away. But then there were other eyes that shone red in the darkness. Eyes that were much higher up than those of a rat, a cat, or a dog. Stormcrow narrowed the beam of his lamp by flicking a tin shutter. The walls around them slipped back into shadow while he sent a ray probing further down the alleyway ahead of them.

Irritated hisses sounded and some of the eyes vanished, covered by clasping hands and shielding arms. Standing exposed by the plague doctor's light were several ratlings. Helchen felt a chill when she recognized the cloaked creature who'd attacked her on the stairway. He had a pair of long knives in his hands. Two of the man-rats with him held crossbows. The others carried swords of every shape and condition.

"Surprising black hat, Khurr is," the cloaked leader chittered, his naked tail lashing from side to side. Alone among the ratlings, he hadn't covered his eyes. Indeed, a strange darkness surrounded him, as though he stood in perpetual shadow. He slapped the flat of a knife against the ear of one of the arbalests. The stricken ratling yelped. Quickly she raised the crossbow and aimed it at the humans. The other arbalest, not wanting the same treatment, squinted at Helchen while lifting his weapon. "Giving Khurr dark dagger, black hat is." The rodent pointed with a knife at the boot where the Dragon's Kiss was hidden.

"Making black hat giving Kraknik magic pages, Darkwalker is," a wizened, bleary-eyed ratling hissed at the cloaked leader. He gestured with a splintered staff at the grimoire hanging from Helchen's belt.

"Hearing Chantchew, black hat is?" Khurr hissed, showing his chisel-like fangs. "Surrendering tribute, humans are. Letting humans live, ratlings will."

Helchen kept her steely eyes fixed on Darkwalker's beady red gaze. She trusted the ratling about as much as she'd trust a hungry troll with a billy goat. Luck had favored them, Stormcrow's lantern exposing the monsters before they could spring an ambush. Khurr was negotiating only because it would mean a fight otherwise. The ratlings were quite ready to ambush and assassinate, but they weren't so eager for a fray where at least some of them were going to be casualties.

"What if I say no?" Helchen said bluntly. "What if I tell Darkwalker to go take a swim in the canal?"

Khurr's eyes narrowed, and his whiskers twitched in annoyance. "Foolish, black hat thinking." He gestured with both knives. "Counting, black hat is. Four, humans are. Seven, ratlings are." The simple math brought amused squeaks from the other man-rats.

"You're not going to trust them?" Gaiseric asked in an incredulous whisper. He had Cryptblade at the ready, but against a living enemy, the sword held no special enchantment.

"What other choice do we have?" Stormcrow said. "They have us outnumbered. Give that Darkwalker creature what he wants."

Helchen shook her head. "That wouldn't buy our lives," she told the plague doctor. Even if it would and she trusted Khurr's promise, she knew she couldn't give the Dragon's Kiss to him. The dagger was a profane artifact, a thing of absolute evil that drove those who wielded it mad. Desperation had made her use it against the archmage Vasilescu, and it was desperation that had made her use it against Flamefang. The blade was too murderous to set loose into the world, especially in the paws of so sinister a creature as Khurr Darkwalker.

"Counting, black hat trying?" the ratling sneered. His ears perked up in an attitude of superiority. "Thinking, black hat trying?" He made a raking motion with his knives, scraping the blades together.

A rustle behind them made the humans turn their heads. Helchen realized that Khurr wasn't negotiating because he was afraid of a fight. He was keeping her talking while another group of ratlings closed in behind them.

There were five man-rats in the second group, but one of these was a brutish beast as big as Ratbag had been. The rest were lightly armored and carried swords, all except the ratling in command of them. The chieftain had the heaviest armor in the entire pack, a steel helm lashed to her elongated head and a massive falchion clenched in her paws.

"Counting, black hat is?" Khurr cooed. "Twelve, ratlings are." His eyes glistened in the shadowy aura clinging to him. "Dying, humans are."

The jeer signaled the ratlings to attack. Prepared, Helchen quickly extended her hand and invoked the frost spell. Her target was Darkwalker. With him gone, the other man-rats might flee.

Khurr was prepared, too. The moment she began to cast her spell, he drove his knives into Chantchew and whipped the shocked ratling around. With a kick he sent the old rodent staggering toward the witch hunter. "Protecting from magic, Kraknik is!" Darkwalker laughed at his own treachery.

The mockery proved accurate. The bleeding Kraknik stumbled into the path of Helchen's spell, blocking most of the icy blast. The wizened ratling was frozen solid only a few feet from her. When one of the arbalests shot a bolt at the witch hunter, it struck Chantchew and exploded his brittle body into chunks.

"Killing humans, ratlings are!" Khurr screeched. In a surge, the warriors with him scurried forward, swinging their swords.

Helchen dropped the first of them with a bolt. The ratling fell immediately, his body tripping one of the others. The last of the sword-rats lunged at her, his sword slashing the brim of her hat as she dodged back. The vermin drew his arm back for another attack, but before he could swing, Helchen brought her mace crashing down, breaking his arm. The sword clattered to the flagstones and the ratling cringed against the wall, squeaking in pain.

Behind her, Helchen could hear Gaiseric and Stormcrow contending with the second group of ratlings. The savage snarls of rodents mixed with the crash of steel. She didn't know how long a plague doctor and a thief could hold against such odds, but she also knew she couldn't turn her back on Khurr's pack to help them.

A crossbow bolt slammed into her chest, knocking her back. Her brigandine armor had absorbed most of the impact and prevented the missile from going too deep, but it had hit with enough force that she was sent reeling. Powerful claws closed around her from behind, digging into her waist. She craned around to see the ratling bully leering down at her, his fanged jaws open in a vicious growl.

"Spinesnap! Mine, black hat is!" Khurr screeched. Darkwalker shoved the arbalests ahead of him and they scurried toward the hulking man-rat.

The bully appeared in no mood to listen, however. He drew Helchen up toward his mouth, his grip tightening until she felt blood streaming down her legs. It seemed the monster intended to bite her head off.

Helchen disabused Spinesnap of that idea when she swung her mace up into his chin. The bully stumbled back against the wall, his grip around her waist relaxing enough that she twisted free. The huge ratling glared and grabbed at her, launching away from the wall, but the witch hunter's mace swatted the groping paw, the flanges slicing deep into his fingers.

"I'll attend to that one," Stormcrow called to Helchen. The plague doctor's clothes were spattered with blood and the slender sword-staff he carried had been snapped in half, but from the way the man moved, Helchen didn't think he'd suffered serious wounds. His beaked mask turned her way for a moment, then his focus was completely upon Spinesnap.

The bully lurched away from the wall. Now that Helchen got a better look at him, she could see the many stab wounds in the ratling's flesh. The other half of Stormcrow's staff was lodged in the beast's hip. Given a choice of victims, Spinesnap was more interested in settling with the chymist.

Stormcrow had never impressed Helchen as an especially brave man, so it puzzled her that he would stand so defiant before a brutal adversary like Spinesnap. He didn't flinch when the monster rushed him. When the bully opened his bloodied mouth to roar, she saw why he'd been so calm. Faster than her eye could follow, the plague doctor flung the glass vial he'd palmed into the rodent's bleeding maw. It shattered on impact and released a whitish vapor.

The gas didn't faze the huge ratling, but then it reacted with the fresh blood dripping from the slashed gums and tongue. As it settled, the vapor bubbled into a black foam, rapidly sizzling past Spinesnap's lips in a steaming froth.

The bully forgot about fighting. He clamped his hands to his throat, clawing at his flesh as though trying to dig through his own neck. Helchen realized with horror that the chemical Stormcrow had used wasn't just dribbling from the ratling's mouth, but was also rushing down his throat, burning him from the inside.

Helchen and Stormcrow backed away from the huge

ratling as he flopped to the ground. It was a lingering and hideous death. One that impressed the other ratlings with terror. Frightened squeaks rose from the warriors who had Gaiseric surrounded farther down the alley. The armored leader took one look at Spinesnap and her ears flattened against the sides of her head, her eyes widening with alarm.

"Retreating, ratlings are!" she wailed, leaping out of reach of Gaiseric's sword. The warriors with her quickly followed suit, scurrying down the alleyway toward the square.

"Coward, Slashstab is!" Khurr raged. The remaining ratlings with him started toward Gaiseric and Stormcrow. Helchen heard the arbalests crack off a final set of shots before rushing in with drawn daggers.

Khurr charged at Helchen. She swung her mace at him, but she was weak from her injuries and the mace only glanced off his cowl. From the way it rebounded, she was sure the ratling had an iron cap hidden under the black leather.

Darkwalker slashed her arm with one knife, then kicked her knee with a clawed foot. To ensure she tripped, Helchen felt his tail behind her ankle in the moment before she fell. The ratling sprang on her when she hit the ground.

"Dark dagger, Khurr belonging!" he snarled, whipping one of the knives across her boot, opening it from shin to heel. Helchen swung her mace again, but the ratling blocked it with his other knife.

"Black hat dying," Khurr growled at Helchen, pinning her hand to the ground with his foot. He thrust one of his knives at her throat, nicking the skin when she twisted away. His eyes gleamed with murder as he raised his arm for another try.

Frantic squeaks sounded from the direction of the square. Slashstab came rushing back down the alley, only one warrior accompanying her. The ratlings ignored the melee between the humans and the rest of the pack. "Zombies killing!" Slashstab shrieked as she ran past. "This way, zombies coming!"

Slashstab's panic infected the others, and they gave up the fight, quickly following the chieftain. Khurr snarled and leapt away from Helchen, but not before his paw snatched an object up from the ground by her feet. The witch hunter raised her head in time to see the ratling slip the black blade into his cloak. She felt a wave of guilt and despair.

Khurr Darkwalker had stolen the Dragon's Kiss.

Even as the terrible thought tormented her, Helchen noticed the other ratlings had stopped farther up the alley. It was difficult to see in the dim light, but it seemed their escape had been cut off by someone. A shadowy figure that the man-rats hesitated to attack. Someone whose mere appearance was enough to make them cower.

The images of the undead abominations she'd faced since the onset of the Black Plague flashed through Helchen's mind. Any one of them would be enough to stop the ratlings in their tracks. Such a monster would mean death to them all, for there wasn't any other way out if the square was infested with zombies.

The quest would fail and Korbara would eventually fall.

There was no hope left to them now.

Ratlings scurried down the alleyway in full retreat. The vermin were so desperate to escape that they didn't notice the figure who stood in their path until they were right on him. When one of the arbalests had her stomach slashed by a sword, her agonized squeak alerted the others of their peril.

Alaric wiped the blood from his sword and took a step toward the rest of the pack. He saw the terror in the verminous faces, the flattened ears, the rounded eyes. The ghastly, rotten condition of his face evoked horror even in the ratlings.

"Should not... attack... my friends," Alaric rasped. The zombivor moved toward the most formidable-looking of the man-rats, an armored chieftain with a heavy falchion in her paws. Takwit Slashstab took a step back, intimidated by the undead knight. Behind her, the remaining arbalest raised his weapon and sent a bolt slamming into Alaric's chest. The impact staggered him, but that was all. The ratling squealed in fright at the ineffectiveness of his shot.

"Can't kill... the dead," the zombivor scolded.

The cold, rasping voice only set the vermin into a deeper panic. Takwit grabbed a ratling with a broken arm and spun him at the knight. Alaric slashed the howling creature, leaving it a twitching corpse on the ground. The brief diversion, however, gave the chief a chance to attack. Her heavy falchion chopped down, smashing Alaric's shoulder. His arm hung useless, popped from its socket by the blow.

"Fighting! Killing!" Takwit screeched at her warriors. The sword-rats were emboldened by the disabling of the knight's arm and rushed in to carry out their chief's orders.

The first of the man-rats fell with her throat ripped open by a sidewise sweep of Alaric's blade. The second managed to stab him in the gut, driving his sword through the knight's surcoat and mail.

"Can't kill… the dead," the zombivor repeated, bringing the edge of his sword cleaving through the ratling's skull.

Alaric stalked toward the remaining enemies, the sword of his last adversary sticking out of his belly. His lidless eyes roved across the ratlings. Keeping his gaze on them, he slammed his shoulder against the wall and popped his arm into place, all without making the slightest sound or show of pain.

"Shooting! Killing!" Takwit snarled. She seized the last arbalest and threw him at Alaric. The hapless man-rat had time to voice only a single squeak of terror before the knight's sword was thrust through his chest and his limp body slid to the ground.

Alaric stared at the two remaining ratlings, the armored Takwit and the cloaked Khurr. He could feel the fear wafting off the creatures. "Which… is next?" he demanded.

"Next, Takwit is!" Khurr shrieked. The treacherous ratling copied the chieftain's tactic and shoved her toward the knight.

Alaric's blade scraped across Takwit's armor, giving her time to retaliate. Her heavy blade crunched down into the zombivor's shoulder. He could detect bones breaking under the blow, but there was no sense of pain. He pivoted with the falchion still caught in his body. The movement jerked Takwit closer to him. The chieftain stumbled and crashed against the knight. Terror in her eyes, she tried to draw away, and might have done so had she released the trapped sword.

Coldly, Alaric brought his sword slashing into Takwit's back. The first blow cut through some of the straps, the second dented the scavenged plate. The chieftain wailed as the tortured metal was pounded out of all shape and jagged spurs were driven into her flesh.

The zombivor pressed his attack, hammering away at Takwit's armor, driving more spurs of steel into her body. The chieftain became frantic, her fangs snapping at Alaric. A strip of flesh was torn from his jaw, another off his cheek. Takwit ducked and wove her head, trying to come at his throat. Viciously she clamped down with her teeth and tried to worry the knight's neck, but the mail coif resisted her fury.

Finally, the frantic efforts slackened. Takwit's body went limp. Alaric let her slip from his grasp, but found he had to break her jaws to release the ratling's hold on his neck. He extracted the falchion and tossed it onto the carcass.

Alaric looked back down the alleyway. He could see Helchen and her companions… far fewer of them than he'd hoped for. There wasn't any sign of the last ratling in that direction, but he could see the zombies creeping into the alley from the square. Waving his arm to Helchen, he motioned his friends to hurry. Then the knight turned. There was only one way Khurr could have fled. He'd taken advantage of the fight to slip past Alaric and flee toward the canal.

The zombivor sprinted down the alleyway, watchful for the least sign of the enemy he pursued. The cloaked Khurr was peculiar in that his vital aura was dull, somehow obscured in a way that was distinct from yet reminded him of the aura Gogol had emitted. Alaric didn't think it was murky enough to conceal the ratling from undead eyes, though, should the vermin be lying in wait for him.

Ambush wasn't on Khurr's mind. Only escape. When Alaric emerged from the alleyway, he found the ratling cautiously making his way toward a footbridge. The creature's slow, slinking steps confused Alaric until he noticed the reason for such stealth. Mobs of zombies were prowling the pathway to either side of the bridge, only a dozen or so feet away from where Khurr crept.

The zombivor watched the slow, silent flight of Khurr. The ratling hadn't noticed his presence yet. Alaric decided to change that. He reached to his stomach and withdrew the enemy sword wedged there. Taking it in hand, he struck it with his own sword. The sharp crack of steel on steel caused the man-rat to spin around. The sound also drew the notice of the zombie mobs. They turned and started moving toward Alaric. He knew he had nothing to fear from these undead; many of them he recognized as the same ones he'd originally lured away from the cathedral. Now he had a different use for them.

Alaric crashed the swords together a second time. The zombies became further agitated by the noise. Then he looked straight at Khurr. His route to the bridge was quickly being cut off. He could see the ratling evaluating his chances. He was bracing himself to make a run for it.

The zombivor's ruined face contorted into the echo of a smile. The moment Khurr started to move, he threw the captured sword at the bridge. The steel blade clattered noisily against the paving stones. The zombies, before intent on Alaric, now converged upon the bridge instead.

Khurr tried to slip past, but the undead were upon him before he could cross the span. He buried a knife in the eye socket of one zombie, dropping the creature. Then the rest of the mob rushed over him. Alaric saw the ratling struggle to free himself, but the zombies pressed him back against the railing. The mass of weight proved too much for the wood and the railing snapped, plunging Khurr and his attackers into the canal.

Alaric hurried to the bridge, shoving zombies out of his way. He stared down at the polluted water, but there was no sign of either ratlings or the undead.

Only the sluggish flow of the current as it wound its way through desolate Zanice.

EPILOGUE

Gaiseric emerged from the alleyway first. He'd had to argue with Helchen, but there were too many points that made it clear he had to take the lead. The witch hunter was wounded, for starters. The ratlings had battered her terribly in the fight and he didn't think she was going to hold up too well if they had another battle ahead of them. On the other hand, with Cryptblade, Gaiseric could more than hold his own against the undead. The most poignant argument, though, was the same Helchen had used with Shareen: the witch hunter was carrying the papers that might let the monks at Korbara replenish Mournshroud's power indefinitely. If anyone in their reduced warband needed protection, it was her.

The thief left Helchen in Doctor Stormcrow's care and slipped forward. There were zombies at the other end of the alley, killing any idea of retreating back to the square. The stench in the air, however, indicated there were undead in this direction as well. When he stepped out from the alley, Gaiseric found one of them standing right beside the wall.

He nearly stabbed Cryptblade into the rotten, hideous creature. Only Alaric's quick reflexes prevented the blow from landing. The knight grabbed him by the wrist and pulled him onto the pathway.

"Alaric!" Gaiseric gasped. He winced, fully looking at the knight. His face was even more mutilated than ever. "You look awful."

The knight nodded. "Gogol... looks... worse," he declared, and made a slashing motion across his neck.

Gaiseric couldn't help but smile. "Then you've taken vengeance for your family," he laughed. He clapped Alaric on the shoulders, so overjoyed for his friend that he forgot the zombivor's monstrous condition. He stepped back and gave the knight a worried look. "For sure this time?"

"No... head," Alaric said. He pointed to the left, then turned to the right. In each direction, Gaiseric could see mobs of zombies making their way around the villas to reach the ruined cathedral. "Many zombies... little time... Get... others."

Gaiseric nodded in understanding and ducked back into the alley. He helped Stormcrow bring Helchen out to the pathway. The witch hunter was as shocked as the thief when she saw Alaric's condition. The zombivor brushed aside her questions to ask one of his own.

"Anyone... else?"

"We're it," Gaiseric said. He at last accepted that Ursola had perished along with Flamefang. His only consolation was that if the dwarf were to choose her manner of death, it would have been to take the dragon with her.

Alaric turned and pointed at the canal. "Skiff... carry us..." he rasped, leading them to the edge of the waterway.

Helchen pulled back. "What about the ratlings?" she demanded. "What about Khurr, the one in the cloak? He stole the Dragon's Kiss!"

Alaric jabbed his thumb at the canal. "Sank… with zombies," he told her. "Didn't… come up… again."

Gaiseric gave Helchen a sharp look. He hoped she'd be satisfied. Buried in the slime at the bottom of Zanice's canals wasn't as secure as the vaults of the Order but it wasn't a place someone would have an easy time in finding it. "It's lost," he said. "Besides, we need to get the documents to Korbara."

The witch hunter sighed in resignation. Gaiseric helped her down the wooden ladder to a small dock where a battered old skiff was tied. Stormcrow and Alaric soon joined them. The zombivor poled them around the side of the square and back toward the cathedral. From that point, Helchen and Gaiseric could provide directions to the sewers and their route out of Zanice.

"Long… way… back," Alaric hissed as he navigated the skiff. "Save… Korbara."

Gaiseric didn't like the hint of emotion in the zombivor's speech. "You'll go back with us," he stated. "We won't leave you here." He turned and stared at Helchen and Stormcrow. "There has to be something, a spell or a potion, that can restore him."

Stormcrow simply turned his back to the thief and stared out across the wasted city. Helchen was a bit more forthright. "No magic I've ever heard of can return life to the undead," she said. She laid her hand on Alaric's leg. "But that doesn't mean we won't try. Wizards and priests of every school and faith are sheltering in Korbara. Between all of them, surely we'll discover some clue."

Gaiseric could hear the doubt in Helchen's voice. It was a dubious hope she was offering Alaric, one that she herself didn't believe.

"You have to return with us," Gaiseric insisted. He wasn't certain when it had happened, but somewhere along the way he'd accepted that the zombivor wasn't a mere shell of Alaric but was indeed his friend returned. He couldn't face losing him again. Not after the other friends he'd lost in Zanice. "Without you we could never have accomplished the quest. We'll make them understand that in Korbara."

Alaric stared at him with empty, desolate eyes. "Do... as you... wish," he told Gaiseric. "Whether... accept me... in Korbara or demand... I be... destroyed... matters little." He turned his gaze to the silent streets of Zanice.

"I'm... already... dead."

Khurr lay flat on his belly, arms and legs straddling an overturned rowboat. It rested low enough in the water for him to paddle with his hands and feet, but not so deep that his body was vulnerable to the carnivorous eels and other rapacious inhabitants of the canals.

It had been a close thing, squirming out from under the zombies when they plunged into the water. The undead sank like stones and dragged him down with them until he managed to break free. The Dragon's Kiss, the mighty dagger that was infused with the powers of Darkness itself, had made short work of his enemies once he used it against them.

How foolish to be afraid of such a weapon! Khurr berated himself for his trepidation. It was prudent to respect any relic of Darkness but sheer idiocy to let that respect restrain him from using the dagger. The zombies had failed from the merest nick of the blade, corroding into a scummy slush that dissipated in the current. Such a mighty weapon!

Khurr looked back at the sprawl of Zanice. Almost he was tempted to go back, find the witch hunter and that undead knight and use the Dragon's Kiss on them. He fought down the murderous impulse. It would be reckless and petty. He had no moral objections to such indulgences, but not when he had bigger things to do. With the Dragon's Kiss, he could go back to the south and return to the warrens. The threat of the power he held in his paws would bring many packs of ratlings under his dominion. He would bind the vermin into service to the Darkness and create a shadow kingdom of his own.

The harbor opened up to Khurr as he paddled his way out from the canal. He paused, letting the tide carry him further out. It wouldn't do to become exhausted. He'd have a good deal of paddling left before he was out of the bay and could steer back toward land again.

While he rested, Khurr scratched at his ear. There was some vague detail he was forgetting. Something the humans were always jabbering about back before the zombies came to Zanice. What was it exactly?

Khurr was still scratching his head over that niggling detail when motion in the water arrested his attention. A tiny wave, but it was troublesome because it moved against the current. He watched with mounting unease as the wave closed the distance, from a hundred yards to fifty. At fifty, he saw a shape behind the wave, a big brown scaly hump. There wasn't any question that what it belonged to was coming straight toward him.

Khurr's ears flattened against the sides of his skull and his eyes widened with fear. He remembered now what he'd almost forgotten. The humans had always been talking about a giant sea serpent that lived in the bay. A creature they kept docile by regular feedings.

The ratling's hand tightened about the Dragon's Kiss as the scaly hump drew nearer.

A sea serpent that hadn't been fed in months.

Ever since the Black Plague struck Zanice.

ABOUT THE AUTHOR

Exiled to the blazing wastes of Arizona for communing with ghastly Lovecraftian abominations, C L WERNER strives to infect others with the grotesque images that infest his mind. Cinephile habits acquired during a stint managing a video store have resulted in a movie collection that threatens to devour his domicile. An inveterate bibliophile, he squanders the proceeds from his writing on hoary old volumes – or reasonably affordable reprints of same – to expand his library of fantasy fiction, horror stories and occult tomes. When not engaged in reading or writing, he is known to re-invest in the gaming community via far too many Kickstarter boardgame campaigns and to haunt obscure collectible shops to ferret out outré Godzilla memorabilia.